ALSO BY RICHARD BAUSCH

NOVELS

Before, During, After
Peace
Thanksgiving Night
Hello to the Cannibals
In the Night Season
Good Evening Mr. and Mrs. America, and All the Ships at Sea
Rebel Powers
Violence
Mr. Field's Daughter
The Last Good Time
Take Me Back
Real Presence

SHORT FICTION

Living in the Weather of the World
Something Is Out There
Wives & Lovers: 3 Short Novels
The Stories of Richard Bausch
Someone to Watch Over Me: Stories
Selected Stories of Richard Bausch
Rare & Endangered Species
The Fireman's Wife and Other Stories
Spirits and Other Stories

POETRY

These Extremes: Poems and Prose

PLAYHOUSE

PLAYHOUSE

Richard Bausch

ALFRED A. KNOPF   NEW YORK   2023

THIS IS A BORZOI BOOK PUBLISHED BY ALFRED A. KNOPF

www.aaknopf.com

Knopf, Borzoi Books, and the colophon are registered trademarks of Penguin Random House LLC.

Library of Congress Cataloging-in-Publication Data
Names: Bausch, Richard, [date] author.
Title: Playhouse / Richard Bausch.
Description: First edition. | New York : Alfred A. Knopf, 2023. | "This is a Borzoi book"—Title page verso.
Identifiers: LCCN 2021040262 (print) | LCCN 2021040263 (ebook) | ISBN 9780451494849 (hardcover) | ISBN 9780451494856 (ebook)
Subjects: LCGFT: Novels.
Classification: LCC PS3552.A846 P58 2022 (print) | LCC PS3552.A846 (ebook) | DDC 813/.54—dc23
LC record available at https://lccn.loc.gov/2021040262
LC ebook record available at https://lccn.loc.gov/2021040263

This is a work of fiction. Names, characters, places, and incidents either are the product of the author's imagination or are used fictitiously. Any resemblance to actual persons, living or dead, events, or locales is entirely coincidental.

Jacket images: *The Storm* by Georges Michel (detail).
The Art Institute of Chicago; (theater seats) Paleha/Getty Images
Jacket design by John Gall

Manufactured in the United States of America
First Edition

To Lisa and Lila.

And in loving memory of my identical twin, Robert Bausch—brilliant writer, artist, teacher, raconteur of matchless genius, and, by whim, whenever he felt like it, a superb satirical cartoonist. Also, always, a kind and tough counselor, a completely trustworthy and wise confidant, my lifelong friend and healing presence—a calming, encouraging, cherished companion in sorrows and in laughter, a continual spur in this art, and the sanest man I ever knew. Oh, Bobby, you stopped and gave me a turn at that pinwheel, over and over again, all the years.

Give me an ounce of civet; good apothecary, sweeten my imagination.

—SHAKESPEARE, *King Lear*

Cast of Characters

THE THREE MAIN CHARACTERS

Thaddeus Deerforth—General manager, Shakespeare Theater of Memphis

Malcolm Ruark—Former TV news anchor, new member of the company

Claudette Bradley—Company actor, Shakespeare Theater of Memphis

AND THE PEOPLE AROUND THEM

Gina Donato—Thaddeus Deerforth's wife, chief of set design

Mona Greer—Malcolm Ruark's ex-wife Hannah's niece, new company actor

Dylan Walters—former box-office clerk for Shakespeare Theater of Memphis

Ellis Bradley—Claudette's father

Geoffrey Chessman—Claudette's ex-husband

Gregory Ruark—Malcolm's much-older half brother, chief accountant of the company

Hannah Ruark—Malcolm Ruark's ex-wife

Pearl Greer—Her sister

Franny Bradley—Claudette's stepmother

Willamina McNichol—Home-care person for Ellis Bradley

Reuben H. Frye—Visiting artistic director, Shakespeare Theater of Memphis

Kelly Gordon—Former student of Frye's, and visiting assistant director

Arthur Grausbeck—Chairman of the theater board, Shakespeare Theater of Memphis

Jocelyn Grausbeck—His wife, also a member of the board

William Mundy—Slated lead actor in *King Lear* at new Globe Shakespeare Theater of Memphis

Lurlene Glenn—Thaddeus Deerforth's assistant

Salina Berrens—Billionaire donor to the theater

Miranda Bland—Her wife and partner

Eleanor Cruikshank—Novelist, friend to Malcolm Ruark and to the theater

Martin Cruikshank—Her brother

Mary Cho—Stage manager, Shakespeare Theater of Memphis

Quincey Blair—Geoffrey Chessman's LA friend

Company actors: Ernest Abernathy, Mickey Castleton, Michael Frost, Maude Gainly, Terence Gleason, Gaylen McCarthy, George Poole, Don Seligman, Peggy Torres, Henry Yates

I

Exits and Entrances

Monday, June 1

(SIXTY-FOUR DAYS TO OPENING)

Thaddeus

Last night, Gina said, "I swear, after all these years, I'm beginning to see the actual contours of your capacity for worrying. My mother's got nothing on you. Come on. We had a good spring, and now we're in the money. What is it that stresses you about a new, fully funded, and expanded theater for the fall? We got *King Lear* in the fall. You keep expecting the other shoe to drop."

True.

And he had gone to bed determined to do better, had kissed her, murmured "Night," and pulled the top sheet up over his shoulders, hearing the breezes outside, and appreciating that the spring season had indeed been successful. He fell asleep almost immediately—unlike the previous five nights—and slept deeply. But the predawn hour had come with a sensation of having dreamed someone put a finger to the middle of his chest and then pushed him away, followed immediately by anxiety over the theater going dark through the whole summer season while the renovation and expansion took place. It had already been dark for nine weeks (the renovation had at last begun after several delays) and it would be dark on into August. They would have a new theater, true, and the first production would be *King Lear,* the one play in the world he loved most; but a whole season was a long time. People might drift away; there were so many other things to do; audiences could dwindle. The board hadn't included him in most of its decisions as the new circumstance unfolded. He had not even met the principals, and he was the theater manager.

Not yet five o'clock. The moon was bright. From the bed, he saw tree shadows on the lawn outside the window. She slept peacefully at his side, though a train horn trailed across the dark like grief. He lay quiet and quite still. He had no memory of what had been in the dream that woke him. He drew a long breath and whispered the word he had lately taken to repeating, inwardly or aloud, like a sort of verbal amulet or charm: "Ridiculous."

Gina stirred now, turned, and put one arm over his chest, sighing. He breathed the fragrance of her hair. When she shifted again and snuggled with her back to him, he reached for his cell phone on the nightstand and looked at the day's news. A Norwegian cargo ship had sunk off the coast of Vietnam. Eighteen dead. "The first thing you do in the mornings," she had also said last night, "is look at the bad news on that phone. Leave the phone at least until you've had some time to collect yourself." But collecting himself meant worrying. He put the cell back down and, soundlessly as possible, rose from the bed.

Anxiety was a natural enough response to the times, wasn't it? Well, he was a man approaching forty with a profound increasing sense of frailty and susceptibility. *Ridiculous.* His heart skipped a beat. He realized that was what had awakened him from whatever the dream was.

She yawned and moaned, "Not yet."

"I'll wake you in half an hour."

He padded downstairs, turning on lights as he went. Opening the front door on the cool, moonlit morning, he collected *The Appeal* from the front stoop. (Nothing on the net would ever replace the morning paper; he was a man of certain set habits.) He put coffee on, and stood under the kitchen light, thinking of people going down in the South China Sea. He would drink the coffee and lose himself in the sports page.

On the dining room table was a collage Gina had put together made of articles that had appeared over the years, a picture history of the Shakespeare Theater of Memphis from the years on Monroe Street through the move to the converted Cotton Exchange warehouse, where it presently was. And she had laced in snippets of the magazine bios of the two women, "Cosmetics Tycoons" (as members of the company now called them), who had given all the money for renovating the place. Thaddeus sat drinking the coffee and looking at the jigsaw fragments of photos in his wife's artful patchwork. They had met at City Stage on Monroe, in its fourth year. He was the young assistant theater manager and she was a staff member in set design. She was three years older, and sometimes teased him about that. (Lately, because she had turned forty—she was forty-one now—the teasing had gone the other way: Thaddeus would ask if she remembered when she was his age.) She had kept her last name: Donato. They were Deerforth and Donato.

She came downstairs as he was making more coffee. She had put on jeans, and a muslin top he liked, and tied her straw-colored hair back in a ponytail. She took a cup down from the cabinet and held it out for him to pour.

"Sorry I woke you," he said.

"You didn't wake me, dear."

They sat across from each other at the table. She looked at the collage. "Can't decide if I like this."

"I'm gonna hang it in my office."

She smiled, shaking her head, running her hand softly over a picture of the present theater with its old art deco façade, part of which had already been taken down. Members of the company had been dispersing for the summer. Gina would substitute teach art classes for a special summer program at Shelby County elementary schools. Their friend Claudette, the company's best actor, had taken a job as a receptionist at the Williams Gallery on Main Street (though she had also scored a couple of local commercials). And the theater's long-standing artistic director, Miles Warden, had decided to take a year's leave of absence—which meant he would miss the fall season and the gala opening production. But he had already directed *Lear,* and even played him once. ("At thirty-eight," he had told Thaddeus. "In five pounds of makeup.") He was back in Sydney, where he had grown up, to write a book about the man who raised him—his paternal grandfather. The old man had survived the Bataan Death March and went on to become a long-distance runner in the Olympics. The board had selected Reuben H. Frye, chair of the drama department at Holliwell Academy in Boston, to replace him for the fall. The board chairman's wife had known Frye since he was her student at Harvard, where she taught literature for a few years. She had kept in touch with him. According to her, he was "preternaturally gifted" and had directed both on and off Broadway.

"Of course," Deerforth had said at the time, "a lot of things in Jocelyn Grausbeck's world are preternatural."

The board chairman's wife used the word a lot.

"So," Gina had said. "The distinguished Reuben H. Frye's been preternaturally on and off Broadway."

"Mostly *far* off," Deerforth answered, nodding with fake gravity. "Beijing." And she laughed in that high, cackling way he loved.

The professor from Holliwell had become an aggravation.

And this was his day of arrival. He had already been pestering Deerforth on the phone and in emails about matters that couldn't be dealt with in any case for weeks.

"Can I fry you a couple eggs?" he asked Gina now.

"Think I'll just have this." She held the cup to her lips. Then she indicated the paper. "There should be an article in there about the Cosmetics Tycoons. Claudette said she got interviewed, too."

He paged through and found it under the heading "Memphis Girls."

"Why didn't they talk to *you*? You're the theater manager."

"It's 'Memphis *Girls*,' babe. Claudette's a Memphis girl, too. And anyway, I haven't even met the Cosmetics Tycoons. It's all been Arthur Grausbeck and the board."

"Well, they should talk to you. You can help them fill up with dread."

"Ha."

A moment later, he said, "You know, they're gonna ask Malcolm Ruark to join the company."

"The guy from WMC news? DUI with his niece?"

Thaddeus lifted one shoulder, a half shrug. "Apparently he was an actor with the company before. Celebrity sells, I guess. Frye wants him."

She dipped her chin and did the former TV anchor's sign-off line: "'That's today's story, so long and have a pleasant evening.'"

Thaddeus smiled. "You know he's Gregory's younger half brother."

"I think I missed the connection." Her tone might have been mock wonder. He couldn't tell. Her eyes showed him friendly chiding. Then she frowned, considering. "But they're not even in touch, are they?"

"I've never heard Gregory mention him. Have you?"

"Not once."

"But Gregory's never mentioned a lot of things. Like the fact that he's the ex-husband of one of the Cosmetics Tycoons."

"You're kidding. Is that why they—"

He shook his head. "I shouldn't've said anything about that. It's—not general knowledge. Yet. And anyway the two ladies are a happy couple. I mean it's ancient history. They were in their twenties. Gregory's as surprised as everybody else about the, um, largesse."

He skimmed through the article while she sipped the coffee. Presently, he said, "Vietnam was in the news this morning. Boat sank in the South China Sea. First thing I saw."

She said, "I don't like the phrase 'going dark' about a theater."

"Did you hear me about the boat sinking?"

"Christ, can we not dwell on that, please? Mother?"

"Right, sorry."

Presently, he said, "I've got the whole morning with contractors about permits and the new wiring. And Frye's arrival."

"Take my car in. Remember, yours needs inspection. I'll get it this morning."

"I'd do it," he said. "But." He held his hands out slightly from his sides.

"I said I'd do it and I'll do it on my way to teach my first class in twelve years."

"You nervous?"

"After this morning with you and the terrors of the world. Yes. Craven."

Her car was always so neat. She had hung a little glass pendant from the rearview mirror that caught sunlight through the windshield. It always caused a reminding flicker of exasperation whenever he saw it because he thought of it as a danger: he worried that it might reflect the light in a way that would blind her at a crucial moment in traffic.

When he left for the theater, there was a fetid breeze coming in off the river, and rain was in the forecast.

The Cosmetics Tycoons were life partners and founders of Berrens & Bland Cosmetics, Inc. And after almost three decades traveling and being wealthy and industrious in the world, they had sold everything lock, stock, and barrel for shiploads of money (their words), and returned to Tennessee determined to create a true showplace in the Mid-South for the one thing they were most passionate about: classical theater, particularly, of course, Shakespeare. Right there in the Mid-South by the river (they were Memphis girls, after all), they would create a theater rivaling places like the Pantages in LA, or Lincoln Center in New York.

Along with funding the renovation and the future, they had given a blank check to the board, for all decisions regarding productions. This allowed them to give Reuben H. Frye a free hand for scheduling, and also for hiring from outside the company. Frye had already scheduled a longer run than usual for *Lear,* which meant there would be only two other events for the season: Edward Albee's *Three Tall Women* and a Christmas choral pageant that Frye would also direct, involving the Memphis Symphony Orchestra and the University of Memphis Chorale. Moreover, he had hired a former Holliwell student, a young woman named Kelly Gordon, to direct the Albee. The Creative Committee, made up of Memphis-based actors and directors, hadn't even been consulted.

But this apparent slight was eased by the fact that he had managed to land William Mundy for the role of Lear. Mundy, lead character in the Netflix smash hit *Home Away,* had been a reputable stage actor for a long time in England, but his celebrity was the result of six seasons as the irascible kindly grandfather in a Yorkshire family sheltering children coming from London during the blitzkrieg. The run for *King Lear* would be from Tuesday, August 4, to Saturday, October 24. More than seventy performances.

The theater board had been pleased that Frye was concerning himself with the fall season while continuing with his duties at Holliwell; but his offhandedness with members of the company had been the cause of some grumbling. He had requested portfolios from everyone, financial records from previous productions going back five years, and summaries of past strategies regarding promotions. He asked Gina and her staff for ideas and sketches regarding set design for the fall productions, and then rejected them all out of hand, the last with a thud of a joke ("You *are* the theater manager's wife, so you're all right no matter what, am I right?"), plus he had besieged Thaddeus himself with innuendos and complaints about the people in development and finance, community outreach and programming.

Perhaps the crowning thing was the postcard sent from New York in the first week of April, a picture of the newly opened Freedom Tower at night, on the back of which was Frye's thin, slanting script, expressing the hope that things were going well, and mentioning his recent visit in New York with his great friend Al Pacino. He went on to say he planned to rejuvenate the dramatic arts in Memphis, and then, in nearly unreadable miniature, designated the brand of tea he would like served in the mornings after he took up residence.

Malcolm

Calls from the theater board had missed the former TV anchorman for almost two weeks. He kept erasing them, believing it was someone trying to sell him something—a robocall, since the number wasn't recognizable as being that of anyone he knew. Finally, he listened to a message. "Hello, this is Jocelyn Grausbeck of the new Globe Shakespeare Theater. Please call us at your earliest convenience."

He thought it was a fundraising call and deleted it. Later, he received still another, and he picked it up, intending to say he was sorry, but it must be clear that he was not going to be a source for any kind of donation; but the voice this time was a man's voice. "Bub-bub—uh, please don't hang up, sir. This is Arthur Grausbeck, chairman of the board for the new Globe Shakespeare Theater of Memphis."

"I don't have any spare money, okay, Arthur? I can't help you. *Quit calling me.*"

"This isn't a fundraising call, sir. *Please* don't hang up. I—bub-bub-bub—I'm calling to offer you a place in our company. Reuben H. Frye, our distinguished visiting artistic director, specifically asked for you. He wants you for *Lear* in the fall."

"He wants *me* to play Lear?"

"He wants you for the *play*. And the theater board wants you for our regular company. We're offering you a job, sir."

"Do you know my recent history?"

"We know your recent history," Grausbeck said, after a slight pause. "And we know you were one of our best actors before going to WMC. We also know you've been clean for a year. Can you come in and talk? The pay wouldn't be what you're used to, of course."

"My half brother runs your finance office. I haven't seen him in years. Is this his doing?"

"Bub-bub. All I know is Reuben Frye asked for you, we as a board met and discussed it, and considered several other candidates, and we decided on you."

"When do you want me to come in?"

"Well, Frye gets here today, at noon. I'll have our general manager call you. His name is Thaddeus Deerforth."

"Well, then, I'll look forward to hearing from Thaddeus Deerforth," Malcolm said.

A year ago in April, after working at WMC sixteen years, ten of which had been as anchor of the evening news, he had been in an accident, driving drunk, with his wife's underage niece in the car, also drunk. He had spent time under house arrest and then in rehab, and he'd been fined a thousand dollars each for three Class C misdemeanors: driving under the influence, contributing to the delinquency of a minor, and recklessly (this was stipulated in the charge) causing the accident in which the minor, whose name was Mona, suffered a bruised vertebra at the base of her neck and a ruptured spleen, requiring time in the hospital. The house arrest was a provision of the court until depositions from concerned parties and witnesses and interviews with the girl herself and her parents established beyond doubt that there had been no sexual involvement. His marriage was over, after twenty-four years; he'd had to settle at disadvantage a damage suit from Mona's mother (who maintained, along with his now ex-wife, that sexual predation was indeed intended, if not realized); and, at fifty-four, he was living on severance pay, all but ruined financially. In truth, even if a job with the theater company came through, some sort of part-time work was going to be necessary. He'd been putting off the search out of pure despondency about his situation.

The furnished efficiency where he now lived was a converted garage with rust-stained sinks, threadbare places in the one rug, and roaches the size of hummingbirds. It was adjacent to a large ramshackle Georgian house in Central Gardens. His landlord was a seventy-four-year-old dealer in antiques who did not deign to own a television and seemed unaware who Malcolm Ruark was. Mostly, the landlord left him alone. Malcolm, even under the circumstances, felt lucky to have the place and thankful, as time went on, to be left to his own devices. His own devices turned out to be mostly staying in while the severance pay sufficed, reading books, and cooking for himself, trying to pay as little attention as possible to the news. He wanted nothing to do with the cycle of horrors and titillations he'd lived by all those years. He'd unplugged the radio and the portable TV. He was reading Chekhov and Winston Churchill's six-volume history of World War II. His wife, Hannah, had claimed the house, the lake cottage, and everything else. Her niece had been undergoing physical therapy, for which he was also paying (the settlement). That whole side of the family, except the girl, Mona, had closed ranks against him. And he was barred from any communication with her by an order of protection (sworn out by her mother).

Hannah now lived in New Hampshire. She had joined a self-styled Buddhist commune with several old school friends. This after a life of devout Catholicism. Her bible now was Thomas Merton's *Zen and the Birds of Appetite*. But she had often been inclined to unpredictable turns and changes. (Indeed, it was her impulsiveness that attracted him to her in the first place, when they were both young and relatively fresh.) He missed those years sometimes, and, as a therapist had put it to him, he was like so many men in late middle age, for whom memory was a palace of youth, and whose habits of mind were too sentimental and romantic for their own good.

The therapist didn't know everything, of course.

For instance, in his early twenties, before college, he had been a pugilist and had suffered a partially detached retina from receiving an elbow to his right eye, a foul committed in a bout he won. (He had won fifteen of seventeen fights, all on points, and the two losses were also decisions.) There was a small scar at the ridge of the eyebrow, where the hair didn't grow. It was scarcely noticeable. An optometrist had told him he might one day go blind in that eye.

Neither his therapist, nor, in fact, Hannah, knew this about him. No one, not even a wife or a therapist, ever knew anyone completely. He believed being aware of this had made him a good journalist.

Claudette

She sat at the three-mirror dressing table in her bedroom, *The Commercial Appeal* open to the classified section, and a steaming cup of tea before her. She had been looking for job opportunities. The gallery on Main Street, after only a week, was killing the light in her heart. At first, the hours of peaceful silence sitting at the reception desk had seemed like respite; but it had soured quickly with all the slow movement of tourists walking through looking for depictions of Memphis attractions—Graceland, Sun Studio, the Stax Museum, the Peabody, Beale Street. The art in this gallery was mostly disarranged shapes, clashing or blended colors, and sculpture that looked like postaccident twistings.

Her phone buzzed. It was Thaddeus. "I'm at the theater," he said. "They're wrecking the old office wing. It's all gonna be new. Why am I sad?"

"It's your nature? I'm going over to see my dad in the home at ten. But I'll be there for the grand arrival at noon."

"Have you heard they've signed Malcolm Ruark?"

"Yep."

"Did you know him back when, at City?"

"He left the season before I started."

"Have you talked to his brother about it?"

"Gregory's not somebody you hang out with and talk about hiring decisions. Or family, for that matter."

Thaddeus said, "Think you can do scenes with a guy like that?"

"If it's lines, I can say them. Right? And you'll recall, I've already had the experience of playing opposite a guy like that."

"How's *that one* doing?"

"Oh, still making me glad he left."

"Did you tell me he was thinking about New York?"

"He's still in LA, still driving for the escort service. And is he jealous about our good luck with the money."

"So you did tell him. Gina said you were planning to send a card or something with hearts."

"I just told him over the phone."

"Did you tell him about Miles leaving for a year?"

"Never, ever mention that name to him, Thaddeus."

He gave a little laugh.

"Anyway, I'll come directly there from Memphis Commons."

"Gina and I haven't forgotten about going over there to visit."

"He's still in the nursery wing, Thaddeus. It's like a hospital room. Visit him now and you might could end up simply watching him sleep. These days, you know I feel resentment every time I see someone *else* in their eighties doing well."

"I still feel envy," Thaddeus said.

"Anyway"—she sighed—"I got him a lower dosage of this antianxiety drug they've had him on. It's what's made him so sleepy, I'm sure."

"What's the drug? I'm thinking I'd like to see about getting ahold of some myself. I don't like us going dark all summer."

"Tell me about it. Aside from these commercial shoots, I'm a receptionist in the gallery. But we've got Frye today, and soon the great thespian dirty old man Mundy'll be here."

"Dirty old man."

"That's what I hear."

After they hung up, another call came in: Geoffrey. She decided not to answer it. He would call back, she knew.

She had said to him more than once, not completely joking, that the distance was a good thing for their relationship. "Our divorce is working," she'd said. But in fact there were times when she did miss him, missed the carelessness, the laughs. They'd actually talked around this a little.

She poured a cup of coffee and sat putting on her makeup. The window of her apartment was open just enough to let the morning breeze in. She could smell the honeysuckle under the window. She went into the kitchen and poured the dregs of the coffee out, and the phone startled her. "Just wanted to check in." Her father's gravelly voice. This was what he had always said calling from home when he was younger and she was out in the world, living with Geoffrey and then married to Geoffrey.

"Hi, Daddy," she said, as she always had.

"What's going on over there, Little One?"

"Just getting ready to come see you this morning. How're you feeling with the new dosage."

"I miss Esther."

"Mom's in England."

Silence.

"A long time now, Dad."

"I know that."

She left a pause.

"Just been thinking about her lately. We all ought to be in closer touch."

"Yes," Claudette said.

"Don't let go of anybody, Little One. Where are you? Come see me again."

"I am, Daddy. Today. I'll be there in a little bit."

"I'm getting sleepy now. Just wanted to hear your voice."

"I'll be there before you know it," she said, her heart sinking.

"I didn't sleep much last night," he said. Then: "You tell Esther I miss her." And he was gone.

She stood hearing sirens far off, the world out there with its constant alarms. She wiped her eyes with a napkin, then went back to her dressing table to fix the running mascara.

Thaddeus

His full name—that is, the name on his birth certificate—was Wolfgang Amadeus Thaddeus Deerforth. His mother had just turned eighteen when he was born. She'd been with only one man, once: a young clarinetist she met at a concert in Alexandria, Virginia. The clarinetist's name was Thaddeus T. Deerforth, fresh out of Juilliard and newest member of a rather well-known ensemble touring the East Coast. The concert was part of a summer festival of the arts. They played Mozart's *Clarinet Quintet*. She was just out of high school, winner of an essay contest sponsored by the festival. After the concert, she struck up a conversation with him because she liked his looks and his playing. When he talked about playing the Mozart, his eyes shone. "I love Mozart," she told him, lying only a little: she had loved the quintet (and now she loved Mozart). They spent a languid afternoon walking along the Potomac and then lying on the grass in the shade of a silver maple. They watched the sun go down. She still maintained it was love at first sight.

The young clarinetist lost his life the next morning in a train accident on his way north. She never knew what the *T* stood for, but she took the name Deerforth, because she was in love and because to her Deerforth sounded far better than Ealey. Naming her child Wolfgang Amadeus came from what she later called the harebrained idea that her child might be brought to a life in music with it, since his father had been a musician whose playing of the great composer's clarinet piece had caused her to notice him in the first place, and because, in her grief at his loss, she had listened incessantly to Mozart during her pregnancy. After nine months and one week in the womb, with Mozart's music flowing every day over his little space of warmth, Thaddeus was born with a distinct taste for Aretha Franklin. It was Aretha from day one, his mother would tell friends, laughing proudly. But she had named him Wolfgang Amadeus anyway. She married a man named Strekfus who claimed he was happy to have an "instant family," as he called it, but in whose heart there lurked a strand of judgmental cruelty; she had been dreaming for more than a year of taking her little boy with her to Tennessee to live with her aunt Anna, when he told her he was in love with someone he'd met on the road. She laughed. Hysterically. He thought it was grief. He couldn't believe it was anything else. Thaddeus was three. He had no memory of Strekfus.

And by the time he was in kindergarten, it was clear that he'd inherited nothing of his biological father's musical gift. Plus, he possessed no real interest in music. So, his mother, now Effie Deerforth, started calling him Thaddeus.

Gina, now and then, called him Wolfie, an endearment only she was allowed.

It had seemed to Thaddeus that all of his wife's darker moods were tied to the winter months. In spring she slept better, even with the bedroom windows open to the nightsounds—the hum of things, the ruckus of night bugs, and the distant moan of the trains crossing the delta. She would wake in a cheerful mood, seeming rested, up for anything.

But it was June, and though she still slept deep, there was a recurring flatness in her disposition. Watching her from his office window as she crossed the street below to come into the confusion, mess, and clatter of the theater's transformation, he held on to the hope that the flicker of vexation he saw in her face was attributable to the noise, and only that. She paused at the bed of flowers bordering the entrance, picked one, and went on out of sight, into the doorway beyond the west side of the building. That was Gina. *Girl of my dreams,* he often called her. This time, thinking the words, he might've spoken them aloud, standing there in the noise. But now it seemed that something in the noise itself, abruptly compounded by the battering of a jackhammer against concrete out on the sidewalk below, moved bluntly through his body. There was a quick shift in his chest, under the breastbone. A skipped heartbeat. Again— what had awakened him this morning. It was exactly as if someone had put a finger there, pushed, and then taken it away. And now it happened again. And then, more pronouncedly, once more. He sat down at his desk and waited for it to stop. But it went on. He knew something about palpitations and their causes—his mother had dealt with them periodically from her twenties through her forties. He took a breath, and remained stock-still. These were palpitations. He took a deep slow breath and tried to turn his attention to something else.

He considered the anxiety level of the last few days, and absurdly, in a helpless spasm of grief as if he'd known every one of the victims personally, he recalled the deaths in the South China Sea. Gina was right. Somehow the sad news in the world had begun going deeper into his psyche. When he could look at it coldly, the images that came to him in sleep or lying awake were often nearly qualifiable as visions. And that could certainly explain palpitations. Then, too, there seemed no time to deal with all there was to do in the days: the darkened theater seemed overcrowded with tasks complicated by construction, dealings with contractors, the finance office, and the several local colleges about the new works contest, a prize for new drama, the winning play to be performed in the black box theater. The renovation was proving more stressful than a full season.

Almost an hour earlier than expected, Reuben H. Frye strolled into the far-from-finished central lobby. People began going back and forth letting others know he'd arrived. The young director he'd chosen for *Three*

Tall Women was with him, and they walked around the lobby looking at things, as if they were tourists. He was surprisingly short. He had on a red bow tie, and a light blue suit, with black tennis shoes, and he wore a factory-abraded baseball cap from the Gibson guitar factory. The hat was slightly askew on his head. She was slender, fair, with almond-shaped brown eyes, shoulder-length auburn hair, and a sprinkling of freckles across her nose. She didn't look old enough to be out of high school—though according to her portfolio she was thirty-four. Gradually everyone collected in the disarray of boards and cans of paint. And after quiet handshakes and a brief tour of the new venue with Jocelyn Grausbeck (whom he embraced, to her clear embarrassment), he introduced Kelly Gordon. There was a smattering of applause. "Yes," he said. "Well."

For an awkward interval, everyone waited.

Then he strode back into the crowd, greeting people, shaking hands, talking individually about airline flights, rental apartments, the attractions of Memphis, and the summer heat so close to the big continent-running river (his phrase). Nothing but small talk, all around, like a polite party on a patio. Then, turning in a circle, taking in the faces, he said, "We'll convene precisely at noon, on the main stage, such as it is. Give everybody an hour or so to get themselves together. Thank you." And he nodded at Jocelyn Grausbeck, who led him down the side hall to Miles Warden's old office. He hugged her again, then entered and quietly closed the door. It looked like he was shutting her and everyone else out.

Kelly Gordon seemed unconcerned. She kept shaking hands all around. And she made a near curtsy to Thaddeus, who, in the exact instant he offered his hand, received the discomforting sense that his hand might be clammy. He was unpleasantly aware of his own heartbeat. It seemed regular now, but it was beating in his neck—thudding there. "Has Frye told you he's close friends with Edward Albee?" she asked him with a crooked little smile.

He was unsure how to react. "Well, no."

She seemed faintly disappointed.

"There *was* something in a postcard about visiting with his great friend Al Pacino during the holidays," he said.

Her response was almost lazy. "Oh, yes, that too. And the thing is, some version of both is actually true. He does know both men." Her small, knowing smile only involved her lips. "Be funnier if it was a lie."

They gazed at the closed door where the visiting artistic director had gone.

"Is this your first visit to Memphis?" he asked, reaching for casualness.

She nodded. "I've already driven around a little to look at things. I'm figuring to stay at one of those places near the river. I'll be at the Peabody till the end of the week, at least. I'm giving that to myself. Always wanted to stay there and go down in the lobby in the morning and watch the ducks get ushered out to the big fountain."

"So you know about that. I've lived here most of my life, and I've never seen it."

"Maybe you've missed something wonderful." She nodded at him, as if agreeing with herself. His assistant, Lurlene Glenn, walked up. She was a quick, fluid-moving, clear-eyed woman near seventy. "I'll show you to your office, dear," she said.

"I have my own office?"

"You're one of our distinguished visitors."

"Distinguished." Kelly smirked.

The theater manager went back to his office, and almost immediately Lurlene joined him. "Looks like a kid," she said about Kelly Gordon.

"I had the same thought."

The two of them went through menus and possible suppliers for preview nights, deciding on wine and refreshments, snacks, and soft drinks, guest lists for receptions and dinners. This was interrupted by the contractors, who had encountered new wiring problems—and then he had to deal with the several members of the company who were upset at the new situation. The longest-standing company member, Maude Gainly, who had from toddlerhood performed with one group or another at all the venues in the city's theater life, had been passed over for the part of Cordelia because, she told Thaddeus, Frye said she was too heavy, and not young enough. ("I can lose this weight, Thaddeus. What the hell. And I'm only thirty-eight.")

The oldest member of the company, Terence Gleason, said, "This about-to-be new, shiny Globe Theater already feels like a small country with a corrupt dictator." He had believed, not unjustly, that he would be Lear, or at least Gloucester. He hadn't been cast at all.

Through all this, Thaddeus kept surreptitiously pressing two fingers against his wrist; there was the strong regular beat the first few times, but then suddenly he felt another shift. He sat at his desk, taking his own pulse. The strong beat made him think it must be laboring. Then it paused. He was certain it stopped for a second. A few strong beats later, it paused again. And started again. He breathed deeply, slowly. And it happened once more. Finally, he closed his office door and called his mother to ask about her experience of the phenomenon.

"Did it ever feel like your heart stopped?"

"Yes," Effie said. "That's what they feel like, honey. It's a little scary, but it's not serious."

"A *little* scary."

"Well, for the anxiety-prone—dear—maybe more than a little scary."

"I can feel it actually stopping."

"That's the way it *feels*, but it's not stopping. It's actually not even pausing. It just *feels* that way. A missed beat. It's a prematurely contracting ventricle, sweetie. A PCV, they call it. No fun. But everybody gets them now and then, and it usually goes away on its own."

"It's extremely disconcerting," he told her.

"Well, go to the doctor. The doctor'll tell you what I just told you, and that'll help your anxiety about it."

"It makes me feel elderly."

"Well, come on, dear. You were an old man when you were nine years old."

"What happened when I was nine?"

"You know, Thaddeus—my darling boy—the first thing that happens when you get this sort of anxiety is you lose your sense of figurative speech. And look at you, a lover of Shakespeare."

"Okay," he said. "But you said since I was nine. You were very specific."

She sighed. Then changed the subject. "Your aunt Anna and I are going to Europe."

He did not want to talk about Europe. "I've got a meeting I've got to get to."

"Bye," she said.

At noon, everyone gathered on the main stage. The smell of fresh-cut wood was in the air from the scaffolding all around. Reuben Frye walked down the long center aisle of shallow stairs to the front, where they were all seated or standing near the orchestra pit. He climbed up the makeshift steps to the littered stage, turned, and addressed everyone: "Okay. Well." He made a gesture as if to indicate the sweep of the room. "Here we are. As per my contract, I'm planning to have some people from outside the company for this production. Mr. Mundy you know about. He's finishing up a commitment in London, but he'll be with us in a day or two. And Mr. Ruark. Who's in fact joining us as the newest member."

The former TV anchor, who was sitting on the steps leading up to the stage, nodded and smiled and seemed, to Thaddeus, rather pained. Thaddeus looked away to allow the man his unease. "And," Frye resumed, "I'll tell you that I plan to cast Cordelia, if I can, from the community of actors at large." He paused again. "We'll be conducting auditions through the next few days for the other parts, and I've opened them up to the city. It'll be a few days, especially since our circumstances are rather—um, in a word, circumscribed. I've decided to edge up on table readings and rehearsal, anyway. This play, as I'm sure you all know, is about a king whose vanity brings him to ruin, and of course it's through this catastrophe that he reaches his best self, and maybe even a kind of salvation. I know some of you probably think salvation as a concept is arguable, and that this play is the most hopeless of the man's dark plays, nothing more than the progress of a king's downfall by his own folly, but I'm one of those people who believe that Lear's last words, as he stares at his dead girl, his youngest and previously most favored daughter, Cordelia, show that he actually believes she's breathing. Maybe you all know the line? *'Do you see this? Look on her! Look, her lips! Look there! Look there!'*"

Frye paused, straightened, adjusted the ratty-looking cap on his head. "So, we're clearly meant to see that the mad king's last breath is happy—in fact positively ecstatic. And we know that in the belief system of the time—and I suppose that system still carries weight for a lot of us—the way to that salvation has been through suffering. Now consider this: The play, *King Lear,* this massive creation, was first played before a new and *very* nervous actual king, back when kings had absolute power. When the belief in the divine right of kings was general. You know? The king was a fellow named James the First—and the show took place only days after the failure of a thing called the Gunpowder Plot. Guy Fawkes and all that. The gang of Jesuits trying to blow up Parliament and kill him. Assassinate him. A conspiracy to assassinate the new king because he'd begun making sounds about Catholics and Protestants coming together to live in peace under one crown. Now. Think of this—they still wear Guy Fawkes masks in England on the anniversary of this plot, each year, and it's been *four hundred* years. Now, imagine the audaciousness of Mr. Shakespeare, to give his made-up king the line *'There thou mightst observe the great image of authority. A dog's obeyed in office.'* Imagine that night, that performance." He paused again. "I want us to reach that kind of audaciousness. So let's think about that as we begin, and then try to forget it, and simply go on working the play we're doing, as we do other plays, you know. Yes, it has this monumental quality, and yet it was written by"—he gave another consciously dramatic pause—"a man." Then he smacked his lips. "A human somebody. With balls." He smiled. And let this pause go on. There was even a smattering of applause beginning as he quickly took up again. "Anyway, I have some unusual plans for this *Lear.* As I said, I wanna go outside the company for Cordelia, but it's going to have to be someone with particular qualities. A very particular quality, actually. I'll have more on this when we convene everyone and things are set for starting in earnest. For now, I don't really have anything much else prepared, or any great detail about the technical matters. But understand this: I'll be asking a lot of you. Of course, for the time being, we'll make several accommodations to things while the renovation's being completed. And until we have a stage, and a finished rehearsal hall, a lot of our preparations will have to be piecemeal. I'm going to depend on you to work with each other individually for a bit, getting familiar with things, and with each other. I'll have a prompt book and full script within the next few days. I welcome you. And, once more, let's all welcome our new company member, Malcolm Ruark."

Thaddeus saw again the disquiet in the former TV newsman's face as the applause went around.

"Very good," Frye said. "Now, I'll be asking for individual meetings just to get to know you all. We'll have an all-call meeting on Monday, the twenty-second. That's three weeks from now. Other than that, all the actors whose names I call may consider that they're in the cast, and are therefore released until then. The rest of you—we begin auditions tomorrow morning. Seven o'clock sharp. And a casting call's already gone out, so I'd get here early. Any questions?"

No one spoke.

Then he read the names. Claudette and Malcolm Ruark were on the cast list, along with several others.

Everyone filed out into the street. Thaddeus and Gina walked with Claudette down to the Sunshine diner across from the Madison Hotel, and looked back up at the broken-looking scaffolded façade of the theater. "Hard to imagine it's all gonna be finished in time," Claudette said. "Gives me a headache thinking about it."

"I've got new respect," said Gina. "He's a pain, but he knows his stuff."

Thaddeus said, "Come on. That's high-school-level stuff."

"Anyway, we're not studying the literature of it," Claudette said.

"Should we go in and get a coffee?" Gina asked, moving to the door of the place.

"I should head out," Claudette said. "I've got a commercial this afternoon. And the same one the next three afternoons. I've got to stand and look sexy leaning against a used car, a new car, and an SUV."

"How'd the visit go with your dad this morning?" Thaddeus wanted to know.

"Oh, he was asleep when I got there. And drowsy. He's not quite out of the daze. Sometimes he thinks I'm my mother or my older sister." Her voice caught.

The theater manager reached over and touched her wrist. "Sorry," he said.

She gave forth what sounded like a sob, mixed with laughter. "He calls me Esther, or he calls me Meryl. Sometimes." She smiled at him, and the smile deepened his old admiration for her. "And then sometimes—he seems clear."

"Hold on for the clear times, kid," he said.

"It's hit or miss, you know. And this isn't Alzheimer's—as far as they know. It was a mild stroke. But my stepmother, and my sister and her—" She stopped. "My family thinks he should be in that place."

The theater manager said, "I'll never forget *Henry IV* in History. Mr. Bradley led me to Shakespeare, Claudie. I know I've told you this, and

I know you want me to call him Ellis. But he'll always be Mr. Bradley to me."

"Oh, Thaddeus," she said. "You can tell me over and over. I hate that they wouldn't let his own daughters take a class from him."

"Stupid," Gina said.

"I loved knowing he was in that school with us. Meryl used to complain about it, but I loved it. We'd say, 'Ellis is in the building,' or 'Ellis has left the building,' like Elvis. Only for her it was always a bother."

They saw Malcolm Ruark cross the street and get into his car, the license plate of which was still ANCHOR 1.

"I felt bad for him when Frye singled him out," Thaddeus said.

"I don't think he wants to be a headliner for a while," Gina put in.

Claudette said, "Anybody talk to him?"

"He doesn't look a bit like his older brother," Thaddeus said.

"'Movie star handsome' is what our board chairman's wife says about him. I, for one, don't see it."

"I have to say I agree with Jocelyn," said Gina. "I wonder what the circumstances really were with the niece and drinking."

Wednesday, June 3–Monday, June 15

Malcolm

He had begun the search for part-time work, going over the job listings in *The Appeal*, and in headhunting publications. Over the next three days, he spent time at the theater, too, watching the auditions, sitting in the far back, being very quiet. Kelly Gordon perched on a crate where the seventh row would be, notebook open on her lap. He admired the luster of her hair. The other company actors attending remained mostly separate, almost as if alone. Clearly, they all knew one another well, were like family. Others, people answering the casting call, stood in line, looking ill at ease and determined at the same time.

The new café wasn't operational yet, so people wandered down to the Sunshine Café on the corner, or across from that to the Madison. Some drove to Midtown, and places like Corky's, or Otherlands.

Kelly Gordon approached him and inquired if he wanted to have lunch. It felt like she was asking for a date. He almost pointed out the age difference, thinking of his niece. The impulse worried him for its accession to the idea everyone seemed to have about him and the girl.

"I'd like to try Iris," Kelly said. "Come on. I'll drive."

They said little on the short drive over to Monroe. She wanted to know what it was like being on TV all the time and then not being on TV. "It must feel strange."

"I guess it did at first."

At the restaurant, she ordered a bottle of Torrontés. He drank two cups of iced coffee while she went on about her plans for directing *Three Tall Women*, and joked about getting William Mundy to do the A part—the old lady—in drag. She was already settled on Claudette Bradley for the B part. "We've got all this money from the tycoon ladies, I'm actually thinking we might could afford somebody like Glenda Jackson or Ellen Burstyn or, hell, even Jane Fonda for the A part."

"Be worth a try," Malcolm said.

"Is this bothering you?" She held up the wine. In fact, it looked perfectly beautiful in its blond shimmer as she tilted the glass to drink.

"No," he said.

"I think there's something going on between Deerforth and his wife."

He didn't know enough to remark about it, and he didn't want to know. It was nobody's business.

"I don't think Deerforth knows he's adorable. And he seems unnecessarily uxorious."

"Well." Malcolm stared. She drank. The wine gave back the sun in the windows.

Into the silence between them, she said, "How is it a guy as phlegmatic as you ends up doing the news?"

He smiled. "I was reading it, mostly."

"I'm curious about Deerforth and Donato, you know. I'm a student of human nature."

"Aren't we all, in our way."

"Well, you especially, being a TV journalist."

"That's just being a student of human actions."

"I'm thinking we could be friends."

He sipped the second cup of coffee, in which the ice had mostly melted; it had already formed a knot of discomfort in his upper abdomen. "That's the great thing about this profession," he got out.

"Oh, don't be pompous or anything." Plainly she meant to tease him, but it was difficult not to see the remark as a rebuke.

He took the last of the coffee. "I'm only talking about lasting friendships from working together."

"I want gossip. Tell me about your niece."

He shook his head. "And how do you know about that?"

"Research. I know more than you'd think."

He didn't respond.

"Come on," she urged, pouring the last of the wine into her glass.

"Are you getting a little crocked?"

"Frye hit on me when I was his student."

Malcolm waited. He had the unwelcome sense that this was the real reason she had asked him to lunch.

"I'm not kidding."

"You must've both got past it," Malcolm said. "Is there some reason I need to know this?"

She shrugged. "Guess not." She drank.

He looked at the backs of her hands, the veins there folding over the straight bones.

"I had to have a conference hour with him at his house," she said. "He drove. Big mistake. His wife was out somewhere, or in one of her stops in the hospital. She needs rehab now and then, you know. Very fragile personality. Anyway, he got drunk on vodka tonics and said he wouldn't drive me back to campus. It was play or walk."

"So, what'd you do?"

"Walked. Of *course*. Three hours."

"Did you tell anyone?"

She shrugged again. "The next day I went in as usual and he took me aside, asked me into his office, where he sat behind his desk, all officious and magisterial, and said he had meant it as a form of testing me. To see how I'd react. It was all *improvisation*. Then he apologized."

"What'd you say?"

"I said—" She stopped and cleared her throat. "'Professor Frye, I could maybe find a way to forgive last night because you were drunk, but I can never forgive this apology because it reduces me to an experiment and it's also a cheap lie that you obviously thought I was dumb enough to believe.' And I got up and left. And after that he became my biggest fan, if you know what I mean."

Malcolm signaled the server for the check.

"I've never told anyone else about that. I'm pretty sure it's why I got the gig in Portland with *Driving Miss Daisy*. That troupe, I mean. That *really* changed my life. He was the one who turned them on to me."

"And that's still your troupe?"

"I've left them. I don't know where I'll go after this. Three different places are interested because of the Portland thing."

"How does that make you feel?"

She reached into her purse, brought out a fifty-dollar bill, and smoothed it on the table like a napkin. "Lucky, I guess."

"Well," he said. "I've got to go look for some part-time employment."

"You're kidding."

"I wish I was," he said, getting up.

"I'm gonna have a coffee," she said. "You sure you gotta go?"

"I've had all the coffee I can drink," he told her, forcing a smile.

Claudette

Friday, the visiting director showed up at the gallery, with William Mundy. Claudette was at the front desk, and saw them approaching through the big window along the right wall. The sight of them startled her. She stood as they came in.

"I know you're on the job," Frye said to her, "and I gave everybody the time. But I just thought I'd see if I could make it easier for you. And then Bill here wanted to meet you."

Mundy extended a soft hand—what Ellis used to call a dead fish. "Looking forward," he said.

"Could you take a short tea break or something?" Frye asked, looking around the place.

"There's no one here, right now," she said. "We can meet here. Have a seat." She indicated the settee against the wall to the left of her desk. They moved to sit down, and she turned the plastic chair adjacent to the desk to face them. They both sat cross-legged, hands folded on their knees. Frye's gaze wandered to the walls, while Mundy stared appraisingly at her. His gaze was unsettling; it made her feel unpleasantly exposed, and she remembered a magazine article about cast members of the hit series calling him *old grandfather goat*.

Frye rubbed the ridge of his nose and coughed. Then he glanced at Mundy. "Lot of abstract stuff."

"Yes," Mundy said. "Very modern."

"You like that sort of thing?" Frye said to Claudette.

"Sometimes," she said.

"Well. Anyway. I wonder how deeply you're versed in Shakespeare."

It seemed an absurd question. She had the notion that he was joking. But his expression was serious, without a hint of anything but sober intent.

"I played Lady M here, five years ago. And I know the major plays."

"You know *Lear*?"

She nodded. "Of course."

"You can play Goneril, do you think?"

"Or Cordelia," said Mundy. He held both hands up as if to provide a frame for her from a distance. "There's Cordelia."

"I'm a little too old for the youngest daughter." She nodded as she spoke, looking straight back at him.

"Goneril," Frye said. "Or Regan."

"I have the feeling we're going to be great friends," Mundy said to her. "I've very much liked what I've seen of yours on YouTube."

"Thank you."

"But Goneril's a more subtle part, I think," Frye said. "Maybe you two should get to work on the back-and-forth pretty early."

"Perhaps at my apartment," Mundy said. "I've just moved into a place on Riverside. A loft."

She said nothing. It struck through her that the two men were actually seeking to bring something about between her and Mundy. She could imagine their talk about her: divorced, living alone. Apparently no male companions.

"Or—where is your place?" Mundy said.

She spoke through her teeth. "It's true that you gentlemen were school chums?"

"Oxford," Frye said. "Long ago."

"Well," she said. "I prefer to keep work confined to the theater if it's all right with *both* of you."

"Really." Reuben Frye smiled stupidly.

"I never liked that word," Mundy said. *"Confined."*

"It's so noisy at the shop, now, with all the construction," Frye said.

Mundy stood, and took a step toward her. "Don't you find it so much better to practice in an informal, relaxed space?"

"I'm afraid I need the theater space in order to feel relaxed, thank you. It'll be fine there."

"Well. At any rate, prepare both parts," Frye said. "Regan and Goneril."

"I will. I would anyway, of course."

Mundy stepped closer and offered his hand again, for her to rise. She stood without taking it, but smiled at him. "Tomorrow then."

"I'd like to look around a little. Can you show us around?"

So she took them through the three rooms. Mundy paused for a long time before the paintings, tilting his head and seeming to study each one. He leaned down to read the names and the titles.

"Well," Frye said. "Thank you."

Again, Mundy came close, extending his hand. "We'll make history," he said, smiling. "That's what I always say to a new costar."

"Costar," she said. Then gave her own smile, though she felt nothing but the desire to be shut of them both. "You're the star, sir."

They went out and down the sidewalk, away.

She stood at the window looking out on the street. Several people were gathering in front of the Civil Rights museum, across the way—evidently a large group had come in two vans. She went back to her desk to wait for the end of her shift.

When she left Ellis that late afternoon, she felt she was abandoning him. He had dozed and his hands twitched as though he were dreaming about catching something. When he did wake, he looked at her for some time, and then said, "Meryl?"

She said, "Meryl's living in Knoxville now, Daddy."

He said, "No. She was just here."

"That was when they registered you here."

"Oh. Was that—that was a while back."

"Last month."

"Ah." He closed his eyes again. "Of course."

When he came to, a moment later, his mood was low, sad, almost sullen. As hers was. "Don't worry," he told her. "Things are stabilizing, I'm finding my way around." But his eyes welled up, and he put his handkerchief to his mouth and coughed. "I'm fine."

She got up to leave after he had been asleep for the better part of an hour. A nurse came in, a young woman with straight blond bangs, and just then he opened his eyes. "Esther?" he said.

"My mother," Claudette murmured to her. "They've been divorced for thirty years."

"People say anything coming out of sleep."

"Yes."

A little later as she was getting into the car, he called her cell from his room phone. "Really, everything's all right, Little One. Don't worry about me. I'm gonna read and watch a movie, then see if I can take a little walk around the courtyard, and then I'll come back and have a whiskey. And I hope I see you tomorrow."

"Maybe I'll bring Thaddeus and Gina," she said. "They've been asking."

"That'd be just fine. Who are they?"

She started to explain.

"I think I know who they are, Little One."

She wasn't sure, and it hurt knowing that. She drove to the river and took a walk, and saw the sunset over the water and Arkansas. She returned to her apartment, had a cup of green tea and an avocado with a little olive oil.

Thinking of Mundy's eyes on her and the day's visit by him and Frye, and of Ellis's sadness, and the whole weight and worry of her life, she grew anxious and poured herself two ounces of bourbon, neat. She was sitting down at the small kitchen table with the half-finished tea and the whiskey when her phone buzzed, and she picked it up without checking the number.

"This is your friendly once-husband. How're things with you this evening?"

She had a flicker of gratitude that it wasn't Ellis. "Hello, Geoffrey."

"Tell me how you are, doll."

Most of her phone conversations with him began in this fashion: a question that invited confidence, a quiet, even calming tone, with no slight trace of the distortions that had ended the marriage. But then sometimes what followed was a self-pitying screed. Apparently, this would be one of those occasions. "Thought I'd see if *your* day was better than *mine* was."

"I'm too tired, Geoffrey."

"Come on. First, let me hear *you* whine, and then you can listen to *me* whine."

She lit a cigarette, looked at it, then dropped it in the cup of cold tea.

"Have a smoke," he said.

"I'm trying to quit."

She heard him sigh out his own smoke. "Well, I wish I could quit." He took a breath. "Not the smoking. Desperation is the spur. Right? Just tell me how you *are*."

She told him a little about her father's existence in Memphis Commons, and took a sip of the whiskey, thinking she might have another when this was done.

"Why don't we raid the place and spring him," Geoffrey said.

The glibness bothered her, even knowing this was profoundly his nature. "I've got lines to work on now, okay? And I'm beat."

"Oh, *well*, then you must be a *working* actor. How lucky for you. I'm in the largest group of people in this area of the world: *non*working actors. Yesterday, I had the pleasure of driving a working actor named Robert De Niro around. Some mix-up with his regular guy. Four different places. While he talked business on his cell phone. But we talked about the business, too, you know. He's a regular guy. He told me to keep plugging."

"I really am tired tonight, Geoffrey. It's been a long week."

He cleared his throat and coughed so loudly that she put the phone away from her ear. When she put it back, he was already in midsentence. "—peating myself, but how's the new palace progressing?" When she didn't answer, he said, "I do have a new agent."

"Good." She had heard this several times before.

"An old guy, this agent. And De Niro actually smiled at me several times. We talked. Two guys, you know. Actually, actually like human beings on a strange planet. His cell phone looks just like ours. Just an ordinary cell phone any person might have."

"Good for him." She picked up the glass of whiskey, walked into her bedroom, and sat on the foot of the bed. She yawned.

"Just a little longer?" he said. "You have to listen to *my* whine now, right?"

"I thought I already was." She took another small swallow of the whiskey.

"Can I complain about that talentless fuck Miles Warden?"

She didn't answer.

"Hey, I'm sorry, forget I said that. I'm over that. Let me give you the unvarnished—like that word? I picked it up from two lobbyist types I took around last week. Let me give you the unvarnished truth about today. Today was what you might call a memory day. I had this memory, see, I'm five or six. My mother's still there. Totally out of nowhere, this memory. We're staying at *her* mother's, because Daddy-boy—well. I can tell you about it later." He had heard her yawn again.

"I'm just toast now, Geoffrey. Really, I'm sorry."

He continued, "It's strange, though. A bad winter storm and a lot of snow, my grandmother's house. Well. So this woman was a boarder there, and the whole town was under a foot of snow, and it was March twenty-first. She comes swinging into the house singing, 'Spring is here, my dear,' and my mother laughs. All I really remember is the scarf with snow on it and snow on her shoulders and my mother laughing. And that's one of my few memories of her. Why would that come back to me?"

"It was your mother in the scarf?"

"No. I told you. The boarder. You never listen. Why would that memory stand out? It's one of the few good memories and it's sketchy as a half-drawn cartoon. What does that say about my real life?" He paused. Then: "I've made it so you could sleep, though, right?"

"Yes," she told him. "You have done that."

"I miss you, Claudie." He disconnected the call before she could answer.

A female director had used the phrase *uncut jewel* about him once, before they were married, because he hadn't finished high school. He considered this an indication of worth. He would say he was of the street, that his education had come from the "school of hard knocks." And the fact that he could use such a shopworn phrase in earnest was at the heart of what she came to see as a disagreeable truth about him: he was a man with such complacency and laziness of mind that it sometimes made him dull. He had blue, blue eyes, perfectly carved sharp features, and, like her, an ability to mime different accents and voices. They had made a good show at parties. He could be compelling talking about growing up in a boardinghouse with a woman his troubled father was dating, among other women.

But they were hardship stories, and often enough he harped on them. He was a pretty boy with surprisingly puerile instincts regarding every facet of adult life. Continually self-absorbed and unhappy—one could say aggrieved—about the world's failure to notice his value, he had no real sense of responsibility to anything; life was a continual game with him.

Finally, being married to him had become almost farcical. He depended on her for everything. She earned most of the money, paid the bills, kept the apartment, maintained the cars, did the shopping, the cooking, the dishes, the laundry, all of it. She would end up making Thaddeus and Gina and Miles Warden laugh, talking about Geoffrey's world, as she called it. The world where everyone catered to him. Once, in a group of others, when he asked her for a light, leaning toward her with the cigarette jutting from his mouth, she struck a match and, holding it out, said, "Should I put my foot up your ass so you can get enough suction to smoke it?"

He laughed, failing to see the bitter exhaustion in the comment, and she knew in that instant she would demand that he leave.

But she didn't have to. He was gone a week later.

Thaddeus

Back in late March, someone had made stickers: Frye's arrival date in a bright yellow circle bordered in green, with, below the date, in black letters, LEAR, inside the open mouth of a skull. The stickers appeared on office doors and on the temporary barriers put up around work areas. Thaddeus suspected Lurlene Glenn, who had been with the company since its inception on Monroe Street. The stickers were just like her sense of humor. Her comic sensibility made you forget sometimes that her son and daughter-in-law were now years gone, having disappeared into the streets with the opioid crisis; she was raising their two young girls alone.

And while members of the board and some of the business and tech people assumed that the stickers were about starting work on producing one of the world's darkest tragedies, the actors knew exactly what it meant. A silent commiseration and joke. There were remarks about litter bearers being needed to carry the professor around. Since his arrival, after meetings with him about casting and marketing, and his demands during the hours of conducting auditions in the clatter of construction—his Canadian tea and his takeout sandwiches, and the long delays while he talked to Holliwell people and other friends on the telephone, and after his abrupt changes in each day's schedule—the joke seemed perfectly apt.

"We're stuck with the guy," Thaddeus said to Gina. "Like you're stuck with me."

"Stop that," she said. "Really." She did not look up from the lesson plan she was working on. Tonight, they'd eaten carryout from Jasmine Thai, down the street. He'd had only chicken satay, no sauce, and tea. She didn't have much appetite either. It was a pleasantly cool, calm night, and they had walked there and back. She sat at the table with the little white cartons scattered around, working on a lesson plan.

Sitting down at her side, he said, "The, um, 'disgraced,' as the papers put it, Malcolm Ruark seems like a nice guy. Grausbeck's got plans for him."

Sighing, she put the pen down and sat back. Beautiful, he thought, a beautiful woman, tired after long concentration. The possible title for a painting.

He had an urge to try entertaining her, as he'd done many times, easy as breathing (often, even his casual observations amused her). "That word, *disgraced,* seems a bit priggish, don't you think?" In an exaggerated, High Church English accent, he went on: "I mean, as a *cultyure,* we *hyave* come to undestyand the concept of alcoholism as an afflictshun, have we naught?"

Her small smile was tolerant. "Well. But contributing to the delinquency."

He let go of the accent. "That was just the booze, though."

"Nevertheless."

He let a moment pass, never taking his gaze from her. And there, again, was the sudden tilting-over in his chest. He strove to ignore it. When she glanced up, and seemed faintly startled to see him staring, he said, "I read up a little. One of the newspaper articles said he was no longer welcome in polite society. I mean, really, how weird is *that*? What exactly *is* 'polite society' nowadays? Would you say it's people who don't say *fuck*?"

She laughed softly. "Fuck no," then put her hands stagily to her mouth. "Oh, gosh."

He felt charmed and enthralled, exactly as when he had first known her. But that feeling seemed distant, suddenly. He put his hand to his chest, where the little flutter had begun again. She yawned and picked up the pencil, and tapped the end of it in a tattoo against the open book.

"I liked Malcolm Ruark," he said, simply to keep talking. "When we were outside today discussing the lines of people waiting to audition, I was shading my eyes because I was facing the sun behind him, and he had a baseball cap on and he walked around so the sun was at my back. Considerate, don't you think? And there wasn't the slightest celebrity smugness about him. He just seemed kind of, I don't know, tentative. And, I'll tell you, I hope I can look as good as he does when I'm in my fifties."

"You don't look as good as he does *now*."

He said, "Always nice to know one's looks are appreciated."

"You'd think with all the drinking, he'd have a gut."

Thaddeus gazed out the window at the flickering night sky, and thought of farewells, Ellis Bradley in a nursing home; Miles Warden gone over the curve of the world. Himself possibly keeling over with the something amiss in his chest. *Ridiculous.* "Wonder what time it is in Sydney?"

"It's across the date line. Better to ask what day it is."

"Let's go over and see Claudette at the gallery."

She indicated the work on the table before her. "I'm trying to do this now, Wolfie. I've put it off until now. Tomorrow's Monday, my first class substituting for an old beloved lady who got pinkeye from her grandson, and these kids will not want to see me. I haven't taught a class in a long time, and I'm just a bit nervous about it. You know? Do you just want to sit here and woolgather with me? What is it with you anyway? You're like a clock that's wound too tight."

"I thought I was like a man with an overactive capacity for worry."

"No—you *are* that man. You're starting to remind me of my mother."

"A beautiful lady, Louisa. My friend."

They were quiet again.

Suddenly she turned to him. "You're hovering. It's weird. Is something wrong? How come you haven't had any wine lately?"

He shrugged. "Just haven't felt like it, I guess."

"You're thirty-eight years old and you're acting elderly."

"My mother says I've been old since I was nine."

"Effie's got a point—but beyond that."

"You mean I've suddenly embraced birtherism? Supply-side economics?"

She stared. "You *know* what I mean, Wolfie. Are you keeping something from me?"

"Yes, my poor darling. I've piled up gambling debts. Millions."

"Stop it." Something changed behind her eyes, a sudden deeper concentration.

He poured a glass of Saint-Estèphe, determining simply to go on as usual, working to calm himself by remembering the conversation with his mother. He had seen a news article on his cell phone about the earthquake in Nepal that had killed people in China and Bangladesh. "You remember that earthquake in Nepal?"

A mistake, and he realized it immediately; he drew in a breath to apologize, but she had already gasped with frustration. "Oh, God, Wolfie. Will you *please*." She actually looked like she might cry. "Just please leave me alone a little. I don't feel like talking about Nepal. Or any bad news. I don't feel like talking. Please."

"Okay," he said, holding both hands out, palms toward her. "Sorry."

She shook her head, not looking at him now, or at the work, which was merely notes on a legal pad about the hours of a day.

"Forgive me, really," he said.

"Go. Do something with yourself."

It seemed that he had never heard this tone in her voice, never been made to feel that he was bothering her. "I'd like to help, babe. I know it's got your nerves—"

She turned suddenly in the chair, one arm on the table, one on the chair back. "That is *not*—" She stopped. "Please. Just—let me be."

He went into the other room and tried to call Claudette, but got no answer. He put some music on: Sibelius's Third. One of their favorite classical pieces, and he had introduced her to it.

"Can you turn it down?" she called. "Or *off*? I'm trying to concentrate. Christ!"

He called to her, "It's fifth graders, Gina. Nothing to worry about."

Silence.

He sat reading. The house was quiet. Finally he went upstairs to bed, early. She came up and went into the bathroom to take a shower. His heart thudded and paused again, and he lay there propped on pillows while the walls of the room seemed to be slowly dissolving, actually moving outward as if this were a dream of reality itself coming apart.

His cell phone erupted in the piano blues riff he had it set on. The suddenness of it brought a startled yelp from his throat. He opened it with trembling fingers, feeling its irrelevance, notes from the world of nothing wrong. In its window was a Boston area code. Frye. "Yes?"

"Am I calling at a bad time? Did I wake you?"

"No, sir."

"I'm wondering if we could get an article about Malcolm Ruark in the papers. You know, the fallen local celeb whose older brother gets him a shot at redemption. You know, second chances, and the company as a family. Somebody in publicity could talk to him."

"You should clear it with him. And maybe ask Lurlene. She'll have an idea about it."

"That former student of mine, Kelly—I'm a little worried about her flightiness."

"Flightiness."

"Well. Don't say anything. I'm sure she'll figure it out. But this is Albee. You know. Albee's tough. But her *Driving Miss Daisy* in Portland blew everybody away."

"That's what I heard." Thaddeus merely desired to end the conversation. He had heard nothing about Kelly Gordon in Portland or anywhere else before Frye introduced her.

"Albee was a friend of mine, you know. Real gentleman. But kind of closed seeming. Guarded. Like he expected to be hurt."

"I love his work," Thaddeus got out, remembering Ms. Gordon's sardonic question: *Has Frye told you he and Edward Albee are friends?*

The visiting director left a pause. Then: "Okay. That's it." And the connection was broken.

"Ridiculous," said Thaddeus.

"Who was that?" Gina asked, coming out of the bathroom in a robe, with a towel wrapped around her head.

"Frye. He wants to get an article done about Ruark."

"Jesus Christ on a raft."

"Are we all right?" he said.

"Do you have any idea how often you've asked me that lately?"

He had no idea. "Okay," he said, trying to remember.

She dried her hair, walking back and forth, and then got into her nightgown. She brought out her little nail-polish kit and sat down in the straight-backed, lace-bordered window seat. He watched as she began painting her toenails.

"I'd like some time off," she said. "While the stage is being remade."

"Maybe we can drive down and see your mom." He reached for the day's *Commercial Appeal* on the nightstand and opened it across his legs.

"Could do that. Or maybe just *I* could do that."

He chose to ignore this. "We could spend the weekend. Maybe visit the Faulkner house again, or take Louisa to Taylor Grocery for the catfish."

"I need some time alone with her, Thaddeus. She's got that new 'beau.'"

"Good for her. I think that's great. A new boyfriend."

"Beau. She insists on using the term *beau*. And this is a freaking retired minister who wants *Roe v. Wade* declared unconstitutional."

Her father, RJ, had been gone almost six years. As a young man, he had been among the speechwriters in the Johnson White House, and had written two history texts. The books had earned him a chair at Rhodes.

"Maybe the minister's a nice person," he said now.

She gave him a look. "They've been watching Fox Spews together. He's obviously narrow as a strand of thread."

"Well, then, we absolutely have to go spend a weekend down there. A long weekend."

"Did you hear me? I need one-on-one time with her."

"Oh, okay." He continued watching her perform the little meticulous motions, holding the lozenge-sized bottle in one hand and the brush in the other. In the next instant, without even looking up from her careful administration of the polish, and completely without emotion, she said, "Um, actually—I've been thinking about splitting."

The beginning of the hot twilight was on her hair through the window, shadow-roots in it showing like dark thoughts. She sighed softly and then looked straight at him, an expression matter-of-fact as a weather report. "I was lying on the sofa. And—and you got up to go into the kitchen, and I saw you touch your chest as you went through the doorway, and I *knew* you'd felt something there that worried you. I could see it in your face. And I knew of course that you'd thought of death because that's been *you* lately. Everything death, death, death. And suddenly I saw thirty-five years more, give or take, of that kind of thing, and just like that I didn't know if I could do it. Maybe it's because I'm forty-one. Maybe it's all these years with my mother and her alarms. And—well anyway, it got me thinking."

Neither of them spoke or moved for a moment.

"I'm just being honest, Wolfie. It's just crossed my mind a little, that's all. And maybe I wondered some if it's crossed *yours*."

"It hasn't," he said. "Not once."

Her gaze was oddly full of a kind of curiosity. "Really."

It gave him a chill. It was as though he would have to call her back from somewhere far. "Really," he said.

She left a pause, still polishing her toenails, concentrating on them. "I haven't done anything, you know. I mean, there isn't anybody else."

"Well, that's a relief."

Silence.

"And—but you want to be *honest*," he managed.

Her slow nod was almost solemn. "I've been worried."

He put the newspaper down and adjusted the pillows and settled, still facing her. She sighed, and came to her side of the bed.

"It probably won't come to anything." She sighed again, settling in with her back to him.

He put his hand, quite softly, on her shoulder, and then took it away. Absently, she reached back and patted his hip.

"Go to sleep," she murmured. "It's just woolgathering."

Claudette

Her father had been wounded in Korea, at the Battle of Chipyong-ni. A place no one ever heard of, he would say. Shrapnel from a mortar round grazed the lower-right side of his face, creasing the mandibular fossa, and the necessary corrective surgery left a slight rightward misalignment of his jaw. The experience was quite painful and a bad memory which caused recurring nightmares long after the war, but the small disfigurement had given him a look of perpetual amusement. It became a large part of his charm. He was her closest family tie. She was not very close to her stepmother, or, for that matter, her biological mother, who lived in Paris now, retired. Her older sister, Meryl, was entrenched with her family in a spacious, barn-red house outside Knoxville, and had embraced a form of bastionlike domesticity. Meryl's husband, Colin, was a nice man with a high, outward-curving forehead and small white hands. He worked at Sears. Their boys, aged nine and thirteen, were pleasant, though not particularly outgoing. She seldom saw them. Meryl had married young, and her husband still adored her. She was lucky and she talked about it.

Claudette had come to prefer the distance.

Ellis taught history for more than thirty-five years, and had been a fixture at Central High almost twenty years when Meryl and Claudette came through, two years apart. After he retired, and Claudette had graduated, she went with him on several vacation trips. He was alone, and seemed fine with it, but she worried about him. They fished on Little River, or hiked in the Smokies, and they spent one long winter weekend down on the Gulf Coast, and another sailing on Spirit Lake, up north (Geoffrey accompanied them on those two trips—the last ones, in fact). Ellis's casual remark back in those good days was "We're making memories, Little One, for when we need them—in a week or two." This was his joke about the quickness of time.

These days, the idea caused a stab of sorrow.

As he had got into his late seventies, he was rarely able to attend her performances. It was too difficult negotiating the steps down into the orchestra section or up into the balconies at the theater, and anyway, as he would good-naturedly point out, he usually couldn't concentrate that long anymore. Mostly, though, it was the arthritic knees and the degenerative rheumatism in the hips, the frequent vertigo, the weakness, the slight palsy, and the fatigue. The stroke had increased the short-term memory lapses, and even so, in some passes you almost forgot the deficits. When her stepmother, sister, and brother-in-law all insisted on placing him at Memphis Commons, Ellis had gone along with it, but Claudette saw the discouragement, the disappointment with which he had done so. And there were many sleepy depressed hours in those first days she visited him, though that didn't stop her. She was often the lone, loving presence sitting by him when he stirred and wondered where he was. But the lower dose of the antianxiety drug was beginning to show.

There were times, now, when he was suddenly there as himself. And they could talk. The deficits seemed, for those intervals, to have receded.

And those intervals seemed to be coming more frequently. Sunday afternoon, she made the turn into the circular drive with its trim, precise border of fresh-cut grass and pulled through the bands of shade thrown by the oaks on either side, the shade not quite reaching the building itself. It was a pretty day, and going by the theater she'd seen that the lettering of the new façade was visible inside its scaffolding and the netting of slats and metal flex cable: THE GLOBE, in a two-foot-high font like a giant signature. At the Commons, as she drove around toward the parking lot, she saw, framed in the main, sunlit window, Ellis sitting in a wheelchair, asleep, the whole tableau looking like a terrifying postmodern sculpture, realistic to the point of horror: elderly man, unconscious in wheelchair, head deeply down, the image and imprint of desolation. It was as though, within the space of twenty-four hours, he'd been reduced to the lethargy of his first days there.

She drove on across to the lot, parked, took her cell out with trembling fingers, and called her stepmother.

Franny answered with a musical lilt. "Hello-oh."

"They've got him sitting in a wheelchair in the window, Franny. In the sun. Like a—like an art exhibit." She started walking across the lot toward the entrance. "What the hell."

"I just left there. He wants to sit in that window. A little sun is healthy."

"He *hates* it in that *place*. And he'll take the sun burning him through glass to look outside of it. Is he drugged up again?" It surprised her to hear that she was shouting. She took a breath, and said, as calmly as she could, "I'm sorry for shouting. But this whole thing was wrong, and Meryl and Colin and you wouldn't hear me. Jesus!"

"I asked for a sedative because of his agitation at lunch. He was downright rude. You and he both agreed to him being there. And he asked for the warm sun. He has a window in his room for looking at scenery. He wanted the sunlight."

"Why the wheelchair, Franny?"

"He was unsteady and they'd just waxed the hallway. That's a precaution. He wanted the sunlight."

"Well, if they want to give him sunlight, they should let him walk out and look at it. And of course he wants more than the window in that room—out that window is the interior lawn and the other wing of this place. It's twenty-five fucking feet of grass." She had reached the entrance.

"All right, now," her stepmother said. "There's no need to get upset. Or swear. And there's certainly no need to get snotty. I'm doing the best I can."

Claudette ended the call.

Inside, she saw some staff people gathered in a little circle in the office, passing around pieces of cake; someone's birthday. She went past this, along the hall, and beyond the last room, his, to the grotto-like opening on one side, where the window was. He was there, head down, hands lying in his thin lap. "Daddy?" she said. He didn't stir. She touched his shoulder.

"Oh," he said, low, as if he'd been reminded of something.

"Hey," she said. "Let's get out of this heat."

Raising his head, he gripped the arms of the chair and looked at her. "Oh, hello, Little One. I fell asleep. Had a nap. Am I driving?"

"Dad."

"Just joking. I know you're driving."

"You *are* joking."

He grinned. "Is Big Girl with you?" This was what he'd always called Meryl.

"Not today."

"I know, she lives in Knoxville." He seemed proud of remembering this. She gripped the back handles of the chair. It seemed wedged in somehow, in the little sharp-angled space which was like the balcony box at a theater. She pulled hard, and finally got the chair to move. Pulling it until she could turn it around facing into the wide hallway, she leaned down to look at him, and kissed the side of his face. She felt the heat from the sun there. It was as if he were burning up with fever.

"Little afternoon nap and looking out at the world," he said, still grinning. "Where did it all go?"

"I'm taking you back to your room."

"I'm not as demented as they think I am, you know. I think they might be stealing things from my room. But I keep hiding the important ones. I've got your picture in a drawer."

For an instant, they were paused there, the window behind them, the extended, distorted shadow of them on the shiny floor—as though she were twelve feet tall and the chair was the size of an automobile.

He smiled the wonderfully skewed smile, and then started, with some effort, to stand.

"I can wheel you there."

"Nah," he said, with a little dismissive shrug, pushing himself to standing. "Let's walk."

She took his arm, and kicked the chair back into the pool of sun at the window. They made their way to his room, where the door was open to anyone walking down the hall. They entered and moved to the wing chair across from his neatly made bed. A folded newspaper had been placed on the pillow. His daily paper, apparently untouched.

Turning the straight-back chair at the desk, as usual, to face him, she saw his hands with their knotted veins, and the wide liver patches. It was always unpleasantly as though she had to be reminded about them.

"You hear from Esther?"

"No," she said. Feeling her spirit go down. "She's busy in Paris." She stepped to the bed, got the newspaper, and brought it back. He opened the first fold of it in his lap, glanced at the headlines, then closed it and tossed it back on the bed. "Don't feel like reading now, Little One. My eyes're tired. Hey, this morning, true, I saw a big spider come racing across the ceiling." He pointed. "Right there. Big as a plate, and fast. I got out of the bed with a slipper to kill it and it was gone. Big, bad-looking spider. Black as midnight in a cave. One of the nurses said it's very common. Hypno-something."

Claudette indicated the newspaper. "I could read that *to* you."

He gazed at her. "I remember Geoffrey had a gift for impressions."

"He did," she admitted. And then the words rose to her lips: *I dug him physically*. She'd always been able to say anything to Ellis. She held it back.

"The two of you, in that Pinter play," he said.

"Oh, that was a really long time ago," she said. "Let's not talk about it."

"Well." He straightened in the chair, perfectly happy to change the subject. "You'll find somebody."

Their talk often led here. She was used to it; her reply was automatic. "I don't mind being single. I like it, really." She began talking quickly about her day at the gallery, describing again the progress of construction at the theater, and the work, now that the visiting director was in place. He stared at the room, and seemed far away. She kept her voice cheerful. He closed his eyes, a slow blinking shut. Then he opened them, almost as if startled, and looked at her. "You already told me all this," he said. "Right?" He'd rested his elbows on the arm of the chair, arms folded, hands clasped under his chin.

Forcing an encouraging smile, she nodded. "I can't remember what I told you."

"Years like minutes," he said. "That is the most amazing thing."

She leaned forward and put her hand on his shoulder. Determined to keep to the goings-on of the day, she said, "I think I'm going to be Goneril, in *Lear*."

He brought his hands down and rested them in his lap. "How's the line go? 'I fear I am not in my perfect mind.'"

The fact that Ellis recalled the passage was cheering in the resolute way of holding on. "That's wonderful, Daddy. You nailed it. Yes."

"Always loved that play. What were you saying just then? Don't tell me."

She waited.

"Where's Esther?"

"She lives in France now. Paris. A long time."

"She sure ran off with that dentist fellow."

"You guys had split, though, way before that."

"She went to Europe. France, I believe."

"England. Yes." Claudette didn't have the breath for more.

"Had to be that far away from me."

She looked out the window at the row of windows across the grass, and with feigned nonchalance wiped the tears from her eyes.

Sighing with satisfaction, he said, "You remind me of her, you know. You favor her, as they used to say. You bring her to mind." Then he tossed his head back slightly. "I was happy with Esther." His eyes narrowed. "Not really all that much since." And there was the slow nodding again. "I keep forgetting the whens and hows and wherefores. I wish I knew where everybody was."

She leaned over and put her arms around his neck, and suddenly she thought of walking with him out of Memphis Commons.

She had an image of him as he'd been in that wheelchair, head down, sun blazing through the glass, and she recalled him in the haze and depression and drugged sleep of the first visits, and then she pictured the nights, his nights, alone, no one to turn to in the predawn hours, and the slow afternoons when he could not look out at the world at all. Geoffrey's mock-serious idea rose to her mind, of simply raiding the place. Why not? She could hire a nurse, someone to be with him when she had to be at the theater. "Daddy, you really want to stay in here?" she heard herself say.

Looking around the room, he seemed to consider. "What'll we do with everything?"

This elated and unnerved her at the same time. She heard herself say, "I'll send for it all. Let's just get the hell out of here."

Again, he looked around the room. "I don't know." He sat there.

She reached down and took hold of his thin-boned hands with their rough palms. "I'll do whatever you want me to do."

"Don't leave me?" He worked to stand, with a grip so tight it hurt her fingers. He turned slightly, and seemed confused.

"We have to get you dressed."

His smile seemed sad. But then he laughed. "Oh, of course."

It took almost an hour. He kept stopping to ask her about things, and she couldn't find socks for him; the home (as he called it) had issued warm slippers, and he didn't know or couldn't remember where he'd put any of his socks. They found a pair in one of his suitcoat jackets, balled up, caked with dry mud. "I don't recall where I went with these."

She shook them, rubbed the cloth against itself over the sink, and helped him put them on, worried the whole time that one of the staff might walk in. At last, the two of them stepped out into the empty hall. The abandoned wheelchair sat in sunlight from the window at the far end. It looked like another kind of art piece, one meant to inspire: empty wheelchair in bright light, shadows falling away from it. They walked the other way and out the exit, into the side alley. There were dark shrubs bordering the lane. The shrubs had been recently trimmed, and dry brown branches jutted from the leaves with stark, sharp, twisting edges. Very slowly, stumbling slightly, they made their way along to the parking lot and the car. As far as she knew, no one had seen them. She actually had the thought that they were safe now, and then she considered the thought. All around her, Memphis was imperviously going on with its day.

Fighting back tears, she helped her father into the car. "Here we go," she said.

At the apartment, he asked for potato chips. All she had was a jar of dry-roasted peanuts and she shook some into a bowl for him. She poured him a glass of orange juice. "Is Franny going to come by?" he asked, smiling.

"She doesn't know about this," Claudette told him. "Yet."

"Esther?"

She had a moment of pure dread. Perhaps this had been the wrong thing to do. She thought of Franny and of Law, and the power and reach of Memphis Commons with their personnel, some of whom had looked like guards to her. "I'm okay, Little One," he said. "You go on and do your work."

"I'll be right in the next room," she told him.

"Sure." He put the TV on. She went into the spare room, which she had used as an office, and put fresh sheets on the bed there, then stored the things from his bag in the dresser, the middle drawers of which hadn't been used.

When she stepped back into the living room, she saw that he'd fallen asleep. Again, the dread reached through her.

She called Gina's phone, and got no answer, so she punched in Thaddeus's number. And Gina answered.

"Hey, I was trying to call you."

"Sorry," Gina said. "My phone died. Thaddeus gave me his because he's in a meeting with the contractors about the new restrooms. Listen. Do you think anxiety might actually be a form of pathological self-regard?"

"Are we talking about your mother?"

"We're talking about Wolfgang Amadeus Thaddeus Deerforth. My one and only."

"Did you have a fight or something?"

Silence.

"Gina, tell me."

"God." Gina paused again. "Look. It's nothing. It's this—this craziness. Trying to do anything with this construction going on and now Frye and the lines of strangers wanting auditions and now Thaddeus is worrying in all the *minutes* of the day. He's getting to be like my mother. I feel smothered. I'm sick of it."

"You're sick of Thaddeus?" Claudette paused. Then: "Like I was sick of Geoffrey?"

There was another silence, followed by Gina's voice, quite small. "No." The word dissolved into the faint static in the line. Then: "I love him. I do love him. But I'm afraid we're both falling out of it. And there's—oh, nevermind. I'm afraid we're getting weary of each other."

"*You* two?" Claudette gave a little mocking laugh, intending it to be soothing.

"You know what happened at the school this morning?" her friend continued. "I had one class, substituting for this old lady with pinkeye. I'm reading a story to the kids and in the middle of a sentence I start crying. Now go ahead and ask me what I was reading to them."

"*Sweetie*. Come *on*."

"*Green Eggs and Ham*, Claudie. I'm in the middle of fucking *Green Eggs and Ham*, saying the line 'I do not like them, Sam-I-am,' and suddenly I'm sobbing."

Claudette laughed. "I can't help it. I'm imagining the looks on their faces."

Her friend gave a small sigh. "It wasn't funny when it happened. What do you need?"

"I called *you*. To tell you I walked out of that place with Dad."

"You—you went for a walk?"

"No. The Commons. I walked out of Memphis Commons with Dad. I brought him home."

"But—what'll he do there? What'll *you* do?"

"We'll *live* here, Gina." She felt the words like a weight in her stomach. She took a breath. "We'll hire somebody for home care. It'll be fine."

"Is he well enough—"

"It's been better since they started on the lower dose. I just couldn't—" Her voice caught. "Couldn't leave him there anymore. And the lower dose is *my* dose, and I've got plenty of it, since I don't take it every day. Hell, I don't even take it once a week."

They said nothing for a beat.

"Claudie, why should Thaddeus's voice irritate me? I mean, all this good stuff is happening and all the money and support and we're about to come apart. We don't have any right to this kind of self-indulgent crap."

"It's a feeling, Gina."

"Can I—is there a way we can meet for a coffee?"

"You'll have to come here."

"Oh, right. Yes. I'll come there. Be good to see Ellis."

As she put a pillow under her father's head, he woke up. "Think I'll go on in and take a nap," he said. This calmed her. He was going to do something as normal as taking a nap.

Fifteen minutes later Gina arrived, looking harried, hot, and weary, her hair held haphazardly in a white scarf.

They looked in on Ellis, who was lying on his side, legs up, snoring lightly.

"Are you gonna get in trouble?" Gina whispered.

"Don't know. I guess I'll see."

They went into the little kitchen. Claudette brewed coffee as her friend cut up a pear and made toast with marmalade. She made enough for Ellis if he woke. They sat across from each other. Gina brought a handkerchief out of her purse and held it crushed in her palm. She put the handkerchief to her mouth, and then wiped her forehead with it.

"So," Claudette said. "You and Thaddeus."

"I'm eight days late, Claudie. I've never been more than a day or two. And I've got these symptoms. I looked it up. I'm only forty-one, and I've got all the signs of perimenopause."

"You can't talk to Thaddeus about *that*?"

"Not the way I feel now. Christ, the other day I said I was thinking of leaving."

"You did *what*?"

"I know. But I was. I was thinking of it. Then. That moment."

"Gina."

"I know."

"What about now?"

"Now I just feel so low and blue all the time. Whole thing's crazy. And he keeps watching me, of course."

"Well, could it be he's afraid you're gonna leave him?"

"It was stupid. But I *have* been thinking about it. I can't stand anything right now. It's crazy, I know. I'm sorry. You don't need this."

Claudette poured more of the coffee for them both.

"Ten years ago, I would've been thinking, you know—*Maybe this is a baby*. It would've been exciting. He wanted a child so bad. But the doctors said I had 'low ovarian reserve.' And—but he was so good about it. Sometimes I think he's just—" She paused, searching for the word. Then: "So much *nicer* than I am."

Claudette said, "I never saw two people more in love."

The other appeared not to have heard this, but sat there muttering to herself. "Walking around in this morbid state all the time." She sat back and looked at the room. "It was heartbreak for him. When we got the report, my father hugged me and said, 'Honey, the first one's God's, no matter what the doctors say.'"

"That sounds like RJ, all right."

"But I saw the look of hope in Wolfie's eyes, that it wasn't over. But it *was* over."

"It was *ten* years ago, honey. What the hell."

Gina rocked forward and back slowly, then stopped. "I know," she said, barely audibly.

"Missing a period now and then's not unusual, anyway," Claudette said. "Right?"

"I'm so tired, though. I feel like *sounds* drain me. I'm so sorry."

"No apologies, honey. Not to me, anyway, right?"

Malcolm

Arthur Grausbeck convened the Summer Acting Camp for children on Monday at noon. The board had decided that even with the renovation, the classes could take place in the black box (which would be substantially unchanged—one wall would be moved back four feet toward the end of the process, to make room for more seats). Malcolm, stopping by to see more auditions, decided to look in on the first meeting. Thaddeus was there, conducting it, and Malcolm found that he liked the younger man's way with children, though the theater manager seemed vaguely distracted, as well. The sound of saws and hammering coming through the walls was a problem. There were nine children from local schools. Thaddeus had divided them up into three groups of three. Intermittently having to raise his voice over all the noise, he explained how they would be doing improvisations. He would give them the situation, and they would take it from there. It was quite clear as the exercise went on that each of them had talent. "They're stunning," Malcolm said, meaning it. "Do they go through an application process?"

"Teachers at the schools pick them."

"I should've covered this when I was with WMC."

"Maybe you can get somebody—" the theater manager began, then halted. "Sorry."

Malcolm smiled. "I'm not on speaking terms with those folks, Thaddeus. Um, their choice."

In the wake of the accident, the three days of house arrest, and the month of rehab, his firing had been sprung upon him, this after several "strong" statements by the program director and the station owner that WMC was standing by its most prominent newscaster in his illness. They used the word. *Illness*. And within ten minutes on the morning of his return to the studio, he was told bluntly that his tenure was over; two uniformed security guards escorted him out as if he were a threat to safety.

Now, he said to Thaddeus, "You understand."

"I do," said the latter. "Forgive me, really."

Before them, three at a time by turns, the children performed, using different accents for an improvised scene he'd given them, of people from different cultures on a bus.

"Would you like to conduct the camp?" the theater manager asked.

"Oh, yes," Malcolm told him. "Thanks, actually, I would."

The acting camp provided an agreeable surprise: he liked being around the children, who knew nothing at all about him.

During his search for part-time work that week, he received the notion that some people talked to him only because they were curious about the fallen local celebrity. Now and then he experienced a disagreeable sense of being gaped at, like a freak. No one had work for him. But there was the acting camp with the talented children, and he considered that he was at least doing something, which was a change from spending days reading Churchill's measured summaries of the movements of great masses of soldiers and matériel in all the theaters of war, or wandering through Chekhov's beautifully exact portrayals of life in late-nineteenth-century Russia.

One morning, toward the end of the acting camp, he saw a listing for a butler, and on an impulse he drove to the address, which turned out to be an enormous cathedral of a house—the very picture of antebellum splendor—on the edge of the Old Forest, down a long, tree-lined driveway. He saw the big wraparound porch and columns through the trees. He hadn't thought he would actually go through with it—indeed he suspected that the whole thing must be a joke. But seeing the house, he grew curious enough to take the driveway in.

Forsythia and crepe myrtle bordered the structure, and the air was thick with floral aromas. A massive magnolia tree stood to the left of the porch, studded with yawning white blossoms—each looking like some capacious creature with a gaping mouth—and the tree itself put him in mind of a stout personage holding an armful of packages and just managing not to drop one.

The listing, it turned out, was serious.

The person who had placed the ad was a tall, pale-eyed woman with a narrow column of a face topped by wispy white hair. She had a long neck, stretched seeming, as though her height were attributable to some invisible force pulling her skyward. Her stunned expression at the sight of him standing there on her big porch made him want to laugh. After a long silence, she spoke: "What on earth do *you* want?"

So, she had recognized him.

He decided to play it. He stood straight, hands clasped at his waist, and with exaggerated dignity said, "I am here regarding your classified ad, madam. Seeking a butler."

She stared. *"You?"*

In his most sonorous newscaster's voice, he said, "It would seem that your need of a butler can be quite adequately met by myself, madam. Would you not agree?" And when she didn't answer, he bowed, just slightly. She closed the door, and stared at him through its small oval window. He stared back. They remained that way for a time on either side of the door. Finally he bowed again, and walked off.

She opened the door and called to him. "Come here, please."

He attempted to remain in character, as it were, ambling back to the base of the porch steps.

"I *don't* need your service," she said. "But I have a small vacant cottage behind the house that I've put up for rent."

"Wouldn't that be where you keep your butler?"

She folded her arms. "If that was meant to offend, it was woefully short of the mark. I have a cottage to rent. The butler would have *his* own room to stay in, on the premises."

"I didn't mean to offend. May I take down the information and let you know?"

"I was not averse to your work as a television journalist." Her tone was matter-of-fact.

He bowed again, marveling at his own sense of the gesture as being required. "I thank you, kindly."

She reached into her long skirt and brought out a small red change purse, from which she removed a card. She glanced at it before offering it to him with a subtle yet noticeable touch of wariness, like someone offering a morsel to a bear.

"I thank you," he said again, and, once more, he bowed.

A little later, driving down Union Avenue toward the river, he began laughing. It seemed to him that he hadn't laughed like that in months.

And he found that thinking about the tall woman with the television newsman at her door helped his mood. Her card read *Eleanor Cruikshank, Author,* with her email address, and book titles: *White Hawthorne, Little Acts of Retribution,* and *Mrs. Dowling.* They were literary romances, labeled as such, and when he looked them up on the internet, they showed many reactions and apparently healthy sales. *White Hawthorne* interested him most because it was about the last days of Keats, a favorite poet of his since reading Fitzgerald and *Tender Is the Night* in college. The Fitzgerald had led him to Keats. He ordered all three books for next-day delivery, and sent her an email saying that if by chance someone hadn't already snapped it up, he was indeed interested in the cottage. She replied promptly that she had supposed he was, and would not rent it until she heard from him one way or another, or until the end of the month, whichever came first. This pass helped relieve the ache of his notoriety in the circumstances, and at the end of that week, at last, he found a part-time position at Gateway Travel Agency—three mornings a week, booking cruises and flights elsewhere. That was how he thought of it. People seeking to go elsewhere. The pay, along with his salary at the theater, was just enough to get by from day to day.

II

Ghost Light

Tuesday, June 9–Wednesday, June 17

Thaddeus

He was sitting alone in the living room. An old Humphrey Bogart movie he didn't recognize was on TCM. He had made himself a snifter of cognac, and he was holding the drink with its lovely stinging aroma to his nose. He thought of Bogart's death. And the deaths of all the others in the film. *Ridiculous.* When the film ended, he put the snifter on the side table, walked slowly around to the stairs and up to the bedroom, and sat on the edge of the bed. Gina was already lying under the blanket, turned to the wall, reading a magazine. She stirred slightly and looked over her shoulder at him.

He undressed, aware of her gaze, then went into the bathroom and brushed his teeth, disliking what he saw in the mirror.

In bed, he lay with his back to her. A long moment passed where it seemed they were simply listening to each other breathe.

"I want you," he said. "I want you close."

She gave an exasperated sigh. "I'm sorry. I just can't—not right now. Tomorrow morning?"

"Don't know if I could concentrate with this." He put his hand to his chest. "My heart keeps skipping beats."

"Look, Wolfie, I know I'm no help. But I can't stand being around worry over sickness. Not now, okay? When we were living here with Mom and RJ, and then just with Mom, that was the thing. I didn't even realize it until she'd moved south, and suddenly we didn't have the constant talk about all the little upsets and changes in her body. I mean, really, that's been my whole growing up. And I can't take it. I don't know how RJ took it all those years."

He was silent.

She moved a little closer.

"You still awake?" he asked.

Silence.

He doubted he would sleep. But he must've drifted slightly, because when she spoke again, her voice gave him a second's startlement. "Mother says they're coming soon, now."

"To our local theater?"

She didn't respond.

"*There's* something that'll reduce the stress level around here."

"I'm not even sure she and I are still speaking after the last time. But she said, 'See ya,' in that way she has."

"I shouldn't make jokes," he said. "We love Louisa."

"Well, let's don't go overboard."

They laughed quietly. It was a taste of their usual way with each other, and it thrilled him. "You gonna be all right alone with her while I'm gone all day? I've got meetings and dealing with contractors at the theater all day Saturday. And Frye's gonna be putting the new budget together and interviewing effects companies. I'll have to sit in on some demonstrations."

Eyes still closed, she said, "Where do you think I've been, Thaddeus? We're all buried in set work, for all three shows. Jesus."

"I'm just saying what *I'll* be doing all day Saturday, babe."

"Well, Louisa can fend for herself a little. And she'll have her boyfriend with her."

He said nothing for a moment. Then: "Beau?"

"Cut it out," she said with a little smirk.

He waited.

"That couple across the street," she said. "Those friends of hers, they need a house sitter."

"She's not gonna stay *here*?"

"They need a house sitter. That's how she broached the subject of coming up."

"What about the dog?"

"The dog'll stay with somebody down there, I guess. But the reverend's coming. Another kind of dog. When she calls me now, he's always there. The Right Reverend Whitcomb."

"From the ministry of St. Sebastian of the Corrective Shoes," said Thaddeus. It was a name she had made up for the man.

She gave a little scoffing laugh, then spoke through a yawn, "Yeah. The ubiquitous Rightwing Reverend Whitcomb. The man who thinks Jesus is a Republican."

After another pause, he said, "Let's at least plan the dog's demise."

She sighed. "Do you know how many times that rodent has bit me over the last seven years? And to think of it: a fucking *dog* named Marcel."

Now we're ourselves, he thought. "I have an image of the first time I met Louisa," he offered. "Sitting in her lounge chair with that other one, Tunk, nestled on her lap, snapping and snarling at anyone who got within ten feet, including RJ. I thought that was the lapdog of all lapdogs, until Marcel."

"I wonder if something in her personality *engenders* that snappishness in her pets."

"There's not a mean bone in the lady's body, Gina."

"*You* get along with her better than I do."

"I love her as my friend and *also* as my mother-in-law."

"If only she liked *me* as well as she likes you."

"She loves you."

They were quiet again. Sleep began stealing over him, and suddenly, she began crying. The sound seemed to come out of his half sleep.

He reached over her and turned the light on. "Gina?"

"Don't," she said. "Turn it off. I'm just so desperately tired, and I need sleep."

But it seemed that she had been sleeping so soundly during his wakeful turns in the nights; he had watched her in his own sleeplessness. He turned the light off, and then lay close, propping himself on one elbow, gingerly running his hand along her hip. She remained still, and in a little while he heard her slow sleep-breathing. The light was still on. Leaning up and carefully reaching past her, he turned the light off, then lay back, resting his hand on her shoulder.

"Don't," she said.

He turned, sighing without sound. She stirred only a little, pulled the blanket high, up to her ears, and was still. A little later, he murmured, "Gina?"

Silence, just the sleep-sighing.

He closed his eyes and kept his head straight so as not to have his ear against the pillow. He could feel the cognac. He waited, sleepless, aware of his pulse, resolving not to attend to it, or to her shifts in mood and tone. And then abruptly knowing, in a discouraging shift of his thoughts, like a door opening on a cold winter night, that he was going to have to find a way to *seem* not to be watching her too closely. He would add an hour before getting out of bed in the morning, let her go in alone, try *seeming* not to worry every minute—as of course he was. He whispered under his breath, "Ridiculous."

He looked at the little too-bright window of his cell phone: the news was terrible. The whole world was going on with its mayhem all the time. He couldn't sleep, and then he kept drifting in and out fitfully. At first light, she rose and started getting ready. "Come on," she said.

"Gonna take a little time this morning," he told her.

"You're okay," she said. It sounded like an opinion. "And aren't you the lucky one." She came over and kissed the side of his face and then left without saying more. He heard her drive off. He sat in the kitchen and read the paper—the sports page—but his mind wandered. It was just a matter of this malaise of hers. She hadn't shown or betrayed interest in anyone else. He was beginning to feel anxious again. He thought how it would be, how things might improve somehow, with Louisa in town.

He was indeed fond of the old lady. Even when she was in one of her panics, she was unfailingly interesting, every bit as good a storyteller as her husband had been. At seventy-eight, she still smoked and drank whiskey. RJ himself had consumed almost half a fifth a day, starting with a dry Manhattan around noon, and going on slowly into the late evenings. She often joined him for the whole ride, from noon to closing, as she put it. When Gina was a child, on visits down in Oxford to that little house where Louisa now lived (which had belonged to Louisa's father, Bo Talbot, the unassuming former mayor of Oxford, who had made it a point to live like any average citizen and who had known Faulkner), RJ and the old man spent sweet slow hours sitting on the porch, drinking Manhattans, telling stories, and laughing. Louisa believed whiskey kept both men alive longer. Bo Talbot died quietly in his sleep at one hundred and five years and fifteen days old, the summer before last. He had outlived RJ, who was nearly twenty years younger. RJ made it to eighty-six.

When she had gone south in order to be with and care for Bo, she talked about how she was starting to believe helping someone in need was a possible cure for her afflictions, meaning her bouts of hysteria (though the ER trips always reassured her and gave her new energy).

Thaddeus had joked with her, "I'm gonna miss you and your afflictions, lady." But his voice almost broke as he said it.

Malcolm

When the acting camp ended, on the tenth, he had his first meeting with the visiting director. The office door was open. Frye waved him in; hewas standing at a high drafting table with blueprints spread out on it, beside an ornate, old-fashioned telephone. He pointed to it. "Like this? Toscano 1929 Antique Brittany. I bought it in Italy a couple years ago. Makes me feel like I could talk to the dead if I really wanted to."

"Must feel strange, dialing numbers."

"Have a seat." Frye moved behind the desk in front of the window.

There were prompt books and playscripts on shelves along three of the walls of the room, which smelled of leather and mimeograph ink and wood. The visiting director was a shadow now, with the sunlight in the window behind him. He wore a white suit and a white shirt with a red bow tie. On the desk was a white panama hat. "Good to see you," he said with his odd smirk (perhaps it had to do with his eyebrows, which were darker than his hair, and arched, giving him a faintly sardonic look). "Good work with the acting camp."

"Thanks. It was fun." Malcolm glanced at the hat.

"Got a lunch today," Frye said. "With the Cosmetics Tycoons, our money supply. Gotta look my best."

"I wondered if I could talk to you about my niece."

"Uh-oh. What's happened now?"

Of course, Frye knew everything. Malcolm took a breath. Then: "Nothing's happened. I had the thought that she might—"

The other gave a little simpering laugh. "You're kidding."

"Excuse me?"

"What're you trying to do here, Mr. TV Man?"

Malcolm chose to ignore the tone. "I thought I might put in—"

Frye interrupted. "Relax, dude. I've got her portfolio. You're gonna love this. She answered the casting call last week and came to see me yesterday morning." He kept the simpering smile. "So now you get to go on being, um, avuncular." There was no expression at all in the face. Just the little eyes, staring, under the curved eyebrows. "Well. Anyway, scripts'll be ready by the end of the week. Opening, God willing, August fourth. Previews the first and second. But we're gonna need to get cracking. And we've got the misfortune of having to mount a production in a construction site."

Malcolm stared.

"Relax," Frye said. "I was joking about avuncular. I like to keep my actors a bit on edge by needling them some. I was impressed by the chick." He sat forward. "Hell, I can tell you now. This is really so cool, man. Keep it to yourself, but she's gonna be our Cordelia. And wait'll you see what I've got planned for her."

"Have you spoken to her parents? There's an order of protection—"

"She'll be eighteen in a week. Nothing anybody can do if she doesn't want it done where that's concerned. And believe me, she wants nothing to do with that."

Malcolm said, "Well. That's good." He stood up to leave.

"Don't you want to know what I've got planned for you?"

"Sorry." He sat back down.

"I have you in mind for Albany. I believe you played Prospero in *The Tempest* at City Stage."

"A long time ago," Malcolm said.

"Your brother sent me a tape somebody made. And some of your TV work, too. I think your, uh, situation gives you considerable—shall we use the term *cachet*?"

"I can play Albany," Malcolm told him.

"Good. It's a start."

Less than an hour later, he was on the phone with Mona. She called his cell, from hers. "The protection order is broken," she said in a singsong voice. "We've breeched the wall again. Hooray for us. How've you been?"

"Where're you calling from?"

"Mars. How've you been?"

"You came in to see Frye and he cast you as Cordelia. Congratulations."

"Hey, what planet in the solar system is *he* from anyway? You see that phone on his drafting table? It's dead. He told me it made him feel like he could talk to people on the other side. He went out for a few seconds and I picked it up and it *is* dead. A fancy dead old-fashioned phone. Why would anybody keep a thing like that?"

Malcolm said nothing.

"Anyway, I'm gonna be Cordelia and we'll have fun."

He heard a rustling cloth-scraping sound on the other end, and then a shout. "Mona?" he said.

There was a tussle, and a door slammed, and another voice started, low, with cigarettes in it. "You're not talking to Mona now. You realize I can have you put away for this?"

Pearl.

Small, quick, fierce, vindictive Pearl. *Pretty little Pearl, vicious as a squirrel,* as her older sister put it in one of her fits of frustration at the woman. Pearl. Whom he had once liked. The one who had moved among the bereaved people at his father's funeral offering a little scented card with a bad misspelling in calligraphic letters adorned by drawn blossoms and hearts, red, pink, and blue: *For you in your greef.*

"Hello, Pearl."

"You've *broken* the order of protection."

"Well, as a matter of fact, your daughter called *me,* Pearl. I'm several *miles* away."

"You got her to try out for that shit at the theater."

"I just found out about that myself. *You* knew about it before I did. I just now found out about it. The whole thing—it's pure coincidence."

"I *hate* you for this."

"She's gonna be onstage with William Mundy, the star of *Home Away,* playing Cordelia opposite his Lear." He heard the beating on the door of the room where Pearl had evidently locked herself.

"I *hate* Shakespeare," she said. "And you're a *pervert*. It might interest you to know that my daughter thinks so, too. You should hear the way she talks about you."

A hot rush coursed through him. His temper rose up the sides of his neck. He said, "Well, fact is, Mona talks about *you,* too, Pearl. You should hear some of *that.*"

"You're a degenerate drug-addict pervert and I've got proof. Hannah—"

He broke in, "Hannah's always thought you were a *flake,* Sis."

Pearl went on, talking over him, "—will testify to it, too. You're a pervert."

"So you've heard from your sister."

"We've been in touch regularly. About you."

"Well, that's very interesting, you know, Pearl? Because the truth is that Hannah always found you annoying."

Silence.

"To her, you've always been comedy central."

After the slightest hesitation, Pearl said, "You go ahead and try separating us."

"*Separating* you. Are you quite all right?"

Another silence.

"Tell your older sister I said hey, all right? And—*not* by the way—*she* happens to *love* Shakespeare."

"Hannah knows things about *you.* You just wait."

"What's she gonna do, testify in the court of public opinion? Take my sins to The Hague?"

"You wait. You go ahead with that egghead shit. Hannah knows everything. And I talk to her every day."

"Good for you. Maybe not so good for *her.*"

The clamor in the background continued.

"Why don't you open the door for your daughter?"

"I'm going to stop you. You won't be successful."

"Successful at *what,* exactly?"

"You won't get away with it."

He could hear Mona protesting and beating on the door. He said, "This is between you and your daughter."

"You should be arrested. You should still be in that room with a bracelet on your ankle."

Mona screamed in the background, "I'll be eighteen in days! You can't stop me! I hate you!"

Her mother spoke icily, calmly. "I'm going to fuck you up, Malcolm."

"Stop threatening me, you quasi-literate—" He caught himself. "Listen—it's got nothing to do with me now. She's about to be *of age*. And you're delusional along with being ignorant if you think there's anything you can do about it. And since we're on the subject of your plans to cause me grief, do you know how to spell the word? You rancorous, small-minded—"

Pearl hung up.

Claudette

The woman they chose after hours of various interviews told Ellis, as he poured coffee to celebrate, "I like it with lots of cream."

"Okay." His hands shook a little. She stood watching.

"That okay?"

"Maybe a little more. I like it as close as I can get it to my own color." Ellis poured more cream, smiling. "Say when."

"That's about right, don't you think?"

She was sixty-eight, but looked younger. She had a sense of humor, and her smile was beautiful, wide and milky white; it seemed to involve her whole being. She explained that she had moved with her family to Memphis from Boston when she was only seven. And Claudette said, "I thought I heard New England in your voice."

"Oh, it's there all right. And I'm not even a Red Sox fan."

Her name was Willamina McNichol. She had three grown children and six grandchildren, and they all lived close. She told Claudette and Ellis she considered herself lucky in life—no, blessed—and Claudette sensed that this notion must have been achieved at great cost: the woman had recently gone through the loss of her husband of forty-one years, to Alzheimer's. (That fact was the first reason for Claudette's interest in her: Willamina had experience caring for someone in the processes of incremental decline.) Ellis just liked her immediately, because, he said, she made him feel so much at ease. Claudette particularly liked her rich, calming, alto voice. It was like the aural equivalent of a color; it brought to mind the amber depths of brandy. Willamina spoke of cherished memories, even from the last years with her husband. She told how, through all their seasons together (she used the word *seasons* with a kind of wistfulness), her husband, Derek, had been a picture taker and had filled many photo albums, which she still kept close. Rows of them. He had been a wonderful archivist of glad moments. The picture albums were treasure, lining the walls of her living room. Dozens upon dozens of frolicking smiles and images of peace. Sometimes in the evening or on a lonesome Sunday morning she would spend a quiet hour with these tender annals; they provided her with a kind of company—sweet solace, of which she could avail herself without troubling the young.

The grandchildren were all fairly close in age. "Perfect symmetry," she said.

She lived alone in a little house on Summer Avenue. The house was paid for years ago and the real estate taxes on it were higher than her mortgage payments had been. "Derek couldn't get over that, you know. Oh my, he'd frown and say, 'Don't get me started,' and then off he'd go anyway." She pronounced the word *started* as *stahted*.

They commenced payments to her out of Ellis's TIAA-CREF account from his many years teaching. That, along with Willamina's Social Security and the money from her husband's life insurance, would enable her to keep the little house. Each day she drove over in her little Civic with the daisies hand-painted on the sides. Claudette would leave for the art gallery early each morning, and Willamina would arrive a few minutes later. And she would be there when, sometimes fairly late, Claudette came home from the theater. Willamina didn't mind. There wasn't anyone at her little house, and her times with the two daughters and the one son weren't regular; most of her visits with them took place on weekends and holidays.

Franny kept calling and getting Willamina. Finally she called the gallery.

"I can't talk now," Claudette told her. "I'm at work. There are people here."

"We are going to *have* this conversation. Do you realize that I can call the police about you? Your sister talked me out of it. I call your place and I get this woman."

"Did you ask to speak to Dad?"

"I asked to speak to you."

"I'll call you this afternoon. On my way to the theater. I can't talk now."

That afternoon at the theater, she got busy at a table reading, paired off with Malcolm, and so she decided her stepmother could wait until the evening, when there would be a glass of wine or something to relax her. She thought Malcolm was a little stiff; she saw him trying too hard. The work was slow, and she was patient, and she looked at his sad eyes and wondered. Finally, just home, her phone buzzing yet again, she stayed in the car and answered it.

"I can't believe you'd just ignore the law like this."

"Look, come see us."

Franny began to cry. "Meryl says I shouldn't involve the police."

"You should listen to Meryl."

"You can't just walk out of a place without clearance."

"We're getting along fine, Franny. It's what Dad wanted. And he's not incapable."

The other took a few moments to gain control of herself.

"You can come see him anytime, you know. You don't have to wait for visiting hours or any of that. And you can rest assured he's in good hands."

"He needs round-the-clock care."

"That's essentially what he has. Come on, Franny. It's been almost a week since we left out of there. He's fine. Why did you wait so long if you're so worried?"

"Because I thought you'd find out for yourself what a load he is, that's why."

"He's never been a *load*, as you put it. Jesus. How can you—"

Franny began talking over her. "Round-the-clock care. Round the clock."

"He needed round the clock in that place at first because he got *put* there, and then because he was full of sedatives."

"He needs doctors."

"He needs what he's got. Come see for yourself."

"We all decided—"

"I've gotta go," Claudette told her. "Come see us." And she broke the connection.

Thaddeus

Figuring heart rate: count the number of beats in ten seconds. Multiply by six.

He muttered, "Ridiculous." He had just pulled into the lot beside the theater and parked. He saw Malcolm Ruark come out and walk down the street, away.

Thaddeus took his own pulse again—the fourth time this morning. One hundred twenty-six.

In his office, he found a yellow rose in a small plaster vase on his desk, with a one-word note: *Breathe*. He thought of Gina, and his mood lifted. But looking closely at the printed letters, he realized it was Lurlene, that generous spirit, worried about everyone but herself. He would have to do something for her, buy her a bottle of her favorite malt Scotch. The Macallan, eighteen-year-old. He folded the note and put it in his shirt pocket to remind himself, then lifted the vase and smelled the flower. The fragrance actually did relax him. He opened the door to her part of the office suite, and saw that she had draped her sweater for the morning chill over her desk chair. He waited, knowing she had gone to get coffee. In a few minutes, she returned with, unsurprisingly, two cups. He sat in the chair beside her desk and they had the coffee together. The morning seemed normal. She talked about last summer's trip to Florence with the girls, who now knew more about Renaissance art than some members of the company.

"They're pretty impressive young ladies," Thaddeus said.

"I'm gonna have a picnic for the whole company on the weekend of the Fourth," she said. "I hope you and Gina can make it. I know her mother's talking about coming up."

"Well, there's talk about it." He smiled. "Thank you for the rose."

"My favorite flower," she said. "My mother's name was Rose."

Lurlene. His ally in all things, and even so he couldn't confide in her. And he would have liked to; it just wasn't part of the friendship. He knew only the outlines of her life and that she was a warm, friendly, thoughtful presence. Everyone depended on her, and she made a point of expressing her impatience with being a walking cliché to people—"No," she would say, "this place would *not* fall apart if I wasn't here, so quit saying it would." She was tough, that much was clear, and she genuinely liked people—which sometimes caused her to say and do things others mistook for sentiment, when in fact it was simple kindness—and she was terribly smart.

After the coffee with her, he spent the first part of the day working on Frye's plans for publicity about all three productions. Already there was a worrisome sign: advance ticket sales were up, but they had slowed. Kelly Gordon had asked to use the black box stage to conduct more auditions for *Three Tall Women*. There were still men working in the orchestra well, repairing the damage from a water-main break in one of the new restrooms. He might have to rent space at the new Performing Arts School on Monroe, built out of what used to be City Stage.

Gregory Ruark's ex-wife, Salina, called asking for a lunch appointment. "I think it's odd the theater manager hasn't yet met us," she said. "Anyway, we've got an idea we'd like to run by you." And she launched into the story of her partner's very old Memphis family and their return to the mansion on Summer Avenue where the partner's father had spent his last days. Thaddeus couldn't break through to tell her he knew most of this from the Grausbecks, not to mention the "Memphis Girls" newspaper article. "I've had to live by my wits," she went on. "I got married off by my parents when I was sixteen to a complete shit, and lived with all *that* for three awful years. He got killed in that plane crash at O'Hare."

"Oh, I'm sorry," Thaddeus got in without quite hearing himself.

"I did *not* mourn his passing. But he left a tremendous load of money, and I gladly took it. Then I was married for two years to your resident accountant, Mr. Gregory Ruark. And I've been with my present partner, Miranda, ever since. Miranda who, in spite of her genteel family, is not your usual type of Memphis society girl."

"She grew up in Memphis?"

"No, honey, a young lady becomes a Memphis society girl growing up in Butler, Arkansas."

He said nothing.

She cleared her throat. "Sarcasm's my fallback."

"Right," he answered. "I think I may have just barely managed to gather that."

"You, too, I see."

He let this go.

"Anyway." She sighed as if nothing could be more exhausting than to go on with this peroration. He almost broke in to say, *I get the idea.*

She talked about living in England, and New York, and about how Miranda's father, Theodorus Bland, had made a fortune selling bacon and sausage, and also had left money behind. Lots and lots of money. "And of course he bequeathed her this big-assed old barn of a house, too, that we've moved into, known in the register of historic Memphis buildings as the Bland Mansion."

Thaddeus said, "I know the house. Well, I'd—"

But she picked up again: "We didn't ask for any of it. We considered ourselves too good for it, har-har. And since we've been back, Miranda and I've doubled it all again, selling our makeup and hair dye company. A whole lot of women want to put a face on, these days, after all that happy, hippie-dippie, natural-as-I-am-and-as-God-made-me, hairy-armpits-and-furry-legs shit. And so we've made a fucking *Symphony of the Seas* full of money—not a boatload, honey. A fucking *cruise-ship-city-on-the-water* load." Again she cleared her throat. "You don't mind my French?"

"No," he said. "It's rather refreshing."

Another hawking sound. "Nobody's ever said *that* to me before."

"Sorry if it's dull to hear it. That's how I find it."

"No, I *mean* it. And thanks for it. So we were looking for some tax shelters, so to speak, and Gregory all those years ago made me want to go to the theater because he didn't have much interest in it beyond the numbers, and Miranda taught me to *love* the theater because *she* does and is interested in *spite* of the numbers, and so here we are. And don't worry, we won't be asking for roles in your productions, even though we're transforming you, so to speak, into a London-style theater."

"I'm sure you know Gregory's kid brother, Malcolm, is one of our actors now," Thaddeus said.

Somewhat impatiently, she pointed out that of course she knew that.

With a soft, nervous laugh, he said, "Malcolm's in his fifties. I think I just made him sound like Doogie Howser with that kid-brother stuff."

She gave forth a surprised chuckle. "You're funny."

He waited.

"Anyway, yeah, he's no kid. He's the, shall we say, *retired* news guy with the niece complex. Of course we know all about him. And to think he was my little brother-in-law. Malcolm Ruark, renowned reprobate.

He wasn't much more than a boy when I left this town a couple of millennia ago with Miranda. Anyway, I called you because we had an idea we want to talk about. And it's time we met you. We've talked to Arthur Grausbeck and Jocelyn and we even had a talk with the rat who left the ship, Mr. Warden."

"He just took a leave of absence."

"I was being sarcastic."

"When would you like to meet?" he asked.

"What's wrong with today. Lunch at Tsunami. Say twelve-thirty?"

Just before he left for the restaurant, Gina came in and closed the door. She sat down in the chair on the other side of his desk, pulled a white hankie out of her slacks, and started to cry. "Mom's in the hospital. She had some kind of episode with her vision this morning. Whitcomb drove her to the emergency room and, Wolfie, they've *admitted* her. He's the one who called me. I'm going down there right now. They've admitted her." She wiped her eyes with the heels of her palms.

"I can leave Lurlene with some of this." He indicated the papers on his desk.

"Please, it's just simpler. This is about my mother and me."

He was silent.

"Whitcomb says suddenly she couldn't see out of her left eye. It sounds like some kind of stroke. They *admitted* her, Wolfie. They've never admitted her before."

"It'll be all right." He felt certain that it would not be all right. He got up from the desk and stepped to the door.

She stood, gazing at him, tears welling in her eyes. "I'm sorry I said that about thinking of leaving you, and here I am, leaving you."

"Are you leaving me? Is that what this is?"

She sobbed. "No. Stop it." She daubed her eyes. "I don't know how long it'll be."

"You think you'll stay down there?"

"I said I don't know how long it'll be. How can I know that? Anyway, I need the time away. Look, Thaddeus, they've admitted her. I'm just saying I have to go down there, and I don't know when I'll be back."

He held the door open. "I'll be right here if you need me."

"I really am sorry." She went by him without a kiss or a touch, and he closed the door. He heard her tell Lurlene that she'd finished all the sketching for the set of *Three Tall Women* and could be gone for a few days.

A little later, Lurlene came in. "Think Frye might pitch a fit?"

"I'm sure the others have been told what to do."

"Are you okay?" she said. "I can manage things if you—"

"No," he broke in. "I've got lunch with the Tycoons."

He encountered unusual traffic going along Union toward Midtown. He put the radio on. NPR. There had been an incident at the university, on Patterson Street. A boy brought a pistol into a voice class. Unrequited love. A girl had thrown him over. The female announcer, who was British, actually used that phrase. He thought of Gina heading south. The announcer said the boy with the pistol claimed to be an incel, short for involuntary celibate. There were many young white males on the internet who apparently considered themselves entitled, and who hated all women, especially pretty young ones, for not surrendering to that entitlement. The NPR announcer, explaining the phenomenon, went on to say that the term *incel* was actually the brainchild of a Canadian woman back in the nineties.

In this case, the boy had turned his anger inward, and shot himself in the left side, a flesh wound. He was suffering from clinical depression. Thaddeus listened to all this, waiting in traffic. His mind presented him with the image of his father-in-law, RJ, rubbing his stubbled chin and talking about Gina's "darks," like fault lines underground.

"Yeah," Thaddeus said aloud, as if RJ were there in the car with him. "I've got my own darks, man." Then, as if speaking to Gina: "Oh, babe. What's wrong with us?"

At last, the traffic began to move. He turned the radio on again and moved the dial away from talking voices to music. He arrived at Tsunami fifteen minutes late and was disappointed to see that the Grausbecks were there, looking harried and vaguely ruffled, as usual. Arthur Grausbeck was as tall and thin as his wife, Jocelyn, was short and wide. There was no other way to say it, or see it. They both had soft green eyes, the same light shade, and while she spoke in a sort of speeding staccato pace that slowed on the last word in any sentence, he had a speech tic, a nonsense syllable that crept into his phrases, *bub, bub, bub.* Thaddeus had made fun of the two of them to members of the company, calling them *Death and the Maiden* and asking people to imagine them at dinner—Jocelyn talking so fast, and Arthur having to try breaking in: "Bub-bub-bub." Gina spoke of them as being examples of immaculate conception because they had three grown children, and yet seemed so clueless about so many things.

Now the two of them smiled warmly at him as he entered. They were sitting with the two women, the Cosmetics Tycoons, neither of whom knew this was what the members of the company called them. They looked rather fierce: white hair, dark eyes, and sharp, untouched-up features. One was slightly thicker through the shoulders than the other. They were talking about the troubled boy with his love and his gun.

"Love and guns, for Christ's sake," the slighter of the two women said, turning as Thaddeus came up to them.

"Sorry I'm late," he said. "Traffic because of the incel boy."

She offered a small blue-veined hand. "Salina," she said. "Good to see you." She had deep-socketed, intelligent gray eyes, and a sharp nose, like a blade, with a little black mole just to the left of it. You could see that she had once been quite beautiful. She was still striking.

He heard himself explain the situation with Louisa, and that Gina was headed south.

"Shouldn't you be *with* Gina?" Jocelyn Grausbeck asked.

Her husband said, "If you need to go—"

"She wanted to go down first," Thaddeus told them.

They all stared, evidently thinking there would be more.

After a few seconds, Salina said, "Tell us your name again?"

He told her.

"Thaddeus. Yeah—you're the one I talked to." He saw the creases bordering her eyes. Although she wore no makeup, the perfume she had on made him think of the rose in the vase on his desk.

The other woman also offered to shake hands. She had thick, inflamed-looking knuckles. Her gaze was frankly estimating. She smiled, showing strangely inward-turned teeth, as if she'd suffered a blow at some point long ago; the edges of them were gray. "Miranda Bland," she said.

"My partner," said Salina.

"Generosity is the soul and spirit of these two ladies," Arthur Grausbeck said to him.

After a slight pause, Salina grinned. "Often thought, yet ne'er so well expressed."

The Grausbecks began to talk at the same time and then stopped. "Sorry," he said, nodding to his wife, who then rushed through a stream of indistinguishable words, ending with *theater,* pronounced *theahh-tuh.* She was clearly quite nervous.

"Excuse me?" Miranda said.

"Bub-bub-bub, well, as we were saying, everybody's just so grateful for all you've done."

"You don't have to keep telling us that," Salina said.

Miranda said, "We happen to love the hell out of Mr. and Mrs. Shakespeare's boy Billy, that's all."

Thaddeus refrained from saying, *Often thought, yet ne'er so well expressed.* Instead, he muttered, "You're on a first-name basis." It came out before he could suppress it.

Fortunately, Arthur Grausbeck had already begun speaking. "I think you'll both be excited with what our visiting director's doing with *Lear.*"

Salina said, quite evenly, "He's not fucking with it, is he?"

There was a pause. The Grausbecks gawked. Their expression, Thaddeus might've said in a more relaxed circumstance, was that of two people who have just learned that the airliner in which they are traveling has lost an engine.

"As I think I made clear in all those meetings with you board people and the city, I'm a purist about *Lear,*" Salina added. "I hate all the *fucking around* these newfangled fancy-pants *aw-vawn-garr* directors feel driven by their own overstuffed egos to do. You know what I mean?"

"Don't sugarcoat it," Miranda said, smiling. "Tell it like it is."

Salina went on without the hint of an answering smile, "I saw it played once as taking place in a big ultramodern, high-tech university science department. With everyday speech. In fucking *talk.* They took all the poetry out and put in other words, stupid words. A fucking translation into day-to-day, flat, dead-in-the-head-and-heart *American* English, full of slang phrases like 'You're too moody,' or 'He's not into that,' and 'The king's cray-cray,' no kidding. The fucking king's cray-cray. Somebody told me it was supposed to be funny and campy, but they gouged out Gloucester's eyes and I didn't hear any laughing. 'Cordelia, don't go away yet.' Actually, *really.* 'The king's cray-cray.' Like those stupid 'translated'"—she made air quotes—"versions of King James. 'At the start, there was the word, and the word shined in the dark but the dark didn't know the light was there.' Jesus. Dull, pseudo-ordinary, middle-class-shitbird *talk*. I wanted to buy that theater and then have it burned down."

"Bub-bub, bub—"

"Reuben H. Frye's not doing anything like that," Jocelyn Grausbeck said. "Do you know his work?"

"We don't pay much attention to directors' names," Salina said. "We know what we like. And we've learned not to soft-pedal things, as you've probably noticed by now."

What Thaddeus had noticed was her way of using strung-together hyphenated phrases.

Ms. Grausbeck offered another nervous stream of words sounding like one word that ended, again, with *theahh-tuh*.

"I didn't get that, quite," Salina said. "Why don't you slow down, deary."

The partner, Miranda, snickered into the heel of her palm.

Arthur Grausbeck rather quickly said, "My wife's excited about the new Globe Theater. That we're actually going to be calling it *the Globe*." He put his hand on Jocelyn's upper back, and rested it there. Thaddeus noted this, and the fond look they exchanged. It went through him.

"Well," Salina said, "*are* we gonna like what this guy's doing to our favorite play?"

"It's my favorite, too," he felt compelled to add. "Ms. Grausbeck helped me and my wife convince the board to commit to it."

Jocelyn turned to him with a warm smile. "We did that, didn't we. And that brought Reuben to us."

Salina folded her arms across her chest. "So what's Reuben doing to it? He's supposed to be here, you know."

"Bub-bub-bub—"

The server walked up, and they all became preoccupied with ordering. Salina asked for a bottle of Albariño. "Have you ever tasted it?" she asked Thaddeus, who had no appetite at all.

"I haven't," he told her.

"Three glasses," Salina said.

"Make it four," said the board chairman.

"Do I hear five?" She gave Jocelyn Grausbeck a look.

"Oh I—" Ms. Grausbeck began.

"My wife doesn't drink in midday," Grausbeck broke in. "And she's nervous."

"Well, I'm enthusiastic, dear."

He spoke to Salina. "When she's nervous or enthusiastic, she tends to run words together."

Salina looked over at Jocelyn. "I can't quite keep up with you, sweetie. I don't mean to be rude. But why do you let your husband speak for you like that?"

Jocelyn nodded, incongruously, evidently meaning to let the other know that she understood the question. But she said nothing, and with a look of severe mortification folded her hands in her lap.

Grausbeck patted her wrists, smiling at everyone.

"Well, how many glasses?" Salina demanded.

"I'm not having any either," Thaddeus put in. He thought again of Gina heading south, and had a strange moment of seeing the full import of the word *estranged:* even a marriage that looked for all the world like a true good marriage could have areas of divided life, of unspoken separation and neglect. The notion stopped him, and he looked at the Grausbecks again with their obvious closeness, and breathed through the next moment like a person in a dark room when someone suddenly blasts open a door on daylight: neither he nor Gina deserved this. Except as the price for some kind of idleness of soul? The thought made him queasy.

They had gone to England in spring, year before last, to Manchester, and driven through the beautiful countryside north of London, and down to the city itself, where they walked in Trafalgar Square and saw the statues and those figures who appeared to be levitated, and who collected money simply by seeming to observe from their apparently baseless height the people walking by them. A new kind of busking. And in the little hotel room off Piccadilly they'd made love and she wept and told him how happy she was. And he lay in the half-light, staring at the ceiling, hearing "Purple Rain" somewhere in another room, and wondered why she was crying. Tears, any tears, to him, meant sorrow. And she'd never before cried after lovemaking. So he'd asked her, "Is something wrong?"

"I'm just happy," she told him. "Listen." She was concentrating on the faint sound of the music coming through the wall. And, well, she had indeed been happy; *they* had been happy. And that was only a little less than two years ago. Two little years.

He came to himself, and remained quiet while the others talked. He couldn't catch the thread of it. He was thinking about England. And then he thought about the celibate and his gun. In the seconds of woolgathering, he saw the boy's ignorant sexual bigotry as perhaps having some faint trace in the psychological coinage of his own life. The world's troubles were seeping into his psyche again.

"Don't you agree, Thaddeus?" Jocelyn Grausbeck said to him.

"Excuse me?"

She smiled at the two ladies across from her. "Thaddeus is our dreamer."

"You're worried about Gina's mother," said her husband.

"I was just thinking about what happened today at the university myself," Miranda said. "This is the craziness of the internet."

"America the shoot 'em full," Salina said. "Russian poet said that."

"I was saying," Jocelyn persisted, with a kindly nod at Thaddeus. "Shakespeare's best experienced when you see the plays performed, and it's seeing the plays that enhances the reading of them."

"Well," Thaddeus managed, "it's fairly obvious he didn't care about publishing the plays. It wasn't normally done back then. He did take the trouble to see the sonnets and the poems published."

"Who was the Russian poet?" Arthur Grausbeck asked.

"Yevtushenko," Salina said. "It was after one of our famous assassinations."

"Wonder what Yevtushenko would make of us now," Miranda said.

"They filled stadiums in Russia when Yevtushenko gave readings."

Thaddeus saw, through the side window showing the street, Reuben Frye walk up, looking like an antebellum relic.

The board chairman had seen him at the same time. "Our visiting director's arrived."

"Why doesn't he come in?" Miranda asked. "He's late. Look at that bow tie."

Frye seemed to be expecting someone else. And now William Mundy and Gregory Ruark came into view.

"That's the big Netflix star who's opening for us," Salina said. "And I *know* the other one rather well." She gave a little smirk. "And he knows me rather well."

"A meeting of the principals," said Miranda. "Mundy looks heavier around the jowls in person."

"Look how old Gregory got. Do I look that old?"

Jocelyn Grausbeck asked the waitstaff to move another table over, which was accomplished without much trouble.

Salina said, "Samuel Langhorne Frye. Panama hat and all."

They all watched the visiting director make his way in, with Gregory and the Netflix star. There seemed something stagy about the way Frye looked around the room; he was a man aware of being observed. His gaze settled on Thaddeus, and then he gestured for the others to follow him. They took seats at the newly extended table. The server was a blond, narrow-faced man with cold eyes. He asked what they wanted to drink. Frye said, "Elijah Craig, neat." Then he ordered his lunch as well. And a bottle of Puligny-Montrachet. "The salmon here is excellent." He looked around the table. "I saw that no one was drinking. I thought a little white wine with lunch."

"We're already having a white wine," said Ms. Grausbeck quickly. Then: "Well, *they* are."

"Bourbon for me first. Always. The true American drink."

"Well," Salina said. "A pronouncement." She looked over at Gregory Ruark. "Hello, Greg."

He said, "Hello."

"Good to see you."

Gregory nodded. Thaddeus thought he looked uneasy, and glanced at the others. They were all watching Mundy settle himself.

For a few seconds, no one spoke. The awkwardness was palpable, like a draft of air.

She turned to Frye. "So, you're the guy who's directing *King Lear* in our new theater."

"That's me." He did not look up, arranging his serviette in his lap.

"Hope it won't be too aw-vawn garr."

Frye chose to ignore the remark. "I like this place. I eat here a lot now."

Salina smiled. "So do we, in fact. We'll have to try running into each other."

"It's a cool place," said Miranda.

They all went on politely—you would almost say gingerly—about the decor, the high ceiling, the noise level. All their inane talk. Thaddeus looked at each of them. He thought of Gregory Ruark and Salina, and wondered if this was the first time they'd seen each other since the Cosmetics Tycoons returned to town. In the next instant, his curiosity was answered.

"How long's it been, Greg?" she asked.

He looked at her with a flat, noncommittal expression, as if she'd asked him what time it was. "Oh, I'd guess—forty years?"

"You two know each other," Frye said.

"Once husband and wife," Miranda said proudly.

"I think you said something to me about that, Gregory. My brain is Swiss cheese lately." Frye sat back languidly in the chair, and regarded Salina. Mundy started a conversation with Grausbeck about an actor who had won a prize in LA for a one-man performance called *Walt*. Frye broke in to remark that he'd met the son of the famous subject of the performance. Then said, "Disney."

"No shit," Salina said.

For a brief spell, it was as if the Cosmetics Tycoons, Frye, Mundy, and Gregory were alone at the table. Thaddeus watched the Grausbecks, who were holding hands. When the server brought Frye's whiskey and the two bottles of white wine, he asked for a whiskey, too, then changed his mind. The server crossed it out like a teacher making a correction on a student paper full of such mistakes. He packed the bottles of wine down into the crushed ice in a large ceramic bucket.

Salina turned to Frye. "So, Professor Frye, tell us about your lead female actors. Are you sleeping with them?"

Another moment passed.

"A bad joke," she said. "Sorry."

The server poured a taste of the Albariño into Salina's glass; she took a little swig of it and nodded. He poured some into Miranda's, then filled Salina's. Gregory held a hand up to refuse the wine. Then the server showed the Montrachet to Frye, who nodded. Everyone watched Frye swirling the poured taste of the expensive wine. He finally breathed it, then took it in and seemed to move it back and forth there.

"It's not mouthwash, is it?" Salina said. She held her glass to the side of her face and smiled. "Well, how is it?"

"Superb."

"I meant sleeping with your actresses."

Miranda burst out laughing. Thaddeus saw the gold fillings on one side of her mouth. Gregory Ruark shook his head, but was laughing softly.

"I don't sleep with my actresses," Frye said. Miranda had spoken at the same time. "Excuse me?" he asked.

"My husband's a direct person," she told him.

"Husband."

Miranda, lengthening the letter *y*, said, "Yyyyyep."

"I see."

"I kept my maiden name."

He tossed back his whiskey and put that glass down. Then he took the stem of his wineglass and moved it, gazing at the sunny color of the wine.

Thaddeus stood. "I should head out. I told my wife I'd follow."

"What is it about your money," Frye said suddenly to Salina and Miranda, looking at one and then the other, "that makes you such experts about the dramatic arts?"

Thaddeus sat back down.

Without any hesitation, and smiling viciously, Salina clasped her fingers under her chin, and tilted her head slightly to one side. "It's green," she said. "And there's so much of it."

"Bub-bub-bub—"

"More than four billion. So. We gave sixty million to this theater. Right?"

"Yes," Frye said in the tone of someone who was acceding to being given a riddle to solve.

"Okay—" Salina began.

"Don't," said Miranda. "That's bad luck. And it's bad manners."

"I'm just establishing a sense of proportion, darling."

There was another interval of silence.

"So," Salina continued. "Talking proportions, shall we say—if a billion is one *thousand* million, then 4.8 billion—just as a ballpark figure—is four thousand eight hundred million. And we gave sixty million. Now—bring it down to thousands. Say we have four thousand eight hundred dollars. Proportionately." She looked around the table. "We gave sixty bucks."

No one said anything for a time.

Presently, Mundy cleared his throat. “A proportionate—” he began.

Thaddeus broke in. “How about another sixty bucks?” he heard himself say.

Everyone looked at him, and Miranda gave a soft laugh. “There’s a man with ambition.”

“So, have I answered your question for you?” Salina said to Frye.

“How many plays have you seen in your young life?” Frye asked her, evidently trying to be charming now. He took a delicate little swallow of his wine.

“Oh, I don’t know. Too many to count. And I bet I’m older than you are.”

Frye seemed to think she would say more.

Thaddeus put his hands in his lap, waiting. They were just going to go on as if this were a contest, and not a business lunch. He saw Gregory looking from one to the other of the two women. His heart went out to him. He had a bad instant seeing himself, years hence, long divorced from Gina, having to watch her with someone else. He thought he had seen pain in the older man’s eyes.

“Actually,” Salina went on, “Claudette Bradley’s father taught history where I went to high school. Right here in the river city. Mr. Ellis Bradley. A wonderful man. Of course he was just starting out—a young man.”

“He was my teacher,” Thaddeus felt compelled to say. “A terrific teacher. He gave me Shakespeare.”

Mundy shifted in his chair. “Small world.” He looked at Frye and then looked down.

“We hear Ms. Bradley’s very talented,” Frye offered.

“We all think the world of her,” Grausbeck put in quickly.

“Have you talked with your TV cohort?” Salina asked Mundy. “The one who got caught trying to seduce his niece?”

“That isn’t true,” Thaddeus said quickly, and more loudly than he meant to.

She gazed at him as if he were saying something endearing. “That business with the niece sounded true enough.” The thin smile seemed meant to allay the malice in the gray eyes.

“What’s true is what the court decided.”

“You sound like his lawyer,” Miranda said.

"What Thaddeus says is true," Gregory said. "And I happen to be Malcolm's brother."

"Well, that's not what I saw in the papers," Salina said. "And how would you know, Greg? As I recall, you never had much to do with the kid. Did that change?"

"Um, fact is," Frye said, "he sold us on signing *the kid*, as you call him."

"Malcolm Ruark's a very strong addition to this company," said Thaddeus, meaning to end the exchange and feeling the shakiness in his own voice. "He did a fine job running the summer acting camp."

Salina turned to William Mundy. "And you, sir—I guess you're used to television-land craziness. Tell us. None of this stuff bothers you at all?"

"Madam." Mundy drew himself up. "Since your intent here is obviously sardonic, I don't suppose I'm obliged to speak to it." He held his drink out as if to toast, and she picked her glass up and clinked it against his.

"To Lear," she said. "And madness."

"Would you care for some of the Montrachet?" Mundy asked her.

Frye said, "Yes, please have some."

"I like your Netflix show," Miranda said to Mundy. "And my Albariño."

Salina took the last of her own glass. "I think I *would* like to try that Montrachet."

Frye poured it.

"Anyway," Mundy said to the table. "Let's get down to food and pleasantries." He gave a tight smile. "We do have an afternoon's work rehearsing ahead of us. And we didn't come here to talk business."

"Oh," Salina said. "But this *is* a business lunch. We want to discuss involving the city's schools in our new theater. The fact is, Miranda and I are actually interested in *doing good*. You know?"

"I'm only here to play Lear."

Salina ignored this. "I'd still like to know what you think of Mr. Malcolm Ruark."

"I haven't had a chance to get to know him that well, personally. I like his professionalism. And his deep voice."

"I like his deep past, here in our little town. Separate from the niece thing."

Mundy looked at the others.

Salina continued. "Feels weird. I remember him when he was a kid."

"Anyway," Miranda said to everyone, "we think we can help literacy here."

"A new renaissance for the city's schools."

"What do you think of the wine?" Grausbeck asked Salina.

"How much was it? A hundred?"

"A hundred fifty," Frye said.

"I liked the Albariño as much. Twenty-six bucks."

"Well, the eye of the beholder and such."

Salina nodded. "And such."

Mundy said, "To what do we owe this rather obvious hostility, madam? I seem to have encountered that quite a bit in some Memphis women."

"You don't say. Not women in general, everywhere you go?"

"It is decidedly not the case elsewhere. Anywhere."

"I'm just fooling," said Salina. "Relax." She smiled. "I read an interview of Professor Frye, here, not long ago. How he likes to needle his actors, to get them on edge and primed for excellence. Thought I'd like to do a little needling myself, since I have the money to do it."

Frye leaned forward, and spoke slowly, through his teeth. "People will be talking about this production for years."

"Disasters get talked about, too."

Still another pause.

"Needling again." She smiled.

"You must've noticed," Miranda said, "my sweetheart likes to clown around."

Frye folded his serviette and set it next to his plate.

"A little razzing," Salina said. "It's what you can do if you have a big bank account."

"She's teasing," said Miranda.

Without looking at anyone, Frye said, low, "Why don't you both trundle on down to the theater and have a look for yourselves when we open."

"You said *trundle*." Salina proclaimed. "I swear some people *require* needling. And you hold a chair at Holliwell?"

Once again, Frye's demeanor was that of a man not backing down.

"Yes, I do indeed." Then he addressed Miranda: "Would you like some of *my* Montrachet?"

Miranda nodded, lifting her glass. "Why not. And we don't trundle. We never trundle."

"Of course not," Ms. Grausbeck said. "Noonewould*dreammm* of saying you truuundle."

"Ridiculous," Thaddeus said, low.

Salina looked at him. "Did you have something to add?"

"I'll be glad to talk about programs for the schools later on, but I really have to go now." He stood again and moved off, actually hurrying for fear of being called back. But no one said anything. Out in the breezy sun, he strode to his car, and then sat behind the wheel, breathing heavily, his heart drumming in the sides of his head. He took his pulse. Ninety-one. Just ninety-one beats.

Arthur Grausbeck crossed the street to stand at his car window. "Going south?" His smile was both tentative and benign.

"I think I might just go back to the house and clean up a little. Been a crowded week. Gina wanted the time, just her and her mother."

The older man smiled. "Seems they all need that now and then."

Thaddeus smiled back, and, as kindly as he could, said, "It didn't look like there'd be time to get any real business done."

"Tough to think there would be." The board chairman looked back at the façade of the restaurant. "They're just word-fencing now. And I hate that sort of thing." He faced the younger man again. "I thought your request for another sixty bucks was golden."

Thaddeus smiled at him.

"What a couple of unpleasant ladies," Arthur said. "For all their largesse."

"Maybe they think the money entitles them to be rude."

The other shook his head, but didn't respond.

"I'll see you tomorrow," Thaddeus told him. "Thanks, Arthur."

A few minutes later, driving up to the house, he thought he could feel the tightness leaving his chest, as if the sight of Louisa's old house with its lattice-railed porch were itself somehow restorative.

Evidently, Gina had stopped there before she headed out. In the bedroom, clothes she must have decided not to pack were strewn across the bed. Down in the kitchen, unwashed dishes cluttered the counter and stood with water in them in the sink. The dining room lights were on, and she'd left the back door open, with just the unlocked wrought-iron screen door.

He secured everything, spent the afternoon straightening the rooms. There was a lot to do. He ran the vacuum on both floors, dusted the surfaces, made the bed, and thoroughly cleaned the kitchen, even mopping the floors. All of it only to keep busy.

In late afternoon, Gina called. "It was floaters in her left eye," she said. "A cloud of them. Harmless. The doctor said it happens sometimes. We're still in the hospital."

He heard Louisa say in the background, "I still have the headache."

"CT scan's fine," said Gina, clearly relieved and exasperated at the same time.

"Apparently, I'm healthy as a horse," Louisa called. "I want a cigarette. One cigarette."

"She's hooked to an IV and they put a nasal cannula on her."

"Why the oxygen?" Thaddeus asked.

"Anxiety," Gina said in the same even tone. "She's calming down now. You heard her. She wants a cigarette."

"Tell her I love her."

"He says he loves you."

"I love you, too, Young Fighter," Louisa called.

"I left the lunch," he said. "Turns out I could've come along if you'd wanted me to."

"We'll talk later," Gina said.

"Can you get where we can talk a little now?"

After a brief silence, she said, "Okay. I'm outside in the hall."

"You know what happened today?" he said. "At that lunch? I looked at the Grausbecks, and really saw them. And you know what? For all my aping of their little idiosyncrasies and making such fun of them and being so *witty* about them, I saw that *they* have real *kindness*. I realized I was looking at the real thing."

After a silence, Gina said, "All right."

"It rocked me, Gina. And I *know* that *we've been* like that. I remember."

"Oh, Wolfie."

He waited.

"Well." She sighed, a little wearily, he thought. "Louisa's fine. Nothing seriously wrong."

"Gina," he said.

"Nobody did anything wrong," she told him. "That's what Louisa says."

"Louisa knows?"

"She's guessed. She thinks I'm funny for feeling like I want to fix something she never thought was broken. *I'm* the one who's broken. And she thinks it's funny. She says it's just my darks, like RJ used to call them. The fault lines, she says, in my makeup. My own private temblors."

He said nothing.

"She's relieved she's not dying," Gina said.

"Right" was all he could think of to say. Then: "Well, I'm relieved, too."

"Yes and she's just the way she always is after one of her emergencies. She wants a cigarette, and she calls me a narc for telling her not to smoke."

"Make fun of it. Tell her it's Marcel who's objecting to it."

"I've even started feeling sorry for the fucking dog."

He walked into the kitchen, still holding the phone to his ear, and turned on the lamp over the sink. "Is the dog there in the hospital with you?"

"Out in the car."

He said, "I guess I'll see you when I see you."

"The nurse is here to discharge Louisa. She wants to rest a few days. I'll call you."

"I'll be here," he said.

Malcolm

The efficiency apartment, after more than a year, still felt like a place he was only visiting for a few days. It smelled of cleanser, basements, dirty clothes, the sweat-infused leather of old shoes, and isolation. As far as getting things into some kind of shape for moving to the novelist's cottage on the edge of the Old Forest, he had signed a two-year lease here, purely out of hopelessness. He remembered this with chagrin, now. He had determined to find someone to sublet, and had tacked on the company bulletin board a notice whose bottom edge was cut into little slices with his number on them. So far, there had been no takers.

He slept in a small recliner by the entrance to the tiny kitchen space. The recliner was across from the bed, which he'd made when he moved in and had yet to use (the chair was just easier). He slept fairly often in his clothes, partway elevated, so his acid reflux wouldn't bother him. In the weeks just after the accident, he'd called the hospital to inquire about Mona, but couldn't get through. She wasn't receiving calls or any visitors except her mother, and of course that was her mother's doing. Pearl had evidently barred even the girl's father. And she'd sworn out the protection order.

He had kept up with Mona's progress through the physical therapist. And he had gone to see Frye about her because he knew of her interest, and he wanted simply to help. To show his disinterested intentions regarding her.

Several times just after the accident and the divorce, he'd driven to Swan Ridge Circle, Pearl's house. He made the turn slowly and parked a few houses down. Once, he'd seen Mona come out to sit in the sunlight of the front yard. He watched her until he began to feel guilty and wrong. Another time, she came out and walked slowly, without a limp, toward the top of the street; she seemed fully recovered. He drove away, determined not to return.

Through that bad time, he kept receiving an image of himself walking with mother and daughter, almost eight years before, when, as part of a communications class at school, Mona had taken the assignment of interviewing him as anchor of *The Memphis Evening News*. The image was like part of a dream, but in the always-present way of dreams, it would unfurl, and he would see the three of them walking down the steps outside the studio on their way to Brother Juniper's, for breakfast. One of the first warm days of spring. He had joked about the advantage of having a television personality in the family, and Pearl nodded and laughed, touching the girl's shoulder. "Tell Uncle Malcolm how happy you are that he agreed to help you."

Mona paused, turned, and, with her mother's hand still gripping hers, curtsied. "Thank you, Uncle Malcolm." As they continued down the stairs, he saw the small bones of the girl's ankles, and experienced a rush of breathless affection, tinged with regret—with a troubling sense of what life might be for someone like her in a world with men like himself in it.

That moment constituted the smallest particle of the flow of his life, yet was blindingly bright in the timeless way of all occurrences from which a host of other things come.

By then, he had begun periodically ingesting substances other than alcohol: cocaine, and some painkillers, and even heroin, injected, after cooking it in a spoon. He had done that twice. Even that. And there had already been several episodes with women whose interest in him was transparently a product solely of his local fame. In other words, he'd become a lie. And there Pearl and Mona were, walking down the shallow staircase, just ahead, full of trust and admiration.

That was the memory, the instant, seeing the fine bones of the girl's ankles and experiencing that powerful tide of affection and regret and anxiety, all at once. In the moment, he quickly dismissed it as being only the fervid jangling of his mind after the morning's drug. And yet he knew the memory would never leave him. It was the beginning of his special attachment to her. His love for her, really. As if she were indeed his only daughter.

Though he had finally come to the disquieting sense that there was more to it than that.

Over the months and then years, he found himself repeatedly thinking about the woman she would be—was already growing into—since he was by then obsessing about all women; it seemed that he was constantly having to unthink enticements.

It was around then that Hannah began manifesting a new, profound interest in the church, getting up every morning for mass and communion. She had drawn inward, away from him, and somehow unsexed herself. He understood quite well that this was no excuse. He couldn't conceive of himself as acting out of any need, or deprivation, even knowing that some men did so. This was far more complicated, so much more than mere need. And it was at least possible that something in him, some subliminal herald of the carnality which gripped him, had pushed Hannah away. She'd begun a friendship with a priest, Father Hemphill, a kindly, chain-smoking, wiry, and intense man with a Scottish accent and a way of sounding lighthearted even when what he had to say was serious or sorrowful. The lilt was appealing and Hannah felt calmed, hearing it. She'd joined several parish organizations he ran, and she was seldom home. Often enough, she elicited Malcolm's help with one of these good causes—more use of him as a TV personality. He didn't mind, though there were his own organizations and functions to attend. The two of them had begun to have less time for each other. They even spoke of it.

"We're so busy all the time," Hannah said. "Don't you wish there was more time?"

"I wish we could have a week—seven days, just to *be*," he said, feeling the sentiment as the lie it was without looking directly at it.

Before these changes, he hadn't been a man inclined to much introspection; so it was all surprising to him. He hadn't seen any of it coming.

One evening, at the station, he worked long on a report about sexual abuse by a priest named Walsey at St. Catherine's in Collierville. The instance had led to the discovery of other cases of this crime that for some time now had been increasingly exposed across the world as the one thing most obsessively wrong with the institution. He did a report about how there were abuses throughout the Memphis diocese, by at least sixteen other priests. He felt soiled, depressed, and furious when he finished the broadcast, disgusted with the extent and the persistence of the offenses and also, given his recent forays into infidelity, with himself. Sitting alone in his office off the studio with its news desk, he ingested some cocaine in hopes of lightening his mood. And then, to offset the coke, he drank most of a half-pint of bourbon, one swallow after another, beginning to feel ill. But beyond the supposed dulling effects of the alcohol, he continued to experience the aura of invincibility the drug had always produced in him. He went out and drove slowly the three miles to Beale Street. At the Rum Boogie Café, he ordered black beans and rice and drank a beer. As he finished the last of his meal, and a second beer, he saw Hannah at the entrance, waiting to come in with Father Hemphill. The priest was blowing smoke toward the night sky while Hannah talked animatedly, with a distressed, brow-knitted expression. The blues band was on a break, and the place wasn't quite as crowded as it shortly would be. Malcolm ducked behind one of the standing columns near the stage, as the young man at the door waved in Hannah and her friend. Hemphill flicked his cigarette out into the street, and Hannah playfully chided him, holding one hand up for the man at the door to wait, and moving to retrieve the cigarette butt, which she crushed out on the sidewalk and then handed back to the priest, who shamefacedly put it in his pocket. The whole thing was comical; they looked like a familiar couple on a date. Malcolm went out the side door, which was open, past two of the musicians lounging there with their own cigarettes, and along the street. He stood a few feet away in the dark, and saw his wife and the priest through the Rum Boogie neon sign as they chose a table. It had been two days since he and Hannah had spoken at any length—they had simply been moving in their different spheres. On impulse, he returned to the front of the place, waited the few minutes to be let back in, moved through the growing crowd, and sat down at the table with his wife and Father Hemphill.

"Well," Hannah said, surprised.

He saw her shining dark eyes and the shape of her mouth, and all the years of admiring her features swept through him. He almost reached over to touch the side of her face. He felt a tremendous urge to get to the bottom of everything, and to change back, to find some way home from the long drifting away. Oh, what was it? Where had it all come from? Was it simply some form of midlife crisis, as the therapist had said it might be?

"Just finished up at the station," he managed. "Thought I might have a drink."

"You look like you've had several already," she said, trying to appear amused. "Your irises are needle points. Have you been staring at a bright light?"

"The bright light of your beauty."

"Oh, stop it." Her smile was fleeting. She scoffed, then spoke quietly, eyes widening a little, her tone thinly civil. "Maybe you should take a cab home."

This angered him. He caught the server's attention and ordered a brandy. When he looked back at Hannah, the whole room swung toward her. "I had a beer," he said. "One beer." Then he turned to the priest, and the room swung that way. He concentrated, blinked. The priest was folding his nervous yellow fingers in and out of themselves under his sharp chin, smiling at him.

"I wonder, Father, if you saw my broadcast tonight."

"No," Father Hemphill said. "I'm sorry, I don't watch much TV." He had a stubble so close to the skin it looked like coloration. "Black Irish," Hannah had said, describing him.

Now she spoke, direct and firm. "We're talking about charity, Malcolm. And you smell of whiskey. And you're high."

He addressed the priest: "Excuse me, Father. Do you happen to know a Monsignor Walsey?"

"Pardon?"

"I'm wondering if you know a Monsignor Walsey of St. Catherine's in Collierville."

"I don't believe I do. Maybe he's new?"

Malcolm sat back and regarded him, and wondered what a priest could be doing coming to a bar at that time of the night. He decided to press him. "Monsignor David Walsey."

"No, really I'm sorry."

"You don't *all* know each other? Aren't there events or convocations you attend or diocese meetings with the bishop? Do you know the bishop?"

"Are you working?" Father Hemphill asked, evidently trying for a light tone.

"Malcolm," said Hannah, "go home, why don't you. I'll be along in a few minutes."

"If you don't mind, Father. I'm not working, no. But for my own edification. Or education. I'm wondering if you know about Monsignor Walsey and *sixteen* other gentlemen of the cloth in our fair city. My report tonight and everyone else's, too. About an old matter, by now, of *ruined lives*, though it persists. Oh, my Lord, but it does persist. Across the diocese. And actually all over this forsaken world."

The priest was silent, staring.

"Malcolm," Hannah said. "Stop this."

"Sorry for the attitude," Malcolm said.

"I really am so sorry," Father Hemphill said. "But I'm afraid I don't know fully what you're talking about."

"You actually *do* know *something* of what I'm talking about, though, right?"

Hannah broke in again. "Malcolm!"

"Well, yes." Father Hemphill turned briefly to her and raised a pacifying hand. "I do have some sorrowful knowledge of—you say, 'all over this fors—all over the world.' Yes, about that—what's been discovered to have been going on. Of course we all know *that* now. These—these days. But I was unaware of anything new in Memphis."

He was probably a good man, probably innocent of any wrongdoing. Malcolm reflected that he himself was not a good man. He leaned over and kissed his wife on the side of her face, which was what she turned to him. "See you at home, my love."

He nodded at the priest and went out. The street was clamorous with guitars and organs and drums from all the clubs. He made it to the car and, with increasingly worsening ability to perform any task, drove very slowly back to the house. It was dark. No light anywhere. And when he got inside, there was no sign of her having been there during the day.

He went to sleep on the couch, and only partially awakened when she came in. "How dare you," she said. "You embarrassed him. And you humiliated *me*."

"Read about Monsignor Walsey, darling. I bet your friend knows more about him and the others than he's letting on. *Embarrassed* him. Christ. Poor guy—but the fact is there's at least *ninety-three* ruined lives in this city, children and *former* children, with just a little more than embarrassment to look back on, you know? Way, way more than embarrassment." He shook his head. "Embarrassed him. *Fuck* him, okay?"

"You just want to break everything up," she said, low. "Ruin everything. You're as bad as anybody you condemn. You don't really care about these—victims. You don't care about anybody but yourself."

"Sorry," Malcolm told her, without quite being able to sit up. He called after her as she stormed out of the room. "Mea culpa, mea culpa, mea maxima fucking culpa."

A door slam. Her crying. He saw himself rise to go in to her. But he didn't move.

Just before first light, when he woke and felt the effects of the previous hours, the whole underpinning of his life seemed to shiver inside him. It was an unendurable, quaking hour, filled with a lost-feeling nisus for resolution, for the will to change things, to go back, to get right. He heard Hannah getting up, and felt sorry for her. Yet it wasn't pity; it was remorse, rising from the long love and the once-happy passages. Hadn't he loved her? There was nothing to say, nothing for the forays into the secret life, the infidelities, the deceit. Because he was certain that she knew, and that she'd been living with the pain of knowing.

All this was a full two years before the accident.

Mona had been performing in community theater since she was six, and she decided early on that she wanted to pursue a career as a performer. She took dance, and musical theater classes, and studied mime, and acting, and she became a regular member of the company at Bartlett Community Theatre. He had managed to get her a local television commercial for Kroger. She was sixteen then, and a year later there were stand-up cutouts of her at all the entrances.

She was ambitious and shrewd, with a passion for books and music, and she possessed the subtle emotional intelligence of someone twenty years older. Perhaps elements of her social acumen came from her mother, who had navigated a difficult marriage through the child's growing up. It was as though Pearl had trained her; there were stratagems and inclinations, ways of attending to shifts in tone or body language. It looked like poise; it was astuteness approaching a form of dissembling: she could manipulate responses, and he saw that she was indeed a gifted actor, beyond her interest in film, or her impressive knowledge of movies and of movie history. In her last year of high school, after she had played in a primarily female version of *Twelve Angry Men* (titled *Twelve Angry Jurors*), he offered to see about using his connections in town to get her an audition at the theater. "Uncle Malcolm," she said. "I've been doing that forever, and the whole time I've had no interest whatsoever in stage acting—especially after this mess of a production."

"I thought it was wonderful."

The truth was that he had thought *she* was wonderful.

Shortly after she graduated, her parents reached the end of their mutual tether and broke apart in rancor and a series of upsetting scenes. Mona weathered all that, or seemed to, and she came to Malcolm for solace and, at least minimally, to confide. There was the sense, never quite acknowledged, that she was holding something back, letting him in on things selectively. "The trouble with my dad," she said when her father moved out, "is that he always wanted everything so squeaky clean. *Unsoiled.*

That's the word. *Unsoiled*. You couldn't just live in our house. It was like a *museum*. And Mom, the artist—*artiste*—" Mona said the word bitterly. "The *creative* person with her paints and drawing paper everywhere and her self-importance and the plates with food still on them, and the overflowing trash cans and the garbage. And her so-dull hippie sensibility with the woven shawls and the moccasins and the braided hair, like she's an Indian maiden just off the reservation when in fact she was born in Baltimore and raised in Thurmont, Maryland, and hasn't got the slightest trace of Native American blood, and he gave her hell about it, but no matter how crack-ass things were, she held on like death. Miserable, and holding on. Everything was all right with her as long as he played the husband part in her little drama about counterculture domestic bliss. And now she's behind the perfume counter at Macy's all day wearing pantsuits, with her long red manicured fingernails, and he's moved into his new apartment in Bartlett, a complete—" She breathed. "He doesn't even know all he really needs is to go home and go back to cleaning up." Abruptly, she gave forth a small tearful laugh. "I come from weird, weird people."

This was an afternoon in early August 2013. They were sitting on the patio outside Bluefin Restaurant. He saw the tears coming to the lower lids of her eyes, and he reached over to put his hand on her shoulder. The firmness of the bone there under his palm, the exquisite, solid, now-grown woman sitting so close, separate from him, yet unnervingly near, made him quickly take his hand away, as though fearful that his own heat might cause a burn. How he wanted to hold her! The realization shook him. For a moment, he lost the power of speech.

"Say something," she said, and raised one dark eyebrow.

"Well," Malcolm managed. "They're—they're human."

"That's so lame," she said. Then, with rueful sarcasm: "But gee, thanks, anyway."

He was an unfaithful husband with intrigues, abusing alcohol and taking drugs, emotionally and physically estranged from his wife, and he began seeing to it that Mona could reach him when she wanted to. By her own account, he was the one family member she could talk to, really be herself with; and everything she said betrayed aspects of an appalling household, filled with unspoken depredations, days of freezing silence whelmed in the commotion of the blaring television. And he found himself lying to everyone so he could see her, talk to her, listen to her.

The afternoon of the accident, he took her to lunch, and as she got into the car he smelled alcohol on her. He himself was aware of the effects of the bourbon he'd just had in his office before starting out. They went into town, to Automatic Slim's. He ordered a big sandwich for her, and another whiskey for himself. The server brought the whiskey, and Malcolm sipped it while she talked about giving lessons in signing to a guy whose sister's little stepson had hearing loss. "Look," she said to Malcolm. She moved her slender fingers in a series of quick motions. "I got a D in it at school, and look at me. Do you know what I just said?"

He shook his head.

"They didn't require classes in ASL when you were in school?"

"No."

The server brought her sandwich, and she took it without quite looking at him. The server was a balding young man with reddish muttonchop sideburns. "Enjoy," he said to her. And waited. Then he looked at Malcolm, who saw the recognition come into his eyes. "Anything else I can bring you, sir?"

"Another one of these."

"Got it."

Malcolm took the last of what he had, and set the glass down.

"What's that taste like?" she asked.

"It's an acquired taste," he told her. "And I've acquired it."

She seemed to sigh this away. Then she repeated her signing gestures while he watched. "So, do you want to know what I just said?"

"Sure."

Delicately taking a potato chip from the pile of them bordering her sandwich, she put it in her mouth, looking at him as if trying to decide something. "Well, the young man I'm teaching how to do ASL is twenty-three, his name is Dylan, he's a playwright, and I just spent the night with him. Perfectly without any funny business."

Malcolm couldn't breathe out for a few seconds.

She took a bite of the big sandwich, nodded at him, as if this were merely some kind of puff interview for TV. "It's perfectly all right. I'll be eighteen soon." She appeared about to laugh. Then her tone became nearly chiding: "He's twenty-three—about to turn twenty-four."

"Your mother knows about you spending the night?"

"She thinks I spent the night with Eileen Clemminger. Look, I'm done being a child."

He thought to take hold of her wrist, but then held still, feeling the measure of her distance from him like a blow to his chest. It was absurd; he had no claim. He told himself he'd never presumed anything or wanted anything, only to help as he could, however that was possible, to protect her and to be there for her—though he also knew (he admitted this to himself) that it was so he could look into her eyes and hear her voice.

He sat there, speechless.

The server returned with the bourbon. "Anything else I can get you?"

"No," Malcolm managed. "Thank you."

The server hesitated, then seemed to collect himself. "I'm studying communications at Christian Brothers. I watch you every night, sir. Never miss."

"Well," Malcolm raised his glass. "Here's to you. And wishing you luck."

"Thank you so much. Do you mind—could I have your autograph?"

"Sure."

It took only a moment. The young man went off with his little signed piece of paper, and Malcolm took a good swallow of his new drink.

"You like that stuff," Mona said.

"Signing autographs?"

She sniggered, and pointed at the drink. "That. I'd like to try it."

So, a little later, he stopped at Buster's and, while she waited in the car, went in and bought a half-pint, feeling pleasantly supervisory; she could have a sip, and form an opinion. He was already a little drunk. He told himself she was bound to try it anyway. They sat in the parking lot at Mud Island and looked out at the wide, brown, going-by of the river, trading small sips from the bottle. "I like it," she said. "I like the corn-sweet aftertaste. Once you get used to the sting."

"I haven't tasted anything in it for years." He drank.

The accident happened on the short drive back to her house. He had in fact never so much as hugged her. And this was in its strange way the clearest indication of what actually troubled him about it all.

Thaddeus

In the early morning, in gray light, heart racing again, he turned over on his back and felt his wrist. Nothing at first, then the violent thrumming. He lay still for a minute, believing that he'd dreamed something, since he'd felt anxiety again as soon as he opened his eyes. He took his pulse. One hundred seventy-four. This wasn't his mother's palpitations.

He went into his study off the bedroom, to his desk and the computer, googled this heart rate and blood pressure, and read the first three articles. *See your doctor. Tachycardia. Hypertension. Irregular heartbeat. Heart failure.*

He called Gina's cell, but ended the call before she answered. He drove himself to the hospital. It was down Park Street, five miles from the house. The sun was obscured by a flat, slate-colored, hot sky.

Gina called as he pulled in. "Is everything all right? It's so early."

"I'm at the hospital."

"What?"

"Yeah, so now there's two of us running to the emergency room."

"Your palpitations."

"Not palpitations. It's racing."

"Well, I'm glad you're getting it checked out."

"I'm glad you're glad, Gina."

"Hey," she said. "Do you hear that I'm calm? I'm calm because I'm sure it's fine. I actually asked a doctor down here about what's been going on with you, and he said if there's no pain it's most likely nothing to worry about."

"A hundred seventy-four beats a minute, babe. It doesn't feel like nothing."

"Well," she insisted. "He told me if there's no pain it's probably nothing. Anyway, now you'll know. You want me to call them at the theater? I'll call the theater. What should I tell them?"

"Say I got drunk and had to be put to sleep."

"Well, you still have your sense of humor."

"Will you come back, Gina?"

She hesitated. "Give me a call after they've seen you."

He got out of the car and looked at the pale morning. A dark couple was strolling along the sidewalk, a boy was cutting grass in a yard, and some men were replacing shingles on the roof of a house across the street. He thought of the busy world of living human beings as if he were no longer part of it. Pounding his fist into his palm, he took a breath, and headed to the entrance. It was difficult to keep from thinking his heart might give out, yet it was true that he felt no pain or wooziness. He wished he knew more, wished he could be certain. There wasn't anyone in the waiting room, which had perhaps ten blue plastic chairs in a row. He saw magazines lying on little side tables, a row of floor-to-ceiling windows to the left of the entrance. He walked over to the opening in the far wall. A squarish brown woman sat there in baby-blue coveralls, shuffling some papers. She looked up at him. "Yes?"

"My heart's going more than a hundred eighty beats a minute," he said. "It's been like that all morning."

"Do you have any pain?"

A very dark man he took to be a doctor entered from behind where the woman sat. He was wearing the same coveralls. His head was shaved and reflected the light in the low asbestos-looking ceiling. "Chest pain and shortness of breath?" he said. He had an accent; Thaddeus thought, for some reason, of Morocco.

"It's going a hundred eighty beats a minute. I'm breathless."

"Come in through the double doors."

He went over to the slowly opening double doors. The bald man turned out to be another nurse. They walked to the first examining cubicle. "Take your shirt off, and your shoes, and lie down," the male nurse said, pointing at the gurney there. "Make yourself comfortable."

He lay down.

The bald dark male nurse put a light blanket over him. "We'll hook you up to some things, take some blood."

Another nurse came in, a blond woman with veins showing in her wiry lean arms. She put him on a monitor, with a blood pressure cuff. The monitor squeezed, and let go. "Two ten over one fifty. Pulse a hundred sixty-eight."

Yet another nurse arrived, pushing an electrocardiogram console. This one was a stocky, wide-shouldered young woman who looked like a teenager. Quickly and efficiently she put the little electrode patches on his chest and upper abdomen, apologizing for the coldness of them. The paper with the graph of his racing heart scrolled out of the machine.

After a few long minutes, a doctor came in, all business, seeming a bit stressed. He had a gray-streaked, well-trimmed beard and salt-and-pepper hair cut close. He looked like a businessman or a lawyer in a white coat. There was something off-kilter about him. Thaddeus thought, *Emergency-room doctor.* The doctor took the scroll of paper with the jagged-looking red lines on it from the nurse. The tag on the pocket of the light blue smock said DR. SHENK. "Any pain?" he asked. His voice was calm.

"It feels like a squirrel or rabbit kicking around under my breastbone."

He looked at the monitor above the gurney, and Thaddeus looked at it, too. "It's speeding, all right." The rate now showed 174. "This is a thing called sinus tachycardia," Dr. Shenk said. "Your heartbeat's fast but regular." The stethoscope was cold on his chest as Shenk listened. "You don't feel dizzy or sick or breathless."

"No."

"We'll run some tests. Take some pictures. I don't think it's anything serious. Really. We do want to get it regulated, of course. Get the rate closer to normal. But this is *atrial.* We sometimes call it nuisance A-fib. But we want to get it under control. *Nuisance* is the operative word."

The blood pressure cuff tightened, and pinched. "Blood pressure still high," the blond nurse said. Thaddeus looked at her lips, and for an instant saw her in sexual terms, a kind of free-floating anxiety-laden impression of a lovely mouth. It appalled him.

The doctor, the nurses, everyone, seemed calm. He would apologize to Gina for his self-absorption and for being blind to her trouble, whatever the trouble was. Her darks, as RJ had called them.

Dr. Shenk said, "Your EKG also shows a slight abnormality—a bundle branch block on the left-hand side."

"Block?"

He smiled tolerantly. "Not that kind of block. It's like circuitry in a machine. Affects timing. Usually, you feel no symptoms. In fact, I've had it myself at least ten years." He kept the smile, patted Thaddeus's arm, and started away. "I'll be back." He stepped beyond the white curtain beside the gurney. The two nurses remained, one tightening the band around his arm to take blood, the other writing something in a pad while glancing back and forth at the EKG machine.

"Big stick," the one said. And as she put the needle in, the white curtain to their left swelled suddenly inward, took the shape of a head moving down its surface on the other side, and then seemed to fly upward at the hem, revealing Dr. Shenk, on his back, mouth and eyes wide open.

The nurse said, "Oh, hell!" It might have been "Oh, help."

The dark male nurse bent quickly to lift the head, and then the other nurses moved, all three of them immediately surrounding the body on the floor. The only sound was a kind of low whine that Thaddeus realized was himself. He'd sat up—he didn't remember doing so—and was being held from rising out of the gurney by the electrodes and the blood pressure cuff.

"Is it his heart?" he said.

No one answered. Now there were others, two more women, nurses, and an alarm beeper began sounding, a voice talking in the walls. Thaddeus held one hand over his chest, the electrodes there and the little wires. "Is he dead?" he demanded. "Is it his heart?"

In the commotion, the others seemed to have forgotten him. "Is it his block branch?" Thaddeus said. "His bundle?"

"Breathing," one of the nurses said.

More people crowded in—doctors, other nurses. You couldn't see the fallen man. They all seemed to be working on him, and the female nurse returned to Thaddeus and took his arm, still watching the confusion where the curtain had been pulled back. "Dead?" he said to her. "Is it his bundle?"

"Lie back." She glanced at the monitor. Thaddeus stared at it. One hundred seventy-six beats per minute. The blood pressure cuff compressed again, stopped, then loosened: 159/123. He lay back and looked at the ceiling, trying to breathe slowly. The turmoil at the end of the bed went on.

"Is it his block bundle?" Thaddeus said.

An African American man with a thick black mustache and bulging eyes came to him. "We're moving you to another part of the ward," he said, and began wheeling the gurney away. Thaddeus saw Dr. Shenk's legs, the hair on the exposed pallid shins, the rest of him obscured by the others crouched or kneeling by him. They had his shirt off, and one of the nurses injected him with something. In the hallway, Thaddeus said, "Was it his bundle?"

"Don't know what you're referring to, sir."

"A doctor tells me I have something abnormal about my heart and he has it, too, and it's nothing to worry about, and then he tumbles over like a sack."

"It was probably dehydration, sir. I'm sure he's all right. He's not dead."

"He looked dead when he fell."

The man wheeled the gurney into another small enclosure, past another curtain on a circular rod, and pulled the curtain closed around him. Thaddeus saw from the tag on his chest that his name was Brown.

"Nurse Brown," he said. "Am I going to be all right?"

"It's Dr. Brown. Just try to relax. You'll be fine."

"Was it his branch bundle, please."

"Relax, all right? Everything's under control."

"I'm only thirty-eight," Thaddeus said as Dr. Brown walked out of sight. "And I have a blocked bundle. It has the word *block* in it. Or it's a block branch."

Perhaps an hour passed. He lay hearing the goings-on of where he was—the loudspeakers, the chatter in the nearby hallway fading and rising. He said, to the vacant space around him, "Anyone?"

Finally a nurse he didn't recall having seen before came and pushed the curtain aside. "Okay," she said. "Mr. Deerforth."

"Yes?"

She held a pad, as if she would write something down—but she referred to it. "I've been asked to report to you that Dr. Shenk's just fine. He had some dehydration, and he fainted. You're okay. Just let go. Try to sleep."

"I won't sleep."

But he did sleep. They must have put something calming in his IV tube. He went under and down, dreamed peacefully, even sweetly, and when he awoke he saw angles of wall and ceiling and knew he was in a room. There was a television set suspended above him. Somewhere inside his skull, he heard the words *hospital room*.

And he remembered everything. He looked around himself. Then put both hands to his chest. He was still hooked to an IV. His back hurt. He heard himself say, "What floor?"

A moment later, the same nurse came in. He knew the face from before, but it was as if now he could really see her. She wore round-lensed glasses and had soft hazel eyes, a lovely smile. She had the same pad with her, which she glanced at. "I have some notes here. First thing, there's nothing seriously wrong with you, okay? You have a strong, healthy heart. You'll be happy to know that your heartbeat has been normal for almost three hours. We put medicine in the IV to slow it down and it's worked. The doctor—Dr. Morales—checked up on you while you slept. He says everything's fine. All blood tests normal. They'll do an echocardiogram and some other things. But your heart's beating strongly and normally. You have a 'very strong, healthy heart' according to Dr. Morales. We want to keep you overnight just to be sure."

"I can't miss work," he said.

"Well, Dr. Morales'll be here in a few minutes."

He spent the night. When he called Gina's phone, Louisa answered. "How are you, Young Fighter?"

"I'm all right. I've got some tests in the morning. Everything seems fine."

"Gina took a walk. She said it was to get away from me because I lit one cigarette."

"Well, tell her the news."

"I'll have her call you."

"If she wants to."

He slept again, straight through. He had the vaguest sense of someone lightly squeezing his foot. Very early in the morning a new nurse came to give him water and broth. He had the whole morning to go through. He didn't call Gina, and no call came from her. Further tests revealed nothing. His pulse remained steady, within normal range. He had no pain, no discomfort. He had spent the one night in the hospital, and now he was given a prescription for a beta-blocker, and Rythmol, and allowed to go home.

It was another humid, gray day, and the airlessness of it worried him. He stood outside the house and breathed, and put his fingers to his wrist.

Dr. Shenk had been dehydrated from jogging in the heat while hungover from a bottle of wine and three whiskeys the night before. He related this in a faintly boasting tone while affixing a heart monitor to Thaddeus's chest, which he would wear for two days. It was attached exactly along the breastbone by adhesive, running the length of it.

He had no appetite, and though he'd been asleep most of the previous day, he went to bed early. After an hour or so, he woke from a dream of trying to climb a wall, and then spent a restless hour, listening to the little sounds of his body—stomach sounds, little catches when he breathed. In the predawn he got up and took his blood pressure: 110/64. His heart rate was 53 beats a minute. When he called Gina again, she answered by saying, "Health Panic Central." Louisa had filled her in.

"I'm home," he said. Then: "And you can be really cruel, you know it?"

"Well, I grew up in Louisa's house. Medical emergencies that end up being nothing have made me a little calloused. Maybe there's calluses on my soul."

He said nothing, intending that as an answer.

"Emergencies stop being emergencies when they were never emergencies in the first place. I learned that from Mama, who right now is out walking with the Rightwing Reverend Whitcomb and smoking like a chimney."

"How's your despair?" he said, meaning it to sting.

She ignored the question with a little scoffing sound.

He made a cup of decaf and sat in the window seat in the bedroom, looking out at the patchy lawn, aware of the monitor in the middle of his chest. When he was through with the coffee, he went down into the kitchen and sat looking at the newspaper. Calamity and suffering all over the world. As usual.

The following day, he spent mostly at the theater, sitting in his office, dealing with the latest phases of the renovation. Lurlene and the girls were there, and he played cards with them, and told the girls stories about pixies and disguises and charms in forests and mixed-up identities; and he ended up talking a little to Lurlene about the sorrows of the season. She was a good listener, and he felt bad for saying anything, given his knowledge of what *she* was carrying. He marveled at how pleasant and musical her voice was. It was like having his mother in the next office. His mother and Aunt Anna were in Cannes for a vacation. They were going south to Nice, and then over to San Remo, on the Italian coast. He told Lurlene's girls, "You know, don't you, what a great lady your grandmother is."

"You stop that," she said, waving one hand in front of her face.

He spoke with Gina on the phone twice—short, halting conversations about the work of expanding the number of seats in the auditorium. It was going on, noisily, and it was a subject for talk. Her staff had finished with the sets. She spoke of Claudette, and he had the sense that she'd been speaking to her fairly often. He hadn't seen Claudette. She was very busy now with rehearsal and also with her father, who had caught some kind of flu. Thaddeus asked Gina how Louisa was doing, and wondered how everybody was getting along. Whitcomb and Marcel were in the way, she told him.

He said, "I'm sorry."

She said, "Me, too," then paused. "But he's a minister and Marcel's a dog. What can you do."

"Drive Marcel to another time zone and let him out? Accuse the minister of taking advantage of a sweet old lady or make up something about him emotionally abusing the pooch?"

"I'd like to." She actually gave a little laugh; it encouraged him. "I'm emotionally abusing the dog myself. I call him fucking pustule when I'm alone with him. How are *you* doing?"

More encouragement. "Oh," he said, "I'm pretty far down, you know."

Her reply was toneless. He thought he heard something almost dismissive in it. "We each have our burden to carry," she said.

Two days later, he drove to Dr. Shenk's office to have the monitor removed and, a day after that, went in for the follow-up. All the tests were normal. The monitor showed everything normal. They shook hands. He had a sudden urge to confide in Dr. Shenk, and heard himself say, "I'm such a worrier."

"You did the right thing," said the doctor, who left him there in the little room. Thaddeus stood buttoning up his shirt, looking at the picture depicting the inside of the human heart.

Gina and her mother and Whitcomb showed up at the house early the following Monday. Louisa came in with the makings for breakfast, and a bottle of rye, which she put in the cabinet above the refrigerator. There were half-empty bottles of rum and Amaretto in there, and the bourbon that had belonged to RJ.

Gina gave him a detached smile and what he now thought of as her "station platform" kiss. And the dog snapped at him and at the Reverend Elias Whitcomb—at everybody, really. The reverend's manner was exceedingly polite. He resembled one of those craggy, gray, starved-looking figures from movies set during the Depression. Watching him, Thaddeus thought of the Walker Evans photographs in James Agee's book *Let Us Now Praise Famous Men*. Though it also occurred to him that the man's voice was nice enough. It was as though his opinions were some sort of deficit, a handicap he couldn't help. Gina was clearly bent on badgering him about his views to draw him into an argument, but he was having none of it, and Louisa, fresh from her emergency of the floaters, annoyed her daughter by insisting on standing out in the yard with Marcel, and smoking.

Thaddeus had to leave for the theater. Gina waved at him from the entrance to the kitchen, though she was in the middle of an argument with Whitcomb about Islam and Christianity. Thaddeus had tuned it out for the rancorous tone in her voice. "Just as bloody," she was saying. "A little thing called the Inquisition." Then, to Thaddeus as he was going out the front door: "Tell them I'll be in. We have to unload the car."

He lifted his hand a little. "See you there?"

But she had turned and was talking at Whitcomb about the Inquisition.

Claudette

Tuesday morning, the sixteenth, she went into the theater, across the new, paint-smelling lobby to the side hall, with its shining tiles, and along it, past the black box, where Kelly Gordon still was conducting auditions for understudies, to Gina's office. She knocked, and waited. The building was quiet—no sounds of renovation or correction for water damage following the mishap from the new restrooms. There was a distillate of mildew on the damp and still-drying surfaces. The air felt thick, nearly unbreathable. She knocked again, and Gina opened the door. Behind her was Frye, leaning on the sketch table, arms folded, legs extended. He looked red eyed and downcast.

"Not now," Gina said, low.

Frye declared. "I've gotta do some work anyway." He came around Gina and sidled through the door and on past where Claudette stood staring.

Then she turned. "What the hell, girl."

"I've been away. He needed to catch me up."

"Catch you up." Claudette smirked. "How." She gingerly edged past her to enter the tight little space, with its walls covered by framed drawings and sketches. There was no window. The place smelled of paper, and coffee.

Gina closed the door. "I'm redoing the set for the Dover scene."

Claudette waited.

"Okay. The truth is, I'm tired of death and thoughts of death all the time, Claudie. I've lived with it my whole life."

"Who hasn't?" Claudette said. "If we're not crazy or stupid, then we're afraid, right?"

"I'm not joking."

"Okay. Did you talk to Thaddeus?"

"Briefly. It's hard to get anything in with the Reverend Wrong and Marcel and Mama in the house. Marcel took a dump in the middle of the living room, at the exact center of the rug, as if he'd found a way to measure it. Thaddeus doesn't even know about it. And don't tell him."

"I'll be able, I think, to refrain from bringing that up as a subject."

Gina left a pause, gazing at her. "Everything's propagation," she said suddenly, as if in answer to a question.

"Are you all right? What the hell are you talking about?"

"That's all it is, really. Think about it. Propagation. Everything, from the smallest mite to the whales in the ocean."

"Hey, don't go batshit on me, okay?"

"I'm thinking clear for the first time in my life. Procreation. The meaning of everything. The truth. The underneath truth. No, it's the *overneath* truth."

Claudette repeated the phrase as if trying to parse it. "Overneath truth."

"With a capital *O*," Gina said. "Tell me, what sort of God would make a world where it's all just fucking or killing? Or both? Think of it. Black widow spiders and the screeching birds and insects, all those cries, calls, or threat sounds all competing for mates, for fucking. And every living thing has to eat another living thing to stay alive."

Claudette stood there in the center of the little room and stared at her. Then: "Okay, look, sweetie. That's enough."

"Everything on earth. Every living thing, right? Am I right?"

"Okay, let's just shut the fuck up about it all, shall we? You're scaring me."

"You have to take this *seriously*," Gina insisted. "And I'm out of the complete flow of it now, because I know. I fucking *know*."

"Look, stop this."

Gina sat down at her desk and put her hands to either side of her head. "I'm afraid of my own mind."

"Can you please calm down and really talk to me?"

"I'm telling you the only meaning in life is this." She sobbed. "I'm glad I won't have it anymore, but I *hate* it, too. Everything; it's all so *ordinary*." For a bad few moments, the only sound was her snuffling.

"Honey, talk to Thaddeus."

"How can I? He's got his own laugh-riot of an emotional sinkhole. And we're like strangers at an airport."

"Talk to him, honey."

"I'm sorry, Claudie. Could you please leave me alone? I'm all right. I just need to be alone a little. Really."

Claudette went out and closed the door behind her, then started along the hall. She was wiping tears from her eyes. As she went along the hall to the turn on the way out, she came face-to-face with William Mundy. "Oh," he said, noticing the tears. "Is something amiss? Has someone put a spanner in the works?"

"Not a thing," Claudette said. "Allergies to all the paint, mildew, and plasterboard."

"Can I treat you to a cuppa?"

"I'm fine."

"I came to look for you. Thought we might do a little advance work."

"I really can't now." She went on.

He walked along beside her. "You're not angry with me?"

"Pardon?"

"I was hoping we might form a friendship."

She stopped and faced him. There was a rounded, muscular look to his shoulders; his hair was white streaked, parted in the middle. "A working relationship, of course," he said. "But friends, too."

She stared. Then: "A working relationship is a given, isn't it?"

"Well," he said, with a leering kind of grin. "But I was hoping it could be, erm, more on a personal level, as fellow artists. A certain kind of friendship."

"I'm nursing my father through the aftermath of several strokes," she heard herself say. "I'm still working two mornings a week as an art gallery receptionist, and after tomorrow I'm sure I'll be spending most of each day, into the evenings, here. There's really no time for any personal relationship beyond that. I really don't want to be rude, so let's just leave it there, okay?"

Now he seemed faintly aggrieved. He straightened, raised one hand to belt level as if to offer it in a handshake, then slowly let it drop. She looked at it, but did not respond.

"Well," she said, moving off. "Gotta go."

"Wait." He took hold of her arm above the elbow and pulled, turning her. "I think you might've misunderstood me." His grip was strong. He grasped her other arm, drawing her toward him. "I thought we could just get to know each other. A little release. For us both."

There was a moment of straining against his pressure, her arms up, both hands open, trying to push away from his thick chest.

"Let go of me right now, or I'll have to react."

"No, but—just—just really," he stammered. "We can be very good for each other." He leaned and tried to put his mouth on hers, pulling her closer. "Really. I can do things for you. You might keep that uppermost in your mind."

She tried to pull away.

"Just one kiss," he said, breathing at her, gripping her arms. "A kiss.

Where's the harm." She felt his mouth on the side of her neck. "Two artists," he said into her skin, then put his mouth, forcibly, on hers, pushing in with his tongue.

She brought her knee up into his groin with as much force as she could muster.

"Oh!" he exclaimed, his voice echoing in the hall. She had felt his pelvic bone and the softness of what was trapped between the top of her kneecap and it.

His hands dropped quickly to the hurting place, and he faltered back, bending over. "Agh!" The sound reverberated. "Agh!" Then he moaned, almost whispering. "Oh, God. Oh, no. Christ."

She heard the words as something enunciated very clearly, as if carefully.

"You—" he said.

"Do we understand each other, now?" she said with a trembling voice. "Do you see what our real relation is?"

"You cu—oh—you'll never—I'll see to it—never. You fucking—oh, oh, bugger."

"So much work to do," she said. Then, glaring, she added, "And remember, Lear never once touches Goneril. Not once. Keep that uppermost in your mind. And this that just happened might help when you rage against her. You can really get into the *method* now."

He'd turned, still bent sorrowfully at the waist, limping to the wall and along it, almost whining.

She walked away, and did not look back. But instead of leaving, she returned to Gina's office.

"What?" Gina said, opening the door.

"I didn't want to leave it there, honey."

"What's the matter. You're out of breath."

"I'm—well, I'm worried about you."

Gina went to her table and sat down, elbows resting on the scattered papers and drawings, chin resting on her palms. Claudette sat in the tall chair opposite, and looked at her.

Her friend shook her head.

Claudette stood and filled the electric kettle, and made hot tea. It was something to do. She was shivering. She wanted to tell what had just happened with Mundy, but kept it back, fearful of increasing the other's stress. The two of them sat there at the sketch table, Gina sniffling now and then, and drawing figures, like a kind of distracted doodling, on the drafting paper strewn across the surface. "Don't worry about me."

Claudette went around and kissed the side of her face. "You'll call me," she said. "Right?"

At the apartment, she found Willamina and Ellis looking like proud grandparents, sitting in wicker chairs on the stoop in front of the apartment, watching a boy play in the small yard. The boy was dark as a night sky, and very thin; he was tossing a soccer ball up and trying unsuccessfully to catch it. Claudette pulled up in front. The boy stopped and stared. Ellis stood. "Where in the world have you been all this time, Esther?"

"The theater," she said. She was exhausted, yet hadn't quite realized it until she spoke those words.

"I've gotta get Sonny back to his mother for lunch," Willamina said. "I'll be back."

Claudette went on in and changed into a T-shirt and shorts. Ellis had come in and put a movie on, TCM, people arguing in a courtroom. He was drifting off, holding a glass of water. Claudette put it away and then went into the kitchen to prepare a sandwich. Her hands shook. She kept seeing Gina's distraught features, and hearing again the echo of the Netflix actor's cry in the hall. She wondered why Gina hadn't heard it—why anyone else hadn't heard it. She was still hearing it. Willamina returned, and when they were sitting in the kitchen and Ellis's movie was playing, she told her about it.

"You're serious," said Willamina, beginning to laugh, leaning across the table. "My, my. I would like to congrat-u-late you on your initiative."

"Don't say anything, please." Claudette gestured at the sound of horses' hooves and gunshots and Indians in the other room.

"Of course not," Willamina said. "Oh, of course not." She took a breath. "I'm just picturing it—the big-time TV star getting a politeness lesson in his chumblies."

This made Claudette laugh. She spoke through it. "I never heard that before."

"My husband's name for it—them."

"I'll remember that. Ellis would say I kicked the bastard in his fruit bowl."

Willamina laughed, both hands over her mouth. "Lord. Oh, Lord."

His voice came from the movie Indian battle in the other room. "What are you two laughing about in there?"

"We're coming," Claudette said.

Willamina poured Bushmills into two shot glasses. She and Ellis had been having it like that, sipped slow, each lunch, movie watching, and then in some evenings. She looked at Claudette and with a sly smile, and laughter in her voice, said, "Have a glass with us, honey? Celebrate a little."

"I can't," Claudette told her. They returned to the living room, where Ellis had paused the movie. "Got my last shift at the gallery for a while. I'll celebrate with orange juice."

Willamina held Ellis's drink toward him. "Here's your Bushmills, Captain."

Ellis took it, smiling proudly at Claudia. "Calls me Captain."

"I'm the bosun," Willamina said.

"I love it," said Claudette, sitting down.

"Sometimes I'm the captain and *he's* the bosun."

"That's about the size of it," Ellis said.

Willamina held her glass toward Claudette as if to offer a toast. "Your father and I have decided we're gonna be in the front row on the first night of *King Lear.*"

"That would be wonderful," Claudette said.

"No, it's *go-ing* to *be* wonderful. We're coming. Opening night. It'll be glorious."

"I believe it," Ellis said. "I do."

The three were quiet for a time, Willamina and Ellis enjoying the whiskey.

Presently, Claudette's father said to her, "Don't know how you can study, with me here—"

Willamina spoke. "Here's to doing *King Lear.*"

"King Lear," Ellis said.

"Have there been any calls?" Claudette asked.

Willamina said, "No calls."

"I thought Franny called," Ellis said. "I was pretty sure."

"Oh, that's right. She did, Captain. We told her to come on ahead."

"Yeah," he said. "I yelled it—'Come on over.'"

"Yes, he did," said Willamina. "But we haven't seen any sign of her."

"Well, I guess she's not coming." Claudette looked from one to the other. "She's gotta come quick—I've gotta get going."

"I'm tired," Ellis said abruptly. "Esther isn't coming, is she—I mean Franny."

Willamina gestured for Claudette to remain seated and helped him into his room.

Perhaps a minute later, Franny drove up and came striding to the door, a woman with a purpose. Claudette saw her through the window to her left. Opening the door, she feigned surprise. "Well, hello."

"You just gonna stand there?" Franny wore a Kauai sun hat with her hair tied back very tightly, so that her large, outlandishly protruding, pinkish ears showed. The ears were oddly circular, and, looking at her, you could not help thinking of those cartoon pictures of mice, nor could you help expecting something funny to come when she spoke, even looking at that drawn, wearily aggrieved but resolute face. She frowned at Claudette, stepped back slightly, and took off the hat, heightening the comic effect of the peninsular ears. She wiped her forehead and put the hat back on.

Claudette stepped aside to let her in.

"Where is he?"

"Willamina just helped him into his room for a nap."

"Did the social workers pay you a visit?"

"You'll have to ask Willamina, his nurse. I just got back from the theater."

Franny moved to the divan and sat with a hand clutching each knee. Claudette saw her swollen, bluish ankles, and the belt she wore with her new-looking, still-store-creased jeans. The belt was twisted on the right side, at her hip. "I'm having some papers drawn up. Since you're so completely sure you want to keep to this—this nonsense. After all, I have the power of attorney. And there's the will. And money from his retirement."

"I honestly don't care about the will, Franny. I never have. You all can have whatever there is that comes, really. I haven't asked and I'm not going to ask him to change a thing where that's concerned. And as far as TIAA-CREF and his pension goes, I think he's still capable of deciding how he'll use that."

"But we need everything in writing."

"It already is, mostly, isn't it?"

Willamina came into the room, folded her arms, and leaned on the doorframe. "Resting comfortably," she said.

Franny glowered at her. "I don't suppose you have a résumé or something this person"—she indicated Claudette—"was probably too busy breaking the law to check carefully."

"Breaking the—" Claudette began.

Willamina spoke calmly, "She has my résumé, yes, ma'am."

"I have it," Claudette said. "And I haven't broken any laws, either."

Franny was unmoved, still addressing Willamina. "And you're being paid—how much?"

"I never share that kind of personal information with anyone, ma'am."

"Well, he needs expert care and he should be under full supervision."

Willamina said to Claudette, "I don't think he'd like it, hearing himself talked about like he's an Airedale in a veterinarian's office."

"That is *not* what we're doing," Franny insisted, with some heat.

"Well," Willamina said, quietly. "As Claudette pointed out, no laws have been broken."

Franny took a deep breath. Then: "He's my husband. And he's Meryl's father, too."

"Meryl's welcome here," Claudette said. "Always has been. So are you."

"I guess I'm a coward." Her stepmother brought a handkerchief out of her purse and held it in her fist at her nose. "I don't mean anything. I want to be nice. I *am* nice. I'm a nice person. I wanted him in that place because it's the place where he can get the best care. Twenty-four-hour care. Where he can have doctors and nurses. And his insurance covers it."

"Nobody disagrees with you about the doctors and nurses, Franny. Willamina's a registered nurse."

"I love him, you know."

"Nobody's contradicting that. And you *are* welcome here anytime. We've got unlimited visiting hours here."

The following silence drew out, lengthening.

Finally Claudette sighed, breaking the spell. "The point is Dad's in good hands. He wants to be here. He's happy here." She stood, as her stepmother did, and forced herself to put her arms around the woman, breathing the odor of sweat poorly camouflaged by perfume. She thought of lonely nights. She had an image of Franny sitting in the silvery-blue light of the television, ingesting the hectic umbrages of right-wing news. And here were her clownish ears sticking out. She wiped her nose and stuffed the handkerchief back into her purse. Claudette touched her rounded elbow as she went out.

"Poor woman," Willamina said. They watched her drive away.

"She's feeling guilty," said Claudette.

"I wasn't talking about her."

She turned. "I've gotta go into the gallery."

"Are you okay?" Willamina said.

"Don't worry," Claudette told her. "Really."

Willamina took a breath, and it was suddenly clear that the visit had cost her. She ran one hand across her gray-streaked hair, and seemed to gather herself. "It's nice to feel useful again, you know?"

Claudette said, "I know, yes."

Willamina folded her hands at her waist. "We've gotta try as much as possible talking to him as himself. The doctors and experts'll tell you that. There's still so much of him there, as you know. You've prob'ly got a good amount of time yet."

"It's not Alzheimer's," Claudette reminded her. "This is vascular."

"I know, I remember," Willamina said. "He and I actually talked about that a little."

"I guess it comes to the same thing."

"There'll be times. When he goes off, just try and talk around it if you can. That's the love of it. And it won't make it one bit easier, either. But it can help you through. At least he's not locked up in some room dying of loneliness."

"I wish I'd been able to know your Derek," Claudette said, close to losing her voice. "To know the two of you together." She watched the other woman touch the corners of her eyes, and in the same moment, they both heard Ellis make a coughing, throat-clearing sound in the other room, followed by a low, muttered curse.

Abruptly, Claudette felt susceptible. A surge of anxiety seized her. Somehow, she summoned the will to speak. "Thank you, so much."

Willamina McNichol sighed, reached over, and touched her wrist. "You're up to it. You've got a lot of strength. I admire your strength."

"Willamina," Claudette said. "That's such a lovely name."

"It's German. My mother picked it out of a book. It means 'protector.'"

She saw the back of Willamina's hand, the bones and veins just intimated under the latte-colored skin. Willamina took out a handkerchief and daubed at the little beads of sweat on the side of her smooth face. Claudette thought she'd never seen a more beautiful face, nor hands so shapely; they did not look like the hands of a woman nearing seventy.

"What do you use to keep your hands so perfect?" she asked, opening the door to leave.

Willamina smiled. "Regular soap and water, honey."

III

All-Call

Saturday, June 20

(FORTY-FIVE DAYS TO OPENING NIGHT)

Malcolm

Two days before all-call, he rose from the recliner and made himself black coffee as he used to when he was drinking. Black coffee at night or in the early-morning hours, after drinking, and then again after the hours of half sleep. He'd never been sick from drinking, or from doing the other substances, either—never blacked out, and never, until almost two years ago, been cited. As far as he knew, no one at WMC ever saw anything about his performance on the job that would indicate impairment.

The fact that he had taken this morning's coffee to give himself a boost for the day was a bitter reminder, though, of his former life. He felt downcast and lethargic, full of aches, nerve pain in his knees and down his shins. The day looked dreary. Gray light came in the window like judgment. He took a long shower, inhaling the steam, adjusting the water to nearly scalding before turning it off. Sitting in the hard chair next to the entrance of the closetlike kitchen, he rubbed ointment onto his calves, and pulled a neoprene brace over each knee, then reheated the coffee, and drank the rest of it down. He wanted a drink. He wanted to drive over to Mona's house and wait for her to come out. And then he was thinking of going to Macy's at Oak Court Mall, to see Pearl. *Hello, Pearl. I'm actually harmless. And clean. Why don't you stop now, Pearl? Everybody's okay.*

He had awakened from a dream of Hannah as she was when they were in college together—or a dream version of her, anyway, an intimate shadow-woman; she was present and absent at the same time, Hannah at twenty, and the set or stage of the dream was college. Some college he had never seen. It all existed in a haze. He woke with a headache.

The coffee helped, though it upset his stomach. He took several antacid pills, then shaved and dressed—jeans, and one of the white shirts he used to wear on-camera. A silk shirt, which felt good on his arms. And a sport coat, for work. When he opened the door to go out, he was startled to see Gregory coming up onto the stoop. The latter had his head down, and was therefore startled, too, looking up to see his younger brother in the doorway. "I was in the neighborhood and thought I'd stop to see how you're doing."

By the time Malcolm had been old enough to know his older brother existed, Gregory was already out in the world. Sometimes, in those growing-up years, Malcolm would see him at family gatherings; there was something nearly mythic about him, then; he seemed no more knowable than their father had been—the artist, Albert Ruark, with his volatile temper and frenetic overbusy life, his ex-wives and his affairs, his days of ignoring everything except his work and his fun, as Malcolm had heard his mother say to him more than once. When she finally divorced the old man and moved with her preteen son to Midtown, and began receiving support payments sent cheerfully through Gregory, Malcolm saw his older brother more often, though he still tended to think of him as an exotic figure, imposing and knowledgeable about everything. Finally, the two were simply not in the same sphere: they had not seen one another with any regularity over time, and not at all since the old man's death. Malcolm knew from his mother that Gregory lived alone in a big loft apartment on Riverside Drive.

"I'm on my way to the theater."

"Got time for a short coffee?"

"I'm sort of on my own clock until Monday."

They took Gregory's car to Brother Juniper's. The sky had become stormy, the air still hot and heavily humid, with steamy-feeling breezes, carrying the creosote odor of the railroad track behind the building. In the café, there wasn't much of a crowd at that hour, midmorning. Gregory asked for a table in the small back room. Malcolm was glad of it. People watched them make their way through.

"How have you been?" his brother wanted to know.

"Today, not so good. Woke up with a headache."

"You look tired."

Their server was a dark brown, broadly built young woman with heavy round elbows and thick dreads held by a black-dotted red bandanna. Malcolm Ruark smiled warmly at her, recognizing her from other visits to the place; she didn't make eye contact. Gregory evidently noticed. After they'd ordered their coffee, he said, "I guess you're still getting that kind of stuff?"

Malcolm shrugged. They waited quietly. The woman brought the coffee on a tray and set it down. "Y'all wanna order breakfast?"

"No, thanks," Malcolm said. Then, smiling: "I used to work right up the street."

She nodded slightly. "That so?"

"Used to come in here almost every day. WMC-TV. Come on, you remember me."

"You believe in God?" she said.

"Do *you*?" Gregory put in.

"Sure." She was already moving off, nodding, with a sardonic smile. "If you need anything, jus' lemme know, gentlemen."

"She used to chatter at me," Malcolm said, low, watching his brother stir his coffee.

"Maybe she wants to draw you into salvation as she conceives of it. Maybe she's acting out of kindness—"

"Feels like judgment."

"Only thing to do is pick yourself up? I seem to recall you doing that several times."

He had a sudden urge to mention seven years of silence, no calls or cards. Except that he himself had been silent, too. "Yes," he managed. "Picked myself up. Knocked down three times. In seventeen fights. Got up each time."

Gregory looked at him. "I was talking about you and the old man. Not the boxing."

"Oh, yeah. He knocked me down more than a few times, like I imagine he did you."

"Once or twice," Gregory said, grinning. "When Mother wasn't around."

"Same here. I think I learned to fight because I was afraid of him."

"He was pretty much of a bastard."

Malcolm said nothing.

"I should be more in touch," Gregory said. "I've wanted to do better. Really, since the old man. I know, it's a long time. I thought about it back then, you know. And I—oh, hell, I don't have the girl's name. Your sister-in-law's Pearl. What was Hannah's phrase? *Pretty little Pearl, vicious as a squirrel.*"

"Oh, yes," Malcolm said. "Vicious *little* squirrel. That's *one* of her riffs on Pearl. They're in friendly touch now, according to Pearl."

"I remember Pearl at the old man's funeral, handing out that card she made. Everything was about her and her"—he made air quotes—"art." He shook his head. "Always about getting next to the old man, for what he might do for her career."

Malcolm said, "She's working the perfume counter at Macy's, now."

"Some people's failures provide at least a little sense of revenge."

He laughed. "That sounds like something I'd say."

"I'm afraid I don't remember the daughter's name—I know she was in the stories—"

"Mona. She's a talented actor."

Gregory nodded. "I've seen the posters at Kroger."

Two young men walked in, amiably but animatedly disagreeing about music. One carried a violin case and set it down against the wall beside his chair. They each wore a Redbirds baseball cap, and in unison they tipped their hats at the brothers sitting across the room. The one with the violin said to Malcolm, "Tell my pal here that Baroque is not boring."

Malcolm looked at the other one and said, "Baroque is not boring."

"You're Malcolm Ruark," that one said.

"Yes."

"Where's your niece?" the boy with the violin asked with a leering smile.

"You guys know *King Lear*?" Gregory asked the violin one.

Each pointed to the other. "He does." They'd spoken in unison, which made them laugh. The boy with the violin said to Malcolm, "Hey. News guy."

"Cool it," his friend said. "Jesus."

"I'm talking to you, news guy. Where's your niece?"

Gregory said, "She's working at the new Globe Theater. Gonna be in *King Lear* opposite William Mundy."

The violin boy was concentrating on Malcolm.

"You guys know *Home Away*?" Gregory asked them.

"That television series," the other boy said.

"That's right."

"Home Away," Malcolm said, not looking at them now. "Netflix."

"I know that one, yeah," the one without the violin said. "Never watched it, though."

The violin one said to Malcolm, "Man, I wanted to know about *how* your niece is doing, not *what* she's doing."

"Should be pretty obvious," said Gregory. "Didn't you hear me tell you? How do you manage to hear that violin, boy?"

"Ha." The violin one kept his eyes on Malcolm. "But weren't you dating her or something?"

"How much did you spend for that violin?" Malcolm asked.

"Not a penny. It was a gift."

"I'll bet you'd like to keep it nice, then."

"Are you threatening my violin?"

"How would you like to wear it around your neck."

"Ha."

The other one said, low, "Man—cool it. Come on. Be nice."

"Shit. I'm nice. I'm religious. Hey. Newsman. Are you religious?"

"Saintly," Malcolm said.

"Hey, old son," Gregory said to the violin one. "Are you tough? You wanna stay pretty?"

Malcolm kept looking down at his folded hands on the table.

"My brother here was a professional fighter before he was a newsman. You wanna go a round or two? Though it wouldn't get to two."

After a tense few seconds, the other one said, "He thinks Baroque is fascinating."

"Well." Malcolm looked at him. "It is."

Gregory said, "Okay, guys. That's all. Let's part as friends. Enjoy your lunch."

The two young men sat there quietly, looking at the menus, and then in surprisingly polite tones, almost chastened sounding, went on with their discussion.

Presently, Malcolm, calming down, said, "So, to what do I owe this visit? Beyond the fact that I owe you for everything lately?"

Gregory shook his head slowly, smiling, still stirring the coffee. "Anyway. My ex-wife—Salina—you know the story."

"My mother told me some things."

"Adele talked about Salina to you?"

"She told me what happened. And something about you still having Salina's picture on your mantel, back when Dad—"

Gregory took a second to acknowledge this with a look. "Yeah—I kept it. Still have it there. Anyway, she and her life partner want me to handle their money."

The heavy dark waitress walked up to the next table and spoke low to the two young men, taking one's hat and putting it on. They were all friends, all being young and uncomplicated and carefree together.

Gregory folded his fingers lightly around his cup, as if to warm them. "It's strange, really, her being back in town. I was devastated when she walked out, you know. And I shouldn't've been, really. I was in the hospital with complications after an appendicitis operation. I felt deserted. But we were a mismatch from the start. I'd talked myself into thinking I loved her. Anyway, their chief financial consultant disappeared down in Tampa, in a small plane accident somewhere over the Gulf, so they've decided they want me to handle their accounts, since I'm connected to the theater anyway and I still live here. I'm a little worried, now, though. I wonder if I'll be up to it. They've got enough money to buy the whole state of Tennessee."

Malcolm saw the lines around his brother's eyes, the network of wrinkles at his mouth. This person who had seemed to be going on in his distance through the years. At the next table, the two boys were leaving.

"Sorry about those two bozos," Gregory said when they were gone.

Malcolm smiled. "That little violin bastard got to me, I'll admit it. I haven't lifted a finger to fight anybody, not even drunk, in a very long time. Ages."

His brother sipped his coffee.

"Why keep the picture?"

"It just seemed easier. And then it was a habit. A persona I kept, for business, I suppose. No, I don't suppose. For business, period."

"Persona."

Gregory leaned toward him, across the table. "Heterosexual, abandoned husband."

Malcolm was quiet for a moment.

"Actually, in this, our forward-thinking home state," his brother said, "a person like me could have been arrested just for being me right up to my fifty-second birthday. And I had a business to run."

They were quiet for another space. A woman walked in, put her hat and a light sweater on the next table, and then turned and went out again.

"How're things at the theater?" Gregory asked, plainly desiring a change of subject.

"Oh, delays, repairs, wiring. It's gonna take us right up to the day."

They'd finished their coffee.

Malcolm told him about Eleanor Cruikshank and her cottage. "A dolichocephalic lady straight out of Gahan Wilson, and I liked her."

"Dolicho—what?"

"Cephalic. Dolichocephalic. Longheaded."

"Why didn't you just say *longheaded*?" Gregory asked. Then: "Anyway, I've actually read a couple of her books. She's a little too acerbic for me. P. G. Wodehouse without any gentleness. In fact, I think she's rather profoundly trivial." This was the authoritative, self-possessed version of his brother that the younger man had grown up watching. It dawned on Malcolm that he had used the esoteric word in a half-conscious bid to impress him.

"You've actually read her," he got out.

"Couple of them," said his brother. "A while ago. She grew up here, you know."

"Right. Well, I've got them. I'm enjoying them."

They moved slowly through the now-crowded space to the cashier's counter. Gregory insisted on paying. Dropping Malcolm off at the apartment, he said, "You really okay?"

"I think I'll make it," said Malcolm, though he was suddenly filled with doubt.

At the theater, he saw the words THE GLOBE in the new façade, framed in scaffolding. Men were sitting around eating sandwiches and drinking from thermoses. They were working on Saturday to make up for time. It was just past noon. He parked the car in the lot and went in.

Several people were in the offices—or lights were spilling into the halls from them—he heard no voices. Apparently, everyone had adjourned for lunch. He entered the auditorium space, walked halfway down into the orchestra section, and took a seat. It was quiet. He sat with his elbows on the seat arms and gazed at the arc of the wide stage and the fly loft, the wide high space. During his years in television, in the occasional features with local and visiting people in entertainment, there were a few segments with actors and others involved in theater, here and in Chicago. He thought of that, now. What surrounded him here seemed for a moment to be the sign and representation of the whole intellectual edifice, Dramatic Arts: the history and grandeur of civilization's playacting expression about itself.

In a Chicago segment for WMC once, he interviewed Peter O'Toole, who spoke about the long, riotous, vibrant procession of people pretending to be other people, all in service to the idea of giving forth the fullest experience of far-flung lives. And by extension, through the mysterious alchemy of the thing, to produce in the audience a heightened sense of each one's own life, no matter how petty that life may have seemed before being in the theater looking at serious play-pretend. "Play-pretend," said the great actor, "that celebrates and portrays the majesty of human suffering, and raises it to the level of the sublime. You leave a tragedy like *King Lear* or *Hamlet* with a sense of being inexplicably *accompanied*—somehow, at least for the moment, no longer alone; the possibility even exists for some sense of belonging. All beautifully present only in the perpetually tossing cauldron that is art. Glorious." He sipped an Irish coffee supplied by Malcolm, and seemed endued with the light of belief; he was a man professing utter faith in the work of his life—the struggle to put on memorable plays, no matter the subject or theme. "I always wanted to be among the best actors in the world," he said. "Remember Polonius's words in *Hamlet:* '. . . either for tragedy, comedy, history, pastoral, pastoral-comical . . . tragical-comical-historical-pastoral . . . or poem unlimited; Seneca cannot be too heavy, nor Plautus too light . . .' and so on. You get the idea." He smiled, and drank.

"Yes," Malcolm Ruark said, having laughed progressively harder as O'Toole had gone on.

Because the actor was gregarious and already a little tipsy, they did their thirty minutes on-camera and then spent three hours in an Irish pub on State Street. They formed what felt like a profound friendship; they exchanged cards, talking enthusiastically about meeting up sometime in Ireland and getting together in Nashville, where O'Toole was scheduled to play Henry V at the Ryman. Hannah could meet O'Toole, and the latter promised Malcolm that he would certainly make a pass at her; and then, asking for his forgiveness in advance for the promised trespass, he insisted on springing for a last glass of Irish.

Saying so long that night, they embraced firmly, slapping each other's back. And after helping his new friend slump into the back seat of the escort limo, Malcolm, trying to close the door, accidentally caught the poor man's foot. O'Toole put his hands to his face, clearly in pain. "Ow," he said. "Ouch." He reached down to lift his leg, gingerly. "Listen, old chap. I seem to recall giving you my card."

"Yes, sir. You did, indeed."

"Well, actually, I think now, given this quite recent *new* circumstance of your unprovoked attack on my person, namely my poor metatarsals, my dear fellow, if you don't mind, I'd rather much like to ask for it back."

They laughed, and the laugh hit all the registers of the evening's hilarity. Malcolm leaned in and embraced him, still howling with it. They had come to a place of total human accord and affection. They waved to each other as O'Toole was driven off.

Three months later, O'Toole was in Nashville, for his scheduled performance at the Ryman; and that same day Malcolm was in the city to interview a group of session musicians living there. He spent the afternoon and evening, but did not go to the Ryman. Later, he read that the actor had begged off interaction with the press because he was suffering an attack of bronchitis, but that he performed bravely in spite of his weakness and fever, and, the next day, flew to Amsterdam. And that was that. Even possessing the excuse to write him (inquiring about his injured foot? his bronchitis?), Malcolm had never written; nor had O'Toole.

He thought about that now, and about how Hannah had laughed when he told the story at gatherings. But there could be no good in entertaining such thoughts. He remembered the line from Lear. *That way madness lies. Let me shun that. No more of that.*

He almost spoke the words aloud, and now, as if summoned by his sober ruminations, Claudette Bradley walked out of the wings and stood in the scarcely lit space where a spotlight, if it were on, would shine on her. Center stage. The place where the ghost light would be in the empty theater when the theater was finished. She seemed deep in thought, even troubled, and perhaps she was remembering something gone, as he had just been doing. Slender as she was, she made an imposing presence, even in that wide space; it was as though she were encased in the iridescent vessel of his admiration for her talent. Yet when he was introduced to her the afternoon of Frye's arrival, and spoke about how, one chilly fall evening at Shelby Farms Park five years earlier he had very much admired her performance in the Scottish play, she had reacted with a kind of smirking self-depredation that seemed rather too polished. "Oh, that one," she said. "That was a disaster. It never got above forty degrees those nights."

"I know," Malcolm had responded. "My wife and I were sipping brandy in the front row to keep warm and we thought you were amazing."

"Ah, but you were both drinking," she said, and her facial expression immediately betrayed her embarrassment. She gave a self-conscious smile. For that bad moment, his recent failures were between them like a wall.

He said, "Well, to keep warm, you know."

"I'm sorry. I hope I haven't offended you." Her aversion concerning what she thought she knew about him showed forth even in the apology.

And then there had been the awkward passes at doing the dual table readings alone. He hadn't been able, quite, to forget who she was, or how it had gone when they'd been introduced.

Now, seeing her at center stage, a part of him entertained the notion that she must be too self-absorbed to reflect. A type. The Diva, staring into an inner mirror of self-regard, webbed tightly by an exacting and far-more-powerful urge to perfection.

The idea discouraged him because it was unfriendly, reductive, and depressing. He thought suddenly of Mona. "Jesus Christ, stop it," he murmured under his breath, then cleared his throat. The sound of his throat clearing startled her.

"Oh, sorry," he said.

"Did you say something?"

"Just talking to myself. Didn't mean to scare you."

Their voices echoed in the hollow reaches of the space.

"It's all right," she said. "Actually, I've been wanting to talk to you."

He walked to the stairs leading up from the orchestra seats and stepped over the stack of planks at the top. She moved to meet him.

"You did a piece not too long ago, when you were—before—" She stopped.

"It's all right," he said. "Really. You can talk about it all you want. You can *think* about it all you want. God knows, *I* have."

After a slight hesitation, she said, "I really didn't mean anything."

"It's fine."

Her smile, again, was self-conscious. She brushed back her dark hair. "Thank you."

He waited.

"Well, if you don't mind. It was a segment about Memphis Commons Senior Living. My family checked my father in there. And recently I—well, I just walked out with him. And I was wondering if you know someone, or if they have any authority—I'm sorry—my stepmother's talking about family services and lawyers and courts."

"I think it's up to the people responsible for him."

She pondered this. Then: "That might be a problem." Her eyes welled up. She ran the heel of a palm lightly over one and then the other, sniffled, and took a breath. "Sorry."

His heart went out to her. He tried a soothing tone. "You want to keep your father with you."

"We've hired a nurse. I just don't know if—if they can do anything to us, or her, for the fact that I took him out of there."

"I think that must be between your stepmother and you. Or, really, him and you. I wish I knew more."

"She's—they're pretty mad at me. But he wants to be with me." Her smile was mirthless, and anxious, too. "Well, I just wondered if you remembered anything I might be able to use about the place."

"It just seemed a little lonely."

"Yes. That's it. That's what I thought. And felt."

"Then you must've done the right thing."

She left a pause. He saw the olive tint of her perfect skin, the green eyes, lustrous, as if made of gemstones. There was something almost unreal about her, as if she had walked out from his own mind. When she touched the side of her face, her hand trembled.

"I think it's brave and good, what you're doing," he said.

"You're a nice person," she said. "I don't believe the stories."

His heart sank. "Are there many? How many have you heard? Tell me about the stories."

"Oh," she said. "Just—talk. The buzz after the news reports. People guessing things, you know."

"What was the buzz. You must know some details."

"I don't know any, really—look, people do talk."

"Price of being known." He heard, to his distress, the self-congratulation in the phrase. "I didn't mean that the way it sounded."

She seemed to smirk, shaking her head.

He wanted to end the conversation and walk away. She could believe whatever anyone else believed, or everyone else. He wanted a drink. He thought of the boy with the violin at Brother Juniper's. Everybody could go to hell.

He said, "I only meant that people know more about your personal life than you know about theirs."

"Yes. I've felt that."

"It seems unfair sometimes. I know that's a spoiled way to look at good fortune."

She nodded.

"Shall we go?" he said.

They made their way out into the hot street with its breeze from the river. The street was filling up with people headed for AutoZone Park and the Redbirds' afternoon game.

She walked to her car at the curb. Then she turned. "Need a lift anywhere?"

"I've got my own," he said.

Monday, June 22

(FORTY-THREE DAYS TO OPENING NIGHT)

Thaddeus

Late morning, before the all-call, Thaddeus was heading out to walk down to the Madison for some coffee. As he went along the hall, past Gina's office, he thought of knocking to ask if she wanted anything, but decided against it. He crossed the lobby. Several people were standing outside the just-finished conference room where the meeting would take place. Frye was standing at the entrance of the auditorium with a young woman Thaddeus recognized, though he could not place her.

"Thaddeus Deerforth, meet Mona Greer."

Thaddeus shook hands. She had a strong grip. She smiled. "Pleasure," she said.

"This is our Cordelia," Frye said.

"Congratulations," said Thaddeus. "I've seen you somewhere before."

"Been to Kroger lately?" Frye gave a sly smile.

"Oh, yes," Thaddeus said, not really understanding. Then: "I'm just going down to get some coffee at the hotel."

"Nothing for us," Frye said.

Thaddeus went out on the sidewalk; in the thin fog, he paused and called Gina's number.

"What," she said.

"Ah, I do love your sunny disposition in the morning."

"Where are you?"

"I'm walking down to the Madison. Where I bet I'll want to keep going for coffee even after the café's finished at the Globe. Would you like a cup?"

"I have one I brought from the house."

"I just met our Cordelia. What does Kroger have to do with her."

"I don't know what you're talking about. I met her too, not a half hour ago."

"Frye introduced you."

"That's right. Reuben introduced me. She strikes me as a firecracker."

"You and Reuben," he said. "Huh."

"You can cut it out, now, Thaddeus."

"Call me Wolfie," he said. "See you at the meeting."

The new, larger conference room was at the other end of the long hall past the auditorium, in the freshly built wing. All but one of the main players, the supporting ensemble, and the tech staff were already in the room when he got there. Several tables were arranged in a wide U at the center of the room. William Mundy and two cast members were leaning against a stack of plasterboard near the window. One of the two was the company veteran Don Seligman, who would play Gloucester. The other was a recent Memphis drama student, Ernest Abernathy, slated to play Oswald. He had performed Othello at the college a year ago, and left school to join the company; he looked very much like a young Richard Pryor, with the same slight build and the same facial structure and mannerisms. He was very talented. Seligman was holding an unlit pipe, talking low and earnestly to Mundy about something. His features had a pinched quality, the flat brow seeming to weigh down the deep-set eyes. You never looked at him without thinking of headaches. Peggy Torres—or Regan—was sitting on one of the tables, swinging her polished-looking tan legs. Standing near her was Malcolm Ruark—assigned to play Albany. He looked weary around the eyes. And Thaddeus, glancing at him, thought of the older man's general melancholic air as if it reflected something in his own mood. Two other young cast members, George Poole and Henry Yates, who would play Edmund and Cornwall respectively, were seated on opposite sides of the U. Two years ago, they had played Lucky and Estragon in the black box theater version of *Waiting for Godot*—a weeklong run launched almost entirely by students from the university.

Thaddeus remembered how, that week, he and Gina had gone south to swim and picnic at Lake Sardis, in Mississippi. They found the place empty—abandoned looking, really. They swam together in the chilly water, then set out a little picnic. Cheese and fig croquettes with walnuts and a bottle of bright cold Viognier. They had been wholly, uncomplicatedly happy. Thinking about this now, he felt low and blue.

Mickey Castleton, or Lear's Fool, was standing just inside the door, hands in his pockets, as if he'd wandered in by mistake and decided to stay. If you saw him from behind, you would say he was a twelve-year-old boy. He'd been with the company for eight years, and was customarily so consistently sarcastic that some people, at least in the beginning, missed his essential benevolence, not to mention his depth. Glancing at Thaddeus, he grinned. "Ready for a big surprise?" You couldn't tell from his tone whether he felt the occasion deserved celebration or scorn, though he seemed aware of whatever the surprise was, if there was indeed a surprise.

Arthur Grausbeck and his wife had pulled chairs back and were seated side by side, waiting quietly. Lurlene and the stage manager, Mary Cho, sat with notebooks on their laps, against the near wall under the windows. Gina was seated on the floor next to them with her own notebook on her knees. Others began taking their places around the U—more regulars, Michael Frost, who would play Edgar; Gaylen McCarthy, who would play Kent. Much of this had been set during the past two weeks. There were several others, interns from the university, young men Thaddeus didn't know very well, who were assigned to fill lesser roles. They were all side by side at the bend in the U. Thaddeus took the chair at the near end of the U. He saw Claudette enter and step to one side of the door, looking over her shoulder. Reuben Frye followed, with the young woman who seemed now rather brazen in an unconscious way; something in her expression partook of the sort of stance people assume when they know something about you that you do not want known. Gazing at her face, he suddenly understood Frye's comment about Kroger, though there was nothing of the lightsome smile of the young face on the posters.

Frye called the meeting to order. "Well," he said, standing with the girl in the open end of the U, "I'm sure some of you may have figured this out, but I want you all to understand, I had the idea the minute I took this, uh, gig."

"My sister's hearing impaired," Castleton/the Fool broke in. "And I told him about it."

"Well," Frye said, "be that as it may, I did indeed think about it from the first." He turned and indicated the girl. "This is Ms. Mona Greer. Mona's taking a gap year before entering college, studying drama, of course. But she's had long experience acting, and she's a pro. Also, I should add, she's related, by marriage, to our new company member, Mr. Ruark, our Albany."

In the ensuing silence, everyone regarded her. Certainly some in the room, perhaps most, knew the history. There was a sound of someone stifling a titter. Thaddeus saw the muscles of Malcolm Ruark's jaw clench. Malcolm was directly across from him.

Reuben Frye put his hand on Mona's thin shoulder. "Anyway, this lovely young woman is our Cordelia. And ladies and gentlemen, we are going to play Cordelia, the real crux of the play, as deaf—" He had said the word, and he paused, looking around at everyone with an expression of sly, privileged knowledge about each of them. "And," he went on, dramatically. "Mute."

Silence. People looked back and forth at one another, and then they fixed again on the girl and Frye.

He continued: "She'll sign all her lines, and the Fool will say them. The others will speak to her, and the Fool will sign what they say."

There was a low stir.

He raised his voice above the comments and increasing exclamations in the room. "I plan—I plan . . ." He paused, waiting for quiet. "I plan for this production to symbolize the suffering of women, and their *fate* all over the world, as it's been since time immemorial, in the inevitable and perpetual scheme of things—that is, to be, effectively, mute. *My* Cordelia will be trapped in this fate, while having to depend on a fool to express herself."

It seemed everyone looked at Mickey Castleton/the Fool, then at Thaddeus, then over at Gina. It occurred to Thaddeus that, knowing how hard he and Gina had pushed to get the board to decide on the great play, everyone was expecting some reaction from one or the other. He remained still. Gina only glanced his way, and then wrote something in her notebook.

"Remember," Frye went on, "Cordelia's the youngest daughter. And according to the play's own—shall we say—psychological *ground*, it's Cordelia who forms the crux of everything. Because it's all—isn't it—triggered by her in that first scene. 'I love you according to my bond,' she tells the old man. And he says, 'So young and so untender?' And what does she say? 'So young, my Lord, and true.' And the old king fails to understand her. She tells the straight truth in that first scene, and she's misunderstood. And banished. And in the destruction that follows, she loses her life. She's going to be seen, in my—in our, this—production, as the real victim of this tragedy. Lear gets what he bloody well deserves."

After a long, staring silence, Ernest Abernathy/Oswald said, "Cordelia can't make a fucking sound?"

This occasioned a wave of nervous laughter.

"She'll sign her lines," Frye said. "Just as I've indicated. And the Fool will say them. And he'll sign the lines to her that come from the others. I've been working very hard on the Fool's part, because of course he'll have his own lines, and Cordelia's."

Again, everyone looked at Castleton/the Fool.

"And so, now at last, we have our full complement of players," Frye said. "And we can really begin."

There was a smattering of discordant applause.

"You can't do this." Michael Frost/Edgar looked around seeking support from the others. "Can he?"

Someone else muttered, "Director's vision," as if to explain.

Frye nodded, as though the comment were addressed to him. "We're going to practice remaining in character while there's silence, because there'll be silence at least as she starts to sign. It'll be a bit different."

Castleton/the Fool said, "I'll be the one saying her lines. She'll sign them, and as she signs them, I'll say them, the play's lines. She'll be using ASL to sign the thing. And of course William'll say Lear's lines, as written, and I'll be signing them back to Ms. Greer in the ASL. Same goes for Goneril and Regan. Say the speeches as they are, folks, and I'll just be signing them in ASL to Cordelia, and then she'll sign her lines while

I say them from the text. Like that. And we'll all play it as if Cordelia's deafness is familiar. As if the Fool's always spoken for her that way. Otherwise, she'll express her feelings with her face and her body language." He looked at Frye and paused. Then: "Right?"

"Right. Yes."

"Do we have people who can do ASL to be understudy for the two roles?" Michael Frost/Edgar asked.

"It's taught in the schools here," Gaylen McCarthy/Kent said. "We've got people."

"So." Peggy Torres/Regan looked at Castleton/the Fool. "You'll have the two parts."

"That's right."

"Crikey," William Mundy said.

Michael Frost/Edgar said, "So now the Fool has to be at Dover with Kent and Cordelia, and also in the scene where she and her father are taken away to prison, near the end. I really don't see how you can do all that without falsifying the whole thing."

"Well, but I've always wondered what happened with the Fool, haven't you all?" Frye looked up and down the table. "Lear says, 'My poor fool is hanged.' But we don't have a thing about how it came about. Or really even why."

"Sure we do," Mundy said. "Sure we do. Look at all that shite the Fool says to Goneril."

"You're going to write it *in*, though?" Peggy Torres/Regan said. "The Fool at Dover? You?"

No one said anything.

"Damn."

"Take it easy, sister," Abernathy/Oswald said, laughing.

"You'll be falsifying it," said Frost/Edgar. "Like Nahum Tate."

Frye's tone was faintly parental. "No. Nothing of the essential plot will change. And the lines won't change. It's just a matter of getting the Fool in without calling too much attention to it."

Michael Frost/Edgar spoke to Mona, "You know about Nahum Tate?"

She didn't hesitate. "Of course I do. I've read that version. And I know the source play. And I'm proficient at ASL. I've been teaching it."

There was a pause. Everyone was clearly impressed.

"Well, the change makes him too obviously a device," Frost/Edgar said.

"He's a device, in any case," Mundy said. "He's not even *in* some productions."

"But he says some pretty important things," Abernathy/Oswald said. "Like, 'Thou shouldst not have been old til thou hadst been wise.'"

"'I would not be mad,'" Thaddeus heard himself begin the quote. Everyone looked at him. "'Not mad,'" he went on. "'Sweet heaven, keep me in temper. I would not be mad.'"

"Imagine it," Abernathy/Oswald said. "Praying to keep sane. Good thing we don't have to sign that line."

"All the lines will be said aloud," Frye said.

"This is absurd," Michael Frost/Edgar muttered. "We're supposed to be doing Shakespeare."

Jocelyn Grausbeck spoke up: "There's an entire section of the Folger Shakespeare Library dedicated to Shakespeare in American Sign Language."

"I know about the Folger," Michael Frost/Edgar said. "But this is *one character.*"

"I think it's a wonderful new wrinkle," Arthur Grausbeck put in. "And we're hiring a person to stand house right to sign the whole thing. We'll advertise it as a performance for all. Bub-bub—hearing impaired–friendly, you might say. Inclusive."

"Tickets *starting* at seventy-five freak'n dollars," Abernathy/Oswald said, with a nervous grin. "Uh, excuse me, but we're not exactly inclusive at *those* prices. And come to think of it, here we are. Everything brand new. How come there's no place for groundlings? I think that'd be cool. Why not do the Globe as it really was."

"The Globe as it really was burned to the ground," William Mundy said. "In the middle of a performance of *Henry VIII.*"

"Okay," Frye said, putting his hands together, "we've all got a lot of work to do so let's—"

"Actually," said Castleton/the Fool, "a version of deaf Cordelia *has* been done, you know."

"Yes," Frye said. "But with much more elaborate sets, with nothing of the fluidity we're going to have." He looked at Ms. Grausbeck. "You won't be sorry."

"I think it'll be *marv*elous." She nodded proudly at him.

"But everything else will end up being subordinate to the deafness," Frost/Edgar said, low. He wasn't looking at anyone; he kept making a small circle on the surface of the table with the index finger of his right hand.

"Well, we'll just have to contend with that," Frye said.

Later, several members of the company strolled down the block to the Madison Hotel, and the bar off the lobby there. Thaddeus decided to go along with them because Gina was going. Perhaps he would get drunk. Mundy and Seligman/Gloucester headed somewhere with Abernathy/Oswald in a limo. "Well, they're thick," Mickey Castleton/the Fool said. "Where're they headed?"

"Do you know the blues bar Wild Bill's?" Peggy Torres/Regan asked him.

"Never heard of it."

"Wonderful place," Lurlene said. "Great band. In a neighborhood, actually."

"They rock the world," Peggy Torres/Regan said. "Every night but Sunday it's packed tight. A place narrow as a hallway. You gotta edge past the band to get in, and the band is the bee's knees. You're shoulder to shoulder with the bass player, when you step in the front door, and start looking for a place at one of the long tables. And you feel like you're *in* the band."

"I've been there," said Claudette, "and I like it as much as any of the places over on Beale Street."

"Ernest's taking them there. I heard 'em talking about it."

"Mundy could get beat up in a bar," Mickey Castleton/the Fool said.

Lurlene said, "Not this bar. This is a very friendly place."

"You coming with us to the rooftop?" Mickey Castleton asked Lurlene.

"I'm going home to watch *Downton Abbey* with my girls. We might turn the sound off and see if we can read lips."

"We got that many hard-of-hearing folks, you think?" Peggy Torres/Regan wanted to know.

"It's not really about the hearing impaired," Gina said. "It's more of a statement. And maybe an important one."

"And what's the statement again?"

No one answered. As they reached the hotel, a wedding party came streaming out, people getting into cabs or walking down toward Main Street. Daylight was failing under gathering storm clouds. Late afternoon looked like dusk. The theater people stood under the marquee for a few minutes, watching the sky roil on the other side of the river. Thaddeus, Gina, and Mickey Castleton went in and took the elevator to the rooftop terrace. There was a little bar on one side with stools and two rows of umbrella tables arranged along the wire-topped wall overlooking the city. The tables on the left side faced the river. They sat together at one of the tables, in a kind of unexpressed lethargy. Mickey ordered a bottle of Cabernet and three glasses. Their server was new. A tall, elegant young man who did not look old enough to serve alcohol. He brought the bottle and glasses on a little tray. Opening the bottle was clumsy and took a while. Mickey had stepped to the wall to look over at the street, so the server poured the taste for Thaddeus, who held the glass to his nose and could smell nothing. "Good," he said. The young man poured.

Mickey, sitting down again, put his hands to the sides of his face, as if to peer through something, as they watched the young man go to the elevators and get on.

Thaddeus said, "Looks too young for the job," and had a momentary, disagreeable sense of faking things, trying to be his usual self. Against this feeling, he drank down half his wine in a gulp. He determined, without quite expressing it to himself, that he would have enough to get calm, sitting there watching his wife explain to Mickey, charmingly and with wit, Louisa's recent battiness concerning arrangements about house-sitting nearby; the old woman had decided not to do it. "Not exactly," Gina said. "She's going to stay in her own old house. Our house, and visit the one across the street where she was going to house-sit." Thaddeus felt a pull to go home and see Louisa, who had lived so well through all her emergencies.

Mickey seemed only vaguely attentive, holding his wineglass under his nose and breathing, putting on a show.

Thaddeus thought again of fakery.

"It's the house wine, Mickey," Gina said. "I'm trying to tell you about my mother."

Having set his own glass down, Thaddeus watched the storm clouds gather. He checked his pulse while they talked. It was habit now. He consciously called to mind Dr. Shenk's voice: "Your blood pressure's stone-cold normal and even the couple of places where things rush a little are innocent." Nothing of what Gina and Mickey were saying got through. He was seeking to slow his breathing. *Ridiculous.* He swallowed more wine. This was simply an anxiety attack. He emptied the glass, and poured more. Gina would need him, with her mother and the new right-wing boyfriend and all the rest. Then he gazed out at the gathering dark roil of cloud. It seemed the whole sky was staggering toward them out of Arkansas, laced with lightning. A thick curtain of rain swept to the far edge of the river, and then seemed to pause there. They were all three quiet now, as if waiting for some prearranged event. They watched the rain.

Suddenly, Gina spoke. "I have depression." Her hands were folded on the table. It was as though she'd offered this as a subject for conversation.

"What're you depressed about?" Mickey wanted to know.

Thaddeus said, quickly, "You've left the subject, Mickey."

"What?"

"Somebody says 'I'm depressed,' and the question immediately comes: 'What're you depressed *about*?' You don't need a reason. There's no reason to it. It's the thing itself."

Mickey Castleton simply stared, holding his glass of wine under his nose. Then he cleared his throat and put both elbows on the table. "What?"

Gina kept her head down. "Nothing. Let's talk about something else. I shouldn't've said anything."

"You say you have depression," Mickey said. Then, looking at Thaddeus: "And when I ask about it, you tell me I've left the subject. Are you guys speaking in metaphors?"

Thaddeus looked at Gina, then looked away. "Forget it, Mickey."

"Well, what the hell. Are you having a fight?"

"I just said there's no *aboutness* about depression. It's depression. Right, Gina? You're not depressed, you have depression."

She didn't answer. She was looking out at the gathering sky over the river.

To Mickey, Thaddeus said, "RJ, her father, called it her darks."

"Please, can we stop talking about it?"

"I thought there was no 'about' here," Mickey said. "Jesus Christ."

For an interval, they all three looked at the towering thunderheads approaching.

Thaddeus drank down his wine and poured more, and had some of that. It gave no pleasure, now. But he was beginning to feel its cheering effects. He felt like needling his wife. But aimed his remark at Mickey. "What about this aboutness disturbs you?"

There was another silence.

"How about Mona Greer?" Mickey said, obviously reaching for a change of subject. "Pretty impressive."

"I hate her," Gina said. "I've always hated precocity."

He laughed. "Yeah, right?"

"I'm glad she has to be muted."

He laughed again.

Gaylen McCarthy came out from the elevators with his own glass of wine and took a chair. He was square faced, with a cinnamon beard trimmed so precisely it looked fake. He had been with the company for twelve years without ever playing a lead, and he didn't mind that. Almost sixty years old, he lived with a woman few people in the company had ever seen because she disliked theater, and theater people, too (especially theater people). But she liked McCarthy. She managed the money in his household, and allowed him the one extravagance, life as an actor. He required time to hang with the other members of the company, drinking wine and trying new recipes. He was dependable and easygoing, and everyone liked him as much as his lady friend did.

He poured a little more wine into the glass he held. "This theater-dark crap eats it."

They watched the laden clouds continue to build up on the Arkansas side of the river.

"Aren't *we* a foursome," Thaddeus said. The wine was swimming behind his eyes.

Mickey leaned toward Gaylen McCarthy. "Our friends, here, seem to be having a spat."

Gaylen patted the back of Gina's hand. "Life's too short, darlings."

"And brutish," Mickey said. "How's that for depressing? You know

Kierkegaard's line? The terrible thing about despair is that it's unaware of itself as despair. Well, it works both ways if you think about it: the sad thing about happiness is that it's often unaware of itself as happiness."

"Christ," Gaylen said. "I can't even know if I'm fucking happy?"

There was a flash of lightning, and a clap of thunder followed close upon it.

"I've got an idea," Gaylen said to Gina. "Why don't you and Thaddeus go on with your spat, but confine yourselves to sign language? It'll be a complicated quiet. A—a gestural storm."

As he said this, a circular motion began at the top of the sky and a thin whitish funnel descended from the lowest fold of cloud; it struck down into the river and whirled in the eddying water and then drew the surface darkly around it, into it, pulling it skyward. It looked like a giant wavering cable going all the way to the turning zenith. Screams and frantic shouts came from the street below. The column of water remained where it was for what seemed an impossibly long time, then collapsed with an unreal battering splash, and the whole mass of cloud and rain just stayed there at the far side of the river. Deerforth waited, aghast, for another tower of water to be sucked up. The wall of the storm itself looked like a mile-wide funnel. At last it broke into separate squalls, moving off, leaving a sky the color of coal ash.

"Never seen a waterspout before," Mickey said in a shaky voice.

"I thought it would come at us." Gaylen said.

"Some part of me always wants to see stuff like that," said Gina. "The terrors of the earth."

"Some of the terrors of the earth are interior," Thaddeus muttered. But he, too, had felt the whole thing as a thrill.

Lightning licked across the sky at the broken line of the horizon, downriver, and then thunder rolled again. Above them, the cloud cover was moving off.

Thaddeus finished the last of the wine and looked around for the server.

Gaylen McCarthy said, "I saw a deaf Cordelia version done in Washington. It was years ago, but it was exactly the way Frye's asking us to do it. It was before I started acting."

"Why didn't you say something when I brought it up?" Mickey asked him.

"Nothing to say. At first the whole thing seemed kind of average, really. The guy who did Lear was good. But he was good for reasons you could see. I mean, I got the idea his fury was more his rage at being stuck in that production than the old king's at his daughters. But the whole thing ended up being an unmitigated *clusterfuck*. The poor guy really didn't have to act *at-tall* in the storm scene, and you wanna know why? It stormed. That very night. And the venue—are you ready?—was a freaking *amphitheater*. No shit. *On cue*, guys. Rain, thunder, and lightning, like the judgment of God himself and all the angels, too. The fucking whole host of heaven. Talk about life imitating art. Thunder loud as volcanic explosions and the guy was some *kind* of *yelling* at it all. I mean *yell-ing*. And the audience, everybody, was trying to duck out of the rain. *Everybody* in that place really *felt* what the mad king felt. And this poor drenched girl, house right, bravely signing through all that uproar. I couldn't believe they'd keep on, but they did."

"Bet the thunder wasn't a distraction for the deaf who were present," Gina said.

"Yeah, but the lightning sure was."

Somewhere out in the night a siren began wailing. It was joined by another, and still another. They had finished their wine and were waiting for the waiter to come back out.

"Anyway," Gaylen added. "Remember. It's not even really the little bastard's idea."

A heavyset waiter whose forearms were covered with thick black hair came out, carrying a big tray of cheeses, a bottle of Barolo, a small pot of coffee, and cups stacked neatly one upon another. Someone down in the bar had ordered all this for them. He set it on the table. "Compliments of the new Globe Theater." His voice was very deep and rich.

"Do you sing?" Mickey asked him, but he'd already moved off, and didn't hear.

"Which member of the board do you think ordered this for us?" Gaylen asked.

"No board member," Gina said. "Claudette. I'd bet money."

"I thought she went home," said Mickey.

"Let's get to the bottom of it," Gaylen said. "Come on."

He and Mickey went on downstairs; it looked like a pretext, so the married couple could continue in private with their spat.

Frye had taken to spending time in Gina's space, supposedly supervising the development of set designs, drawings he asked her to do from photos he'd pulled down off the net, of other productions, including one of his own from Holliwell, for *Julius Caesar.* Twice he called in lunch for them and worked with her on designs for all three productions, sitting close at her drafting table. Deerforth saw them like that.

The evening before the all-call, Louisa and the Reverend Rightwing went out to walk Marcel, and they were going to spend an hour at the house across the street, watering the plants and dusting the furniture. Thaddeus and Gina were sitting across from each other in the living room, sharing a bottle of Chardonnay. It was supposed to be a little time alone for the two of them.

"I think I'd like to have Reuben over for dinner," she said. "So you can know him better."

"You go ahead out to dinner," Thaddeus said crisply. "I'd rather he not come here."

"But I've already suggested it. And he's accepted."

"Well, then, unsuggest it and he can unaccept."

"You're being unreasonable."

"All right, I'll be reasonable. You eat here with Frye and I'll eat out anywhere else."

They were both silent for a time, not looking at each other.

Presently, she said, "He's not as bad as you all think he is, you know. He's a person. He's actually trying his best, and his life at home—he's got troubles, like all of us." Her eyes narrowed. "The man's wife has a problem with opioids and booze. Just like Ruark had. He's working to get his wife to join him here."

"You're feeling sorry for this preening, middle-class bully."

"You can be *such* a fucking snob," she said.

Neither of them finished the wine. She went upstairs to bed, and he sat reading at the window looking out on the street, so he could make his way quickly upstairs when he saw Louisa and Whitcomb returning from the other house with Marcel. He slept on the daybed in his study, after leaving his wife a note: *didn't want to wake you.*

Now, in the moist, rain-smelling breeze of the rooftop patio of the Madison, he touched her wrist, determined to be gentle. "So, how are you feeling?"

She gave him a bland, mildly unconfiding look. "Tired. Sick. Worried. Depleted."

"Me, too. All of the above."

"No. You don't get to claim this."

"Oh," he said, his blood rising. "Forgive me. I don't feel any of those things. I'm peachy."

She said nothing, staring at the wine she was swirling in her glass.

He said, "Because, of course, this is not about *me*. I do know that. I do get that. None of this and nothing *ever* is about me."

After a pause, she said, "I'm sorry. I know you're disappointed."

He waited a moment. Then, attempting a mollifying tone: "We'll have to make do, I guess. At least it's not Lear as a CEO in a business suit."

"I wasn't talking about the fucking show."

"Well, let's do talk about it."

"Let's not. And I don't want to talk about us, either."

"Okay. Your mother. The Reverend Wrong. Marcel."

"None of the above."

"Okay. I know—the fucking *weather.*"

She didn't respond. They were silently watching the squalls in the distance beyond the river. She took the coffeepot and poured some of it into one of the cups.

Thunder boomed and startled them both. The sirens kept on out in the turbulent night.

"How long do you think it'll be this way between us?" he asked suddenly.

Her sigh was pronounced. "Oh, God. How's your heartbeat?"

"Why ask that now?"

"Because I'm your fucking wife." She reached around her own glass, took up one of the glasses of wine on the tray, and sipped from that. Then, pressing her hands down on the table, fingers spread, she frowned at him.

"Does Louisa seem happy?" he asked.

"You're not listening to me. I don't want to talk about it."

"Okay." He took his phone out. "I can ask her myself."

"If you—" She took his wrist. "Please."

He put the phone back. And waited.

"The guy's several yards to the right of Hitler," she said. "And he calls himself a Christian. No—a Crushtian. That's the way he says it. Crushtian."

"Tell me about you and Frye."

Her eyes narrowed. "What." It was a flat, harsh pronunciation of the word, sounding the last letter.

"Well, let's talk about that a little?"

"I will not talk about Reuben."

"It kills me it's first name, now."

She left a pause.

"What's he call you, Schnookums?"

She looked away. "Fuck off. Just fuck off."

"Okay, well, here's my experience," he said. "One peaceful early evening you tell me you're thinking of splitting. Like that. A flat announcement, like a bomb. And I'm just supposed to leave it at that, just go on as if you never said it, or any of the rest of what you said, while you start up a friendship with this—this—"

"He's a person, Thaddeus. A human somebody. And I do like his ideas. And you've made an object out of him."

"Well, not quite. But let's do that. Let's call him—" He paused. Then: "I've got it. Let's call him the Enchanted Stump. There. What do you think."

Again, she said nothing.

He was absolutely certain that he had done nothing wrong.

Several people came out and crossed to the other side, laughing and talking. He thought of the chambers of his own heart. "The thing is, I still love you," he managed, just as she coughed. She hadn't heard him.

He started to repeat it, but Claudette came from the elevator, carrying a half-finished bottle of white wine and three glasses. She set this before Thaddeus, then said, "Oh. That's right. I already sent the red." She pulled a chair over from the next table, and straddled it. She had gone to her apartment to see her father and Willamina, and to change clothes. She wore ragged jeans, now, and a T-shirt with the words I AM NOT

JEJUNE emblazoned across the front. You could see her nipples through the cloth. "So," she said to Thaddeus and his wife. "You can pour whichever one you want. Or there's the coffee."

"I don't want any more," Gina said.

"Are you all right, sweetie?"

"I'm fine."

Claudette filled one of the glasses with the white. "Willamina's staying late. She's making chicken *à la grande*, a New Orleans dish, and they're gonna watch something on TCM. I'm on my own for a while."

The three of them sat there looking at the wine.

"I'll have some of the coffee," Thaddeus said.

"All my adult life, I've had a friend in my father." Claudette smiled, lifted her glass, and sipped the white. "But I was a little afraid, I guess, of him living with me—in this—with what's happening. And, you know, it's been fine. Lovely, in fact."

"I'm numb," Gina said, staring out at the river. "Isn't that remarkable."

"There are things you can do for that, you know." Claudette's tone was faintly caustic.

"I'm sorry," Gina said. She picked up one of the glasses of red and sipped it. "The sets are done, anyway."

"You know what Frye told me today?" Claudette said. "Right before the meeting—which is why I was the last person to come into it? He said I look too sexy to be Goneril or Regan. I'll have to ugly-down. He actually used the phrase. *Ugly-down*. He'd obviously been talking to his chum. And I swear, even so, I thought *he* was about to hit on me. Anyway, first full table reading tomorrow morning. That's what I came up here to tell you."

Mickey Castleton sauntered back out, looking happy, carrying a snifter of cognac. "Hey all, apparently, Lurlene's still on the job. She just sent an email with the winner of the play competition for the black box. And I know the work."

Thaddeus, having secured the judges and set up the panel, had left it to Lurlene. He felt a moment's gratitude for her.

Everyone waited for Mickey to go on.

"It's that kid who used to work the box office." He held up his phone.

"This is from the press release. 'The winner is a recent graduate from Memphis College of the Dramatic Arts, Dylan Walters. And the play is called *Dear One*. It's about a TV newsman who's the fifth husband of a woman sex counselor."

"Where's Malcolm Ruark?" Gina asked.

Mickey said, "He walked off with that harpy of a niece. Anyway, he wouldn't be in the bar. As I'm sure you know, he's a teetotaler now."

"Isn't he supposed to, um, stay away from her?"

"Well, they're colleagues now. I don't know how it works. Anyway, downstairs, we've agreed that Cordelia's deafness is glib and obvious as a cowbell about the statement Frye wants to make."

"I'd like to make a statement," Claudette muttered. "In his balls."

Thaddeus laughed. He lifted one of the glasses of white and took a swallow.

"You've already made a statement to Mundy in his balls," Gina said.

Mickey laughed softly. "Yeah." He folded his hands protectively in his lap, smiling with feigned wariness at Claudette.

Claudette shook her head at him. "I wish it was funny." She took a slow sip of her wine, and said something they couldn't quite hear, about her father. Then: "I should do something where I don't have to be near Mundy. Maybe see about a part in the black box play."

"I've read the winning play. I've read all the finalists, in fact. And the winner is a cut above. It's got a good female lead. She spends the whole play on a chaise lounge, though. Woman conducting counseling sessions for the sexually troubled, and her troubles with her five husbands."

"And the whole thing's in pantomime and ASL, right?" Claudette said.

"Five husbands," Gina said.

"Four exes and a current," Mickey told them. "The TV anchor. And all of them have erectile dysfunction."

"You're making that up," Claudette said.

Mickey smiled. "It's not stipulated. There's just a lot of *wink-wink, nudge-nudge* hints and innuendos."

"How do you *wink-wink, nudge-nudge* a thing like that?"

"Oh, easy. The bacon's not crisp, bread dough doesn't rise. A lot of things sagging. It's funny."

"What's funny about impotence?" Claudette asked.

Malcolm

Just outside the theater entrance, Mona had turned and, gesturing for him to accompany her, murmured, "I need to be away from this." So, he followed her to her car on Front Street. He got in, moving the books there to the floor. She got behind the wheel and looked over at him. "I didn't like the way that felt."

"I think Frye likes to make a show out of everything."

"Wanna see where I'm staying now? We could walk if it wasn't gonna rain."

"All right," he heard himself say.

She put the car in gear and looked out, to pull into the street. He saw the perfect shape of her, and then took his gaze away. She had asked him to come with her and he had said all right. There seemed no will in him now, only reaction. No history. He felt a chill, a sinking. He knew he should ask her to turn around. And he also knew he would go on with whatever this was going to be. If he could have a drink, it might make the stillness he craved. And he knew exactly how dangerous that thought was.

He worked to put it away. And to breathe once, fully.

"I should go home," he heard himself say.

They had reached Union, and a half block past the intersection she turned into a wide driveway. There were low-slung, flat-roofed apartments ranged along a fence and a hedge bordering the highway beyond. The rain was starting. She parked in front of the end apartment, and they got out. "Guess what lady *doesn't* know where I live now," she said, reaching into her bag. The doorway was made of dark metal, corrugated like the door to a garage. She led him in. The apartment was larger than he expected. It was badly cluttered and smelled of cats. There was one window giving off onto an alley and the adjacent street. "I have two roommates," she said. "Phil and Marta. They're not here now. And I just moved in, so it's kind of a mess."

"Well. It's nice," he said.

"I've got coffee. And Pellegrino."

"No, thanks. I really should go."

"Sit down." She quickly removed a confusion of clothes from the sofa. "Come on. I wanna talk a little. I'm nervous. I don't like the way they all seemed to think of it as a goof. Me getting the part. Everybody looking at me so funny. They were staring. Like they were thinking about *us*."

"I think they were impressed by you," he managed, sitting on the edge of the sofa.

"What about you? Right now, you look like you're gonna run."

"Well, I should go, Mona."

"Why? It's not like I'm trying to seduce you or anything." She gave forth a tremulous laugh, then scooched to the other end, lifting herself to remove a throw pillow, and tossing it across the room. Her nervousness filled him with heartache. He thought of what her mother had said: *You should hear the way she talks about you*.

"Come on," she urged. "You can tell me. They think I'm just a stunt, don't they?"

"No."

"Well, but they know about us. They know what happened."

"Some, I guess. Sure."

"That doesn't bug you?"

He shrugged. "Nothing I can do about it. We got past it, right?"

She sat back, not looking at him. "I don't have any friends, you know that?"

"Don't be silly."

In fact, her classmates had too often tended to see her precociousness as a form of arrogance. She was moody and kept to herself much of the time. She had read more than most of her teachers, many of whom thought her scornful and vain. People still saw the Kroger ad, and the poster picture of her at the store entrances, the sweet smile that was actually nothing at all like what was behind it, and they were envious. Nobody understood her. Her present roommates had advertised for someone to offset rent; their paintings, figurines, bric-a-brac, and books all suggested religion. "You're going to be wonderful in the play," he told her, looking at a crucifix on the wall over the entrance to the small kitchen. Beneath the crucifix was a bronze plaque with bold black lettering: I ASKED JESUS HOW MUCH HE LOVED ME AND HE SAID "THIS MUCH" AND HE SPREAD OUT HIS ARMS AND DIED.

She saw him looking at it, and said, "I know. Did you ever see anything kitschier?"

They both laughed; it felt wonderful, and it filled him with dread. "God," he managed.

"Not much conversation between me and them, as you can guess," she said.

He was still marveling at the unease he felt. "Well. You'll be surprised how many friends you have and they'll all come see you in the play." This sounded so flatly routine, so insultingly avuncular, that he almost apologized. Thunder beyond the trees waving in the wind outside saved him.

"My mom was talking to Aunt Hannah the other day."

"*You* didn't talk to her?"

"Aunt Hannah hasn't been close since I was four or five. Besides, she hates me. Like she hates you—come on, Malcolm."

He shook his head, but said nothing.

Shifting her weight slightly, she said, "Something happened this afternoon, right after the meeting. I was in the restroom, and when I came out, Mundy was waiting for me—lurking, you know? Suddenly he was John Gielgud with the accent and everything." She pursed her lips, and mimicked: "'Come let us lift you and see how't will be,' holding his bony hands out. I said excuse me and walked around him, and I got a few feet away and he said my name, like we're old friends or something. So, I turned. And he gives me this—this *look*. Fake sad, and says, 'If you have poison for me, I will drink it.'"

"That's from the play," Malcolm told her.

She looked at him. "I *know* the *line*. But he wasn't rehearsing anything. I mean it was just whacked."

"I'm sorry that happened," he said, because he could think of nothing else.

"My friend." She smiled.

The rain swept at the one window, the wind picking up.

"Well, what should we do now?" she said.

"Excuse me?"

"I'm just wondering what we should do now."

He took a breath. Then: "Your mother said some things—your talk about me."

"Oh, I bet she did. I'd love to hear *that*."

"You say you heard Aunt Hannah talking to your mother. But she hasn't talked to you?"

"Oh, she's done with me, Malcolm. I told you, I haven't talked to her or heard from her in a long time. You know what *she* thinks. Or thought. I mean even before everything. They never got along."

Again, he was silent. The quiet went on. They were not three feet apart, looking at each other and then not looking. She played with the cuff of her blouse, and shifted slightly.

"No one's coming until later tonight," she said.

He stood. "Well, I've got to get going. Got a shift at the travel agency."

She gathered her purse, the car keys, then suddenly put them down and, with the air of someone meaning to settle something, went up and, wrapping her arms around his neck, kissed him on the mouth. He froze. She let her mouth linger on his a second longer, then let go and stepped back to gaze at him. Everything of his whole history faltered under the bones of his face. When she seemed about to move toward him again, he took her by the upper arms and held her there, at the slight distance. "Mona," he said. "This isn't—please."

"This isn't what?" she said. "What're you saying? I'm glad you got me the part."

"I've really got to go. I've always had trouble with thank-yous. They make me nervous."

She sat down on the sofa again. "What do you think I am?"

Through the thin rasp of his breathing, he said, "I think you're a gifted actor."

"I'm here for you," she said, with that smile.

He was momentarily without breath. Then: "Ah. I really should go now."

"You don't really have to go anywhere."

Perhaps another half minute went by. He couldn't look at her.

Abruptly, she gathered the purse and the keys, and moved to the door.

He said, "Mona—"

She interrupted him. "Don't say anything else, please."

He moved carefully wide of her, and out into the drizzle that was left of the storm.

In the car, settling behind the wheel, she ran one hand through her wet hair, not looking at him.

"Well," he managed. "It's a nice place. I'm glad for you."

"We're such good friends," she said. "I'm glad I have you. I wouldn't be doing this if it wasn't for you. I only wanted to thank you. I was only hoping to please you and give you what you want. And Pearl can go to hell."

He decided, with a sinking at his abdomen, to go past this. "Has she canceled the order of protection yet?" He could hear the stiffness and formality in his own voice, and added, "I hope so."

"Pearl and I aren't talking much. I'm seeing someone now—well, you know that, and I did tell her *that,* just to bug her. And I think she wants to swear out a protection order on *him*."

He thought there would be more. After waiting a little, he said, "You're seeing the one you've been teaching to sign?"

She nodded. "You don't know him. But you will. He's a young playwright. I've known him for years. I knew him in school."

She started the car. Sirens were sounding in the city, and the rain had begun anew. The shadow of it trailing down the windshield was on her face in the grayness. She turned the wipers on and put the car in gear and then paused to look at him. "I can do this, Malcolm. Even mute."

"I think you can do anything you want." He saw the rainy street through the streaks the wipers made.

"Really—back there at the place—well. Nevermind. I—I don't want to do anything more than talking with anybody for a long time."

He thought of her father. They had come to the red light at Union and Third.

"No sense talking about it," she said.

"You're strong." He felt the glibness of the words, and added, "I'm not just saying that. You can do anything you want. And this—" He stopped. "This—playing Cordelia. You can do it in your sleep." He paused, and she sniffled, coughed. She was so young, a girl still, for all her swagger and her complications. She was shivering, both hands gripping the wheel, watching the storm. He understood with a kind of interior quake that for a very long time he had seen her only in light of unrealized and unexpressed yearning. A thing of beauty; an object of desire. *Thing. Object.* It was as if he must find some way to see her as herself, separate from all that. He almost reached over to touch the back of her hand. The traffic light changed, and she drove through. The storm was moving off, blundering down the river. When she stopped the car at the theater, he turned, and breathed, and held on. "The whole thing's—" He stopped again.

"The whole thing's what?" she said. "Tell me what you mean."

He thought of Gregory and the picture on the mantel, and pretexts, and lifelong deceptions, and he felt woozy, full of grief, ashamed. He had been about to say, *My fault*. Instead, he heard himself say, "Whole thing's something you can easily do. Like I said."

Thaddeus

At dinner after the Madison, Louisa told a couple of stories over the salt-and-pepper-crusted sea bass she had made. Gina was mostly silent. Thaddeus, coffee-sober after all the wine he'd had, only wanted to listen. Louisa had opened a bottle of Capri, which he sipped gratefully, coming to the point of not caring that his heart was stamping in its cage of bone. He considered it that way. A normal battering under his breastbone. He could stop thinking about it. And in any case, Louisa's cigarette voice called him back, talking about RJ. "He was staying at this woman's house in DC," she said. "Some congressman's daughter. This lady who'd tried to have her son at home with a midwife, but it was a breech birth, so they had to rush to the hospital for a C-section. Now—she *said* all this while nursing this kid standing between her legs—something like four years old, this kid. I mean he could walk up and stand there"—Louisa indicated one of her breasts—"and express a preference, you know? 'I'll have this one tonight.'" She laughed, and had to take a sip of the wine to clear the cough that came. "So, while this kid who can speak perfect English sentences is nursing, his mommy keeps squeezing his skull with her fingers. Massaging and squeezing his cranium with her whole hand, fingers pressing on both sides, like it's a softball or a grapefruit. And RJ—well, I wish you could've seen him tell this."

"I remember this one," Gina said flatly. "You're doing a good-enough job."

"Well, RJ wants to ask her what the hell she's doing—whole business, you know, nursing a kid that age. He starts to, but then the squeezing really gets to him, and so he points—" Louisa laughed again, struggling to finish, and glancing in Gina's direction. "So—so he points and *almost* says, 'Are you trying to get blood to come out of his fuck'n eyes?' but instead he just says, 'Excuse me. What're you doing there,' and the lady—as if it's a perfectly reasonable thing—says, 'Well, he was born by C-section and denied a vaginal birth, so he didn't get any time—any time—'" Louisa had covered her face with her hands. "Oh, God. Sorry. 'He didn't—didn't have any time in the birth canal, getting his head squeezed. And I'm trying to provide the experience as much as possible.'"

"Good Lord," the Rightwing Reverend Elias Whitcomb said, laughing.

Louisa was coughing. "Lordy. I can't stop laughing when I try to tell the end."

"That laugh's always charming," Thaddeus said, meaning it. He glanced over at Gina, who was clearly far off in her mind. It struck him as another indication that she was going away from him. She was going away from everyone. He said, "Babe? Isn't that amazing?"

"I remember it," she said.

"So you tuned it out."

"I guess."

"Well, that's what makes you so easy to be with."

"We're not her favorite channel anymore," Louisa said.

"RJ certainly met some interesting people," Whitcomb put in.

"He was a storyteller," Thaddeus said to Louisa, "and you were a perfect partner." It was an attempt to go past things, though what he had said to Gina was perfectly true and he felt justified in having said it.

"Where've you been in that head of yours?" Louisa suddenly asked her daughter. "And you haven't eaten."

Gina threw her napkin down and then, reconsidering, picked it up and folded it neatly. "It's been a long day. I'm going to bed."

Later, lying quietly in the bed watching as she brushed her hair, he said, "Can we talk about today—the meeting? The bar? Claudette's T-shirt?"

"Oh, Wolfie, please. Go on to sleep."

"I loved that T-shirt."

"Jejune." She smirked.

"How about that tornado in the river," he said.

"Wolfie."

"We didn't even have time to think it might kill us."

"I did. Now please."

As he watched her, it occurred to him that honesty itself could constitute a failure of love, perhaps even a form of aggression. The idea was evanescent as breath fogging a window. And it was nothing new, of course. He had a moment of bitter detachment, still watching her. *Such dull, obvious thinking. Ridiculous.* But a flicker of eerie gratification followed this, and he received an urge to tease her, as if she'd been in on this selfish woolgathering—part of a game they were playing. He resisted the impulse, seeking to hold on. "I'm such a fool," he managed.

"Cut it out."

He might've murmured "See you in the morning," or he might've dreamed it. He woke once in the night, saw the darkness, and felt her slow breathing at his side. His heart was hammering in his ear on the pillow.

Tuesday, June 23–Thursday, July 2

Malcolm

The first reading/rehearsal was stumbling and troublesome, and they worked on through the late afternoon. There were many problems to iron out regarding timing with the aspect of Cordelia being voiceless, and sessions had been riddled with interruptions and confusions. Everyone was restless and tired. In the early-afternoon read through, Frye stopped Claudette three times in midline, and told her to start again. "It's not quite right. You have to enunciate better. Remember, you're the marble-hearted fiend who's lying to your father the king. Flattering him shamelessly. Keep Cordelia's line to Goneril and Regan uppermost in your mind as you begin saying yours. *'I know you, what you are.'*"

Claudette said, "I can't *half believe* the professed love, here, in the first scene? There can't be a hint of what used to be real daughter-love here?"

"I think you may be complicating it too much, dear."

Claudette cleared her throat. "I would *very* much prefer that you not call me *dear.*"

"At my age, I call every woman *dear.* You must've noticed."

"No, I don't notice that much about you, sir. And all the same, I prefer that you *refrain* from it, in my case, please."

After the slightest hesitation, and with a glance at Mundy, he said, "Soytenly," pronouncing it like Groucho Marx.

"Well, and, regarding the lines here, it's Shakespeare. The language *soytenly* supports *many* nuances, doesn't it."

"Just—no nuance, *here*," Frye insisted with an edge of annoyance. "Crisp, straightforward *lying* is what I, as director of this particular production, require. I take full responsibility." He smiled, curtly. "So. If you'll just play it as I've asked it to be played."

"Butter won't melt in my mouth."

"Precisely."

She went on with the scene, without expression, enunciating each syllable with a scarcely discernible touch of hostility which, if Frye noticed, he didn't comment on.

Now, in the new rehearsal hall, Malcolm sat next to her at the long table in the center of the room. They were going through a scene, another of the paired readings Frye had assigned. They were doing Albany and Goneril, and again it hadn't gone well. Malcolm sat back and decided to say something about the afternoon. "I agree with you about the note of once daughter-love, you know. Shakespeare understood human nature well enough to know it would be there, I think."

"Oh, well." She waved this away. "He wants me to be Snidely Whiplash, I'll be Snidely Whiplash. Interesting, isn't it, for a man wanting to emphasize society keeping women down."

"I think plays consciously set up to make some point or other end up *missing* the point."

"What's the point?" She smiled.

"The story."

"Good point. Except, you know, the history plays are making a bit of a point."

He laughed softly. They were quiet for an interval.

The new hall had been built out of the old one, so the smell of fresh paint and plasterboard mingled with the odor of old wood and stone. Late-afternoon sun poured through the windows. Acoustic panels jutted from the opposite wall; two large whiteboards on stands were ranged to the right of the entrance, next to a booth with technical equipment in it—microphones and speakers, cables and wires, a quartermaster's desk with two PCs on it.

"Okay." She took a deep breath. "Let's try it again. Ready? Albany and Goneril. Act four, scene two." She fixed him in her green gaze, and took on the expression of prideful spite. "'I have been worth the whistling,'" she recited.

"'O Goneril,'" Malcolm came back. "'You are not worth the dust which the rude wind blows in your face. I fear your disposition—'"

She held up a hand. "Do you think he'd be closer to *dismay* here?"

"Oh, sure," he said. "Let me try that."

They repeated the exchange.

"No," she said. "Sorry—it was better before."

"Okay."

"Let's stop, why don't we. I'm played out."

"You should be directing us," he said.

"Funny."

He sat back. "I'm actually enjoying this. Being involved in it again. I'm remembering how much I liked it all. Don't know why I left it, really."

"You must've enjoyed doing the news, too."

"There was more money in it," he said. "And I did enjoy the, uh—the celebrity status."

"I wouldn't've thought you were the type."

"Oh, I was the type, believe me."

After a brief pause, she said, "I shouldn't've said that about *type*."

"How's the situation with your dad?"

"He's so much better than he was. Thanks for asking. Though there's an ominous silence from my stepmother."

"I'm glad to hear he's better."

"Are you in love with someone?" she asked suddenly.

He was slow in answering, gazing at her. Then he shook his head, smiling a bit. The fact glared at him that not long ago he had been very much like William Mundy where women were concerned. "No." Then, keeping the smile: "You?"

She shook her head, also with a small smile. "Didn't mean to get personal."

"We were just talking about your dad."

"Well, anyway, it's always personal, acting, isn't it."

"Right now, it feels like personal *failure* to me."

"What do you want out of life, now, Malcolm?"

He couldn't return her gaze. "That's a strange question."

"Sorry."

"Something you'd ask a kid, isn't it?"

She said nothing. And so to relieve her embarrassment, he said, "But, in fact, I guess I really still can't say. Exactly. Get from here to next week, maybe. Usually. How strange is that?"

Her eyes in this light were the color of two near patches of deep seawater. "Not so strange, really."

He said, "Mundy made a try at Mona, too, you know."

She nodded. "Right. So, then—everybody knows."

"Has anybody else said anything to Frye?" he asked.

"Well, *I* haven't. But grandpa goat has been awarded the roundest rejections by all of us, and so maybe that'll be the end of it. Unless he makes a run at Lurlene."

"Lurlene will hand him his liver," Malcolm said.

She laughed softly. Then: "I nearly did just that."

After a small space, he told her about Eleanor Cruikshank and her books, the cottage he wanted to rent on her property. "Trouble is, I can't seem to find anybody to sublet the place I'm in."

She nodded. "I saw the notice on the bulletin board."

"Do you know Eleanor Cruikshank's work?"

"I may've seen an excerpt somewhere."

They went out into the corridor. At the far end they saw Lurlene locking the theater manager's suite. Her two granddaughters were with her. Lurlene waved and got the girls to wave. Claudette called out, "We're looking forward to the Fourth."

"We are, too," Lurlene said.

Claudette turned to Malcolm. "Good luck on the cottage."

"I'm heading over there right now," Malcolm said.

The sky was threatening rain again, and there was thunder in the gray distance. He drove toward the Old Forest. As he turned down Poplar, a police car pulled behind him and followed for several blocks. He felt like a fugitive, worrying about the protection order and what Pearl might have done seeking to beleaguer him. The police car veered off onto a side street, and he drove on. As he made the turn into the long drive, he saw the novelist out in her garden to the right of the house. She stood straight when she saw him, rested her wrists on the stand-up weeder she'd been using, and waited for him to approach. In her gardening clothes and straw hat, she looked imposing. Somewhere close by, music was playing. He didn't recognize it: brass and violins and timpani, crashings. She propped the weeder against the little garden fence. "Well, aren't you the typical southern boy, just driving up. Why don't you call someone with a little warning?"

"I really am sorry."

"Well, it's the southern way, isn't it." The music was building to a crescendo. "Do you know Mahler's Third?" She opened the gate and stepped out.

"I seldom listen to classical. A failure of mine."

"Does this bother you?"

"Oh, no. It's rather interesting, actually."

"Rather interesting. Yes. Mahler. That's a little like saying Shakespeare is rather engaging. But I think Mr. Mahler would approve. The cottage isn't ready to be looked at today. It's a mess."

"I promise I won't mind the mess," he said. "Pretty messy myself."

"Well, nevertheless. It's dirty."

The music ended with an orchestral cascade, and timpani that sounded like the thunder now lessening in the far sky. She stood there in the silence that followed, gazing at him, and once again he felt the urge to bow. He controlled it, turning, giving a little wave, and moving off.

"Tea?" she said.

He turned. "Excuse me?"

"Would you care for some tea?"

"I don't normally drink it."

"What do you normally drink?" She smiled. Her teeth were the color of sweet corn. "These days."

"Sparkling water."

"I have plenty of that."

He followed her into the house. It was as though she were leading him on a guided tour. They entered an arched foyer and he saw a console table where two polished, dark burgundy bottles stood with roses in them, flanking a small bronze-based lamp. A white-cushioned bench was just beyond the table, and a staircase wound up to the left. Photographs hung in frames along the right wall, groups of people in seated rows. It looked like one of those galleries of the long dead.

She indicated them with a slight waving motion, walking through. "These are classes of mine at Christian Brothers school. I always ask for a sepia photograph and that everyone in them keep as much as possible to the stunned-serious look of the nineteenth century. It's a little peccadillo of mine. I've kept in touch with a lot of these young people."

"What do you teach?"

"Fiction writing, of course. I call it lying. When people ask me what I teach, I say I teach lying." He thought she had bestowed a witticism, but as they moved through, she went on, "There was no *actual* Good Samaritan, you know. That's a story. A lie, made up to arrive at a truth. Whatever else Jesus was, he must've been an absolutely spellbinding storyteller."

They entered a large, high-ceilinged room full of light from four palladium windows. There were two limousine-long divans on either side of a wide coffee table, with a carousel bookcase on either end of both, flanking a marble hearth with a mantel holding two more wine bottles with blooms jutting from them. She sat at the end of the divan closest to the windows, picked up a small porcelain bell from the side table there, and shook it. An elderly man appeared in the arched passageway in the adjacent wall.

She introduced him as her elder brother, Martin. He came over and shook hands. The flesh of his palm was quite cold. "That's Malcolm," she said to him. "Tea for me, please, and a Pellegrino for Malcolm."

"Yes, darling." He turned slightly, gave Malcolm a nod, and went on.

"He likes bells," she said.

"You've decided to hire him?"

"He's been with me a long time."

Malcolm looked at the carousel bookcases. There were bookcases on either side of the hearth, as well. "You haven't found a butler, then."

"Times are hard."

"Still looking at candidates?"

She nodded slightly, with a disinterested half smile.

The older brother came back into the room carrying the sparkling water and ice in a glass. Malcolm thanked him and watched him go back through the passageway.

"Not much past elementary school," she said, low. "Head injury. Fell off an ordinary playground swing. Nine years old. An afternoon's outing. I take care of him, now. And he takes care of me. Until recently, we had someone who did that for both of us. But that gentleman's gone back home to care for his lady mother."

Malcolm simply attended, nodding slowly.

"In the Bahamas," she continued. "A place called Eleuthera."

"Are there placement services for butlers? I should know, I guess."

"We interviewed four people from a service." She sighed. "None of them quite satisfactory, I'm afraid. So I placed the ad in *The Appeal*."

"Anybody other than me answer it?"

"Several. Not one fit the bill. And we seem to be getting along nicely without one."

He shifted slightly forward, resting his elbows on his knees. "Well, you know, I really don't mind a mess, if you want to show me the cottage."

"That's absolutely out of the question. You should call and set up an appointment."

"All right, then. I'll do that." He took in the room, the brightness from the tall windows, the furniture casting sharp shadows. Everything immaculate. The marble hearth looked freshly polished.

He took a swallow of his sparkling water, and immediately hiccuped. This was not in itself surprising—it happened often enough whenever he drank anything carbonated—but the volume of it was; it was as though he'd suddenly barked, or shouted an obscenity, and it brought a startled little cry from the back of her throat. She sat up.

"Are you working on a novel now?" he got out, trying to seem unruffled.

She took a few seconds, waiting politely in case there might be another eruption. And a second hiccup did burst forth, even more loudly. Her eyes were wide as a child's might be at the sound of a gunshot.

"Excuse me," he managed, and let go a shaky laugh. "Sparkling water sometimes does this to me."

"Do you want something else? Regular water?"

"No, I think that was it."

"I don't think I've ever heard a singultus that loud."

"Singultus."

"Yes, indeed. What you just did was way past hiccups. *Singultus* is the only word for those spasms. I first heard it used in England, actually. In a lovely village called Edale."

One more of what he now thought of as a singultus issued from him, slightly less loud. He drew in a gulp of air and held his breath while she watched.

Presently, and a little doubtfully, she said, "So, what part will you play in *Lear*?"

He told her.

"Goneril's good husband. That's a juicy part."

"Claudette Bradley's doing Goneril. She was Lady M, wonderfully, in the Scottish play, several years ago." He smiled and drank, with, to his relief, no hiccup. The cold, carbonated water felt good now going down, pleasantly thirst quenching.

"I actually saw that *Macbeth,*" she said. "The one outside in the park. I remember the fellow playing him had a bad cold and kept throwing phlegm during the scene when Banquo's ghost appears. I felt for him because he didn't see at first how it added to his performance. So odd—and enlightening—to see an actor discover, in midline, how an accident is actually helping him, and then finding himself able to dissolve *inside* it all enough to have his mortification add to the overall effect." She paused, seemed to ponder, and then: "I've probably only succeeded just now in being obscure."

"No," he said. "Not at all."

She left a pause.

"The night I saw it," Malcolm said, "was a very cold night. And Ms. Bradley was just terrific."

"Yes, I remember her. I think she got the madness and evil balanced just right. Best I've seen since Judi Dench on BBC."

"Can I tell her you said that?"

The lady novelist nodded, smiling. "I never refuse the opportunity to be quoted."

He took another sip of the water, and a small hiccup followed it.

"You really ought to give that up along with whatever else you've given up."

"Doesn't always happen," he said.

"I'm working now on a novel set in England," she told him, still smiling. "In Edale, as a matter of fact. It's not going so well, though—which is normal enough—so I'm spending more time gardening."

"Time to think."

"Time to *avoid* thinking. Mindless activity."

It seemed they were becoming friends. The older brother brought her tea. "Thank you, Martin."

Martin went out.

Her eyes became thin, amber slits suddenly, fixing him. "How are you managing your desperation?"

Malcolm stared. "Excuse me?"

She put the cup down in the saucer, and it made a little glass-clinking sound—the sound, he had once remarked while standing at a party trying to seem sober, of civilized life all over the world. "I'm just wondering how you're handling your trouble. I think it only fair that I be able to assess the stability of my tenant."

He finished the Pellegrino and held the glass of ice with both hands. "Well," he said. "As for the state of my general well-being, it's not quite ready to be looked at. In fact, it's a mess."

"I see." The smile came back. "I do like witty people."

"I can afford the rent," he said. "I'm employed, and my divorce is final. I'm doing as well as can be expected. I'm working. I don't drink anymore."

"Are you ever tempted?"

"No," he lied. "I'm still too frightened of it to be tempted." This, he realized, was also true.

"Are you seeing anyone?"

He set the glass down on the edge of the coffee table and stood. "Not so it would affect anything having to do with the cottage."

"I didn't mean romantically."

"Oh," he said. "Not just now, no."

"Are you still in touch with your niece?"

"Pardon me?" He was standing there, half turned toward the doorway.

She seemed momentarily exasperated, and gave a little shirking motion with her shoulders. "I do read the papers and look at the news, Mr. Ruark."

"I'm—I was never 'seeing' my niece in that way. I never touched her, except to let her cry on my shoulder about the mess her parents were making of their lives—and hers."

"I just meant are you *in touch* with her."

He explained about the protection order, and then talked about Mona's role as Cordelia.

"So, how is *that* for you under the circumstances?"

"Is this why you were—why you offered me the place? To help answer your curiosity?"

"I do not dissemble, young man. I told you I liked your television work."

He said nothing for a moment. Then: "It's rather nice to be called young man at my age."

"I'm twenty years older than you are. What should I call you?"

"*Young man* is fine."

"I am curious, though," she went on. "Nothing to do with the cottage. It's friendly curiosity, let us say."

He waited. And then slowly sat back down.

"Honestly," she said.

He let the quiet go on. A crow protested from a tree outside, a repeated, insistent squawk, like impatient comments on the silence. He took the last of the water around the melting ice from the glass, and set it down again.

"I truly meant no offense."

"None taken," he said.

She stood. "Perhaps it'll serve to show you the cottage after all. If you don't mind dirt."

"I don't mind at all."

"Hey?" she called. "We're going to show the cottage."

Her brother joined them. As they went along the wraparound porch to the side of the house, Malcolm thought of seeking an opportunity to say something about liking what he'd been reading. They stepped down into the big lawn. The cottage stood close to the back fence, a koi pond on the left, and a tall river poplar on the right; it would be in shade much of the day. Four small rooms, each painted Egyptian blue—bedroom, bathroom, main room, and kitchen. Twice as big as the little efficiency apartment with the reclining chair and the bed. Big wing chairs, plush, heavy furniture; a padded sofa in the main room; a table in the kitchen with four tall-backed wooden stools. A double bed and a cedar chest in the bedroom, with a chifforobe and a shallow closet. There was a faint mineral smell about the place, and the wood-grain floors were water-stained along one side of the narrow hallway. She explained that there had been a small fire six years before, which the fire department had put out just in time; there was only a little water damage, and no mold. In fact, the little place looked immaculate. "Well?" she said.

"I don't see the mess you spoke of," he said.

They were standing in the kitchen. She ran two fingers along the countertop, and showed him the dust.

"Well," he said. "It's very nice."

"After what *you're* used to?" Plainly she meant the house and the lake cottage, with its wide windows looking out on the water.

"*Especially* after what I'm, uh, *lately* used to."

She smiled, then nodding at her brother turned and went on back to the house. The brother, also smiling but seeming vaguely tense, showed him the small back garden and the koi pond.

"You're doing Shakespeare now. Not the news anymore. We love seeing Shakespeare. I like to watch them arguing and fighting."

"Me t—" Ruark began.

But the other wasn't finished. "I like the special effects a lot. That's why it's more fun as a movie. Do you like it when it's a movie?"

"I do."

"I like the special effects. And the sounds. I like the sound of the words. 'And when he shall die, take him and cut him out in little stars, and he will make the face of heaven so fine that all the world will be in love with night . . .'"

Malcolm was pleasurably surprised and impressed.

"How beautiful." The brother held up his hand, indicating everything around them. "'All the world will be in love with night.' Wait here."

Malcolm watched him walk across the lawn to the house and in.

A minute went by, and then another. The birds sang. He heard the murmurous sound the leaves made in the stirring delta breezes. Overton Park looked droopy, the flowers all bending in the hot air. A humid near twilight. He was standing alone in a yard, in the disappearing shadow of a house. Finally, deciding he'd been forgotten, he started toward the entrance drive. As he came within a few feet of the place, the brother beckoned him from the side door, and led him into the big room with the palladium windows. "She thought you might wish to adjust," the brother explained. Malcolm wanted to thank him, and to indicate somehow his pleasure in listening to him talk about Shakespeare. But suddenly the name was lost to him. He searched his mind, angry with himself, and now Eleanor Cruikshank walked in, stood over the side table, turned the lamp on there, set the lease down, and signed it. The lamp had brought night to the windows. She pushed the lease toward him. "Occupying this week?"

"A week from Friday?" he said.

"Anytime after this Friday."

He turned to the last page and signed.

"You ought to read it," she said, low. "What if I've put in a clause requiring you to empty your bank account?"

"Then I'll empty my bank account."

She didn't respond.

"Wouldn't be much," he said.

"Enough to pay the rent, I presume."

He tried a smile. "I liked *White Hawthorne* very much. And *Little Acts of Retribution*, too. I found them very absorbing."

"What about *Mrs. Dowling*?"

"Haven't started that one yet. I'm feeling pretty sure I'll like it."

"You got them out of the library?"

"I ordered them online."

"You *are* industrious."

"I was curious. And of course if I hadn't liked them I wouldn't've said anything."

"Very wise, I'd say." She smiled, and then took the smile away with a sigh and a little turn of her head. "I'm impressed that you have them. I really am. And I'm very glad you're liking them."

"It's probably bad form to compliment an author to her face."

"Oh." She smiled the brief smile again. "I can bear any amount of affection for my work expressed in any way, anywhere you choose, with me or without me."

He said, "I understand completely."

"Well, as I said at the beginning of our—" She paused. "Our relation, let us say, I did tell you I admired your work. I was sorry to see you go."

In the next moment, to his own astonishment, he found himself telling her everything—the drinking, the accident with Mona in the car, her injuries and Pearl's reaction, the DUI and the police, all of it. The protection order, and his feelings for the girl, fatherly, as he expressed them, yet also remembering to say that Mona was not blood related, and realizing as he spoke how it really sounded, the obsessiveness in it; the tawdriness. He thought of the awkwardness of Mona's pass at him in the cluttered apartment. It stopped him. He was still for a few seconds. Then he heard himself going on about rehearsals with her as deaf Cordelia.

The novelist stood there, staring, with what he saw was a faintly discomfited but kindly gaze. He felt pulled into it.

". . . so, it's been an adjustment for everyone," he said, finishing.

Eleanor Cruikshank bent down and picked up her now-cold tea and, after another pause, asked, "Would you like another water?"

"No, thanks."

Silence. She drank the rest of the tea, then sat down at her place on the divan, still holding the cup.

"Forgive me," he got out, still standing. "I don't know what brought that on. I really am sorry."

"Well," she said after still more silence. "You just signed your life away."

"Were you ever married?" he suddenly felt emboldened to ask.

"No," she said.

He waited a second. Then: "It's none of my business, of course."

"That would be my estimation of it." Her smile now was a bit sardonic. Once more, she put the cup down on the saucer, with that little sound. "But the fact is, you've told me things, quite honestly, that are none of *my* business."

"Well," he said. "Anyway, I'm glad about the cottage. And I really am sorry for unloading all that. I really—I'm not the divulging type, usually, you know?"

"Nothing to worry about," she said. "I like to know my tenants. Maybe one afternoon I'll find myself divulging with you." She rang the little porcelain bell again, and the old man appeared. "Martin, see Malcolm to the door."

"Thank you, Martin," Malcolm said.

Martin. Yes.

There was something curiously almost dancelike in Martin's stride as he led the way out. At the door, he looked at Malcolm and smiled, so Malcolm waited for him to speak. But Eleanor Cruikshank's brother simply held out one hand, indicating the outside as if it were a display he had arranged, and started slowly to close the door. Malcolm felt shut out; it was a strange, irrelevant moment bringing the whole bad last two years home to him. Walking away from the big house, he wanted a drink; it was suddenly a terrible thirst. He saw himself going somewhere and ordering one drink. He took deep breaths, tasting the air, working to dispel the thought.

Claudette

She said, "Should I call Franny and invite her?"

They were getting into her car, Ellis being helped into the front passenger seat by Willamina, who had let him nap most of the afternoon. He was a little groggy. "Franny's often annoyed," he said. "She doesn't want to come over."

It was the last day of June, and they had got into a pattern. Dinners out on Tuesday nights, usually at the Madison, since it was near the theater, and Claudette could walk down there sometimes and meet them. This evening, she had come home early because three effects companies were conducting trials in the auditorium, and the fight coach had begun his meetings with the actors about the sword fights and battles. So they were going to drive together back into the city center. As they headed down Poplar toward the river, Ellis gazed out the window and spoke about the beauty of Memphis summer evenings. "The light's always marvelous heading west," he said.

That morning, she'd come from her room to find him standing in his robe at the little table in the kitchen, gripping the back of one of the chairs.

"You're up," she'd said. She was in her nightgown.

He only glanced at her. "For God's sake put some clothes on."

Ignoring the tone, she said, "Oh, I will, when I've had some breakfast."

"You know I'm not peppy in the morning, Esther. Let go of it."

"I'll make you some French toast," she said.

"I never liked French toast. Is Meryl up?"

Claudette ignored this, too. "French toast has always been my favorite."

"It was Claudette who liked the French toast." He turned. Briefly they were simply standing there in the light from the window, staring at each other.

"Say hello to Lear," he said, and smiled, and then looked down at his hands on the back of the chair.

"Hello to Lear," she said.

"I got a terrible headache."

"Can I get you something? Did you take your Coumadin?"

"Gave me a headache. So I took a Tylenol. One tablet. Then a Xanax."

"Let me get dressed."

He lifted one hand to wave this away, and she saw the strain in the muscles of his other forearm where that hand still held on to the chair. "Don't worry about it, honey. I'm back."

"No, it's all right."

"Don't tell me no!" He'd gripped the chair again.

She left him there and went into her room and dressed, quickly, in jeans and a sweatshirt. When she got back to the kitchen, he was at the stove, supporting himself on it, peering at the knobs.

"I can't read these," he said. "What the Christ and god*damn* it to fiery hell."

She went and took him by the shoulders, and gently pulled him back to the table, where he sat down and put his hands to his face. "Couldn't sleep. I'm sorry. I was feeling good."

"I'll make you an egg in a cup."

"I like egg in a cup. That's the name of it. Only yesterday morning I wanted to ask for it. Couldn't remember the name. I was wounded at Chipyong-ni. Awful, awful."

"It's all right," she said, opening the refrigerator. "We're fine now."

He sat there with his arms folded. "God, I'm sorry. What day is this?"

"It's Tuesday."

"And—" He paused. "The month?"

"Last week of June."

"Yes. I see that. I'm sorry, Claudie. Was I short with you?"

"No."

"You were in a nightie. You oughta be able to be comfortable in your own house."

"I'm fine, Dad. Really. I'm so happy to have you with me here."

He looked around. "That's right. It's better this way. It is better. I'll be better."

"I think you're great," she told him, and he smiled at her.

Now, she pulled the car in front of the Madison and watched Willamina and the doorman help him out of the car. It took a little doing; he seemed stiff. "Go on in," she said. Then she drove up the block to the theater and parked. As she walked down toward them where they waited in the light of the hotel marquee, she saw that her father had one arm across Willamina's shoulders. Ellis reached and pulled her to his other side as she came up to them; it was not for support, but purely for affection, and he seemed anxious that she know that. "My two best people," he said. "Do you know each other?"

"Let's go in," said Willamina. "It's too hot under this marquee."

The three of them made their way in, past the bar, where Claudette saw Mundy with a young woman at a table with a bottle of wine between them. Claudette felt a twinge of dread. In the elevator, her father held tight to the handrail and gave forth a low sort of tuneless hum. He had never liked elevators.

They emerged and were led by the hostess, whom Claudette knew, to a table nearest the wall overlooking the street. Claudette accepted the menus and wine list with a smile. Ellis stared at the open menu, like a man holding an open newspaper. It was a point of pride with Ellis that his eyesight and his hearing were still good. He scrutinized the choices. Willamina sat to his right and was gazing over his shoulder, frowning, concentrating. Claudette saw the depthless brown of her eyes.

"We played Scrabble today," Ellis said, folding the menu. "Didn't we," he said to Willamina. "And I didn't do so bad. Except I couldn't remember the word *oxygen*. Like I never heard the word before. *Oxygen*. Seemed like it might be just a noise you'd make with your mouth. *Ox-ih-gen*."

"You had the letters for *oxygen*?"

"With two wild-card tiles," Willamina said.

"I didn't remember it was even a word. Willamina had to show me."

A bell sounded somewhere off in the city. They looked at the tops of the buildings across the way, and at the hazy sun nearing the line of trees beyond the river.

"I like coming here," Willamina offered. "It's nice."

"Sunset, so pretty," Claudette said.

Ellis picked the menu up again, glanced at it, and put it down. "Order me the usual, darling, I've got to use the toilet." He got to his feet, and then hesitated.

"Dad. The usual?"

He seemed confused. "Fine," he said, too loud.

Willamina stood and held out one hand for him. Not seeing this, he moved with wobbly paces toward the doorway into where the elevator was, then stopped and half turned. Willamina started toward him. He made a throat-clearing sound, caught the attention of the hostess. "The amenities, please, young lady."

She indicated a doorway. He went there slowly, still not quite steady on his feet.

Willamina came back and sat down. "Maybe I should think of an excuse to go stand by the door."

Claudette watched her go. The other tables on this part of the rooftop were empty, though she heard talk and laughter beyond the angle of the inside partition. She saw the young hostess lead an elderly couple to a table on the opposite end.

A few seconds later, Geoffrey Chessman walked in from the elevators.

Her heart went down.

He wore a white shirt rolled halfway at the sleeves and tan pleated slacks. But the clothes looked slept in. His hair was cut shorter than she'd ever seen it. Walking confidently over to her, as if this were all planned, he said, "Relax. I'm not a ghost," and bent down to offer a kiss. She leaned away from it.

"Wow," he said. "Fright, and then avoidance."

"What the hell are you doing here?"

"I came to inform you that you got me pregnant."

She stared, glowering.

Settling into Ellis's chair, he said, "You're not delighted to see me?"

"That's my father's place."

"Oh, Ellis escaped?" He looked briefly around. "I'll move when he comes back."

She took some of the water before her, not looking at him, trying to breathe.

"Anyway," he said. "I'm pregnant, and you'll have to do the honorable thing. It's only right. Society still expects it."

"You should've told me you were coming."

"The obstetrician advised against it. He thought you might flee."

"Stop it, please, Geoffrey. I mean it."

He let a few seconds go by, looking around at the other tables. Then: "I thought this might be a happy surprise. I thought you might even fall into my arms. I drove all the way here in the Subaru. Packed with my whole bundle of riches."

She stared.

"Four days, straight through. Slept in the car. Hamburgers and hot dogs all the way."

"Look, I can't deal with this now, Geoffrey. So cut it. Please."

"I'm telling you the truth."

A moment passed while he looked around the room.

"Saw William Mundy downstairs," he said. "With a foxy lady. Is he in this production?"

"I told you that over the phone way back in January."

He left another pause, fumbling distractedly with the tablecloth. "I thought, you know, little surprise might be good. Sorry. I'm a little desperate. A tiny bit. Sleeping by the roadsides was tough, you know." He was not looking at her now, concentrating on his hands, moving them, palms down, lightly over the tablecloth, as if to smooth it. "Anyway, William fucking Mundy. Wow."

"Everything's already set with casting, Geoffrey. We're in rehearsals."

He considered a moment. "Well, anyway, I'm in the last stages of a breakdown. So I don't think I'm available. I mean I'm probably not right for the part. Too sexy to play Lear."

"How much've you had to drink?"

He leaned toward her, clownishly opened his mouth, and exhaled. She smelled only a faint mingling of peppermint and the metal of his fillings. It nauseated her. "You don't drink when you're driving a couple thousand miles, you know?"

"Well—what're you doing here?"

"I think the breakdown about covers it," he said, low, without inflection. "Mr. Miles fucking Warden's all the way in Sydney. You sure nobody needs me here?"

"Did you hear me? Everything's settled. It doesn't matter where Miles is."

He ignored this. "I have to admit I haven't come back to Memphis as much as I've left LA. You were right about it being a mistake to go out there."

"I never said anything about it, Geoffrey. One way or the other."

"Well," he said. "Anyway, everything about it was wrong, you know? So, I'm back. And I can still act as good as anybody. I'm pretty good for a guy off the street, with no pet degree. Oh, I'm sorry. Pedigree." He smiled, but his eyes glittered. "I've been out in the elephants. Oh, pardon me, elements. Elephants, elements. Remember that?"

It had been a repeated joke between them when they were happy together, something from Dickens's character Micawber that she knew first from her father's reading to her in childhood. *David Copperfield* had been a favorite book of hers since. Now she simply stared at him.

"Barkis is willing," he said, from the same book, and another joke they used at times, about whether or not they would make love.

She shook her head in the purest dismay, and looked down at her hands.

"Incorrigible," he said, with a self-congratulatory smirk. "I know."

"Please."

"Warden's in Australia," he said. "The great impediment's on the other side of the world."

"I told you. Everything's cast," she said. "The whole season. That's how it is."

He nodded, and smiled. "Pedigree," he repeated. Then: "What do you call an actor with two brain cells?"

"Geoffrey, stop it."

"Pregnant." The smile was now almost a leer.

She kept silent.

"You don't find that funny? Well, but I was also making a point."

Looking beyond him, she saw Ellis and Willamina coming back from the restrooms.

"Well, lookie here," Geoffrey said, turning.

Ellis was leaning on Willamina's arm. They got to the table, and she helped him sit down. Claudette's former husband had stood out of the chair, and now he reached for one at the next table and brought it over. "Hey, Ellis," he said. "Hey, man. You look great."

Ellis squinted at him. "Geoffrey?"

"My ex," Claudette murmured to Willamina.

The two men were exclaiming and making over each other, shaking hands. "Good Lord, boy, where've you been all this time?" Ellis said.

Geoffrey stood and leaned over awkwardly to embrace him. "I've been so far away, man. Other planets, you know."

"Well, you're back. You two—" He looked at Claudette, and seemed suddenly confused and uneasy. "I don't—"

"I was telling Claudette my sad story," Geoffrey said. "Years, man, and nothing, not a blessed thing. It makes me sick when I think of it. Once—when I first got there—man, I had six callbacks in a week. Four of them for one damn part. Four. For the same part. Couldn't make up their tiny minds or something. But all that went kaput."

For a few seconds, no one said anything.

He looked at each of them in turn. "Oh, Ellis, I've got a joke. Sorry, Claudie. It's as follows." He paused and, after taking a hesitating breath, told the joke again. Claudette remembered he had often used that phrase, *as follows,* that construction when launching into a story. It always irked her, even when she was in love with him and wanted him in the nights.

"Well, how *are* you, anyway, Son?" Ellis said suddenly, quite loud, having only smiled at the joke, while Willamina politely chuckled. It was as though he'd just noticed that it was Geoffrey sitting there. "How long's it been? Gee, it's good to see you. This is my friend Willamina, and how long do we have to wait to order here?"

Claudette signaled the hostess, who walked over and, perceiving the problem, volunteered that the server would be right with them.

"I'm really hungry," Ellis said. Still quite loud.

"I think they heard you, Dad," Claudette told him. "It's all right."

He slapped Geoffrey's shoulder. "I haven't been quite tip-top lately."

The server arrived. He was a tall, bone-thin boy Claudette also knew. "Hi, Tim," she managed, and Willamina reached over and touched her wrist.

"I'm so sorry," Tim said. "We're slammed downstairs. Some summer program thing."

"I was in Korea," Ellis said. "Feels like yesterday. No, feels like *earlier today.*"

A siren sounded in the street below.

"Ah," Geoffrey Chessman said. "Nice to be back in my hometown. Wonder who's been shot."

Tim took the orders and left. They were all feeling the slight breeze, hearing the strains of music coming from Beale.

"So, you're through with Hollywood, then," said Willamina to Geoffrey.

Geoffrey nodded thoughtfully. "I hate to say it, but yeah. I guess."

"I'm so glad we could all be together," Ellis said. "There's times, I tell you, I expect things to fold up and blow away like smoke."

"That's poetic," said Willamina.

"I feel the same way," Geoffrey said, looking at Claudette.

She wiped her serviette across her lips and was silent.

Tim brought the bottle of Syrah Claudette had ordered. He poured the three glasses. Ellis gulped his down. He tried to stand. "Gotta visit the amenities again." He held the back of his chair and seemed momentarily dizzy.

Willamina rose to help him. "You drank that wine pretty fast," she said.

"Want a glass of Irish, now," he said. "What we should've had." They moved off, carefully.

Claudette had a small drink of the wine, and watched them. Geoffrey sighed at her. "You don't like the Syrah."

"I'm tired."

"Why're you so sharp with me? All I did was come home. I lived here once." He paused. Then: "I thought you'd be more friendly. We've been friendly enough over the phone."

"There's nothing for you at the theater, Geoffrey."

"You think I'd try to use you like that?"

She looked at him.

"Nothing in the black box?"

She tilted her head and smiled.

"I was teasing. Trying to get a rise out of you."

"Well, there's nothing in the black box, either."

"Well? Maybe put in a word with Thaddeus and the Grausbecks for me? Something? Somebody's understudy? Work in the offices?"

"You do remember how it was before you left."

"Okay," he said, low. "But probably I wouldn't have to lie hidden under a sheet in a bed onstage again, right?"

He'd been drunk or high on something through the run-up and preview night of Megan Terry's *The Gloaming, Oh My Darling*. It was a disaster of a night, and brought about the end of his career with the company. The drama depicts two elderly women in a nursing home who have spirited away a demented old man (Geoffrey, thickly made-up), hiding him in their room to be their play beau in polite turn-of-the-century flirtations. The first scene opens with the two women seated side by side in rocking chairs downstage, talking about keeping secret what they've done, while behind them, in the bed under a sheet, the old man character is hidden, keeping completely still, so the audience remains unaware of his presence until, about twenty minutes in, he sits bolt upright and begins mouthing accusations about the murder of Roosevelt, and memories of driving cattle across dusty, dry western plains. That preview night, Geoffrey, already half drunk, lying under the sheet in the bed upstage, keeping still, waiting for his cue, fell asleep. And snored. Loudly. Midscene. The two women had to drop what amounted to more than two pages of dialogue, get out of their chairs, and move to the bed to wake him. Geoffrey came to, dazed and groggy, bolted upright, and saw with sudden terror the four hundred people looking and laughing, and he forgot everything for the better part of a minute while the two women struggled to fill the time by improvising lines.

Miles Warden raged at him after it was over, even though the audience—many of them—had assumed the snoring and the frantic reaction were part of the comedy. Warden—after Geoffrey said, "Did you hear those laughs?"—fired him on the spot, saying, "It's cheap, and unethical, and it does violence to the play. It made the evening into a farce, and it makes you into a whore." The rest of the run was conducted with Mickey Castleton in the role. Geoffrey never performed again at the theater, and a month later headed for Hollywood. "I'm good-looking," he had said. "I'll make it there. Watch."

"Go," she had told him calmly. "Go. And stay gone. And best of luck."

"You'll be the first to know," he told her.

Now, he shook his head, frowning. "I was good. You know I was."

She said nothing.

"So that's it, then?"

"I don't know what else to say. I'm not in charge."

He took more of the wine, and made a smacking sound. It occurred to her that perhaps he'd ingested something other than alcohol before he walked in. He gave a sour little smirk. "So, here we are. I think the wine's good. You don't like the wine."

She had another sip, not looking at him.

"You say to-*mah*-toe. I say to-*mate*-toe."

An elderly couple walked toward the door and she watched them.

"You guys in that big, fancy venue, with all that money, and me out in the fucking street."

Now she turned to him, and looked into his wild eyes. "Are you on something?"

"I wish." He sighed. "No, I'm dry as a bone and clean as church. Are you that mad at me?"

"It makes me crazy that you showed up without letting me know and then presumed on me, like I owe you anything. We're not together anymore, Geoffrey. It's been four years. Our lives don't intersect the way you're trying to make it seem they do. And with my father in this—" She stopped. "It's just typical and selfish and wrong and not fair. Look. This is not an old rom-com movie. I am not Julia Roberts and you are not Hugh Grant."

"I love those two."

She said nothing.

"I love your dad."

Again, she was silent.

"And he always liked me."

"It's no use, Geoffrey."

"What does *that* mean?"

"It means we're done with each other that way. Come on, what do you think it means?"

They sat quiet for a time. There was just the low music in the walls of the restaurant, and on the summer air from Beale Street, and the chatter of the others at neighboring tables.

"We haven't been on such bad terms," he said.

"I'll admit I didn't mind talking on the phone. But it was never gonna be anything else."

Ellis and Willamina came from the restrooms and crossed to the view of the city.

"I wasn't planning on moving back in with you if that's worrying you. I think after the good things I did in that theater, though, they could give me another chance. I did very well playing Brick in *Cat* in '09. Everybody talked about it." He sighed, gazing off. "That was *us*."

"Don't." She was fighting tears now. But the feeling was of helpless fury. "Please," she said through her teeth.

"I know I fucked up a lot, later on. But I was going through the end of us—"

"That's *not* true," she said, managing it, arms folded tight. "You were on something for days, even during *Cat*. Nobody could trust you."

"I'm not asking you to take me in. I got a place. I actually, actually have a studio apartment an LA friend offered me for cheap rent. He left it six years ago to be a star. Kept it for revenue. He was in that movie they filmed over on Union back in '04. That's where he got the habit. And he's been in some commercials, and got some modeling gigs, so he's sticking it out. Those are actually, actually his words. *Sticking it out*. Imagine sticking it out standing in jockey shorts all day for the department store ads. Man, that is not for the likes of me."

She remembered this other tic of his, repeating the word *actually*, as if somehow to make something *more* actual. She could recall when this, too, was a grating thing she forgave him in the nights.

How arid the space was where her love for him had once been.

Ellis and Willamina were making their way back from their rooftop gazing. They took a while, and now Tim arrived with a big tray, all the food they had ordered. While he set it out on the table, Geoffrey talked about driving mega-celebrities all over Hollywood and Beverly Hills and Brentwood. He embellished his story about De Niro—how they laughed about the business, and how he used the famous actor's cell phone. Claudette watched him, and caught herself feeling sorry for him.

Now he turned to her. "So, Claudie. Tell me about your visiting director."

She said, "Not gonna talk about work."

"How will that be for you two?" Ellis asked. "Working together again."

The next night, late, her cell phone buzzed on the stand beside her bed. She ignored it, turned in the blankets, and tried to go back to sleep. But it buzzed again. She sat up, looked at it, and saw that the area code was the same as Geoffrey's in California. She opened it. "Hello."

"Geoffrey Chessman, please."

"Who is this?"

"I'm trying to get ahold of Geoffrey Chessman. His phone isn't answering."

"How did you get my cell number?"

"He gave it to me in case I needed it. And I think I need it. Are you Claudette? The actor wife?"

Claudette breathed out slowly, a soundless sigh. "Ex-wife. That's me, yes, but I—"

"My name's Quincey Blair. I gave him the key to my place."

"He mentioned that. That he had a place. He mentioned you."

"Well, I haven't heard from him. Is he there?"

"I—I saw him last night."

"He said he'd be with you. Said you were separated and he was gonna stay straight and win you back. And he's got my place, there, and now I can't raise him."

"Well, I only just saw him," Claudette said. "And it wasn't what he'd hoped, I can tell you that." She went on and told him everything. "Anyway," she concluded, "I think he should've stayed out there driving De Niro and other Hollywood types around."

Blair said, "That was *me*. *I* drove De Niro around. Did he say they talked about sticking to it? Acting?"

"Yes. Exactly that."

"Christ."

"Listen, I don't know if I'll see him. I suppose he might call."

"Shitsicles. I can't raise him. I've been calling him and calling him."

"He wanted back at the theater here, so I have the feeling I'll see him again."

"Yeah, well, he was heading there to—he—but I needed somebody to occupy that place. Tenant moved out. Like that. He was supposed to do half the mortgage payment. As rent. Said these rich ladies gave you all a shitload of money, excuse my language."

"It's excused," she heard herself say. "I understand."

"You say he mentioned me? What'd he say about me."

"Just that you were—modeling, and that he couldn't see himself doing that."

"Christ."

"Mr. Blair, there's no chance of him getting anything again at this theater. Really. Not the way he left."

"I think I kind of knew that, listening to him talk about the place. Hates everybody there, except you and this guy—the manager. Can't remember his name."

"Deerforth?"

"That sounds right. Everybody else, well, he loathes. Like, that's his word. *Loathes*. The Deerforth guy, he said. Harmless—no, he said feckless. Called him feckless—but a friend, of sorts. He thought maybe you and Deerforth could get him something for old-timey's sake. That was how he put it. Timey. Old-timey's sake. I *knew* I shouldn't've gone along with it, but I was desperate."

"Well, I don't know what to tell you," Claudette said. "But I have your number on this phone now, and I promise I'll call you if I see him or hear from him."

"Please just tell him to call me. Or turn his damn phone on."

She told no one about the call, though she kept the determination to convey the message if and when she saw Geoffrey again. But days passed, and she did not see or hear from him, and this occasioned a surprising amount of anxiety: Geoffrey was a blankness, a silence that loomed.

IV

Run-Throughs

Sunday, July 5–Wednesday, July 22

Thaddeus

Lurlene Glenn's Independence Day party, which was what she called it in her invitation, took place on Sunday. Everyone was invited. Thaddeus and Gina went separately. She had brunch with Claudette, Ellis, and Willamina, at Claudette's apartment. Thaddeus spent the early part of the day at a meeting in the theater offices with the visiting director, the lead actor, and the Grausbecks. The lead actor had a complaint about Claudette. Mundy appeared rather suddenly a lot older than the TV character he played; the rucks and lines in his face seemed deeper. "That woman's celebrity-struck," he said about Claudette. "I was kindly to her and she got the wrong idea. I've decided I've got to report this. She made a pass at me, and when I rejected it, she assaulted me. I know it's late, but we haven't yet commenced full rehearsals, and there are perfectly capable people—"

"It *is* late, Bill," Frye said, very quietly.

There was a tense silence.

"Really," Frye said, in the same calm, quiet tone.

"We've not even had a full run-through," Mundy contended. "We both know better."

The theater manager took a short breath and surprised himself by saying, "I think you'd be making a big mistake, sir. Or you'd be compounding one you already made."

"Oh? I'll bet she's a friend of yours."

"In fact, yes, she is. A dear friend. And I know her very well."

Mundy harrumphed, and made as if to turn from him, tilting his upper body at Frye. "Now listen—"

Thaddeus interrupted him, continuing with increasing urgency as he did so. "And I can tell you, sir, that she's only refraining from charging you with sexual assault because she wants this production to succeed."

Mundy turned and glared.

Thaddeus glared back. "Harassment, at the least, would be the charge. Though she's well aware that she could charge sexual assault."

"Sexual—" Mundy drew himself up.

"Bub-bub, in fact," Arthur Grausbeck said quickly. "I'm afraid there's been another complaint about you, sir. So that's at least two."

Now there was a protracted silence. Jocelyn Grausbeck cleared her throat, rather like an expression of emphasis to the lead actor. "I admire your work, Mr. Mundy, but I wonder what the people responsible for *Home Away* at Netflix might do if this were to get out."

"It would be her word against mine," he muttered.

"*Their* word against yours," Thaddeus said.

After another silence, Reuben Frye said, "Why don't we just—soldier on, Bill. We don't want this to end up in the news. She hasn't broadcast it. And clearly won't."

Mundy just stared. Then, all injured dignity, he said: "Well, tell her to keep her distance."

Thaddeus remained silent, though as the meeting broke up he felt a relieving sense of triumph, and pride, too. He had been occupied the whole morning dealing with separate contractors about the lighting console, flooring in the new restrooms, the just-installed elevators, which were, according to Jocelyn Grausbeck, preternaturally slow. "In fact," he had said to the contractor, "there's time for people to meet, get to know each other, fall in love, and have a small family from the first to the third floor." The contractor laughed.

He could savor that, too. Life was not completely barren of pleasures. *Ridiculous.*

Kelly Gordon arrived in a frenetic rush just as the Grausbecks departed the meeting, heading for Lurlene's. She said, "Hello, Bill," to Mundy, who seemed surprised, and then skulked away. She said to Thaddeus, "Did I do something wrong?"

"Not a thing," Thaddeus said.

"Can I ride with you? I can get a ride back with the Grausbecks."

"Sure," the theater manager said.

As they drove out of the parking lot, he said, "How do you get along with your mentor?"

"Mentor."

He waited. He had only been seeking to make conversation.

She looked over at him. "Have you been talking to Ruark?"

"About what?"

"Nevermind. I studied one semester with Frye. He's not my mentor. After I graduated, he introduced me to the people in Portland for *Driving Miss Daisy*. But he is definitely not my mentor."

He turned onto Union. "It must already be ninety degrees."

"He got me Portland. I didn't want to go that far west, but the play was popular and it was a good company, so I went. And I'm glad I did because it was while I was there that I figured out I'm bisexual."

At first, he wasn't sure he'd heard her correctly. A moment later, trying for polite agreement, he said, "Well, gotta be yourself," and realized as the words left his lips that they sounded empty and vaguely mitigating.

She smirked. "That's the plan."

He left another pause. Then: "Anyway, Frye said your *Driving Miss Daisy* in Portland blew everybody away."

"Oh, but that's such an unwittingly racist play. I think I succeeded with it because I didn't respect it much."

Thaddeus, who loved *Driving Miss Daisy*, couldn't help saying, "It's a *story*, though. About a specific time, and two people *in* that time, both of them subject to the attitudes that exist *where* they live and *when* they live. I mean, what's the sense imposing present-day sensibilities on characters in our own history? The history happened. People lived it and lived *in* it. The *story's* about a black man saving an unwittingly—your word—racist white woman, and bringing her out of her ignorance with his patience, intelligence, and compassion."

"Well. I guess I know where *you* stand."

He said nothing. He was driving down Poplar Avenue toward High Point Terrace.

She said, "At the end of the play, he's *feeding* her. All he's had is a new car every few years that he drove on his *job*. He's still a servant."

"Savior," Thaddeus said. "Servant. Old friend."

"Yeah, like an old dog."

"I think *that's* racist."

"Well, I got it done, anyway," she said. "I'm glad people liked it."

When he looked at her, she looked back. They stared at each other for a few seconds. There were faint shadow-lines going down from either side of her thin mouth; she was already pinched, he thought, clenched on some grievance or other.

They got to Lurlene's. "Thanks for the lift," Kelly Gordon said, already getting out. They said nothing else to each other, crossing to go through the gate into the wide lawn, where two tents had been put up, and pennants flew on a pole wrapped in red, white, and blue ribbons.

Lurlene had hired Rendezvous to cater it, and there were ribs on two different grills, along with hot dogs, brats, hamburgers, pulled pork in an aluminum bin, two large containers of red beans and rice, and platters of salads and fruits. Plus one large aluminum roasting pan of fried chicken from Gus's restaurant, which Lurlene's neighbor, the man she said would provide the fireworks, had brought. She welcomed Thaddeus and Kelly with a wave from across the lawn, as if she were flagging down a train. They walked over to her, and she embraced Thaddeus, and then, after the slightest hesitation, Kelly.

Frye entered a moment later. He offered Lurlene a bottle of Lagavulin as a gift. "I bring regrets from Bill Mundy. He's unfortunately suffering a migraine." This was said without the faintest trace of mendacity. He kissed her cheek. She looked at Thaddeus and winked.

Gina was already there with Claudette, standing by one of the grills. The Ruark brothers were there, too.

Thaddeus stepped to the makeshift bar and asked for a glass of rye. There was no rye, so he said, "Irish?"

"I got bourbon, and I got Scotch," the bartender said. He was burnished looking, rich deep brown in color, thickly built, with little definition. His large, kind eyes were very dark.

"Scotch, then," Thaddeus said. "And can I have another when I finish?"

The big man smiled. "According to Ms. Lurlene, you can have six. To start."

Thaddeus took his one glass, grinning, and then sipped from it. "I thank you, sir, from the bottom of my heart."

"You're welcome, young man, from the bottom of mine."

Gregory Ruark came over. "I see you brought Ms. Gordon," he said, low. "What's she like?"

Thaddeus said, "She's very direct. And Reuben Frye is not her mentor."

A little later, Gina walked over and stood at his side. She had a can of beer.

"Having fun?" Gina asked him.

He talked about the bluntness of Frye's protégé, feeling himself striving for the old feeling of their closeness, as it had always been in gatherings like this, the pair of them appreciating, without malice, the eccentricities and absurdities all around them.

In a flat voice, she said, "You can be so judgmental."

He stared at her. Then: "You mean judgmental as in, oh, let's say, arbitrarily and without friendly intention deciding that somebody who loves you and who happens to be *confiding* in you is judgmental? Is that what you mean? I couldn't quite take it in, love."

She sipped the beer, not looking at him.

"I wonder if you'd have this reaction if anyone *else* said it to you."

Claudette walked over from the grill. "I wish I was hungry. What're you guys jabbering about."

Thaddeus and his wife answered at exactly the same time. "Not a thing," said Gina. "Judgmental people," Thaddeus said.

"Whoa. Hold on. I lost you both. What kind of people?"

"People like us," Thaddeus said through a tight mouth, and moved off.

A little later, Lurlene, fanning herself with a Mardi Gras marabou-feather fan she had brought home from the festival in February, introduced her girls: Dawn, twelve, and Caitlin, ten. They had been to New Orleans with her and were wearing blue-sequin Mardi Gras shorts, the same white T-shirts with a band of bright primary colors across the chest, and green flip-flops. They looked like twins: rosy cheeked, round faces, and blond curls. In those flimsy rubber sandals, they managed to do a dance together, singing "Diamonds are a girl's best friend." It was charming and completely unpretentious, and Lurlene watched them with tears in her eyes. Thaddeus had moved to the drinks table. He looked over at Gina, who'd finished her beer and was standing near the row of grills. He saw the blank way she took in the gathering, until Claudette spoke to her, offering her another can of beer. She took it and drank, and her face became the face he'd known so well, the interested, beautiful face. She laughed softly at something Claudette said. Claudette glanced over at him and, seeing that he was gazing at her, smiled and waved.

The party went on in the swelter of the afternoon. Thaddeus walked over to where Malcolm and Lurlene were standing, arms folded, smiling and talking low. He joked about wishing the real summer heat would arrive, and pretended to shiver. As she laughed politely, he recognized that he had interrupted them.

"I guess it'll work out," she said.

Malcolm, apparently continuing their previous conversation, said, "Anyway. I'm hoping to occupy soon."

"I'm sorry," the theater manager said to them. "I just walked up and barged in."

"Don't be silly," Lurlene said.

They were quiet for a few moments.

Thaddeus saw his wife cross to the far side of the lawn, and sit in the little arbor there, on the bench swing. Claudette joined her. They laughed about something. He lifted his gaze to the white sky, feeling as though he had been spying. But he couldn't keep from looking back at them. Claudette was talking fast, and Gina looked concerned, but then they laughed again. After a few more moments, one of Lurlene's girls approached them, carrying in each hand a cone of already melting ice cream. She offered the cones, and Gina smiled, putting one hand up, palm out. The girl ran off with her ice cream, and Thaddeus wandered over to stand near Claudette's shoulder. He heard her saying to Gina that she adored the nurse she'd hired. The nurse and Ellis were best buds.

"Ellis has a lot of time left," he told her, without looking at Gina. "Especially now that he's with you."

"Franny doesn't think so. And she's brought my sister and her husband into it. She keeps talking about some kind of action."

"There's nothing she can do, though, is there?"

Gina got up and crossed the lawn again, to the table of food.

"Everything all right?" he asked Claudette.

She took a few seconds. "We were talking about our respective parents. Our mothers—hers visiting, and mine, so far away in Paris."

"Nothing about me?"

She looked at him and tilted her head slightly.

"I know," he said. "Isn't it strange that I have to ask you that? And I live with her."

Lurlene had arranged for the neighbor friend to set off his fireworks. He was very tall and had a stiff gray ponytail trailing halfway down his back. Because the crown of his head was bald, he looked as though he had a starched scarf attached to the back of his head. The hot day had evolved into a stifling night, and you could easily believe the flaming coals in the grills had contributed to it. The air seemed nearly incendiary. Even so, the neighbor lit a bonfire in the center of the lawn, and when it was fully blazing, Lurlene walked out to stand within the circle of shifting radiance, smoke rising with live-looking embers in it. Above everything, in a scattering of puffy clouds, the moon looked like a thin white smile at the top of the sky. She got everyone's attention and, after a moment's silence, began talking about the family they all were and thanking everyone for coming. "My girls," she added, "have informed me that they want to say something else. I didn't plan this. I think it's an Independence Day poem? Is that right, Dawn?"

Dawn held a piece of notepaper in her hand. She stepped into the brightness of the bonfire, turned, and drew her younger sister in close. Then, looking at their grandmother, she straightened, shoulders back, handed the piece of paper to Caitlin, murmuring to her. The two of them stood there a moment, Dawn quietly urging her younger sister to begin. Caitlin read in a clear but slightly tremulous voice: "We're glad you're here to help us to behave, and give us everything you have each day. We think you're grand and good and fun and brave. And this is what we both would like to say." She handed the piece of paper to Dawn, whose voice was loud and strong: "Please, dear Grams, we do not lack, don't cry once more, or fret. We love you to the moon and back, and don't forget." Both girls then said, in unison, "We always will."

Lurlene, weeping, gathered them to her, and everyone cheered and applauded. After it grew quiet again, she managed to say, "I hope you like the rest of the show."

The neighbor then began setting off rockets. The streaks of light and fire climbed the sky, then bloomed into exploding shapes of sparkle fanning out and falling.

Through the following several days, the theater manager and his wife went through the motions of being a couple. That was how it felt to him. In the middle of the week, Louisa and the Reverend Whitcomb went across the street to spend some time at Louisa's friend's house, where Louisa would cook trout almondine for the two of them. Perhaps spurred by the sweetness of what they had witnessed at Lurlene's party, Thaddeus and Gina took advantage of the night alone; it seemed to him that it was the first time in his marriage that he had ever thought of it not as making love, but as "having sex." She got up immediately afterward and went into the bathroom to shower. And while she was quietly drying off, Louisa called to say she and the reverend were coming back over from the other house. After his shower, he found that she had simply gone to sleep. The whole house was asleep. He went quietly out and drove to the theater, and worked late, alone in his office. The next day they went separately to the theater. There were more construction delays and he had his own tasks regarding sponsors, and plans for the fall season. He and Gina were polite with each other, considerate, even intimate—there would be an hour or two when she seemed herself, and he could almost believe they might come all the way back. But he couldn't find a way to discern what was missing; and the thought of how it really was between them brought him low, every time. Something would close down in her eyes, usually after something he did or didn't do, and a pall would descend on them. He began wanting a fight. Something to bring it all to a head, some sort of catharsis. But he wouldn't act on it. She was waking in the nights, now, and since he wasn't sleeping much, he knew it. But she wanted no talk about any of it. They went on, sullenly considerate. Her restlessness and the flatness of her spirit seemed more unbridgeable all the time—though he had observed that she was rather steadily herself in company—which was uncanny, and scary. There seemed two distinct versions of her: Gina edgy with Thaddeus, Louisa, and the Reverend

Whitcomb; and Gina the pleasant, beguiling woman with everyone else. He had heard her laughing.

The two of them rarely spoke anymore with the careless confidence in each other that they had once possessed. Everything seemed freighted with the unspoken distress. One night, as he was going in and she was coming out of the bathroom, he tried a joke: "Just ships," he said, "pissing in the night."

Her laugh was more of a sigh.

She was easily made tearful whenever they did come close to talking about anything not directly connected with work or the sensible routines of the day. And finally he didn't want to know what she might be harboring. It seemed clear that she was feeling a pull toward Frye.

He felt this in the walls of his heart.

At the theater, everybody was having to deal with the clutter and rattle of what was proceeding so glacially, the last of the renovation. The heat of July in Memphis took everyone's energy, it seemed; and the whole city lay roasting under a merciless clear white sky, the flowers and blooms losing their freshness, beginning to wilt, the fragrances of magnolia and crepe blossom and honeysuckle fading in the shiftings of wind off the river.

Friday morning he went alone into the theater and to his office, seeing only Lurlene, who had made coffee, and poured him some. She was solicitous, very gentle, without referring to anything. She talked about the girls and their summer; they were on a tour of sites in the city's history, organized as a summer program by their school.

In the late afternoon, back at the house after several wrangling meetings, one with city officials about the problem of black mold in the old downstairs restroom, and whether or not simply to take out the plumbing and turn it into a storage closet, he lay on the couch in the living room with his cell phone and tried calling his mother. No answer.

He wanted very much to quieten his mind. He watched his hand tremble, putting the phone down on the coffee table, and decided that he would require a Xanax. Instead, he took the old bottle of RJ's bourbon from the cabinet in the kitchen and drank from it. A good swallow, which warmed him all the way down. The insects were shrill out the windows, a racket he didn't hear, and then did. He turned on the air-conditioning and sat at the kitchen table with a pitcher of milk. He didn't know where Louisa and the reverend were. He knew that Gina was with Frye, ostensibly going over set designs for *Three Tall Women*. He tried to assure himself that Kelly would be there, too, since she was the director. His pulse was seventy-two. There wasn't anything on television, and he was in no mood for it anyway. He went into the bedroom and lay on the bed for a while, and found himself thinking of being dead in an abstract, adolescent way. He sat up and looked at himself in the mirror across the room. "Ridiculous," he said, and lay back down. The next moment, in a fantastic turn of his mind, it seemed that in spite of everything she was with him there, doing something in the other room. And then it wasn't any house he recognized: the room had folded into night. He watched green shade change into a midnight far from anything he knew. There was a window, and outside he saw night and a street, and sodium-vapor lamps with clouds of insects. He spoke to someone standing in shadow at his side about everything he'd lost—happiness, excitement, the peace of knowing what was expected and what you could reasonably expect in return—and realized the someone was his biological father, gone before he was born. He spoke to the shape, and the words were strangely tinged with an explanatory tone, as if to be reassuring. Except they made no sense, had no context at all. "You must be really late."

He sat up suddenly in the darkness, hearing them all come in. Gina and her mother were arguing. He felt great relief that he had been asleep, and then was cast down by the acrimonious tone of Gina's voice. She was arguing with Whitcomb again, baiting him. Rising quietly from the bed, he went down the back stairs and out into the yard. He saw them through the window, all three standing in the living room, trying to talk over one another. Gina put her hands to her ears. He turned and went out to the sidewalk, and around the block, looking at the houses and yards, and the people sitting in living rooms or relaxing on front porches.

Finally, he drove to the theater. It was quiet inside, with few lights, and it smelled of fresh paint; there had been work on the black box stage in preparation for the four weekends of the winning play for that venue. In his office, the rose in its little vase was losing its petals, but amazingly its fragrance still lingered. Or perhaps he was imagining it. A note from Lurlene said that the winner of the new works contest had interest from

Chicago and may want to withdraw his entry, to have it premiered up north.

He sat at his desk in the pool of light from the lamp and wrote an answer: *Let Dylan Walters take his farce where he wants*. Then, as if simply to be busy, he made a list of possible plays for coming seasons, but finally realized the fruitlessness of it. It would all have to be discussed.

Gina called his cell. "Yes?" he said.

"Where are you? Where'd you go? Your car was here when we got here. Did you sneak out?"

"I didn't have to sneak. You all were making that completely unnecessary."

"Are you at the office?"

"I'm at my office."

"Louisa wanted to have a whiskey with you."

"Next time," he said.

"I'm going to bed," she told him. "Don't wake me when you come in."

Past ten o'clock. He decided to head over to the Madison. As he was coming down the hallway toward the refurbished and expanded lobby, he heard a voice: "So that's it, then? That's—oh, God, that's it? That's fuck'n *it*?" The voice was coming from the new tech booth to the left of the doorway into the auditorium. It was Frye. Thaddeus moved soundlessly to the wall, pressing his back to it, and made a sliding motion, edging back.

"That's all you've got for me? Throw it away like this? You've been using again, haven't you. You're on it now. You were doing so well, honey. I haven't spent time with anybody. I swear to you. I haven't. Everybody's sacrosanct. I haven't touched anyone. I barely see them outside this place. No. Look—for God's sake. Kelly Gordon is *gay*. She's *gay*, Lauren. You know that. She volunteers that information, like a prize she won."

A long pause. Thaddeus kept to the wall, moving back as noiselessly as possible.

"I know," Frye said. "I get that. I know. I'm proud of you for it. But it hasn't even been—you were going to come *here*. That was the deal, right?"

Pause.

"But that was the idea. Wasn't it? Come on, Lauren. Don't—don't."

The theater manager made it to the entrance of the outer office, Lurlene's, got in, and shut the door quietly. Then he moved to the window in his own office, climbed out, and down the fire escape.

At the Madison, it was nearly closing time. Inside, he saw William Mundy sitting alone at the downstairs bar. He took a place, standing a few feet from him. The barkeep was someone he knew, a round-faced man named Pratt with a bald spot that made him look monastic; he was the personality of the place. He passed a bowl of peanuts along the bar. "What'll it be, old son?"

"Angel's Envy, finished rye. Neat."

Mundy was sipping coffee. He ordered another, holding out his cup. Pratt poured more coffee, then brought a bottle of Jameson from the row of bottles along the back and added a little of that to it. "Thanks," Mundy said. "For everything you've done *to* me and *for* me. I will not part with thee yet." He looked over at Thaddeus and nodded, smiling. Then he came over and sat on the stool next to him. "So, lad."

Pratt brought the rye over. "Open an inexhaustible tab?"

Thaddeus grinned. "Yeah, thanks, Pratt."

"To th'ladies," Mundy said. "What?"

They drank.

"Been here awhile?" Thaddeus asked, and there was no disguising the sarcastic nature of the question.

The older man nodded. "Oh, I'm quite drunk tonight, lad. Could say jus' felt like it. But it's an old custom b'fore first run-through. Lends residual courage."

"Really."

"Though one remains a bit destitute of spirit, I mus'say." He rested one elbow on the bar. "Whole mistake of a—" He stopped, held the coffee slightly higher, and drank. "I've decided—don't much like th'river city. Or ne'sarily anybody in it. Present comp'ny, for *c'nveenyence's* sake, excluded." He nodded.

Thaddeus took another sip of the rye. It didn't even sting, and he determined that he would have another when he finished this one.

"Still b'lieve Gone'ril," Mundy said, "should be"—he lowered his chin to his upper chest, belching—"removed."

"A dear friend of mine, as you know," Thaddeus told him, smiling, and keeping the smile. "Think you should head on back to where you're staying, sir?"

Mundy wasn't listening. He'd turned, extending an arm. "Ah!" he said, greeting Ernest Abernathy, who had emerged from the elevator doors coming down from the roof. He wore a white shirt with a bow tie. A moment later, Mona Greer came out, too, also in a bow tie, and a pair of too-tight blue jeans. The bow tie was wrapped around her bare neck. She was followed by Dylan Walters, with his bow tie undone and straggling down his front. He was wearing shorts. They all looked as though they had come from some sort of ersatz costume party.

Ernest, evidently seeing Thaddeus's puzzlement at the attire, said, "We're celebrating the winner of the black box competition, and the fact that it's getting interest all over the place." He turned to the tall complacency of the former box-office clerk, who looked strangely boneless. "There he is."

Thaddeus remembered that when Walters worked the box office, he had a persistent air of being put upon when fielding requests.

"Bravo the winning play, and young Dylan," Kelly Gordon pronounced, coming from the elevators. Her blouse was open beneath her own bow tie, in a steep V down the front, and her hair was in a chignon that had come a little loose. "They've closed the roof. Sent us packing."

"We've all come to understand that our big task is to teach the whole audience how to sign," said Ernest Abernathy. "Curiouser and curiouser."

"I think I should be getting home, anyway. Two morning auditions for seconds in *Three Tall Women*. You all obviously"—she indicated Mundy—"have your work cut out for you." Then she noticed the theater manager. "Well. What're you doing here so late?"

Mundy said, "Bloke's alone 'n' on th'town, id'n ee? Wife gone south? I don'know."

She smiled at Thaddeus. "Wild life?"

Thaddeus started to correct her, but Mundy declared loudly, "Wild life!"

"You're disgusting," Mona said to him.

"Cordelia speaks." He dipped his head still again. "Cordelia has a voice!"

"Fuck off," she said. Then: "Hollywood."

"She had a couple at my place," Dylan Walters said.

Kelly Gordon said, "Well, it looks like you've all got the cards stacked against you." She indicated Mundy again. "First day of full rehearsal, and look."

Pratt asked, "You all want anything to drink?"

"Coffee," Abernathy said, too loud.

"Have to brew another pot."

"I'll have some, too," Kelly said.

Mundy held out one hand, palm up. "Love all th'lady d'rectors. Had good ones 'leven dif'rent episodes've *Home Away.*"

Thaddeus signaled Pratt for another whiskey, and called, "When you get a chance."

"You're all gonna hate yourselves in the morning," Kelly said.

"Actors," Dylan Walters said, and from his tone it was impossible to tell whether he meant derision or tribute.

Mona, Kelly, and the two men were standing so as to make a small circle—Mundy and the theater manager seated, and the little surrounding group. Now they each moved to take a seat at the bar. Pratt brought the rye over and poured more into Thaddeus's glass.

"I'd like another beer," Dylan Walters said.

Pratt got it for him.

"Just a li'l Irish by itself, if y'don't mind," said William Mundy. "While I wait for th'coffee."

Mona, on the other side of Walters, said, "I'll have some Irish."

"See your ID, please," Pratt said.

"Imagine," Mundy proclaimed. "This where they make th'bourbon 'n' she wants t'go"—he dipped his chin again with the silent belch—"Ireland."

She took a wallet out of the back pocket of the jeans, and began looking through it. Pratt stood waiting. At length, she put the wallet back. "Okay. Coffee."

Abernathy said, "Right. You got into some trouble with whiskey before, sister."

"I'm not your sister."

"Term of endearment. *Sister.*"

"Not to me."

"Tell us about the trouble you got in with the whiskey."

"Everybody already knows about the accident at the stop sign," Thaddeus said.

Kelly Gordon coughed into her fist, cleared her throat, and said, "Not me."

"We were drunk," Mona said. "Okay? My uncle was driving. We had this"—she made a gesture as if shaking off an annoying thought—"incident."

Thaddeus drank the rest of his whiskey, and nodded when Pratt offered the bottle.

Mona went on, as though addressing the room. Her tone was that of someone imparting new knowledge. "They all want the same thing and they're stunned when you show them you're just like they are. Even my uncle. He has this—this thing about me. Looks at me, all moony eyed. It made my mother crazy. She hates him like disease."

"You've had something to drink this evening," Thaddeus said. "Haven't you."

"Two beers," Dylan Walters said. "And two bourbons. Our place."

Mona was staring. "Okay," she admitted. "So what? Just fuck you all."

"What a nice—uh, nice person *she* is," Mundy said. "Abs'lutely stellar. Memphis women. Christos."

"I think everybody ought to just calm down," Kelly said. "We're all colleagues."

"Famous news guy, so needy," said Mona. "But when push comes to shove."

Thaddeus sipped the rye. "He's been very professional. And helpful."

"Has Mr. Ruark ever hit on you?" Abernathy asked. "Or did you hit on him?"

"Know 'bout that sort've thing," Mundy said. "Happ'ns all th'time to me. Cert'n ladies hit'n on th'star player."

Thaddeus smirked, and drank.

"What'd you do, Mona?" Abernathy persisted. "Little flirting?"

"Shut up, Ernest," she said. "Just shut up."

"Well, chickee-poo, you make it sound like he hit on you."

"He's been like a sick puppy around me," she told him. Then: "Chickee-poo."

Abernathy laughed softly.

Thaddeus said, "I think it might be best for us to change the subject."

"You still haven't answered the question," Abernathy said to her. "He ever hit on you?"

"Go fuck yourself. *Ernie*."

"Ev'body calm down," said Mundy, holding up his coffee cup. "Le's leave subject people hit'n on people. Unpleas'nt uz hell."

"You're barely able to stay upright," Mona snapped. "You're a walking cliché. The drunk lead actor." Then she turned to Thaddeus. "You don't understand anything."

"What I understand," the theater manager said, "and what I've observed is that your uncle doesn't seem interested in anything but *watching out* for you." He brought his glass up and took a sip, purposely avoiding her gaze.

"You can all just fuck off," she said.

Pratt brought the fresh coffee and poured it for Abernathy, Mona, Kelly, and Mundy. He offered it to Thaddeus, who put one hand up. "I'll have a little more rye."

"More Irish for me, too," Mundy said. "'N'th'coffee."

Pratt took care of it.

As he did so, four people came in, three women and a man, all in late middle age. They were talking over one another, it seemed. He was short, round, and dark, with a shaved head. He wore a navy-blue pin-striped suit and red tie, and the women were in virtually identical electric-blue evening gowns. They had probably come from something at the Orpheum Theatre, past Beale Street, and were all evidently staying at the hotel. The man asked if it was too late to get one drink. Pratt said it wasn't. They sat in a booth along the wall, and he went over to take their orders.

"Here's to all actors," Mundy said. "Here's t'the great old days at th'Vick."

"You all're theater people?" one of the women called out. She was blocky but thin armed. Heavy through the hips. She labored getting out of the booth and approached them, peering at Mundy. "I *thought* I recognized you. You're *Home Away*. The grumpy grandfather."

He smiled widely. "Heyyy. H'lo. How d'you do?"

Everything about her was sharp angled, it seemed; her collarbones showed at the base of her neck. "Yeah, the grumpy grandfather." She turned to the others. "Hey, the *Home Away* guy."

The others merely smiled tolerantly and went on talking low.

Mundy expanded his chest and raised his cup. "I confess t'being that p'tic'lar item of mort—*hal*-ity."

"That show filmed here?"

"No. I'm—uh—here—just now"—belch—"uh, t'play King Lear at th'new Globe."

Mona said, "Can you excuse us, please? We were talking."

"Don't worry," Mundy said quietly to the woman. "Happy t'talk."

"Well, I do have a couple questions. I love the series."

"Thank you from th'bott'm of my—uh, soul. Such as't is."

Mona said to Thaddeus, in a voice that was now a register higher, "Does my uncle talk about me?" Her boyfriend came off his stool, stepped around the thin-armed woman, who flinched slightly as he passed, and faced Thaddeus.

"Yeah. What about that?"

"This isn't your business, Dylan," Mona said.

He stepped back with a facial expression so hangdog that he looked rather stupid. Thaddeus felt an urge to laugh.

The thin-armed woman spoke to Mundy. "Will it have still another season, do you think?"

He nodded. "Ev'body's happy."

"I hope you won't be doing it in this condition," the woman said, starting to move off.

Mona said, "My uncle's a liar if he told you anything."

"We haven't discussed you," said Thaddeus. "What would he have told me?"

Mundy turned to them, looking a little downcast to have been dismissed by the woman. "Think he'll be ex'lent." He held up his cup again as if to toast. "Here's t'Mr. Malcolm Ruark."

"Malcolm Ruark," the woman said, and came striding back. "Oh, I know *his* story. A regular womanizer."

"There," Mona said.

Thaddeus tried to concentrate on his glass of rye.

"How is it," Kelly said to Mona, "that you feel you can talk about him like this—in a bar, no less? He's your colleague now, whatever the family relationship is. Whatever your previous history is. You've had too much to drink. So, maybe, just now, silence is best for you."

"I can talk all I want about him or anybody."

"Oh," the woman with the narrow arms exclaimed, turning to Mona. "You're the girl, ain't you. The one. The girl in the newspaper stories. You're the one."

"I much prefer talk'n 'bout *Home Away*," Mundy said. "Tha's my vote."

"I haven't had too much to drink," said Mona to Kelly and Thaddeus. "So, just forget it."

"Your mama still hate Mr. Malcolm like disease?" Abernathy wanted to know. "Now that you're in this production together?"

"My mother wants to charge him with statutory *rape*." Her voice was loud, and definite.

Everyone stopped, then, even the other people in the booth, who had been happily ordering drinks and appetizers while bantering softly among themselves and with Pratt.

"That's what I thought," the woman said, nodding and putting her hands on her hips. "That's what I thought from the beginning. No matter *what* the newspapers said."

Kelly turned back to her coffee and seemed to fix on it. Thaddeus could see she wanted to remove herself.

Mona said, low, "You don't know anything." Now she sounded sullen, grudging. She glanced at the woman, and across the bar at Pratt.

"Has he ever touched you in an inappropriate way?" Thaddeus asked.

Everyone waited for her answer.

"No."

"Ever tried to coerce you?"

"Look, what *is* this?"

"I'm just asking you, as a colleague, let's say." He nodded at Kelly, who had stood away from the bar.

Mona gave a frustrated sigh. "He looks moony eyed at me, and gets sad, like I said. And when I was recovering from the injuries that *he* caused me, he kept coming over to my house and sitting in his car watching, like a stalker."

"That's creepy," said the woman. "That's really, really creepy."

"S'a bit creepy," said William Mundy.

"My mother thinks stalking's the next closest thing," Mona said.

"S'cuse me?" Mundy seemed genuinely confused, now.

"You know what I mean, no matter what you say. The next thing. The nearest thing."

"Whoa," Ernest Abernathy said. "Let's back that shit up." He paused. "Chickee-poo."

"Stop calling me that."

"Wouldn't say tha's nearest thing," Mundy said. "Nearest thing? Hell. F'give me. Just would never say so. Anyone'n God's pretty green earth say so? An'one in 'mediate v'cinity say so?"

"Are you all just going to gang up on me?"

"Come on, guys," said Abernathy.

"Well, I, for one, think it's creepy," the thin-armed woman said. "Extremely creepy. I mean it would creep me out."

From the booth, the man called to her, "Hey, Marva. Come on."

"Hold your water," she said.

"Poss'bly bit creepy," Mundy said. "No more'n that, though. That Mont'gue lad, Romeo, did spend a bit've time under th'Capulet lass's balc'ny after all."

"She wasn't Romeo's niece," the woman named Marva said. "And Malcolm Ruark sure ain't no Romeo, neither, let me tell you."

Mundy seemed impressed. "You"—still once more, the silent, chin-dipping belch—"you f'miliar wi'the play *Romeo an' Juliet*?"

"Of course."

"Well. So. There't is. Not so"—belch—"creepy, then. Actually. Right?" He looked at Mona. "You're not blood r'lated—i'n' that so?"

"I wouldn't like it," Marva insisted.

"S'jus not that creepy."

"Well, you're—"

Mona spoke over her to Mundy, "You *would* say that. Being yourself the nearest thing."

"S'cuse *me*?" he said. He put one hand, fingers widely spread, to his chest.

"You heard me."

"Man," Abernathy exclaimed. "Let's just calm down. Jesus."

Thaddeus stepped from the bar and faced her. "I'm the manager of the theater. And, pardon me, but you're way out of line."

She glowered at him.

"Hold it, now," the woman said. "Just hold it. Malcolm Ruark is no Romeo. Let's just establish that. He's a womanizer."

"Excuse us," Thaddeus said, and took Mona by the elbow to draw her aside. She pulled away violently, and seemed about to scream.

"I saw that," the woman broke forth. "You all saw that. That's just creepy. Stand your ground, girl."

"May I speak to you, please, Mona?"

"Don't let him, girl. He's creepy."

"Ev'body's creepy by turns," Mundy said. He stood away from the bar and, bowing to the woman, gestured for her to step a little to one side with him.

"If you think someone's crossed a line," Thaddeus said, low, to Mona, "there's a way to deal with it. And it doesn't involve throwing accusations around in a bar, with too much to drink."

"I have not had too much to drink," she said in that sullen tone.

"Has anyone violated your personal space or touched you inappropriately or said anything to threaten or coerce you?"

"This isn't a courtroom."

"I'm asking you as a colleague. And as manager of the theater."

She hesitated, looking around resentfully at the others. Then: "You're not the boss. You just do scheduling and programming and fundraising stuff."

"I'm manager of the new Globe Theater of Memphis," Thaddeus said. "You are the newest member of the company and I have every right to ask you, has anyone harassed you in any way?"

Mundy waved at the woman as she started to move away. "Thank you, kindly. I don' know any more'n you do—y'know, what's'n th'papers."

Thaddeus went on quietly to Mona. "Does your uncle have the slightest idea that you talk about him like this?"

She brought one hand to the side of her face, then looked past him at the bar, where Dylan Walters had put his head on his folded arms, as if shamed into quiet. And where the director of *Three Tall Women* stood drinking her coffee.

Thaddeus said, "Well?"

Even the four other people were quiet and staring, now. The thin-armed woman, Marva, had gone back to sit in the booth.

"We're waiting," Thaddeus said.

Mona stepped toward him, her eyes cloudy and unfocused. "Jesus," she said. "Can you please forget I said any of this?"

Mundy had turned so that his back was to the bar, elbows leaning on it. "I find the man extremely interesting and kindly, myself." The slurring had, for that moment, left his speech. He took a breath, and continued, "An' he seems a little, well, almost sheepish. And just a bit creepy, I c'n admit tha' much. Think he worries some sorta deal uz made 'cause he was a TV news bloke."

From the booth, the woman named Marva said, "Malcolm Ruark, from WMC. A drunk and a druggie. And a womanizer." She touched lightly her own high crown of dark hair. "Let's just say that this city, Memphis, is a major American city and all that, but it's also like a small town, and I've had dealings with your WMC newsman."

"Please," Mona said, looking around. "Please. I didn't mean any of it. I don't know why." She faced Mundy. "I didn't mean—"

Marva said from the booth, "Girl, you said *rape*. That ain't a word you throw around."

Mona stood with her hands tightly clasped at her waist. "I didn't mean it. I didn't. Please. He's always been a perfect gentleman. Please don't tell him."

"You can see she's afraid of him," Marva said. "That's coercion. He's got her so the only time she can say the truth is when she's drunk. If that ain't coercion, I don't know what is. And he's the type. Believe me. Malcolm Ruark is just the type. And his older brother's a homosexual. I know that, too, for a fact."

The others in her booth had paused, and were staring at her.

"Madam," William Mundy said with perfect diction, now. "It is my duty to inform you that you have been preempted by the R'pooblican P—*harrrttay*."

She simply glared as Thaddeus burst into laughter. The whiskey was having its effect on him.

"Unfort'nate state've affairs," Mundy continued. "An' I don' lik't either, but there it is." He belched again, quite loud this time, no dipping of his chin. It was as if he'd hurled it at her.

Thaddeus was trying not to laugh as Mona began talking again. "My uncle"—she stopped, and then reached to grab hold of the bar—"never has done anything but try to help me. He's been my friend and I'm not coerced. He's my friend."

"Well, hell. Some friend *you've* been, then," the woman said.

Pratt approached them carrying a tray with their drinks. "She didn't mean any of it," he said. "Look at her. It was booze talking."

"Booze tells the truth, honey."

"Madam, what was your name again?" Mundy asked.

She told him.

"Marva," he repeated it. "Good." He raised his cup. "Marva. Here's to all us theater folks, tonight—ev'n ones I don' fancy a-tall. And you may now do us"—his chin dipped into his neck (it was almost like a form of gestural punctuation, now)—"the great, the inest—inest—in—in*est'*mable courtesy—of shutting the fuck *up*."

Again, Thaddeus heard himself laugh. Marva started to rise, but one of the other women in the booth took her arm. "Please, Marva. Just let's have a drink and let this alone."

"Marv'lous idea," Mundy said. "Marva."

Mona had put both hands to her face.

For what seemed a very long time, no one spoke. Pratt came to stand before Thaddeus with the bottle of Angel's Envy. Thaddeus shook his head. "Just the bill. And thanks."

"It's all right," Mundy was saying to Mona, facing the bar again, both arms folded on it, and looking over at her where she stood. "You just got li'l tight."

Walters raised his head, where he'd rested it on his arms. "What's happened now."

"Shut up, Dylan," Mona said. She turned to Thaddeus. "Promise you won't say anything. I didn't know what I was saying. I had whiskey before. I didn't mean it." There was something cloying in her tone that made Thaddeus wonder if Malcolm Ruark's feelings mattered to her at all.

Thaddeus paid his bill, thanked Pratt, and went to the door to leave them all there. Kelly followed him out.

"Walk me to my car?" she said.

They went down to Third Street, and over to Union. He saw the reddish strands that had come loose from the chignon. Her gait was slow, almost languid. There was a tiny droplet of sweat on the side of her face. She wiped it away, like a tear. They paused at the corner.

"I've been trying to decide if I should tell you something."

He looked at the ridiculous bow tie at the base of her bare neck, and was silent.

"It would be like a warning, sort of, or a heads-up. But I think you should know about it. There's something going on back at Holliwell."

"Does it have to do with Frye's wife?"

She took a moment. "Well, not directly." The light changed, and she started across. He followed, still slightly behind her. As they stepped up on the other side, she paused and turned. They could look up Beale. Her eyes sparkled in the light from the street; they were the color of hot chocolate. "Some women I know," she went on. "These women—three former students—are talking harassment charges."

"Oh, Jesus. As if we didn't already have enough with Mundy."

"Really." She stared.

He was silent, wishing he hadn't spoken.

"Well, actually, I'm not surprised at that, either. But he's mostly innuendo. He almost never really acts on anything."

"He tried to kiss Claudette Bradley. Tried to force it."

She shrugged. "Normally, he doesn't have to force anything. Must've been a real shock to him. You think that's why he's drunk in there?"

"He said something about it being his custom the night before it all begins in earnest."

"I think I read that somewhere."

They said nothing for a moment. He was looking at her eyes as she gazed back toward where they'd come from, as if wanting to be sure they hadn't been followed.

"Personally, I don't find him all that impressive."

"No," he said.

She sighed. "Anyway, this other business is something I heard from one of the girls. They're talking about making some noise together."

He looked up the street, with its bright lights going on to Main, and the people in front of the cafés, the different strains of music rising to the night sky, and abruptly he was experiencing the full effects of the whiskey. "Can you keep it to yourself?" He wasn't certain that he'd spoken clearly. "At least until your friends actually do whatever they're gonna do?"

She stepped closer, and took hold of his wrist. "You all right?"

"Fine," he said.

"You looked like you were gonna fall over."

"No," he got out. "Fine."

She let go, and spoke from another sigh. "Well, they're worried about his wife. What it might do to her. A couple of them know her. She's got her own troubles, you know. Whole thing's hideous."

He had a bad moment of wondering what she might already have said to Frye. "Have you spoken to anyone else?"

She shook her head. "Not a soul."

"Not Frye?"

"I said not a soul."

"And you will keep it to yourself awhile?"

She gave a little half smile. "Holliwell Academy's rotting from the inside, it seems. Funding in the tank really since the meltdown back in '08. That's really why he wanted this gig."

"Let's hope it doesn't explode in our faces."

Her smile deepened; the dark eyes glinted. It was a subtly burning gaze, an invitation in the soft lamp glow, even with the subject of their talk. Perhaps *because* of the subject of their talk. "Don't worry," she said, one eyebrow slightly raised.

He felt something change in the little space between them, a flicker, but he believed it was certain. As far as she knew, he was alone. He looked at the little smile on her lips. No, he told himself, this was merely how she conducted herself. "Well," he said, moving away. "Thanks."

"I'll let you know." She hesitated. "Bye-bye. And I *did* say I was bi." The brow-lifting smile.

He stopped in the middle of the street and took in her slyly salacious grin, then turned and went on. From the other side, he saw her enter the parking lot beyond that corner, near the entrance to Handy Park. He felt suddenly a little sick. Heading back toward the theater, he said, as if addressing someone: "Ridiculous. A marital spat, and you're tottering. You love your wife. Christ. You are *in love* with your wife."

———

The days passed in a broil of sun and annoyance, with Louisa, Marcel, and the Rightwing Reverend Wrong—as Gina now regularly referred to him—in their part of the house, and Thaddeus and Gina in theirs (*they* were also fairly well separated; he was spending most of his time in his study off the master bedroom). Everyone was trying, rather reflexively, to avoid too much contact. Thaddeus drove into the theater an hour after Gina did each morning, and usually returned a couple of hours before her. All this time he'd kept to himself what he'd overheard of Frye's phone conversation, and what Kelly had imparted. He didn't want to talk about Frye at all. Frye was at rehearsal and with the tech people and the effects companies most of each day. He had said he wanted the play to be muted, along with the Cordelia muteness—the effects would be accomplished mostly with lights, and flashes to suggest lightning, and Lear's raving on the heath would be spoken almost in a stage murmur while the visual tumult went on. All to reflect the state of Cordelia's aural deficiency. Mundy claimed he was glad of this. "It'll be good not to shout for the hurricanoes, which sounds like a football team: Hurricanoes ten, Swansea Thunderbolts zero." He seemed in better humor, almost light-hearted, and Frye said something about how good it was for everyone to be at work. The choreography for the battle and sword-fight scenes was progressing. Thaddeus, for the most part, kept to his own office, dealing with the contractors in the last stages of the renovation; a subcontractor had again miswired something, this time in the control panel, and it kept shorting out. Gina was revising designs for *The Christmas Pageant;* the theater manager and his wife said little to each other when the tasks and the hours brought them into the same rooms.

All the tension and discontent between them seemed to be gathering with a kind of unbearable blind inertia, and he'd never felt anything so powerful as the dread of being without her.

Except that he was already without her.

She was unrecognizable. And still there continued the sense of two versions of her: the one she showed everyone at the theater, and the one she showed him at home, with her mother, and Whitcomb.

She had worked late a couple afternoons with Frye, and maybe Frye was hitting on her, as he had done to the young female students at Holliwell; probably he was already telling her about his own troubled marriage. It seemed logical that she would in turn be telling him about hers.

Troubled marriage.

It was all so terribly ordinary. So ridiculous.

Gina had finalized, and Frye had approved, several sets and scene shifts on the main stage, and she was supervising the last work to complete them. The grand drape—burgundy-colored thick velour, with a darker-reddish teaser—the tormentor and backdrop curtains, had all been hung; rehearsals were getting smoother; the blocking had been finalized. There had been a couple of dry run-throughs, with only a few snags. Presently, they were working the scenes at Dover when the king wakes from his tormented sleep and is reunited with Cordelia, and the scene where Edmund, after the battle, orders that the king and his daughter be slain. The actors had accommodated themselves to the changes involving the Fool's presence. Indeed, they seemed to be taking over a little, probably because of the recent change in Frye's demeanor. Frye had entered a phase of intermittent lapses of attention; indeed, he seemed a little passive. People wondered what was on his mind, and of course Thaddeus knew what it was.

At the house, he heard Louisa cough downstairs, and thought of her and RJ. Their many years together. A long, combative, adversarial-seeming procession of instances. Louisa had often talked about those days. They had lived modestly that whole prosperous time as if financial ruin was looming. According to their one daughter, though they had always been quite manifestly discordant, they were also consistently interested in each other. Thaddeus himself could recall them managing even their hardships with a kind of elemental belief in good things awaiting them, the worth of what they were doing, fighting and quarreling and bickering through the better part of each day.

He sat quiet and gloomily reflective in the little office down the hall from the upstairs bedroom, which was such a dreary place these days, and it occurred to him with the force of an inkling from preconscious childhood memory that, in spite of all their failings and eccentricities, RJ and Louisa had been right about almost everything.

Now he heard Gina come in downstairs, and right away she was arguing with her mother about the increasingly ill-tempered dog. He heard

Louisa say, "I think he senses the unrest in these rooms and your unhappiness with everything."

"I wish I *felt* unhappiness," Gina said. "I don't feel anything. Only this immense weariness."

"I understand love's good for that."

"Oh, God, Mother."

Silence.

Thaddeus waited for the sound of Whitcomb moving around, but there was just the quiet, the little stirrings of air at the window.

The next night, unable to sleep, he poured a glass of cold Tavel and went into the living room. He was sitting on the sofa, thinking of turning on the television, when Louisa walked in, sipping a whiskey. She made a startled sound when she saw him. "Jesus, Young Fighter, are you trying to give someone a heart attack?"

"I'm sorry."

"My dear beau, Elias Whitcomb sounds like a horse with asthma." She sat down in the chair to his left, sipped the drink, and smiled at him. "I should go back and let you have some peace, Young Fighter."

"Hey, beauty, this is your house."

She sipped again.

"Do you mind if I ask—I've never asked this. It always pleased me so much. But why do you call me that? Young Fighter?"

She tilted her head slightly, still smiling. "RJ was Old Fighter."

"Oh."

"You didn't know that?"

He shook his head. "I don't think I ever heard you call him that."

"I guess I'd stopped calling him that when you joined the family. Isn't that odd. He knew what I meant calling you that."

"I always loved it, Louisa."

"Everything okay?" she asked, leaning toward him slightly.

"Sure," he lied. "Couldn't sleep."

"What's that you're drinking?"

"Tavel." He held it up. "Rosé."

They were quiet. He watched her gaze into the whiskey.

Presently, he said, "Forgive me—"

She looked at him. "Forgive you for what?"

"Has Gina said anything to you about Frye?"

She looked down. "Gina doesn't volunteer, and I don't ask."

"What *does* she talk about with you?"

"Nothing to worry about, Young Fighter. She's in one of her darks. Go meet her there."

"I've tried. She doesn't want me there." He saw her thumb moving slightly on the side of the glass. "I'm worried Frye might've met her there."

She smirked. Then: "Sometimes you have to talk *at* a person a little. Keep going till they hear you. That's what I always say, anyway."

"I don't think she loves me anymore." He hadn't known he would say this. He felt like choking. He took a deep drink of the Tavel.

Louisa reached across, over the small space that separated them, and touched his arm. "She loves you, baby."

"But I don't think she's *in* love anymore."

Louisa sat back slowly. "No, she's married. And—but you want Romance. That's your God-given right, too, isn't it."

He hid his distress, smiling. "It's in the Declaration of Independence. *Life, Liberty and the pursuit of Romance*."

"That's the Young Fighter I know," she said. "The man with humor. Let's tell some stories. Be adventurous. That's what RJ liked about you. You reminded him of himself at your age. You were adventurous. Going off to New York to try acting and then starting school, and traveling. God, he loved to travel. You know, when he traveled to the Philippines with LBJ, he ate something called a balut, and he was the only one on the whole staff who'd try it. Adventurous. You know what a balut is?" She didn't wait. "It's a fertilized duck egg. There's a lot of jellylike stuff and yolk inside, and also a tiny duck—head and neck, you know, the whole awful bloody little creature, bones and all." She shuddered. "And he'd say—telling it—he'd say you just pop it in your mouth and chew. Made me sick, him talking about it. Makes me sick *now,* talking about it. But he did it. Claimed he ate three of them. And he said they were good."

They both laughed a little. Thaddeus finished the Tavel and tried very hard not to think about the balut.

"He actually said it was good." She shook her head, remembering.

The old woman's ways, her memories of RJ, always distracted him; it actually lightened his mood being around her.

He stood and leaned over to kiss the side of her face. "I'm glad you're here, Louisa."

Her smile seemed faintly sad. He started upstairs. Perhaps he would sit in his study and read. But reading was out of the question, since every sound divided his attention. In the bedroom, he leaned down slowly and kissed the top of Gina's head, breathing the faint shampoo scent of her hair. She stirred, impatiently, it seemed—or maybe she was dreaming. She lifted slightly and looked at him over her shoulder. "You smell like booze."

"I couldn't sleep. I had a glass of wine. Your mother came in and we talked."

"I'm sleepy."

"Go back to sleep." He kissed her again, and she made a shrugging motion with her shoulder.

He sat on the bed for a moment, thinking about simply lying back. Forgetting everything. Trying just to go on. But sleep wouldn't come. He got up quietly and went into his office, to the computer. On the desk beside it were four copies of different paperback books of *Lear.* One was an old Norton Critical Edition from Gina's college days. He opened it and looked at the little notes in the margins and underlined passages about the play in performance through the centuries. It made him feel close to her, somehow.

He went back and slid soundlessly into the bed, lay very still, marking how quiet she was. "Babe?" he murmured.

No sound.

He said, low, "I haven't done anything wrong."

"Oh, please, Thaddeus. Just go to sleep. I'm exhausted."

The quiet in the room, and in the night, was like a pall. Perhaps a full minute later, he said, "I think I should move out."

There was another long, almost-unnatural-feeling quiet. Then he heard that she was crying. He put his hand to her shoulder, and then took it away. He heard Louisa cough at the foot of the stairs and knew she was crossing to go into the kitchen. She would make herself coffee at this hour of the night, and go out on the front porch and smoke a cigarette while she drank it. And then she would get into bed and fall asleep with the quickness and ease of an infant.

"I'm so tired." Gina sighed, crying.

"Good night," he told her. And he himself was crying, silently, hands over his mouth. The tears ran down the side of his face. Nothing to be done anymore, nothing to say. "Honey?" he murmured.

Silence, just her sniffling. And then her sleep-breathing.

He lay quite still, in awe at how terribly matter-of-fact it all seemed, the words spoken, the fact established. No sleep. He lay gazing at the unreal, moving angles of shadow on the walls of the room, the angles changing as breezes outside moved tree branches across a wide band of lunar light.

Malcolm

He had moved most of his clothes and sundries to the cottage on the edge of the Old Forest. But tonight he chose the efficiency. (He didn't want to see anybody for a time, and Eleanor Cruikshank had been outside when he went by the Old Forest cottage.) He came in and drank most of a quart of orange juice in long gulps, then started pacing and saying lines. New lines. During the day's rehearsals, Frye had decided that Malcolm should play Kent, and Gaylen McCarthy should play Albany. So there was a whole new part to internalize. He paced up and down, and faltered through the saying of the lines. Everything distracted him—the dirty glasses and coffee cups in the sink, the night racket out the window, the whir of the air conditioner. He did the dishes. Then stood thinking of Claudette, trying to construct a pretext to call her. But he wasn't playing Albany anymore. He decided he might go out again, and he called Gregory. "I'm either away from my phone," Gregory's rough-sounding recorded voice. "Or my phone is away from me. Leave your name and number and I'll get back." At the beep, he waited a moment, said, "It's me—give me a call when you can," and broke the connection. He thought about Mona, there was the scene between Kent and Cordelia at Dover—a reason to call her. He started to punch in her number, but stopped himself after four digits. You couldn't practice if one of the voices was mute. But he knew, too, that wanting to call her had nothing to do with the play. He felt the same heart-rush as someone barely avoiding an accident. And there was a brief freshet of guilt, too. Finally, he sat in the recliner and tried to sleep. It was too early, too humid. The insects were mad at the window, an enveloping clamor. Once more, he began pacing with the script, saying the lines, getting them wrong, and then saying them again. He had always, through the processes of line readings, learned most of the other parts, as nearly everyone else did. Nonetheless, the situation of Cordelia signing or being signed to, and the waiting while she struggled to figure out how to emote while signing, had compounded all the difficulties, and set everyone on edge.

Just now, he wanted badly to find a way not to feel so thirsty for a drink. He remembered a line from the poet John Berryman: *It is, after all, very simple. You just never drink again all each damned day.*

He phoned Gregory again, and this time Gregory answered, sounding groggy.

"I woke you."

Gregory said, "That's my 'don't bother me' voice for clients. I was out on the balcony. It's you. How good. What're you doing?"

"Nothing. I'm here trying to get comfortable with my lines and failing at it for some reason." As he told about his new rental, he heard the slight tremor in his own voice. "Anyway, I've moved everything *into* it, mostly. And now I have to get serious about subletting *this* place."

Gregory left a pause. Then: "You all right? What's going on at the theater?"

"Oh, a lot, you know. Frye changed my role. I'm Kent, now. So, stress, you know, one thing and another."

"Come over here. It's about time."

"You don't mind?"

"Should've asked way before this. Get over here."

The flickering neon signs of the liquor stores, it seemed, were purely meant to entice him. At Tennessee Street, he parked, and walked along the road in the opposite direction from the avenue that went up to the theater and the Madison. He thought of members of the company gathering in the rooftop bar, and wondered who might be there. He was curious to know how the other actors, especially Gaylen McCarthy, were reacting to the change of roles. He told himself it was important that he know. (Often enough, this kind of thinking had been his undoing.)

He hurried on, rejecting the thought, hands shoved down in his pockets, as if in flight from the powerful impulse that lurked just beyond the next minute. The hum of the city surrounded him like the hum of a big engine, and embedded in that sound was the music from Beale Street, the notes drifting on the breezeless air. To his right, the river and the bridge to Arkansas sparkled, and he could smell the algae in the moving water. Flat barges glided along slowly in the reflected shore light, looking like giant crocs.

His brother's loft residence was in the old Tennessee Riverside Apartments. Malcolm had been on this street only once, to pick up his mother the week of Albert Ruark's funeral. The artist's last wife, Adele, had been visiting his first son. Walking up to the building in the gray light, Malcolm tried unsuccessfully to remember why it was that he hadn't gone on that visit.

Gregory stood in buttery light on the balcony above him as he approached the first building. There were two women with him. One of the women held a glass of red wine. Both of them moved to the railing to gaze at him as Gregory headed down to the front door to let him in.

Malcolm waved uncertainly at the women, feeling his own deficiency and wondering if he'd made a mistake in coming here. The door opened, and Gregory stepped out to hug him. There was a hint of alcohol on his breath. "This makes me very happy, Malcolm."

"You've got company."

"I've also got plenty of sparkling water and finger food. Come on in."

Malcolm followed him up the narrow stairs, which opened into a big, rectangular room with a massive flagstone fireplace to the left. On the end table next to the couch was Eleanor Cruikshank's novel about Keats. Blue-framed French doors at the far end led onto the balcony, from which the two women presently entered, the one carrying her full glass. The bottle was on the slate coffee table, bounded by an open ledger book with pages spilling from it, and a platter of cheeses, cut vegetables, and dip. The bottle was claret shaped. Malcolm saw the dark shine of it, and then looked away.

Gregory introduced the women. Salina and Miranda.

"Remember me?" Salina joked. She shook hands and then sat in the wing chair next to the couch. "So glad I finally get to see you all grown up. I wish I'd seen you do the news. Just about everybody we run into says you were the best." She took a long slow sip of the wine. "Mmm." There was something so unmindful about the gesture that it seemed a form of cruelty, if not stupidity. He gazed at her sharp features, the strawlike stiffness of her hair. "Ah," she went on about the wine. "Frei Brothers Reserve Cabernet. Delicious."

"Wow, Salina," said Miranda with evident disbelief. "Have a little consideration."

"I reckon our celebrity anchorman's strong enough to be in company."

"My celebrity is overblown," Malcolm said, smiling. "Probably so is my strength."

Gregory poured himself a glass of milk, and offered the carton to him, indicating one of the glasses on the table. "It's almond milk. Vanilla flavored."

"No, thanks."

"That's what I'm drinking," said Miranda proudly about the milk, though she wasn't holding a glass. She plonked down on the sofa and bounced once, rubbing her hands together like someone anticipating a good time.

This was clearly the turn of a fresh mood; the three people were leaving something, some tone or moment, behind. Gregory sipped his almond milk and sat at the other end of the sofa. "It's pretty good," he said. "Maybe a little too sweet."

Malcolm heard nervousness in his brother's voice, and decided that coming here had indeed been a mistake.

"We're celebrating our new program to increase literacy in the schools," Salina said. "The Globe Shakespeare Theater of Memphis will be one of the greatest institutions in this city. Or any city."

"I'm glad to hear it." Malcolm took the benchlike seat next to the couch opposite her, intuitively assuming the manner of someone familiar with the place. To his left was the hearth, and he saw the pictures on the mantel of Gregory with various people, including one rather large one of their father, standing in bright sunlight with a tall, slim woman. Gregory's mother, no doubt. There was no picture of Salina.

On the coffee table, the open ledger book showed columns of figures. Salina reached over, stuffed the loose papers in, and shut it. "That's enough business." She slapped her hands together as if to remove dust from her palms, and poured more wine for herself.

"This is more of a social occasion anyway," Miranda said. "We've signed everything."

"Here's to the agreement," Salina offered, holding up her glass of wine. She drank, then looked at each of them. "I'm sorry. How cloddish of me. I'm the only one with wine now."

Miranda volunteered an aside about knowing when to stop, and then seemed to be returning to the subject that had been interrupted by Malcolm's arrival: "Anyway, we think we can raise the literacy rate by thirty or forty percent. Conservatively speaking. This sort of program has done just that in other cities. And we can run ads with famous people, asking for contributions, so it won't all depend only on our funds."

Salina looked at Malcolm. "You've met a lot of famous people in your line of work. Maybe you can give us some names for the campaign."

Malcolm heard himself say, "Well, I did get drunk with Peter O'Toole once, and ended up shutting a car door on his foot." A panicky rush ascended his spine. He was aware of himself as acting a part, someone calm, with stories to tell. Still, it *was* a true story. "For that particular night, anyway," he added, "we were pals."

"During your drinking days," Miranda said.

"We had a few, yes." He felt the color rising in his face, yet couldn't help the rush of needing to explain. "It was a long time ago."

Salina leaned toward him. "Are you okay?"

He worked the smile. "Fine."

"I know I can be hard to take sometimes. I'm sorry."

He shrugged, and felt the thin line of his own mouth.

"Well anyway," Miranda said, low. "Let's talk about something else."

Salina was still fixed on Malcolm. "I understand none of your former colleagues speak to you anymore. Bunch of cowards if you ask me."

"Actually," he said with a brittle smile, "I'd really like to hear about your school programs."

Noticing his eyes following the motion of her glass of wine, she put it down. "Forgive me. I thought it might offend you if I got all frazzled about drinking in front of you."

Gregory broke in, "It's nothing to make any fuss about."

"You're strong," Salina said. "Anybody can see that."

Malcolm crossed his legs, folded his hands on his knee, and simply smiled.

"Do you mind talking directly about it?" Salina asked him.

"Not at all."

"I can be pretty direct, I know—too direct."

"It's fine," Malcolm said.

"Well, right, because there's nothing about character in it at all. Any more than there is in an ulcer or an allergy. And people talk directly about those all the time. How's your allergy? It *is* a sort of allergy."

He nodded. And forced a smile. "Nothing to worry about," he managed.

"Are you still tempted?"

"I don't drink at all."

"But you *are* tempted."

He shook his head.

"I'm very glad I don't drink like you did, so I *can* drink."

"Well, I don't drink," he said again, forcing the smile.

"Anymore, right," she added, with her own smile. Then: "I'm sorry. Really."

"Nothing to apologize for."

"Well," she said, rising to her feet. "I'll just take this into the kitchen." She took the bottle and her glass and went toward the hallway leading to the other rooms, but she stopped and looked over at Malcolm. "Thing is, I *do* need it just now. We've got a little—well, crisis out in Sonoma. A lawsuit about the purchase of a winery out there. Complications that make for a bit of self-medication." She turned with her glass, and left the room.

Miranda stood, and hesitated. Then, looking at Gregory, she said, very low, "Sometimes I wonder what you saw in her. All the thoughtfulness of a bank, sometimes." She followed.

For a moment, the brothers sat quiet, hearing the indistinct chatter of the two women as they moved around in the kitchen.

"Anything you want to talk to me about?" Gregory asked.

"Was she this—" Malcolm searched for the word. But then remained silent, watching his older brother drink his almond milk.

Gregory put the carton down and said, "Rude?"

"Blunt," said Malcolm. "Or, I guess, direct—as she says. To tell you the truth, I don't really find it rude. I mean it's obviously well-meaning."

His brother went on in a low tone, "A bit obtuse."

"Actually, she's quite unsettlingly honest. I've seldom encountered that kind of directness in the last couple of years. It's refreshing, really."

The voices were going back and forth in the kitchen, indistinguishable talk.

Gregory glanced at the entrance into the hall. "Miranda said something earlier this evening about people coming into mountains of money, and how the very fact of it can make them less prone to subtlety or nuance."

Malcolm quoted Scott Fitzgerald: "Let me tell you about the very rich."

Gregory took it up, smiling. "They are different from you and me."

They were both quiet again. And the quiet extended, while the garbled talk continued in the other room.

"Anyway, she has a generous heart, I know that. And she hates pretense. You should've seen her with Frye the other day at lunch."

Malcolm let his gaze wander to the shadowed loft, with its wall-length bookshelves.

"You seem a little shaky," Gregory said.

"I'm okay."

He indicated the wall, beyond which the two women were chattering. "Not offended?"

"Not at all. Really." Malcolm had a moment of recalling the older man's reserve and the contrasts between them—from personal history to temperament. "No," he continued. "This is just part of my old, usual, um, *obvious* situation."

"I took the picture down after we had our coffee at Brother Juniper's."

"Was it because you knew you'd be seeing her?"

"Well—it's stupid. All those years. This place is pretty much the same, you know, in terms of its look. I never have liked change much. Might be from growing up in Albert Ruark's house."

"You still get inquiries about the paintings?"

"Miranda wanted to buy something tonight. I gave her the address of the gallery in Chicago. I sold the last ones here two or three years ago. There weren't that many, finally. He wasn't very productive in those last years. Spent a lot of time sitting on the sofa in front of the television drawing sketches on a legal pad. Those sketches sold for some real dough, believe it or not."

A laugh came from the kitchen, both voices.

"It's strange neither of us ended up being an artist," Gregory said. "I mean, I've always been able to draw, a little, but I have absolutely no eye for color."

"I don't even have the drawing."

"Well, I never do it anymore. Doodling now and then."

"Did you ever have trouble with alcohol?" Malcolm asked, surprised at himself.

"Now you sound like—" Gregory indicated the voices on the other side of the wall.

"Really, Greg. I liked it that she didn't pussyfoot around about it. At the theater, I get the feeling everyone's watching what they say. Or regretting something they just said. Claudette Bradley, in my first couple of weeks. I could feel her being on tenterhooks, afraid to offend me."

"Okay. Well, regarding my history, I got drunk on vodka when I was sixteen. Made me sick, and I said not ever again."

"It never made me sick," Malcolm told him. "For some reason I never even had hangovers. That was the trouble, really. I was always ready for more."

You could distinguish some of the words the women were saying on the other side of the wall, now. Salina was talking loud about England, then about Sonoma.

"She's—they're trying to buy a winery out there?"

"It's already done. A family business in trouble—one of them offered it for sale and signed papers. That's what I've gathered. The others in the family are suing to have the deal abrogated. They're maintaining the one who sold it isn't quite right in the head. It's going to court soon. Salina's hands-on. She's got attorneys, of course, but she and Miranda are flying out there to be on-site. And I guess they'll be testifying." Gregory put his hands to his forehead and pushed the hair back, a gesture of weariness, though there had been none of this in his voice; just the slightest nervousness, perhaps, of a man not used to entertaining, having to do so for the former wife who was now his employer.

"I started drinking when I was about fifteen," Malcolm said. "Mom and the great artiste, as she got to calling him, were fighting a lot. And I admit I've always liked the taste of it. All of it. All the whiskeys, rums, cognacs, beers, wines. Just nothing mixed. I never liked mixed drinks."

There was another pause. It was as if they were both trying to hear what was being said in the kitchen. "You want a drink now," his brother said. "Don't you. I can tell by the way you're talking about it."

He nodded, and felt suddenly as if tears might come. He took out his handkerchief and wiped his face. "Hot tonight, huh."

"You want a beer?"

"Oh—no, thanks."

"Sorry. I sound like a pusher."

They were quiet again for a space. Then: "I don't know how to thank you, Greg."

Gregory waved this away. He leaned back and said, almost philosophically, "To be truthful, I never liked beer or whiskey that much. A little wine now and then."

Malcolm came close to asking him how he'd done without those things and then saw that he was thinking of it that way—something you must ingest for the strength to go through a day. Any day. In that instant, the long dry skein of weeks, months, and years ahead stretched before him. He thought of the Berryman line again: *all each damned day*. He drew in a breath to ask for the beer, just as the two women came back, carrying cups of coffee. "God bless the Keurig in the kitchen," Salina said.

Gregory said, "Coffee, Malcolm?"

"Shite," Salina said. "What an ass I am. I should've thought of it. Let me get it."

They watched her hurry out.

Miranda sat down with her coffee, and looked at Malcolm. "I hope this hasn't been awkward for you. I apologize if it has."

"No need," he managed. "Really." Gregory was gazing at him. "I just decided to stop in and see my older brother."

"That's what we did," said Miranda. "We decided to stop in and see your older brother. We saw him sitting out on his balcony with his glass of wine and a book. That book." She pointed to the Eleanor Cruikshank on the side table.

"Your novelist friend," Gregory said. "Thought I'd take another look.

I'm enjoying it." The subtle urgency in his eyes was now companion to the disquiet in his voice, and Malcolm understood that his brother was seeking conversation about the book. He tried vainly, through jangled nerves and the desire for the one beer, to think of something to say. "I like reading about artists and poets" was all he could put forth.

"It's fascinating," Gregory said. "She really sets you down there in the time."

"She's my landlord now, so probably you'll be meeting her."

"Meeting who?" Salina asked, bringing in Malcolm's coffee. She handed it to him and then returned to the wing chair, stopping to retrieve her own cup from the table.

"Eleanor Cruikshank," Gregory said. "The novelist."

She glanced down at the book. "You know her?"

"She's my new landlady."

There was yet another lengthy silence. Gregory cleared his throat, seemed about to cough. Miranda sang four syllables on four notes, "Awk-ward *si*-lence." Then she scoffed and added, "Silence extending," as though this were a command and she were directing actors in a scene.

"Tell me," Salina addressed Malcolm as though Miranda hadn't spoken. "What's your exact opinion about deaf Cordelia?"

"I—well, I know she has a lot of talent—"

"I wanted to know what you think about the *idea*."

"I haven't quite decided what I think about it. It's been a stubborn problem in rehearsals."

"I'm beginning to *like* it. It makes a direct statement."

"My wife is happy about all direct statements," Miranda volunteered.

"Well," Gregory said, "then your wife and I agree."

Salina, looking around the room, said, "I swear, this place is almost exactly like it was in the past century. It makes everything feel *foreshortened,* somehow. As if no time has passed at all. And I don't think it's the wine."

"It's the wine," said Miranda.

A while later, after more talk of the speed of time and the emergence of the new Globe and all the exigencies of producing a gigantic thing like *Lear,* and after two more cups of coffee, Salina got up, moved to the table, and brought the ledger book to her chest. "You don't need this now?" she said to Gregory. "We'll go." She looked around again. "It's uncanny, how much the same this place is. I swear I feel like it hasn't been three minutes since I left it."

Miranda had moved to the door and was waiting.

"Well." Salina offered her hand to Gregory, palm down, as though she expected him to kiss it. He clasped it and shook, and then put his hands on his hips, watching her go.

With a nod at Malcolm, she said, "Bye-bye, now, and again, I hope I didn't hurt any feelings or cause you any pain."

"No," he said.

She walked through the open door that Miranda held for her. Miranda, following, closed it quietly.

Gregory took the tray into the kitchen. Malcolm stood at the French doors, gazing out. He saw the lights beyond the river. He heard water running, dishes clattering softly in the sink, and wondered if he should go in and offer to help. His brother returned, settled on the couch, and picked up the TV remote. "Feel like watching something?"

"I should go."

"Come on, let's watch something. Or we could just talk."

The younger man crossed to the sofa and sat where Salina had been. "I'm better," he lied.

"It's weird," said Gregory with a sigh. "She's nearly seventy, and she still gets to me."

"I really did like her honesty."

He gave a soft laugh. "Her lack of guile can be tough on the nerves. Just picks up and does things. She wanted to live in Memphis again, and here they are. She wanted to finance us, and there she is. It's a tremendous amount of money. And she really does want to do good for people."

"And now she wants to become a vintner," Malcolm said.

"Humoring Miranda with that one, I think."

"Do the people at the theater talk about what happened with Mona and me?"

Gregory shrugged. "I suppose." He left a brief pause. "I mean, people talk, of course. But nothing I've heard." A car horn sounded out in the night. Music wafted across the short distance from Beale. Dogs barked and answered one another. He got up and pulled the balcony door shut.

"I better go," Malcolm said to his back. "Long day tomorrow."

"I was never in love with her, you know." His brother turned, and stood there. "Any more than she was with me. We were just young together. Too damn young. But she's always had this weird effect on me."

Malcolm said nothing.

"Even as I see how socially awkward she can be."

"Did she have money, back then?"

"Her father ran some kind of import business, and her first husband, some stockbroker—a guy who died in that crash at O'Hare—he had a lot. And Miranda's father built housing tracts. So, yeah, all along, there was a lot of money. But not even a fraction of what that cosmetics corporation made them. Multiple billions. And they want to live here in Memphis. You tell *me*. They could live anywhere in the world, and *have* lived in a lot of beautiful, exotic places. But they've settled here. They love this city, the two of them." Gregory paused. Then: "Of course, they've also got houses in Sonoma, and Key West, and Madrid, and Nice. But this is where they want to spend most of the year."

"I've always loved this town, myself," Malcolm said.

"We're family—and we've never talked like this," Gregory mused. "Isn't that odd?"

"I'm thinking about that beer you offered."

There was the slightest pause.

"Really."

For another moment, there were only the muted sounds on the other side of the balcony door.

"Really?" It was a question this time.

After a short, dry breath, Malcolm Ruark said, "No. Sorry."

"You're thinking about it, but you don't want it."

"Both."

"You really can't do it, can you?"

"Can't stop? No, I've stopped."

"I mean have one beer."

"I'm terrified both ways," Malcolm said. "Having it, or not having it."

"Want to stay here tonight?"

He let a little time go by. His brother watched him, apparently believing he was pondering the idea, while in fact he was trying very hard to keep from falling into little pieces. "I'm all right." It felt as if he'd hauled the words up out of the whole dark tangle of himself. "I'm gonna head back and do some reading, and drink some orange juice or sparkling water."

"Brave boy," Gregory said.

The worrisome pressure of paying two rents was playing on him. It was one of the things keeping him awake at night, even as he lay, for the first time in many months, in a very comfortable bed, with crisp clean sheets. But here he had barely enough of his meager belongings to function, and that was a nagging concern, too. He sat up in the early suggestion of dawn light at the windows, and breathed slow, feeling the aches in his knees and ankles. Last night, late, Thaddeus had said he might call this morning. Malcolm hoped he knew what it was about.

The call that came was Hannah.

He had lain back, and drifted, and was half asleep when he picked it up. There was her voice, soft in his ear. "Malcolm." Because he was in the bed instead of the lounge chair, it was almost as if she lay next to him, and this was the house they'd lived in all those years. There was a nocturnal intimate feeling about it. "Hannah?" He sat up again, feeling a strange, unexpected, penitential ache.

"Wanted to see how you're doing," she said.

He took a moment. Then: "I'm okay. How're you?"

"I woke you."

"No, it's all right."

"I guess it's too early there."

He looked at the clock on the bureau next to the bed: 5:37 a.m. "Where you calling from?"

"I'm in Bordeaux. I've left the commune, Malcolm."

He listened to her breathing through the strands of static mixed with music.

"I know it's odd to be calling you now," she said. "Especially since you're not awake yet."

"I'm awake," he said.

"I've got a lot to tell you."

"You're living in France, now?"

"Visiting. I'm getting married. Ted grew up here. We're visiting his parents. Both more than ninety and both sharp as a tack."

"Well, I'm happy for you." The words felt automatic. "Really. You and—Ted, is it?"

"Ted. Right. We met in the Saturday farmers market, and struck up a friendship. I liked him right away and I—well, I decided not to train my anger on him." She sighed. "The commune started boring me, you know? It got to feeling—" She paused. "You know. Wrong. Too negative, because it was all reactions—all about what happened—the bad things that happened to each of us. The Buddhism part was really just Harriet, the owner. All the statues everywhere and the talk and the hours of praying. I got tired of it. The meals and the sitting around in the evenings, with a constant thread of victimhood talk. Really it had less to do with the religion than with Harriet's grievances."

"I don't think I'd want to meet Harriet."

"No. Not you. God! Not you."

"I've been spared."

"Anyway, I did make a couple friends. I don't regret it. I mean"—she gave a little laugh—"I met Ted."

He waited, thinking there was more. And the silence went on.

Finally she sighed. "So—I just wanted to say I bear you no ill will."

"That's good news."

"Ted wanted me to clear the decks."

"Clear the decks."

"Yes. And as I'm sure you know, this means you can quit the alimony payments."

"What's Ted do for a living?"

"He's an architect. He's sixty-six years old and getting ready to retire."

"Well, I'm glad for you."

"You should be glad for yourself, too."

"Will you live in France?"

"New Hampshire. He has a nice house there. And so now you really are free and you can do—" She paused. "Whatever it is you and Mona do, with my blessing."

"I never *did* anything with Mona except drink some whiskey and go through a stop sign."

"I hear you're working with her at the Globe."

"You get that from Pearl?"

"We've been talking quite a bit."

"She said you have. In a threatening call to me. Pretty little Pearl, vicious as a squirrel."

"Cut it out."

"That was *your* little rhyme about her, as I recall."

"Well, she *has* always had her ways."

"She called you first, though, right?"

Silence.

"There's nothing at all with Mona."

"I'm surprised."

"You can tell that to Pearl, though I've told her, more than once. Nothing with Mona."

"You were so gone on her, Malcolm. Come on, you can tell me now. You're still gone on her."

"That's funny," he said. "Really. But, you know, it's too early here for jokes. Call me back in an hour and you can go to town on me."

"Are you seeing anyone, then?"

"Yes," he said.

"Care to tell me who?"

Silence.

"Pearl has you dead to rights, you know."

"What're we talking about now?" he asked.

"Nothing," she said cryptically. "Anyway, we'll consider the decks cleared."

"Mona's doing very well acting in *Lear* at the new Globe."

"Just tell me who you're seeing, and that'll take care of things with Pearl."

"Tell Pearl I went gay all of a sudden and I'm sleeping with all three quarterbacks of the Memphis Tigers football team." He ended the call.

There followed the worst hour of his time sober—worse even than the time in house arrest, humiliated and drying out and, as the papers and the TV news said, disgraced.

Before going to the theater, merely to occupy the sleepless predawn hour, he moved more of his things from the efficiency to the cottage. All that remained now were a few books, some of his winter clothing, and the last pictures. He was packing these last things when the call came from Thaddeus.

"Malcolm?" The voice sounded faintly timorous. "If you still haven't sublet your apartment, I wonder if I might take it."

Malcolm quickly and gladly said, "It's vacant, man. You can move right in."

He called the antiques dealer/landlord to notify him of the change, then started loading the last of his belongings into the trunk of his car. As he was putting in the last box of books, the theater manager drove up. Thaddeus had three suitcases and several small cartons of his own books and papers. Malcolm helped him carry everything in. They said very little. When it was done, they stood awkwardly just inside the door. "I'm leaving most of my stuff at the house, of course," Thaddeus said.

Malcolm pointed to the bed. "I've never slept in it. Sheets are I guess as clean as they were the day I occupied this—place. I mean, sheets don't spoil, do they?"

"Probably not," said the other.

Finally, because it might seem unfriendly not to inquire, Malcolm said, "You all right?"

"Fine," Thaddeus said. "Just—like to have this as a place to get away a little." He hesitated, took a breath. "No, hell. That's—that's not the truth."

"I think there's a little orange juice left in the fridge," Malcolm told him.

"Actually."

He dusted off a glass and poured what was left in the bottle. It wasn't much. They sat across from each other at the table.

"Furnished rooms," Thaddeus muttered, as if to himself.

"That's my recent life," Malcolm told him. "Same thing at the novelist's cottage, too, of course. Except *that* furniture looks like it ought to be in an old mansion house."

The other took a sip of the juice, and cast his dejected gaze about the little room.

"It's not much of a place, I know," Malcolm went on. "Something to keep you out of the rain. It's quiet here, though. There's that about it. The landlord is so busy with his antiques business he'll leave you be. You'll never see him."

They were quiet. The theater manager drank the juice, then sighed. "I read *Lear* the first time when I was fourteen years old." He turned the glass on the table, as if it were a curious object he had found. "A whole lot of time alone in the library. I went there after school every day, because my great-aunt Anna ran the place, and my mom worked at Rum Boogie." He brought the glass to his mouth, drank the rest of the juice, and set it down.

Malcolm remembered spilling his own history to the lady novelist. "I saw *King Lear* before I read it," he said. "I was in New York."

The other nodded. "I used to say the lines aloud. My voice hadn't even changed. And Gina and I worked so hard getting the board—" He stopped, and looked down.

"Her set designs look wonderful."

"Right. She and Frye—working well together."

"He's been kind of subdued lately."

"He's—he's got trouble at home. Same trouble I have, I guess. I heard him on the phone in the tech room a while back. Talking to his wife. Begging her."

Malcolm held silent.

Now Thaddeus leaned forward and brought his hands to his head. "Gina—she—it's just better if I'm not there for a while. I think I *tire* her, you know."

"You don't owe me any explanation, Thaddeus. My wife's in France with a guy named Ted who talks about her clearing the decks with me."

"Trouble is, I'm too negative, I guess."

"We go through phases, don't you think?"

"I'm very quick to alarm. Like her mother, really."

Silence again.

"Listen, I'd appreciate it if you didn't talk to anybody about this."

"Absolutely." It was difficult not to think of the younger man's heartbeat.

"I mean, Claudette knows, and I assume the Grausbecks must know because they always know everybody's business. But they're discreet. And Claudette *can* be discreet."

Malcolm said nothing.

"I don't mean to impose."

"Don't be ridiculous, man. You're saving me. I won't be paying two rents anymore."

They were quiet again without looking at each other. Now, for some reason, further speech seemed nearly impossible while at the same time proportionately necessary: the longer the silence, the greater the need to break it. It was as though an invisible bell had been lowered over each of them. Thaddeus picked up the empty glass and turned it slowly in his hand, staring at it now as if some word or idea might be hidden in its dull roundness, discernible only if you looked deeply enough. Malcolm watched, feeling the strain and the unease, wanting now simply to excuse himself and go on out into the brightness of the rest of the day. "How 'bout some water?"

"Sure."

He took the glass, went to the sink, rinsed and filled it. When he came back, and set it down, he began, "Of course I realize," just as the other said, "I don't mean to trouble you." He sat and watched as Thaddeus drank the whole glass.

"It's really nobody's business, Thaddeus." Malcolm felt suddenly very close to him. He almost reached across the table to pat his shoulder. "I'm sorry about it all," he managed.

Claudette

Just after dawn of the last day before tech week, wanting to get there early enough to run through the play herself in her dressing room, she was crossing from the parking lot, when Geoffrey came out of the angle of shadow bordering the alley on that side. He smelled badly of cigarettes, but his eyes were clear and he was in a sport coat and jeans. "Guess what, ex-strife?" he said. "I'm looking for work."

"Congratulations," she said. "That's good. Good for you." When she tried to walk around him, he moved to block her path.

"You don't sound sincere."

"Oh, come on, Geoff, please."

"Well." He shuffled a little and stood back, looking down. "Okay. Sure." Smiling, he shook his head slightly. "Look, I'm here to apologize, okay? And tell you I'm a citizen again. I had a job interview today. I'm getting on with it."

"That's great," she said. "Really. Do you think it went well?"

"Don't know—think I might've not been dressed up enough." He stood there in her way. "I'm here to apologize again for messing up that night at the restaurant with your dad."

She made a move to walk around him.

"Hey," he said. "I apologized."

"Apology accepted. There's no stations of the cross about it, Geoff. You apologized. Now, please. I do have to go in."

He disregarded this. "I'm making a start." He stood straight to hitch his pants up. "And that's just the beginning. It's a ground-up sort of thing, like you say. I'm doing what you want."

"Can you please? I really have to go."

"But, hey, let's just pause for one second to think about it. I mean, I'm giving this to you. My gift. And someday I might even get a part. Maybe fuckhead Miles Warden won't come back?"

Again, she started around him.

"Hey, the least you can do is wish me luck."

"I always have," she said, as calmly as she could. "I wish you luck." Then she remembered the call from Quincey Blair. "Oh, Quincey Blair called me, looking for you."

He stared for a few seconds, then suddenly took hold of her at the shoulders. "Blair."

A small cry issued from the back of her throat. "Let me go."

"How do you know about Blair?" he said.

"He called me. You gave him my number."

He walked her, pushing, to the side of a parked car, still holding her arms tight. She thought of William Mundy.

"Let me go, Geoffrey, or you're gonna wish you had." She could feel the nerves in her leg quickening.

"I'm a forceful, passionate man." He nodded as he spoke, as though proud of having made a point. He was smiling.

"You better let go of me, I mean it."

He did so. But then he reached and grabbed hold again, bringing another cry from her. "I had a woman I didn't even know tell me the other night that I'm a forceful passionate man. She took me up to her room in the Peabody Hotel. A professor type. And you know me. You *know* how good it makes me feel when somebody gets it." His voice was nearly pleading. She smelled something like mint on his breath—a heavy medicinal odor.

"I'm giving you fair warning now. If you don't let go, you're gonna wish you had."

He had stepped back before she finished the sentence. "But listen. *Listen*," he went on. "I'm important to you. I know it. And she meant nothing to me, not even as a friend. You see me as a friend, anyway, right?"

"Yes, okay." She said this just to be able to go around him.

He murmured through his teeth as she did so. "It's simple, sweetheart. It's all so simple." Then he stepped close, nearly bumping her. And he stood there, his hands held wide from his sides. "Nothing to it. I'm just a man talking with his former wife who's still his friend. Well, I hope still his friend."

She couldn't draw enough air to speak. It came to her that the clear eyes were crazy. "Geoff."

"But listen. I've just been thinking, Why not. You know? Why the hell not. I was a leading actor. Why not take charge of things a little."

"Are you on something?"

He took her arms again, but very gently this time. "I'm low, baby. Low and blue and dead and stone-cold sober. The bottom of the tank. This morning I looked around for the rest of me and I'm not there. I went away."

"Please let go of me," she said. "Please, Geoffrey, I swear to God."

His grip tightened. "I think, as a forceful passionate man, I should tell you I want you to stay away from the bad influences of theater." He stepped back and held his arms out again, looking to either side. "I meant to be affectionate. My God, I wouldn't hurt you in a million years."

"You need help." Her throat closed, and she was looking at him now through tears. "Christ!"

"No," he said, calmly, "I'm putting it all together. Don't cry. I'm working on the case."

"Just please, please, let me alone. I mean it. Get on with your life."

This seemed momentarily to confound him. She watched the color leave his face.

His eyes welled up. She saw tears run down his ashen cheeks.

"You need sleep, Geoffrey."

"That's it, all right," he said. "Look at us. Crying from the grief of losing each other."

She wiped across her face with the heel of her palms. "I'm not crying for us," she got out. "I want you to please stop this."

"All I wanted to do was act. That was what I wanted."

She had the thought that he was acting now. "Listen to me," she said. "I've been working most of the summer as a receptionist at an art gallery. Hourly wages. Okay? Do the work you can get whatever it is and keep trying out and *stop* the drinking and drugging and see what happens."

"You're such a pretentious twit," he said suddenly, with a leering, tearful smile.

Once more, she moved to go around him. This time he didn't stop her. But he called after her. "Tell Ellis I said hello."

She went through the rest of the day. She watched Micheal Frost and Ernest Abernathy practice choreography for the fight between Edgar and Oswald. And then later, at lunch in the new cafeteria, with Malcolm Ruark and Mickey Castleton, she said nothing about it. But it was there in her mind. When she could think calmly about it, she saw it as one pass in her complicated history with Geoffrey. She believed he would end up in his own net of trouble, no matter what she did. But the thought of him nagged at her, and hurt.

That evening, her father walked out of the apartment, and down the street.

Claudette, driving up, saw him on the sidewalk, going along in his undershirt, jeans, and slippers. She pulled over and called to him, then got out. "Claudie," he said. "Where the hell have you been all this time?"

"Where's Willamina?" she asked him.

"She had to use the bathroom." Then he murmured, "I snuck out."

Claudette took his arm at the elbow. "Daddy?"

"If I could just go on up to the Kroger, I could get her a sandwich and surprise her."

"Let's go together. I'll take you." She indicated the car.

Down the street, Willamina's voice rang out. "Ellis!"

"Here!" Claudette called.

"Franny's often annoyed," her father said.

Willamina came rushing up, out of breath. "Oh, Lord," she got out. "I wasn't gone more than a minute. I'm so sorry."

"Where the hell have you been all this time?" Ellis said, and seemed to falter.

Both women helped him to the car. He didn't resist. He slumped over on Willamina's shoulder. "I wish I could go home," he said. "Take me home." Claudette drove to the urgent care on Poplar. They walked in supporting him on either side, and sat in the plastic chairs. A young woman with frizzy black hair identifying herself as Dr. Dupree looked into his eyes with a light, and got him to fix his gaze, and follow her finger. She asked him where he was. "I don't know," Ellis said. "But I like what I see right here."

"Kind sir," she said, and then listened to his heart and breathing. "Can you give me a big smile?"

"I've had a flu," he said, smiling. "I wish I could go home."

"Now, can you stick your tongue out?"

"Why would I do that?"

"Open wide, and stick it out for me."

He did so.

She looked at him. "Okay, just a couple more things."

Ellis closed his mouth, then smiled again.

"Good. Now close your eyes."

He kept the smile, closing his eyes.

"Raise both your arms?"

He did that, slowly.

"Now, repeat after me. 'Memphis skies are blue over the Mississippi.'"

Ellis said it back, arms still raised. Then: "They sure are on a sunny cool day."

"You can let your arms down now, and open your eyes."

"Thanks." He looked at her. "How beautiful you are."

"What a sweet thing to say. Do you have a headache?"

"A little one, earlier."

She looked into his eyes again. "You seem all right." Then she straightened and addressed Claudette: "Could've been what's called a petit mal kind of thing. I don't see evidence of anything serious. Of course, there are more detailed tests. But he—" She interrupted herself and addressed Ellis: "You seem fine."

Night had come. The lights in the street outside, with the thousands of flying insects agitating in them, fascinated him. "Look at that," he said. "All that hurrying."

"I'm so sorry," Willamina said as they got back to the car.

"I'm feeling better after the flu. That was flu, wasn't it?"

"It's my fault."

"No," Claudette said. "Now, really. Don't do that to yourself."

There was some construction toward the crossing with Union Avenue—a bright spotlight, and smaller flashing yellow lights. The moon was very bright.

"I can spend the night," Willamina said.

"Oh, are you sure it's no trouble?"

"None at all."

"Let's have a Bushmills," Ellis said. "And I'm hungry. I was gonna get you something, Willamina. I was gonna surprise you."

"I'd much rather you didn't go without taking me with you."

"Okay," he said, simply.

"Promise me, Captain."

At the apartment, Claudette thanked her again, and sat for a while as Ellis went on about the nice lady in the hospital.

Willamina had poured him a half shot of the Bushmills. "I feel so bad," she murmured to Claudette, sitting next to her on the sofa.

"Listen to me," Claudette said. "I think you are the gold standard for home care." She got up and went toward her bedroom, then stopped and turned. "And I love you to pieces." Near tears again, she came close to telling her about the pathology of the morning. But no. Willamina was sitting there beaming, and Ellis was fine, and the day was ending on a good note. "Night," she said.

"Night," Willamina answered.

In her bedroom, she undressed, put on a nightgown, and lay across the bed. She would shower in the morning. Hearing laughter from the TV, she got herself under the sheet, and nestled. Her cell buzzed, over on the dresser, and she decided to let it go. Later, near dawn, when she got up to use the bathroom, she saw that Geoffrey had texted her. *Forgive me. Sorry.*

Thaddeus

Through the days leading up to tech week, he kept to himself. He listened to music on his iPad, or he read or slept—in the recliner, as Malcolm had. He didn't go to the Madison again; he was a solitary, mostly silent resident. Once, Malcolm invited him to lunch with Eleanor Cruikshank at her big house on the edge of the Old Forest, and he reflexively declined, feeling self-conscious at having confided in the older man as he had. He didn't question the feeling, but only acted on it, and he was subsequently self-conscious about that: Malcolm seemed kind; and once more the theater manager was aware of his own odd nature like a condition, an impediment.

The days slipped by toward July 24, and tech week. Now and then he caught himself whistling or humming to something on the iPad. He had made no adjustments, put up no pictures, acceded to none of the normal matters of personal occupation. And as long as he stayed closed up in that cramped, faintly dank-smelling place, he gave little thought to the theater, or to anything else. He did read Shakespeare over and again, *Hamlet, Romeo and Juliet*, and *Macbeth*, but only for themselves, as he had done when he was fourteen, a precocious, nervous kid in the library, turning the crisp thin pages as if scaling the dust from ancient artifacts.

Online ticket sales were brisk, now. The money from the Cosmetics Tycoons had allowed him to get another mailer ready and printed. That had gone out, too. He was in his office promptly in the mornings, preparing budget proposals and expense reports, giving sponsors and donors and members of the board progress reports on the renovation and the production, and gauging possible profits; and when the days were done, he spent nights in the reclining chair, checking his heart rate and being reassured by its steady slow drumming, thinking about Gina, wondering what she might be doing and thinking. He knew that she and Louisa had visited Otherlands; Claudette had seen them there several times, and once, she said, they were murmuring so intently that Claudette pretended not to notice them. She was occupied anyway, with Willamina and Ellis in the evenings. She told Thaddeus that she and Gina were not very much in each other's company now that rehearsals were in full swing. She was concentrating on the issue of William Mundy's depredations, backstage. The veteran actor was still making sly innuendos and indulging in little feathery touches as he moved by her, always played as if they were accidental. She had asked for a meeting with the whole board about it. And the smoldering hatred he felt was evident with every glance. She told Thaddeus, "If looks could kill, that look would kill me and everyone on the other side of me for at least forty-five miles."

To the others, except Seligman and Frye, Mundy was only marginally polite, though the behavior seemed not from anger but a kind of tamped down mortification, attempting to keep from showing what was perfectly obvious: he couldn't wait until the whole thing was over, and he could get out of Memphis.

Thaddeus avoided direct contact with him as much as possible. Mundy's days were the province of rehearsal and publicity, anyway. The theater manager kept busy. And not just with theater business, though there were of course the hours spent arranging invitations and facets of the opening celebration unveiling the finished new Globe Shakespeare Theater of Memphis. Lately he had assumed the role of friend and listener to Kelly Gordon, who had begun an affair with a woman in finance, also named Kelly. The relationship was already in trouble, and for some reason she brought her confusion about it to Thaddeus. She confided openly, exactly as she had about being bisexual on the ride to Lurlene's July 4 party. It appeared that the other Kelly wanted to break things off. There were others who approached the theater manager about the fact that Frye had essentially begun backing down in terms of directing anyone; at times, the man was little more than a passive observer. His wife's troubles had returned, they now knew; she would not be joining him. He had announced this to everyone, without elaborating, as if it were of general interest, like television news.

Kelly Gordon had the wife's story from Mundy. Frye's wife had been arrested after an altercation with a receptionist at a private club. The details had come from Frye's sister, who was there when it happened. The sister, who had known Mundy at Oxford before Frye did, was trying to help the poor woman by distracting her; they drank one more Aperol Spritz than they should have at lunch in the café several blocks down the street from where the sister worked. As they were heading back to the sister's building, Lauren Frye discovered that she required a restroom; they entered what appeared to be a chic restaurant, and the young woman receptionist, perhaps having seen the signs of intoxication, said to them, "This is a private club."

Lauren Frye purred sweetly, "I just need the restroom, darling."

And the receptionist repeated, "This is a private club."

Ms. Frye, politely but with direct and unmistakable resolve, said, "I'm on the verge of an episode of colitis, dear, and by law I believe you have to let me use your restroom." And when she received the answer yet again, in the same toneless voice, "This is a private club," she leaned toward the girl and, lips pulled tight in a snarling smile, said, quietly, "Move aside, bitch, or I'll shit right here on your desk."

The young woman stood and backed away, pale as starvation, while Frye's wife strolled past her to the hallway and the restrooms. She took ten minutes in there, then walked tranquilly out to the reception area and, giving the receptionist a polite, pinkie-finger-raised wave of the hand, went on her way. The police arrested her halfway down the block. She had apparently managed to get herself poised over the toilet seat long enough to leave a pile behind it. She was now incarcerated, drying out again, and, as anyone might be, Frye seemed preoccupied. (Preternaturally so, Thaddeus muttered at Claudette, who didn't get the joke at first, and then did. Her laugh lifted him.) Frye had explained to Mundy that he was self-medicating in the evenings, to calm down, and then told him the whole story.

Mundy told Kelly, who later told Thaddeus.

She did so as they lay in her bed at Gayoso House & Pembroke Square. He had gone to the Madison again, after seeing Gina with Frye walking down Second Street from Automatic Slim's. Kelly was at the Madison rooftop patio, sipping coffee and working on notes. He had intended to have a rye whiskey (or two) and then head back to the efficiency. And yet he hoped fuzzily that he might run into her—or someone from the theater.

There she was.

"Sit," she said, indicating the chair across from her.

He did so, and asked the server for a double of the Angel's Envy rye. The server was a thin elderly man with a large brown mole on the side of his neck. Thaddeus thought of fate, looking at it.

"A double, huh," Kelly Gordon said, putting her notes away. "Gonna drown some sorrows?"

She knew how things were with Gina. Nothing could be secret for long in the company.

"Sure," he said.

"Would you like to drown them with me?"

He felt the stir in his blood. "I guess that's what I'll be doing."

The server brought his whiskey, and she asked for a sweet vermouth. They passed an hour, sipping the drinks and discussing the new theater, and her failing romance with the other Kelly. He spoke of that romance as if it were heterosexual, since that was all he knew—and by his own recent estimation he didn't know much, really, about that. But as he listened to her talk about it, the other Kelly's dissatisfaction with Kelly Gordon sounded similar enough to Gina's dissatisfaction with Thaddeus. Kelly went on and then with a sudden change of tone began talking about making history, which puzzled him. His bewildered frown made her pause.

"Well, really," she said. "I like to think of my life that way. I'm making history—my own history. Night before last I was with Ernest Abernathy in a place over on Watkins Street called the Pumping Station."

"I've heard of it."

"Been there?"

"No."

"I got bored, though." She touched the back of his hand. "I did say I like it both ways."

Her apartment appeared unlived in, like a model for rentals. Which, he found out in the first minute, it indeed was. She explained that the Grausbecks had prevailed upon the owners of the complex to let her have the short lease, there, and that it had never before been occupied; it was one of two inexactly mirrored places used to showcase these short-term flats. This one had a grandfather clock, made of dark polished cherrywood, standing like a sentry at the entrance to the living room, whose walls were packed with the sort of paintings you find in hotel rooms. There were sconces with fake sprays of flowers or electric candles, interspersed with framed city-street photographs. The furniture was thick-padded and solid, flanked by plants in pots. But there was no slight trace of real occupancy. The windows looked out on the city and the Peabody Hotel off to one side with its rooftop sign. All this made him strangely queasy, as though they had walked onto a movie set.

"As you can see," she said, "I spend as little time here as possible."

They went to her unmade bed in a welter of words, talking, talking. He was feeling the whiskey, and none of it made much sense. He agreed with her about all the nuances of her feelings about the other Kelly, and about *Three Tall Women*, and she talked about the essential sexlessness of Frye's *Lear.* They were lying side by side, fully clothed, and she was going on. Finally she wriggled out of her jeans, and quite quickly they were both naked, and he was inside her, and she came, and for a long time he moved in her and they ended with her on top, working, to no avail, to bring him off. When at last it was over, she collapsed next to him and gave forth a long sigh, and said, "Boy, I needed that."

He said nothing.

"I'm relaxed now." She sighed again, and then reached to pick up a magazine on the bedside table.

He lay there with a sense of the whole thing as having been rather distressingly empty. They hadn't even approached intimacy. There had been something almost transactional about it, as if he should pay her now for the afternoon and the evening.

"You took a long time," she breathed, turning the magazine's glossy pages. He saw a luridly bright ad for a truck. "I thought that was the nice part."

"I can't believe—" he began, but fell silent.

For a few blank moments, they were quiet. Absurdly, probably because of the whiskey, he saw the instant at the bar when Mundy so drunkenly mispronounced *Republican* as he told the thin-armed woman she had been preempted by the party. The memory stirred a laugh inside him, just beneath utterance; repressing it, he turned his head, vexed by the capacity of his mind to present him with these completely unrelated associations, random as the fall of a coin. *Ridiculous*. She leaned up on one elbow and put her leg across his middle. "Wanna hear something rich about Frye's wife? I have it in wonderful detail." The smell of what she'd had to drink was on her breath. Her thigh against his middle now felt rather hot and irritatingly sticky.

"I guess." He was still having to repress the laugh. The moment was a bizarre amalgam of conflicting emotions—dizzying, beyond the alcohol, now.

"Oh, I get it," she said. "You wanna be romantic and cuddly now, is that it?"

"Not necessarily."

"What's got into you?"

"Nothing."

"You think you have to divorce Gina and take up with me now."

"No." He made a wordless vow to himself that he would never touch another drop of whiskey again as long as he lived.

She lay back, and then sat up, her back to him. He saw the downy hair at the nape of her neck. "Well, whatever you're thinking—" She let out an exasperated breath. "Look, this is just history. No strings. I don't want any strings."

"Tell me about Frye's wife," he heard himself say.

He didn't stay long. And she seemed perfectly fine with that. He went back to the efficiency and paced and tried to read, and couldn't sleep.

She had said, "History, man. No one else will know. Okay? I don't kiss and tell. Ask Ernest."

"You just told on Ernest," he said.

Patiently she shook her head. "No, nothing happened between me and Ernest. But he knows me well."

He wouldn't argue. Gina was gone from him, anyway.

The full cast was running through the play, now, with Frye halfway back in the middle row of seats, watching, while Mary Cho and two of her assistants sat with the promptbook open, pen in hand, making notes. For intervals Frye might be all there, completely engaged, but gradations of meaning and tone had begun to escape his notice, so the actors were often providing them. His reactions were uneven, and not only because of his wife's troubles; evidently the problem at Holliwell had come to a head.

Yet the work went on, now with full run-throughs. Tech week would start Monday the twenty-seventh. Withal, the play itself was taking on its old force, like an enormous invisible ship on which they were all sailing homeward.

All that—in its way—was pleasing for Thaddeus; it filled him with a quiet, assuaging warmth. If only he could concentrate on that alone, keep it near in his thoughts, and set it apart from the other thoughts that came at him, and at him.

He caught himself saying Gina's name in the mornings. Drying off in the little stall of a shower, he would talk to her. "It didn't matter, kid. It was like going to the bathroom. What's been the matter with us, darling?"

The morning of the twenty-fourth, he ran into her in the hallway leading out of the suite of new offices, down from the rehearsal hall. She actually smiled at him. There was something withdrawn, almost shy, about it, but it was a smile. "Looks like it's finished," he said, because he could not think of how else to begin.

"Hard to believe," she said. "But yeah."

"And it looks great." He took a breath. "I'm—I'm about to go try out our new café."

"I was on my way there," she said.

They went together to the open area with the tall windows looking out on the street, the line of cars shining in the sun and the Cotton Exchange across the way, its door crowned by thick brass wings. They crossed to the wide new gleaming lobby. Everything smelled new. Behind the counter, a large refrigerator cabinet had been built. He and Lurlene had watched three men stock it from Buster's Liquor & Wines only the day before. He took out a Michelob. She reached past him for iced tea. "I shouldn't have this," he said. "Midday."

"Live it up," she said.

He thought of Kelly Gordon. The whiskey. And then tried not to think.

"I hope the newness smell doesn't last too long," Gina said.

"We'll prop the doors open and air it out."

They were dishearteningly like cordial strangers. The place was quiet, with only the slight whir of the refrigerator cabinets. They sat at one of the small tables and drank, looking at all the new surfaces. "It's gonna be something, opening night," he said, swallowing the beer. The beer was ice cold.

"All fancy and bright," she answered.

Again they were quiet.

Finally she cleared her throat and said, "All this might be for naught if Mundy leaves or gets fired. I heard he came at Mona Greer, too."

"The board won't do anything. Claudette won't want them to. Not now, when we're almost ready to go."

This time the silence had a quality of intention, and he felt the moment slipping away. She would finish her tea and he would finish his beer; they would get up and go their separate ways for the evening, and the evenings would, as they already had, continue to add up.

"It'll be official tomorrow," he said. And when she looked at him defensively as if expecting some announcement of a change in the status quo between them, he quickly added, "I mean they're finally putting the street sign up. B.B. KING BLVD instead of THIRD STREET. He'd've been ninety tomorrow."

"A Memphis street named after BB," she said. "So cool."

The silent moments slipped by. He took another swallow, and came close to telling her what had happened with Kelly. Instead, he murmured, "How are you, honey?"

She was silent for another space, looking down.

"I was—" He paused. "You know. I'm sorry. Wondering."

"Well"—she gave a nervous, small smile—"now, I guess it's kind of wait and see."

"Things with Louisa getting better?"

"We argue—exactly like we always did."

He nodded, but she wasn't looking at him.

"It's him," she blurted out. "It's all him. He's always there. And I can't stand him and I can't stand the dog, either, anymore. Well, I never could stand Marcel. But the reverend talks and talks and talks and talks, and it's like a contagion. All that ultra-right-wing, fascist tripe. And the thing is, he's so—he's so goddamn *nice*. This pleasant voice, politely telling me there's a left-wing plot to put Hillary in power, and the Jews have taken over the media. *That* shit. And it's starting to come from Louisa, too, for God's sake. Louisa, who used to say they should break up the fucking corporations and use the money to transform the face of the country."

He felt the urge to say that Louisa's change was not the only change, but that would be arguing, and he was very tired of the argument itself. "I've been having trouble sleeping," he got out. "A little."

She left a pause. Then: "Louisa misses you."

He decided not to respond to this.

"She keeps talking about you."

"Sorry. You don't need to hear her talking like that."

"Cut it out, Wolfie."

"I meant it simply, seriously."

Another silence, which went on.

Presently, he leaned slightly toward her and began speaking just above a whisper. "Are you feeling—" but the words jammed in his throat.

"What," she said. "Am I feeling what."

"Nevermind."

"No—" She made a motion like someone shooing off something bothersome in the air. Then: "I didn't mean that to sound—I'm sorry. Please."

"Are you feeling any better?"

"I'm seeing someone."

His heart moved exactly like the beginning of another tachycardia.

"Not that," she said, and her mouth actually creased into a little thin-lipped, half smile. "A psychologist. Jeez."

"Oh," he managed, breathing out as if having come up from underwater.

"You just went absolutely white."

"Well," he said. "See?" Then: "God. *See?*"

She said nothing.

"Do you think—are you—do you think you'll want a divorce?"

Her voice was almost too quiet to hear. "No."

"The fact is, I'm still—" He stopped. Then: "I still c-care for you. So much, you know." He took a breath, and then managed to pull everything back into focus. "Well, of course you know." He waited.

"It's gonna be nuts from now to opening," she said. "I'll be running all the time."

He took the last of the beer, and crushed the can. "Are you and—" He couldn't finish.

"No," she said, simply. "If you're talking about Reuben, that was all in your head. That whole thing."

"Well."

A moment later, she said, "I'm taking some medicine, Thaddeus. Not the stuff I took in high school, which made me want to kill myself, no matter what my parents told you. This stuff's helping. Your mother actually called me and we talked. I'm sleeping better."

"Effie called you? She didn't say—she hasn't—"

"She gave me the name of the stuff. And I feel, I don't know, roomier, in my mind."

"It was probably that you had to be with me." He heard himself say each word, as if he were repeating a list.

She tilted her head slightly, and grinned. "You mean it was about you?"

"No, Gina. That is not what I meant."

Now the silence was fraught with what the whole six months had been. She sighed, and gently moved a tress of fine hair from her brow. Her eyes shone. "The—the time alone *has* helped. A little. Mom and Whitcomb spent the last two nights at the friend's house. So, I really have been alone. It's felt good."

He said nothing, but managed a small nodding smile.

"What about you?"

"Oh. I'm sleeping in a chair. Alone. And that feels—" He hesitated. Then: "Well, like I'm sleeping in a chair, alone."

"You're sleeping in a chair?"

"Malcolm Ruark never pulled the covers back on the bed, and I haven't either. It's been made and untouched for a couple years. Like it's haunted or something."

"That's ridiculous," she said. Then, holding her iced tea in its can against her cheek, as if for the cool feel of it, she actually smiled; it was as though she were offering it to him, like a gift. "*Ridiculous*. Isn't that your word?"

"That's the right word for it, though, I guess," he said. "It might also be funny, too, a little. I mean I'm just a tad scared of what I'd find if I pulled the blanket off."

She simply kept the smile, gazing out the tall windows to the street.

He went on, "I keep hoping it won't matter finally, you know. That I'm only living there temporarily."

"Well, we'll see, won't we?"

"I guess we will."

"You're not around much for rehearsals anymore."

"No. Do you want me to be?"

She shrugged. "Guess that's up to you."

"I miss you," he said.

She'd begun tapping the bottom of the empty can lightly on the table.

"Me, too, you, sometimes." But her voice was without emotion; she may as well have been commenting on the decor.

"Really?" he said.

"Of course." Now her tone was patient, as if she were relaying something quite obvious to them both.

He gazed at her. There seemed nothing more to say or do. He wanted to reach over and touch the side of her face.

"Well," she said, rising, heading out of the room. "Back to work."

"I hope you've noticed that I'm not—I'm not pressing you," he said.

She stopped and turned, her expression calm, even friendly. "You should pull the covers back on that bed. Temporary or no, you might sleep better."

V

Blaze

Saturday, July 25–Thursday, July 30

Malcolm

There had been new troubles involving the logistics of the mute Cordelia plot, among the many other problems of putting together a thing so massive, but Mona was showing herself to be professional and dependable, working extra sessions with Castleton and Mundy, and with Malcolm, now as Kent. That scene was brief, and the signing back and forth with her had to be done by one of the soldiers attending to Cordelia, the new queen of France. Mona was with the once office clerk Dylan Walters, and often it was Walters who dropped her off in the mornings. Walters had decided to let the new Globe black box premiere his play (it made others wonder if the talk of interest from Chicago or other cities was in fact true), and auditions were proceeding for that. She arrived for work punctually, and she said little, often signing as she spoke, to keep sharp. The whole production seemed to be coalescing at last, despite its complications—something Frye talked about proudly: how the particular, *gargantuan* undertaking (he used the word) somehow always came together in some mysterious way *because* of its particular problems. It was as if Shakespeare had divined all possible complications on into eternity. And regarding the players, somehow they all grew as actors, and as appreciators of the measureless genius with which they were happily involved.

Malcolm went to work each morning from the cottage, and he saw

Claudette at her dressing table putting on makeup. They had coffee in the newly finished café. Her father's difficulties were preoccupying her. Ellis's face, she said, would at intervals take on an expression of shock or amazement that was difficult to witness. Willamina would put salve on the backs of his hands, for the dry skin there, and he would look at her that way. "Sometimes," Claudette said, "I think he's trying to recognize her. And a minute later he'll say her name, as if he's reciting it."

You could see that the hours of rehearsal provided her with a kind of surcease. But there was something else bothering her, too, just under the surface—her gaze seemed to dart in the direction of any unexpected sound. She was strangely watchful.

"You all right?" he asked.

"Oh," she said, seeming faintly puzzled. "Sure."

The triple-decked frame of what would be the area of the finished stage for the opening production and the arching backdrop and giant screen were still in construction. The special-effects team had brought in framed pipes with tiny vents to make the mist that would pass for rain. The cloud curtains were draped, and ready, and the Cubist-looking fake walls of the castle were painted and stacked along the left side of the proscenium space. All that was progressing. Frye was often with Kelly Gordon, and Gina Donato, the three of them leaning over Gina's sketches, and then Gina would be with Frye at lunch, discussing the other productions.

When Malcolm saw Thaddeus in the halls or the lobby on the way in, the younger man nodded, but then averted his eyes. The theater manager seemed to have detached himself from the whole enterprise.

Many of the others gathered at the Madison rooftop bar. Mundy, people said, drank coffee, with Seligman, Abernathy, and George Poole—or Gloucester, Oswald, and Edmund, as he called them each, so close to tech week. (Frye had insisted that they all address one another by their character names.)

Now and then at rehearsal you could still smell alcohol on Mundy. Nobody said anything.

During one morning's session, Mona began to cry. Frye had been trying to get her to temper her facial expression during the king's tirade at her—this after he'd just been asking Claudette to ratchet hers up as Goneril. "But I'm the youngest one," Mona said, and started to cry. It was so unlike her normal demeanor that everyone froze for a moment.

Frye took her aside, and then walked her out and down the hall to his office. Malcolm followed. Frye had his hand at the small of her back, and was talking low to her. They went down the narrow hallway to the empty new offices.

"Please leave us alone," Mona said when she saw Malcolm in the doorway.

Frye turned. "No," he said. "We're okay. Everything's okay. Tell her."

"It *is* okay," Malcolm said. "Nothing to worry about."

"*You* say." She sniffled, and held the tail of her loosely fitting blouse to her face, daubing her tears.

"You're doing fine," Frye said. "We'll solve it, you'll see."

"It's not that."

Malcolm said to Frye, "Maybe let's give her a little time alone."

"Yes," she sneered. "Uncle-Daddy. That'd be just the thing."

Pierced, and with a flicker of irrational dread that some sort of action from Pearl was imminent, he kept silent.

"Just take some deep breaths," Frye said. "Slow, deep breaths."

The two men stood and watched her trying to comply.

"Sorry," she said, finally. "I'm so sorry, Uncle Malcolm. That was shitty. I'm a mess."

"This is normal, for what you're trying to do," Frye told her.

"Let me talk to her," Malcolm said, feeling for the first time that the latter was, after all, someone with qualities.

Frye went out, and Malcolm sat across the table from her. For several moments, neither of them spoke. She was gaining control of herself.

"You really are doing fine," he heard himself say. "And *we're* fine. We're old friends, right?" He felt absurd, and wrong. "You're still my dear niece that I love and believe in."

She said. "Do you love me?"

"Of course."

"Don't be glib."

He kept still while she sobbed and sniffled. He thought of quietly leaving her there.

"Dylan's got a girlfriend in Tupelo," she burst forth. "I found out this morning. He tells me he hasn't wanted to be around me since—since this thing that happened at the Madison."

"What thing?"

She looked at him. "Nothing. Forget it." She began crying again. "I'm sorry."

"There's nothing for you to be sorry about."

"It's all gone to his head. Having his play open. Thinks he's a big shot. And I'm supposed to be in love with him."

"Maybe give it some time."

"Oh, that's rich. Give it some time."

"Well," Malcolm said, "clichéd as it sounds, it happens to be true. You're eighteen. You haven't been nineteen, twenty—forty, or fifty, like I have, so I know. And anyway, that's all you *can* do, under the circumstances. Give it some time."

"You don't understand."

"Try me."

"His girlfriend in Tupelo? She's his *old* girlfriend. And he's been in touch with her all along. They're getting married. He told me this in a fucking text message. At six o'clock in the morning. *This affair is over.* Can you imagine that? 'This affair is over.' And if I see him here, I'm to behave as if we don't know each other. I'm supposed to keep quiet. Like I'm invisible." She sobbed again. "I finally let him, you know. And then afterward—we—we were at the bar. I'd had some whiskey, and—and Mundy was drunk." She seemed to brace herself, holding the cloth to her face, looking away, and then glancing at him as if to apologize for saying anything at all. "It was all so stupid."

"If you don't want to talk about it," he began.

And she broke in, sobbing, "I'm sorry. I'm so sorry. I thought I could make it up to you."

"What? Make what up to me? You don't owe me anything."

Perhaps a full minute went by while he watched her struggle to gain control of herself. Finally Claudette came to the doorway.

"We're coming," Mona said. "Please."

Malcolm stood. "It's fine," he said. Then, leaning a little to catch Mona's gaze: "You're stronger than you know."

"Just leave me alone now. Five minutes."

As he started out, Claudette, standing at the door, gave him a sympathizing look with a question in it. The two of them went down the hall a few paces, then paused and turned. They were looking at the open doorway, where the sniffling sound continued.

"Dylan Walters," said Malcolm. "Is a dick." Then he turned to her. "I'm sorry. He must be a friend of yours."

They started back down the hall. "He worked the box office," Claudette said, low. "It wasn't like we were buds."

"Somebody ought to—" Malcolm stopped, and turned. She did, too.

Mona had come out into the hall, and started toward them, shamefaced now.

Claudette took her hand, and said, "I've blubbered all the way through rehearsals for comedies."

"I feel so stupid," Mona said, looking at Malcolm.

"Forget it, kid," he said.

The next afternoon, as he was headed down the corridor toward the side door of the theater, Claudette came out of the rehearsal hall, followed by her ex-husband. "Ah, the famous TV newsman," Geoffrey said. "Can't believe you haven't met me sooner." He wore a red tie, and a dark sport coat and jeans, and he smelled of cologne. His hair was brushed straight back, and looked wet.

Malcolm glanced at Claudette, who gave a helpless little smile.

"'Home from the hills,'" said her ex-husband, offering his hand.

Malcolm was at a loss. They shook.

"*Beverly* Hills?" Geoffrey explained, though it sounded like a question. "'Home is the hunter, home from the—'" He stopped and whispered, *"Beverly,"* then he finished in a normal tone, "'hills.'"

"Okay."

"You still don't get it, do you."

Malcolm said nothing.

"It's actually, actually, if I do say so, a rather clever play on the verse engraved on Robert Louis Stevenson's tombstone. 'And this be the verse you grave for me, home is the sailor, home from the sea, and the hunter home from the hill.' My daddy used to quote it. All weepy and appreciating the genius of it greatly. That was his word. *Greatly.* He appreciated beauty greatly mostly when he was greatly drunk as a skunk—um, we used to say. Though nobody's ever seen a drunk skunk, far as I know. You ever seen a drunk skunk?"

"Geoff," Claudette pleaded.

He held up one hand. "That's why I never liked books and reading and all that. My old man liked to quote poems when he was drunk. Did it a lot, too, because, you know, he was drunk a lot. And then he wanted everybody to know how greatly well-read and greatly educated he was. You've heard the two categories of drunks, right? Happy, friendly drunk, as opposed to mean and nasty drunk? Well, Daddy was a third kind. Daddy was a *romantic* drunk, softhearted. A softhearted drunk with a greatly big library and quotations galore. Sober? Well, sober, he was meaner than a constipated cop."

"Geoffrey, come on," Claudette said. "That's all."

But Geoffrey went on as if no one had spoken, "Yeah, the old man would start crying, saying a poem he liked. And give you the shirt off his back, too. Total hell of a guy. My entire catalog of poems comes from him. And that particular one, the one I just said, well, that's—that's from a major one in the, um, inebriate catalog. Because the man spent a lot of quality time with the bottle."

"Have you been spending some time there, too?" Malcolm asked.

"Perceptive," Geoffrey said, smiling too brightly. "I see why you're a famous newsman."

"Sorry," Claudette muttered to Malcolm.

Her ex-husband went on, "What this is, see, I'm trying to get my once-wife, my ex-strife, to understand the vast enormity of my mistake in leaving her. An immense unspeakable unvarnished mistake. Playing straight into my destructive tendencies. Just like Daddy—and like all the romantic early death types. Daddy knew the Romantic Early Death Types with a capital *R* and a capital *E*, and a capital *DT*."

"We're going, now," Claudette said.

Geoffrey wasn't having it. "I've got a new job now, anyway. Right?" He took hold of Malcolm's arm. "So I'm celebrating a little. It's allowed, I *guess*." He leaned close. "The Grausbecks felt sorry for me." It was as though he were sharing a dirty joke.

"I'm headed home," she interrupted, addressing Malcolm, taking a small step inside the space between the two men.

Her ex-husband said, "Let me tell him, sweetness. I start tomorrow as a *custodian*. There I was in that interview, smelling like a Spanish whore, and the Grausbecks stepped in and were merciful and I realized I was coming to this, and that I'd actually, actually take it. Janitor slash watchman. From being a lead actor in the company, through to Hollywood and casting calls and driving Robert De Niro around, to home and a janitor's job in the brand-new expensive, beautifully renovated Globe Theater with all the money."

"Have you talked to Quincey Blair yet?" Claudette demanded. "Has he got ahold of you yet?"

"Never heard of Quincey Blair. Is that a musician? Sounds like a musician."

The response apparently surprised her into silence.

"Quincey Blair," he repeated, seeming to consider.

"We talked about him that—the other morning. He called me looking for you."

Geoffrey feigned puzzlement, then threw his arms up and exclaimed, "Oh, right. Quincey. Quincey Blair. Right. He called you, yeah." He stood there frowning.

She turned to Malcolm. "Please come to dinner, Malcolm. Willamina's making chicken soup, Irish-style, with homemade noodles."

"What's Irish-style," Geoffrey wondered aloud, not looking at either of them. "I'm Irish. Does it have whiskey in it? Does it include stepping out in front of a car?"

"His father," Claudette murmured to Malcolm while Geoffrey went on talking.

"Could've been accidental, because he was extremely fucked up. Quoting Wordsworth, I've been told. Talking loud, they said, about 'We murder to dissect.' He used to say that one a lot. 'We murder to dissect,' he says and then steps off the curb in perfect timing for an oncoming car. I wasn't there. Poor girl driving it. Man. She'll never be the same."

"Time to go now, Geoffrey," Claudette said. "Come on, Malcolm. You know you'll just go back to that lady novelist's cottage and stew. I've asked Thaddeus to come, too. And Gina. See what happens." She shrugged.

"I gotta go see those two," Geoffrey said. "Old pals." He seemed to chatter to himself for a moment, unintelligible, as if alone and going over something. Then he said, "Saw a guy wheeling a tall wire-and-canvas basket across Poplar today. All he had in the world shoved down in there. Homeless. That cart was packed tight. That's me, soon. I looked at that jammed cart and thought, Man, what's he got at the bottom of that thing? Stuff he hasn't used in ages? He'd have to take everything on top out to get to whatever's at the bottom. He'd have to put it all somewhere while he rummaged to the bottom. It made me sick to see it. Because what do people do? How can they fucking manage? But I got a fucking job, today, like a punishment. Eleven dollars an hour. Janitor at the new, glorious Globe. What'll I do when people recognize me? Watch for me." He went on to the doorway, pushed out, and was gone.

Claudette said, "He finally got his courage up, and came to see Frye. And the Grausbecks came in. I have new respect for those two. They overruled Frye. Jocelyn said, 'Give him the job. He was good for us once.' I couldn't believe my ears. He'll lose this job if they see him like this. But that's probably what he wants on some level. It makes me sad. He has abilities." She shook her head. "He's got all that *glibness*. But it's a front. He's just—and maybe he always was. I thought it was edginess, for a time. But it's just this empty malice."

Malcolm waited for her to go on, and when she didn't, he said, "I won't go to my cottage and stew. I'll come and have *Willamina's* stew."

She grinned, her eyes becoming twin half crescents of emerald sparkle. It charmed him so completely that he almost touched her shoulder. She said, "You have such a kindly way, Malcolm."

His blood jumped. He said, "Thank you." And then took the slight step closer, looking into those eyes. In the next instant, she moved into his arms. He held her, and felt the breathing, tender length of her. Then he was holding her face in his hands. "My God," he said. "You're lovely."

"Malcolm," she said.

And very slowly, gently he put his lips on hers. It was the softest kiss. He stepped back, but kept his hands lightly on her upper arms. "I feel as if I've just"—he hesitated—"reached adulthood."

She smiled.

"Does that sound stupid coming from an almost-fifty-five-year-old man?"

"No. I think it's a perfectly beautiful thing to say."

"It just came out." He laughed.

A shadow moved across the window in the doorway.

"I was going over lines with Peggy Torres," she said. "And then she had to leave, and I was alone, getting my stuff together, and he walked in. All dressed up, and begged me to take him to Frye. He smelled so strongly of mint that I was sure he'd been drinking."

"I'm sorry," Malcolm said, and looked down. "But don't we have to—shouldn't we talk about *this* that just happened?"

She answered with another soft kiss, then stepped back again. "Of course. Can it wait, though, just a little?"

"I understand," he got out, though he didn't understand.

"Let's not give anybody reason to see us differently, yet."

"Oh, yes. I do see."

They went toward the doorway, where she hesitated, which caused him to hesitate. Then they embraced again, and the kiss was long, and amazingly tactile. She held tight, and then pressed her lips sweetly on the side of his neck. They stood apart in the dim light, gazing at each other. She said his name. "Malcolm." They remained there for another moment, then stepped outside. A car idled at the light on the corner, spilling exhaust into the heat. They crossed the street and walked to the parking lot on that side. She kept looking around. "I feel like he's watching me."

"He was really drunk, wasn't he."

"Three sheets. He went straight from the interview to get a bottle. He told me so. Said he had it on the floor in his car. He used to do that with stuff—whatever he was on. Put it on the floor or the front seat. He'd call it a passenger."

"He didn't really seem—until he started going on about—"

She broke in. "He's always been able to seem less drunk than he is. But he was drunk. Trust me. That's how he carries it. He gets talkative and glib and what he thinks is witty. And now, thanks to the kindly Jocelyn and Arthur Grausbeck, he'll be a regular part of our days."

"I don't care," Malcolm said. "I feel so glad just now."

She breathed out. "Oh, yes. Me, too." She got into her car, and he closed the door. Opening the window, she gave him a confiding smile. "See you." She drove off.

Down from the hotel, at his own car, he found Geoffrey sitting on the curb, drinking from a pint bottle wrapped in a tightly folded paper bag. He was smoking a cigarette. "You get along well with my lady, don't you, newsman."

"You don't want to get arrested and lose the new job, right?"

"I said, you get along well with my lady."

"Look, I know how this is for you. I've been there."

"You've been with my lady?"

"She's not your lady. I was talking about the drinking."

"Hey, what about go fuck yourself, old son. Thrice."

"That's witty."

"Don't press your luck, cowboy."

Malcolm said nothing. He opened his car door.

"Just keep your distance from my lady, bro."

"I think that's more my advice to you," Malcolm told him.

"Well, thanks for the advice. But it's my preference that you leave the lady alone. Since you're the type who goes after the underage ones."

Malcolm took a moment to decide he would ignore this. "I don't think the lady's inclined to consider your preferences."

"What the fuck does that mean?" The other put the bag down, got to his feet, and started toward him.

"Take it easy," Malcolm told him. "You don't want to get hurt."

"Yeah?" Geoffrey gathered himself, shifted a little, and threw a punch. Malcolm slipped it easily, stepped inside the next one, and clipped him with a quick left to the side of the head, reaching to catch him as he was toppling backward. There was a brief tussle, Malcolm holding him up, while he tottered from the blow.

"Easy," Malcolm said. "Easy. You're okay. Let's just get your balance."

The other stared wildly and dazed-eyed at him, one hand up to where the left had landed.

"I haven't fought since a ten-rounder in my early twenties," Malcolm told him. "But I remember every little thing about fighting. So, let's just take it easy, okay?"

Geoffrey's face took on a look of abject horror.

Malcolm let go and stepped back. "You all right now?"

From that face with its drunken, stunned, broken panic, the other man's words were toneless and distressingly incongruous. "Care for a drink, newsman?"

"No—now let's just cool it, okay? No, thanks."

"She's a good lady, taking care of her old man like that."

"Right."

"She taking care of you, too?"

Malcolm moved to the car, got in behind the wheel, closed the door, put the key in the ignition, and turned it. The engine roared. He was aware of these motions as separate instances of ignoring the other. His window was down. Geoffrey had gone back and picked up the paper bag with the bottle in it, watching him.

"I asked you a question, man."

"Oh, you've got a weapon now," Malcolm called to him. He backed the car up. Geoffrey crouched a little, arm back, as if he would throw the bottle. Malcolm called, "You wouldn't want to waste what's left in there."

The bottle came flying, skipped off the roof of the car, and shattered in its paper bag on the asphalt beyond. "There's nothing left," Geoffrey yelled.

"You got that right," Malcolm called back. "And you just made your second application of the day. For a place to stay awhile. I think they call it jail." He opened the car door to get out, and the other man ran off, looking back in fright, and almost tumbling when he went up on the sidewalk.

Malcolm got back into the car and pulled away.

He phoned Thaddeus as he drove to Claudette's. Thaddeus had been going over renovation and repair cost evaluations, and ceremony plans for the opening, and he sounded a little frenetic. "Sure," he said. "I was already going."

"I just wanted to check."

At Claudette's apartment, he saw the pictures on the walls. There was one of the performance in Shelby Farms Park. He gazed at it. Gina Donato was there alone, talking to Claudette about her mother's late romance with the man she called the polite fascist. Ellis sat in his chair with a book open on his lap. A biography of Roosevelt. Willamina McNichol stood with a rolling pin pressing flour-coated homemade egg-noodle dough, part of preparing the dinner; and Mary Cho was cutting bread. Mona Greer was helping her, placing the slices on a platter with the cheeses she'd been cutting into little wedges. Malcolm watched her concentrate on what she was doing, gazing at the smooth skin of her forearms without the usual feeling of interior starvation. It was strange. There was no hunger in it, now. And this fact, this new reality, made him smile. She glanced at him and smiled back fleetingly, then returned to the work. He felt sorry about her hurt over Dylan Walters.

Ellis closed his book, got up, and moved stiffly around the little dining area, insisting on helping his daughter set the table. Claudette kissed the side of his face, and he smiled his crooked smile.

Thaddeus arrived, looking depleted at first, but warming up to Ellis, who seemed to remember him as a former student—more, indeed, than as a longtime friend of Claudette's. To Malcolm he smiled and said, "I've been wondering what happened to you, sir."

Claudette explained. "He's playing Kent, Dad. He's a member of the company now." She gave Malcolm a look that took him in, containing exquisitely what had happened between them less than an hour ago.

"How 'bout a whiskey for Malcolm and me?" Ellis said to Willamina.

"Later," she told him. She had cut the noodles, and was carefully lifting them by sections, letting them gently down in the large pan of boiling water with pads of olive oil folding in and out of the agitating surface. When this was done, she turned to the room and said, "Okay, it's time to mash the potatoes."

"Who wants something to drink?" Ellis said to the room. "Anybody?"

Thaddeus said, "I'll have a Pellegrino." Then, to Malcolm: "Pellegrino?"

"Yes, thanks," Malcolm told him. They exchanged a look.

Mary Cho explained to Willamina about the phrase *off book* after having commented that she was worried how a couple members seemed still not quite there, five days from tech week. Frye had switched to having Lear sign the lines as he spoke them to Cordelia after the battle was lost, at Dover. And he was still reworking the changed blocking in the last two scenes. She talked of all that, and of Gina's set design. Claudette brought the sparkling water, and handed one to Malcolm. She leaned close and said, "You should've heard Mundy this afternoon, complaining about having to speak two languages at the same time in those last scenes. He was trying to get 'Fire us hence like foxes,' and signing the translation annoyed him no end. You would've loved it." She stepped back a little and did a remarkable rendition of Mundy in distress. "'I say, I don't know what I just said. I know perfectly well the Fool doesn't appear again in the goddamn thing but for God's sake, put the Fool in here.'" She laughed, and continued, "It made everybody's day. And that's the phrase now: 'For God's sake, put the Fool in here.' That's our catchphrase." She turned to Willamina. "So, Willamina, we're all hungry." She pointed to her own abdomen. "For God's sake, put the *food* in *here*."

Malcolm said, "He gets more cartoonishly Anglo as he gets more angry." He took a sip of the Pellegrino, and emitted a piercing hiccup. Everyone stopped. "Sorry," he said. "Carbonation. Does that to me at times, for some reason."

"That happens to me, too, now and then," Ellis said, smiling.

"Mundy's more like the Netflix granddad every day," Claudette said, smiling warmly at Malcolm.

Franny arrived a few minutes later, having been invited at Willamina's urging, and she immediately took the tone of the still-involved wife, questioning Ellis about his routines and what he was eating and drinking. She had only glanced at Claudette when entering, and with her busy swarm of gestures and parental urgings at Ellis, she had fairly ignored everyone else.

Claudette murmured to Malcolm, in a voice broken by the effort not to laugh, "For God's sake, put the Fool in here." He touched her wrist, and did laugh softly, turning toward the doorway.

"Willamina's my best friend," Ellis said calmly to Franny.

"And your wife?" she asked in an affronted tone.

He said patiently, "No, Willamina's most definitely not my wife. I'm sure I didn't say that. Though, now that I think of it—" He turned. "Say, Willamina. How 'bout it?"

"How 'bout what?" she said, over the whir of the mixer.

"I meant," Franny said, her lips drawn tight, "if she's your best friend, what about me?"

He gave a broad smile, and touched her wrist. Then, after a brief glance Claudette's way, he smiled and said, "You get my second-best bed."

Willamina shut the mixer off, and everyone looked at her in the sudden quiet. She said, "Who's ready for some soup?"

"I've had this soup before," Ellis said. "This soup is my friend. I'd like to adopt it. Tell them about it, good lady."

"Well," said Willamina, "it's basically chicken soup with homemade egg noodles poured over buttery mashed potatoes. An Irish dish. Mmm-mmm."

"Mashed potatoes with noodles?" Franny seemed incredulous. But she gave a nervous smile.

"Wait'll you taste it," Ellis told her. "You'll be happy."

She looked at him. "I don't want the second-best bed."

Thaddeus explained quietly that Shakespeare in his will had left his wife his "second best bed," and that many scholars believed this was an endearment, a sort of joke from the grave.

"Well," Franny said. "That's morbid." Then, looking at Claudette, "And I don't think *he* means it as a joke."

"It was a joke," Claudette said, simply.

Everyone was silent again.

Franny looked around and muttered, "I feel out of place."

"You're with friends," Ellis said. "Really. You brought me breakfast." His voice was even, but gentle. "Claudette's my best friend, too."

When at length Willamina served up the soup, Ellis found that he could not spoon it into his mouth for the essential tremor in his hands. He made a joke about it. Malcolm saw Claudette's eyes, and sought to distract her with talk about Mundy's flatness of expression while trying to deal with deaf Cordelia. The conversation turned, mostly to talk about the food. Malcolm, sitting next to Ellis, talked a little with him about Roosevelt. History of course being the subject Ellis knew deeply and well. He was quite interesting about it. Malcolm saw that the memory deficits were intermittent, like a cough. He said, "I wish I could've been in one of your classes."

Ellis turned to Willamina. "How 'bout our whiskey, lady?"

"Dad, Malcolm doesn't drink."

"Oh." Ellis looked incredulous for a few seconds. Then: "Have I put my foot in it?"

"Not at all," Malcolm told him.

"I've stopped drinking," Mona said with a little smile, and quick glances around the room. The assertion seemed faintly absurd, coming from one so young.

"That's the truth," Malcolm felt the confidence to say. "We learned our lesson, huh?"

"Right," she said, still shifting her gaze back and forth. "Boy, did we."

She seemed, now, exactly her age. He felt the peculiarity of this, even as he considered with satisfying detachment the depth and subtlety of her talent. And even as he was freshly sorry for the hurt he knew she had been going through. She was family, after all.

The meal went on, with a little less talk about anything, and when it was over he went up to Claudette and said, "Where do you keep the whiskey?"

"What?"

"Let me pour it for him."

She put her hands on his shoulders and smiled, then reached into the cabinet above the refrigerator and brought out the bottle of Old Bushmills. As he poured it, all the others watched him. He went over to Ellis, who had returned to his chair, and offered it to him.

"Thank you," Ellis said. "King Lear."

"Kent, Dad," Claudette said. She moved to his side, leaned down, and kissed his cheek. He glanced up at her, and then held his hand out as if to offer her to everyone. "I want to tell you all about this girl and the bear."

"Dad," she said.

"We were up in the Smoky Mountains, the two of us, for her birthday. And we ran into a bear."

Malcolm saw the look of anxious tolerance on Claudette's face. But then she spoke, "I never saw any wild thing that big up close, before or since." She smiled at everyone, one hand on her father's shoulder.

"You're not going to tell that—" Franny started to say. Then she seemed to realize what was happening, and she actually smiled encouragingly. "The big old scary bear," she said, and looked around as if what she had said were a cough, or an embarrassing noise.

Ellis continued, "Well, this girl didn't give the slightest sign of being scared. We're eating at this campfire we made in a clearing and this huge, little-eyed critter—like a—like a big thug wearing a loose-fitting winter fur coat full of briars and leaf meal from rolling around on the ground all day—raggedy and baggy and fierce—walked up to the edge of the fire like—like God's own reckoning and licked the baked beans off my tin plate. I was afraid to breathe out. And he glared at me with those piggy little eyes, the sauce all over his snout. Like I'd shortchanged him. I can see it clear as a sunny day. I can see *that* sunny day, the very one, and the tree shade. So pretty. And then he turned that gigantic head and looked at Little One, here, and you know what she did?" He hesitated, and seemed momentarily at a loss. His face showed the anxiety he felt in that instant. He straightened in his chair, squeezed Claudette's wrist, and began again. "You know what she did? Well, she stared straight into that bear's little eyes and said: 'If you don't like the food, whyn't you go eat someplace else?' And god*damn* didn't he turn and sulk away, like some big lumbering kid being sent to his room. It looked for all the world like he was ashamed."

Claudette's eyes were welling up. Everyone was quite still for a moment.

"I remember," Ellis said, his voice shaking. "Seems so—close."

"And we got quiet as church," Claudette said. "Because we thought he might come back." She bent down and hugged her father, who said, "You remember."

"Oh, yes, Daddy."

"Of course you do. I do, too."

"Oh, and you told it so well."

When the meal was done, Claudette approached Malcolm with her eyes still moist, and said, "It's the first time in a long time that he told a story like that. He's always been a wonderful storyteller." When she saw that Ellis heard this, she addressed him: "That's why you were such a good teacher."

"I was, yes. But I've been telling that story all the years. And you gave me that. Tell Esther for me. That I remembered the bear."

"Yes," Claudette said, with a glance at Willamina, and then at Franny. "I will."

Everyone talked for a time about the bear, and bears, and the Smoky Mountains, and Ellis's storytelling.

Malcolm looked over at Gina and her husband, who were still seated at the table. They did not seem together. She was looking at her phone, and he was simply gazing miserably at the room.

Claudette

No sleep.

The dinner gathering had been exhausting, but Ellis had told the story so well and with consistency, the story as she had heard him tell it, and it was a story he did tell over and over, but not once since he went into Memphis Commons. She told Malcolm this when everyone else was gone. She walked outside with him, and they stopped at the end of the sidewalk, at the street. She kissed him lightly and stood back and looked at him.

"He used to—" she began. "His normal *talk* was stories. Or that was how it seemed. And tonight it was a little like a recitation. The first time since I took him out of that place. And Franny saw it."

"He must've been an amazing teacher."

She nodded. "I think having everyone together like that."

"He got energy from it, that was clear."

"Well." She kissed him again, just a brushing of her lips against his. "Good night, friend. Good night, my love."

He took hold of her arms, and spoke very softly. "My love," he said. Then smiled and let go. "We'll keep this for ourselves, for now."

"Yes."

He leaned in and kissed her, and then held her close for a few seconds. "Tomorrow," he said.

Inside, Willamina and Ellis were sipping the Bushmills, and the TV was on. "I should go," Willamina said. "I'm beat."

"That was a great dinner," Claudette told her. "And did you notice that Franny cleared everything and loaded the dishwasher?"

"I did."

"Things are turning. I feel it."

"Did you tell Esther?" Ellis said.

Five days later, the whole company had the first full run-through of tech week. It was surprisingly smooth. In Claudette's scenes with Mundy, he was precise, superlatively *present*, and remarkably rather gratifying to play against in sequence. He had inhabited the role. And she saw the faintest glint of pleasure in his eyes as, for her own part, she inhabited hers. The whole expanse of the thing worked, Cordelia's mute delivery of her lines went efficiently with Mickey Castleton's deft delivery. When it was over, back in the halls where the new dressing rooms were, Mundy walked up and congratulated her. "Well done," he said. And then brushed by, his arm coming against hers. She decided to ignore the tremor of disgust that washed over her with the touch, watching him go on, shaking hands with Don Seligman and with Peggy Torres and the others. Everyone was pleased. Frye, giving his assessment, went on about how little he had for them in the way of notes, it had gone so very well. "Everybody, back bright and early tomorrow. And feel good. It's gonna be good."

A small cheer went up as everyone began to disperse.

"Come to the bar for a while for coffee?" Malcolm said to Claudette.

"Sure. I'll be there in a while. But only for a little."

"It's gonna be wonderful, Claudie." He smiled.

She reached over and touched his wrist. "I think that's the first time you called me that. I like your voice saying it."

He kept the smile, and patted her arm.

She went home and changed into her I AM NOT JEJUNE T-shirt. Ellis was asleep peacefully. Willamina made a small caprese salad for her, and talked a little about Ellis's day. "We took a walk," she said. "Two of the grandkids and their mom came by for a little and we all walked down to the end of the block and up, and then back. He and I sort of had to rush back a little, because he had to pee. He was a little bit shaky, then. And angry about it—but anger's good, I think. Anyway, I told him it happens to me all the time."

"He used to complain about having to hurry to the bathroom when he was in his fifties," Claudette said.

"Oh, and he told the bear story to the kids. Just like the other night."

"That's great—how cool that the grandkids and their mom came over, he still loves company."

"Yes, he sure does. Now. Tell me more about today's run-through."

"Well, if I can just stay ten feet away from Mundy, I think it'll be all right—because he really does know what he's doing with Lear."

"We're definitely gonna be there, opening night." Willamina beamed. Then something crossed in her expression, the slightest change. "He is still talking to Esther a bit."

"Esther's in Paris, and hasn't given him a thought in years." Suddenly, she was crying.

Willamina reached across and covered her hand. "He comes back, though, honey. He does come back. And the other night—"

"Yes." Claudette sniffled.

"And we're gonna be there opening night. First one. Preview. Reception and all."

"Thank you. I—you are my dear friend."

"I feel that."

"Sure you can stay longer this—"

"Happy to. We'll watch a movie and have a sip of our Bushmills. For now, he's resting good. Maybe stop and get us a pizza on the way home."

"Thank you," Claudette said. "I won't be long."

At the Madison bar, she found Malcolm in the first booth with a coffee cup between his palms. The coffee was cold. William Mundy was at the bar, with Don Seligman, Ernest Abernathy, and Mickey Castleton. Kelly Gordon was in the next booth with Mary Cho and Mona Greer. Others were seated along the far wall. Everyone looked at her when she came in, and Mickey Castleton said, "Great job, lady."

"Yes," Mundy said, with a wide, insincere smile, "brilliant."

She acknowledged the comments, and sat down across from Malcolm. "You were great," she said to him.

"I've got a lot of work to do, still."

She collected herself to say something about Mundy's subtle physical trespass, but found she lacked the will. She would handle things, in any case. (In fact, if she said anything at all, it might be to compliment the man's professionalism, managing to perform so well under the circumstance, having had his personal dignity wrecked in that humiliating way.) She desired to bask in the good feeling; Ellis hadn't had another stroke, and he had told the bear story; Geoffrey had asked for forgiveness; she and Malcolm were going to be together; the run-through had been smooth. In the noisy bar, the atmosphere was celebratory.

"Did you see Geoffrey?" Malcolm asked.

"Excuse me?"

"He was there. Crouched against the back wall. I felt a little sorry for him."

"He feels enough of that for himself."

"I wonder if he'll come here."

She shook her head. "Works nights." She felt a twinge of anxiety about Malcolm being involved with Geoffrey in any way. "If you see him or hear from him—avoid him."

"He threw a bottle at me after I ran into you with him in the hall."

"Oh, God."

"We had a little set-to. Nothing serious. I didn't think I should tell you about it and now I've told you."

"You should've told the board. Malcolm, he's capable of attacking you."

"Well, he tried."

She stared.

"I'm afraid I had to cuff him, to fend him off."

"Oh, God."

"Really, he's all talk. It's all right. He's harmless to everybody but himself."

She sat there feeling the gladness of the afternoon's work slipping away from her.

"Come on," he said. "Let's marvel at our fine run-through."

She had one glass of wine, then began to feel ill. Clammy, and breathless. He was talking to Mickey Castleton, who had sat down next to him.

"I'm beat," she told them.

Malcolm gave her an understanding look. She stood and hugged both men, and made her way out.

"Glorious work," Mundy called after her. And then smiled poison.

She went out onto Madison, thinking to go back to the apartment. It was getting toward dark; the sky to the west was a smoldering rosy color, the air hot as midday, cooking with the acrid odor of diesel exhaust.

She walked up to the theater. Lurlene was coming out, bundling some paperwork into her laptop case. Seeing Claudette, she tilted her head and smiled, her eyes bright, full of affection. "My, you were splendid today."

"Oh, that's so kind, Lurlene."

She kept gingerly pushing the papers into the bag. "Girls' drawings from a couple of years ago. Don't want to wrinkle them. I've got new ones."

"Is everyone gone for the day?"

"Everyone but some of the tech people and cleaning staff." She got the papers in the bag, and then took hold of Claudette's wrist. "You were deliciously wicked today. Even more than with the Scottish lady." She winked. "I loved it. This is going to knock them all a yard to the side."

"Thank you, thank you, so much. Bless you."

"You know, Geoffrey's in there. They hired him."

"I know."

"He seems quiet."

"Thanks."

"You don't owe him anything, honey."

"I know. Thank you."

Lurlene rushed out into the twilight and along the walk. Claudette crossed the newly finished lobby, and stepped into the auditorium. When she saw him moving along the edge of the stage with a push broom, sweeping, talking low to himself, she had a strong impulse to turn and make her way out. But finding herself drawn toward him, she started down the long passage of shallow steps to where he was. Perhaps there was curiosity in it, or even a measure of nostalgia, since he was reciting lines, very low, the way he used to, and she would wake in the nights and hear him moving through the rooms of the house they lived in then, when they were new and there were excitements and they were always together, so accustomed to their good fortune that each day was full of promise and they were two gifted young artists, on the rise.

He was pushing the broom along, muttering, "'. . . so loving to my mother that he might not beteem the winds of heaven visit her face too roughly. Heaven and earth! Must I remember?'" Then he saw her and stopped, dropping the broom with a dramatic faltering half step back. "Come to see me in my humiliation."

"No," she managed.

He lit a cigarette. "It's come to this, huh." He moved to the edge of the stage, stooped, and offered the cigarette to her. She reached up and took it, drew on it, and blew smoke as she passed it back. He went to stage right and came down, and instead of going over to her, sat in one of the seats. She sat three seats away. He blew smoke. "Pretty sorry sight, huh?"

"No."

"I was drunk the other day."

"I know."

"You must have a weakness for men with alcohol trouble."

She said nothing.

"I was just being Hamlet, did you hear?"

"I heard."

"Hamlet pushing a broom. Imagine. A director could use it. Hamlet believing himself to be trying to clean up the mess of the whole thing.

Sweeping away the ghost." He drew on the cigarette, and sighed the smoke. The quiet went on. He took another draw, blew it out, and offered her another drag.

"No, thanks."

He smoked, tapped his knee as if keeping some inner rhythm, then stopped. He turned his head to look straight at her, and recited Hamlet's words to Ophelia. "'I did love you once.'"

After a pause, she said the answering line, "'Indeed, my lord, you made me believe so.'"

"'You should not have believed me. For virtue cannot so inoculate our old stock but we shall relish of it: I loved you not.'"

"'I was the more deceived.'"

He sighed smoke, paused. And then: "'Get thee to a nunnery. Why—'" He nodded. "'Why wouldst thou be a breeder of sinners. I am indifferent honest'—is that it? 'Go thy ways to a nunnery—' And—and what?"

She shook her head to say she couldn't call it up. She could, but she lacked the will.

He took a long draw this time. She saw the brightened coal. Then: "Shit. You win."

"Geoffrey. I don't remember it either, really."

He sank down farther in the seat.

"I can give you most of *Lear*," she said. "Now."

"I'm lost," he said.

"But you're taking hold."

"I was talking about the *lines*. About *Hamlet*. The lines."

"Oh, sorry. But you *are* taking hold. Right?"

He looked at her, then turned to blow smoke the other way. He held the cigarette tight between his index finger and thumb. "You always tried to put a positive spin on everything."

She waited.

"Used to make me want to kick something out from under you."

"Well."

"Sorry." He offered a drag on the cigarette again, and she shook her head.

"You were there at the run-through today," she said.

"Yeah. Everybody did great. Made me miss it, a little." Then he grumbled, low: "And you're with that—pedophile alcoholic."

She said nothing, but put her hands on the seat arms, thinking to rise and leave him there.

"Sorry. I can't—agh. Sorry. Shit. Wait. Makes no difference now. I'm sorry. It's your life. He's probably a nice pedophile alcoholic."

"Well, you take care," she said.

"No. Really. Wait. I'm sorry, okay? I don't want you having any more bad feelings than you already have about me—and—let's just remember the good days."

She watched him smoke the cigarette.

"Those few times," he added with a smirk.

"Let's not argue."

"No, right. It's your life now."

She nodded, but he was looking at the smoke trailing out of his mouth.

"And this," he said, indicating the large space where they were seated, "is now *my* life." He blew the smoke, concentrating on it again, then looked at her and smiled. "I like your T-shirt."

"Don't remember where I got it."

"What does *jejune* mean?"

"I think it means something like 'dull.'"

"Oh, I get it. You're not dull. Funny you feel the need to announce it."

"I thought it was funny."

"S'funny. I guess."

"I'd better get going."

"Yeah."

"You're gonna be all right, Geoffrey."

"Oh, of course." He blew three perfect smoke rings, each inside the preceding one. "You know what I remember most about us?"

"Being onstage together?"

"Nah. Stage, who needs that." He made a scoffing sound. "That's all gone."

"There's nothing that says you can't bring it back."

"It would be nice if you could avoid the inspirational speeches with me."

"I'm only saying the truth."

"Nevertheless."

"You used to talk about it, Geoffrey. Our hunger for it."

He shrugged. "Not really hungry anymore. Isn't that curious. Not even slightly hungry. Just a kind of—a kind of peaceful sense of, you know, 'this is the given.'"

"Well, maybe that's a good thing."

"Could be. Peace. Taking it all in stride."

"Sort of, sure."

He looked at her. "I asked you something. I asked you if you know what I remember most."

"All right," she said. "What do you remember most?"

"Our morning walks." He shook his head, evidently picturing everything. "Down High Point Terrace, and across Walnut Grove, going by those huge, fancy houses around the Galloway Golf Course, the two of us, talking or saying lines. And in town, with the farmers market and strolling around the loop, and riding the trolley after lunch at Bluefin. Looking at all the people. When I was in LA, I had dreams about it. Did I ever tell you on the phone I had dreams about it?"

"No."

"Right, I was too busy being my witty self."

She was silent.

"I've always been pissed off, you know that? But I'm not anymore."

"Yes," she said. "Good."

"From being a little kid riding around in my father's car while he made calls. A collector's son. Repossessionsville, USA. I saw a whole lot of people getting shit taken away from them. And he's—the whole time, you know, holding forth from his books. All that learning, and it didn't help him a little bit."

She nodded.

"Well, you know all that about my watching him pull stuff away. The charge he got out of it. I heard him tell one of his women it made him feel like all that merchandise—the televisions and stereos and the appliances—like all that belonged to him. Like he'd loaned it all out and was taking it back. And the women. You know one of them took me to bed with her? I was thirteen. It was my first time. I don't think I ever told you that. Talk about mixed feelings." He scoffed, and shook his head. "Stupid joke. But in fact I was curious as hell at first and it felt really great and she was drunk and slavering, and then when it was over she got sick. I ran out of there like Satan himself was after me. But that—that was my first, uh, sexual experience. A drunk lady 'friend' of my daddy's."

"God," she said. "No. You never did tell me that."

"Beat me across the middle of my back with a broomstick, too, he did. More than once." He raised his eyes to the high ceiling, and let his gaze roam the room in the soft red light.

"I'm so sorry that happened."

He shrugged. "Got an early start, huh."

She said nothing.

"Sure you don't want a cigarette?"

"I'm fine."

"Trouble is, you know, not all of it's true."

"Okay."

"What if I told you Daddy was a nice loan manager at a bank. And we had two cars. And Mommy was a guitar player in the orchestra?"

She was silent.

"Of course *that's* not true, either."

"Well, one foot in front of the other," she said, because there seemed nothing else to say.

He half smiled, and sighed. "I've got this steady sort of flow inside."

"Flow. In what way?"

"A river of—of something. Lava? It's exhausting, and I drink to relieve it. Cool it down." He took one more pull on the cigarette, then put it out on the floor, scraping the coal away, and putting the butt in his uniform shirt pocket. "I'll sweep that up." From the other pocket he brought out the pack, and a book of matches, and lit another.

"Rage," she said.

"'You purchase pain, with all that joy can give,'" he quoted.

She kept still.

"'And die of nothing but a—'" He paused and opened a palm at her.

"'Rage,'" she said.

"Score one for the lady. 'Nothing but a rage to live.'" He smiled, nodding. "You always knew me best. But you *don't* know, haven't really *known*. You *think* you do. You're not even sure *any* of it is true."

She straightened, and looked into him. "No." Now she felt the impulse to challenge him, to say the whole last few minutes had been a performance. Nothing of what he had said was beyond his particular style of gaslighting. Yet there wasn't anything to be gained by arguing through it, either, and she had to admit there was a strand of truth in all the stories of his bad past. His father *had* stepped out in front of an automobile; his mother *was* schizophrenic, in and out of hospitals, and then just gone. These things were true. The fabric of assertions and falsehoods he dressed them in was always changing, and you had to sift through it. And the fact was he used it all—if not for his work, then as an excuse. She looked at him and felt sorry again, wanted to say something easing to him.

"I'm glad you stopped in," he said. There was a calm in his voice now, and the usual gleam was gone from his eyes. He sat back and folded his arms across his abdomen, legs stretched out, crossed at the ankles. He was still so good to look at.

As she started to rise, he offered yet again a drag on the cigarette. Once more she demurred, though she let herself back down.

There was another moment, the two of them sitting there silent, three seats apart, she with her hands on the ends of the seat arms, watching him smoke the cigarette and then looking at the thick velour curtain in front of them, the lights along the stage front glowing softly in its thick folds. The only sound was him sighing the smoke.

"So," he said at last. "You just wanted to lay eyes on me as your next triumph unfolded?"

"I'm not sure what I wanted. I had a good day, today."

"I'm having a quiet day. Simply—going over things a little. Saying lines. Seeing if I can still do it. You caught me on a peaceable day. I'm peaceable. I can even look at the awful inner furious ferocious river."

She kept still.

"Furious, ferocious. That sounds cool. Did somebody write that? Dad would know."

"Doesn't sound like anyone," she said.

"I've been a lot of trouble to you," he sighed out the words in smoke.

"We've been trouble for each other," she told him.

He smirked. "Innocence will get no points here."

She kept silent.

"Yeah. It's okay. I won't bother you. Time to move on." He stood. "Well, got work to do."

"Take care," she said.

"You know, out there—LA. When I first got there, I had a bunch of callbacks. Several of them, and I'd go in again, and every single time I'd get the yips. Every time. What is that? You'd think subconsciously I was afraid I might actually get the part."

"Subconsciously," she said. "I thought you didn't believe in all that psychological stuff."

"Mumbo jumbo." He smiled. "Yeah. But it got me, really. Each time."

She started up the aisle toward the back.

"Thanks for the visit," he called.

She turned, and saw him standing in front of the grand drape, smoking the cigarette, holding the broom. He lifted one hand and held it up, then let it drop to his side.

Thaddeus

In the middle of that night, after reading the play yet again (it was an indulgence he allowed himself), then going over the lists of invitations and complimentary tickets for the two preview performances, and checking the orders for food and buffet items and the layout for the snacks and the choices of red and white wines, he gathered the courage to pull the blanket back on the bed in the little efficiency. He looked carefully at the sheet, expecting to see insects or spiders. It was clean and smelled faintly and surprisingly of detergent. As he got in and lay on his side with a book, he heard sirens, and, perhaps ten minutes later, reaching to turn out the light, he marked that there were many sirens. "Life in the city," he murmured, "Ridiculous." He thought of Gina. He would tell her he followed her advice about using the bed, and he would mention the surprising, curiously stubborn laundry detergent smell. He would keep things casual and friendly.

The sirens increased. Closing his eyes tight, he pictured Gina as she'd been when they were in London, her lovely features, the perfect shine of her hair, and he was just drifting off when his phone rang. It was Lurlene, who'd been up late with one of the girls suffering a summer cold, and had turned her television on, wondering about the commotion. "Oh, God help us, Thaddeus. Are you seeing this? Do you have a television?"

He brought his legs around to sit on the edge of the bed. "What is it, Lurlene? Are—has there been another attack?"

"The theater," she said. "Oh, it's the Globe. Oh, God—our new theater, Thaddeus."

He was the first to arrive at the scene. He had to park down on Second Street. Madison Avenue was already cordoned off from Main to Front Street. Standing under the bright canopy of the Madison Hotel, he saw the new, sleekly modern façade of the Globe emit a wide flag of conflagration. Even from this distance, the heat was amazing. There wasn't any way to get closer. He stood there watching it all seem to toss and rise. When a freshet of air from the river caught and cooled the tears streaming down his cheeks, he realized he was crying. The odor of incineration filled the air. He saw the reflecting glare of the street, the sides of the shadowed fire trucks in the hectic, unsteady light, the water in the gutters, the hoses lying in zigzags, and the fallen shards of the roof of the building, the unreachable uproar of the flames hurtling into the lowering clouds, the heavy black smoke mingling with them, so that it looked as though the entire world was ablaze.

Claudette walked up, and then Lurlene, with Mary Cho. Lurlene was crying, too. Mickey Castleton came out of the crowd of others, people streaming over from Beale Street and the cafés. He put an arm around Lurlene. Her face was a pale blankness, a mask of shock. Soon most of the other members of the company were there, too: Mundy, Seligman, Frost, Abernathy, Kelly Gordon, the tech people and office staff. The Grausbecks. And Malcolm Ruark, who moved to stand with Claudette. They were all gathered in the light of the Madison Hotel marquee, watching the spectacle up the street, the fierce plunging upward of the flames, the flashing that looked like electric sparks inside the hurrying smoke. No one said anything. They all lost track of time. At one point, Thaddeus called his mother, just to seek the calm her voice usually generated in him, and she said the kind of reassuring things that were finally more vexing than soothing. "I know, I know we'll be all right," he heard himself say in response. "But it's burning, right before our eyes. It's just going up in smoke." He sobbed, and while managing to reassure Effie that the building was empty, he kept looking for Gina through the moving back and forth of people. "I love you," he said to his mother.

"I'm sorry, Mom." He closed the call. He would call Gina, but, suddenly overcome by a weariness so great it affected his ability to stand without support, he decided against it, imagining her safe in the big old house, and unaware, with *her* mother. He sat down heavily on the curb, and saw Gregory Ruark come up from BB King Blvd., hands shoved down into the pockets of his summer jacket. He reached Malcolm, and the two men embraced, then turned together, arm in arm, helplessly attending. Frye approached from the corner and stood with them. Thaddeus conjured how it would be for Gina in the morning, to learn of this, and he thought again of calling the house. In the next moment, as if produced by the thought itself, Gina and Louisa appeared out of the crowd. He got to his feet as they came up to him, the chaotic light playing over their features. Gina put her arms around his neck and held tight. The crowd kept growing. News trucks were arriving. Cameramen and -women, reporters, TV people setting up for broadcast. The night itself seemed made out of sirens and fright. It all went on, and on.

At length, predawn light began to show over the disintegrating structure, forming a backdrop of dimmed, carmine illumination beyond the roiling mass of solid-looking smoke and cloud troubling its massive way to the sky. Thaddeus couldn't believe they had all been there the whole night. There hadn't been much talk. People questioned where other members of the company might be, and wondered sadly aloud what might have caused the fire, remarking about the intense heat, from a city block away, obliterating whatever breath of coolness might have come with night, after such a blistering day. The whole city seemed to be burning. Now, like a reaction from blank heaven, a vast savanna of cloud moved in and mixed with the smoke, and it began to rain. No one seemed to notice. Thaddeus stood still, and kept crying soundlessly. Gina put her hand inside the crook of his arm at the elbow, and leaned close.

Malcolm

He remarked the two of them clinging to each other, Louisa moving off, going into the crowd in the closed street, and he saw Thaddeus's crying face, Gina wiping her eyes with a red handkerchief. Malcolm thought absurdly of troubled marriages. Claudette was still at his side. She was crying, too. "I can't believe it," she said. "My God. I can't make myself *believe* it."

The sirens, the rushing water of the hoses, the deafening roar of the flames, and now the crashings inside the building itself, structures collapsing, were finally too loud for talk. It was another awful, speechless, watching hour.

Geoffrey Chessman emerged from the crowd at Madison and Main, and came to where Malcolm and Claudette were standing. His face was white and wild looking. "Well," he said. "What'll we all do *now*?" Then, oddly, he smiled, as though embarrassed at having spoken at all. He looked along the disconsolate line of people. "Where's your visiting director?" Then: "Oh."

Frye was standing between Mickey Castleton and Mona Greer, whose dark mascara was running with her tears.

"Goddamn," Geoffrey said. "That is one big fire." He seemed winded, struggling for air. "There goes my fucking job."

They watched Frye start into the hotel. He had to be helped by Mickey Castleton.

Malcolm saw Thaddeus and his wife go in, too. "Let's go in there," he said to Claudette.

Geoffrey followed them. They entered the spacious gold-lit lobby, with its soaring, chandeliered ceiling and its soft benches, red-cushioned chairs, and low, wide sofas facing polished circular tables. Claudette moved through the throng to Thaddeus and hugged him, holding Gina's hand tightly. Then she put her arms around Gina. "God," Gina said. Then, again: "God."

No one else spoke. They moved slowly to the wide windows looking out on the street. People were pressing close, there, without paying much attention to anything else. Some company members went the other way, into the bar, simply for the shelter of it and places to sit.

Malcolm looked at Geoffrey, who smiled, and then wiped the smile away. "I was in the bar, man. A drink after work. I must've left the gas on the stove."

Malcolm stared.

"Wait, there's no stove," the other went on. "Oh, this is just the big, fat, heavy fucking foot of fate. I mean, there goes my nice cushy fucking custodial job."

Malcolm turned away. His brother was standing close by. Gregory shook his head, and said, low, "Salina and Miranda are in California. The lawsuit about the winery. I put in a call."

"The rich ladies?" Geoffrey Chessman looked across Malcolm at him.

Gregory stared.

"Claudette's ex-husband," Malcolm explained.

"Oh, I know."

"I'm a little fucked up," said Geoffrey. "I'm sorry I pitched that bottle at you, man. That's over now. Water under the bridge." He smiled thinly, shaking his head.

Gregory's phone jangled. He turned, and held it to his ear. Frye walked over, accompanied by Mundy and Arthur Grausbeck. Neither of them had been asleep. "I don't know," Mundy said. "I just don't know about this."

"Everything," Frye said. "All that work. My good god*damn*."

Thaddeus

"I don't know what happened to my mother," Gina said, through tears. He touched her shoulder, then took his hand away. "I'll find her." He went back out into the street and across it, through the still-gathering crowd, and saw Louisa, sitting on a stone bench near the doorway of the Sunshine Café, smoking a cigarette. The tumult seemed to increase at the top of the block. The firefighters were spraying foam on the university law building across Front Street, evidently to keep the flames from spreading there. "I lost you all," Louisa said, blowing smoke. "I was going to get a coffee and smoke a cigarette on the way. I was going to bring a coffee back."

"Here." He extended his hand.

"All that life." His mother-in-law put the cigarette down, and stepped on it. She stood shakily, taking hold, and he walked with her back through the confusion toward the packed hotel lobby. Shafts of new sun spilled through a little opening in the still-raining clouds. The rain was lessening. The brightness of the fire, along with the sporadic sunlight reflecting off the windows of the law building, sent blinding glints. And across the horizon line beyond the far trees to the east, a spectacular rainbow shone just under another shelf of dark cloud. He and Louisa stopped. She put her arms around him, holding on. "Is this it?" she said. "Is this the end?" The rainbow dissolved in the folding, heavy sky. In the lobby, he said to Gina, "Should I ask if anyone wants coffee?"

"That's thoughtful, Thaddeus," she said, through tears. "Thank you."

"I was gonna bring back a coffee," Louisa said. "It's like the end of the world."

Mickey Castleton walked up and took Thaddeus's arm. "Come on, we'll order some food from the hotel kitchen. Someone's already offered."

They went over to the check-in area of the lobby, and were met by a small roundish man who had rolled out a large metal cart with shelves of sandwiches. The shelves and the frame of the cart were quite cold; it had come from a refrigerated storage room in the back of the restaurant. The roundish man, apparently the hotel manager, said, "This was all prepared for an influx of guests, a convention of librarians which begins tomorrow. Everybody'll understand." His voice was calm. "No charge for the sandwiches." Each shelf of the cart had a different kind of sandwich. Thaddeus said, "That's a great kindness, sir."

"Does anyone know what happened? How it started?"

"There was trouble with the wiring, but I don't think anyone knows yet." Thaddeus thanked him again and wheeled the cart into where everyone was gathered. The space looked depressingly sumptuous in contrast to the discouraged, grieving crowd, many of whom were merely seeking consolation in numbers. Mickey Castleton followed him with a portable carriage on which were urns of coffee, tea, and water, and a cooler of canned soft drinks in ice. "Compliments of the Madison Hotel," he kept saying.

Claudette

Louisa stood against a pillar nearby. "Too nervous and horrified to sit," she said. Gina sat close, shivering. Claudette saw Geoffrey resting an elbow on one of the giant stone pots of white flowers at the entrance. The flowers were grayish, and she thought of dust before she realized that it was ash from the fire, from the doors opening and closing on the street.

Earlier, she had asked Willamina to spend the night again, and had left her and Ellis sitting in the living room, watching the news coverage. Ellis seemed confused, and his face had taken on that startled look. He was still coughing a little from the flu he'd had, but his fever was gone, and before the news came through he and Willamina had happily sipped their one whiskey apiece. It had in fact been a lovely evening until they heard the sirens, and Willamina turned the TV on to see what was happening. Ellis, as Claudette was getting ready to drive out in the night, appeared to be taking the news as notice of the end of the life they had here in the apartment: there was such sadness and anxiety in his eyes. She wanted the crooked, charming smile. "Dad," she said, taking his hands. "It'll be all right. Everybody's safe."

"Sure," said Willamina. "That's what really matters."

"But are we going?" His stunned gaze was pleading; it reached deeply into her.

"We got it," said Willamina. "We'll do it. You'll see."

"I'll be back," Claudette told them.

"Is everybody all right?" he said. "Did everybody get out?"

She nodded, answering the question for the fourth time. "No one was there. Everybody's out, Daddy. Really. It's just an empty building, now." This made her throat close. She turned to keep him from seeing the tears that came. But he'd seen.

"Oh, come here, Little One."

She went and knelt, and put her arms around him.

Willamina sobbed softly, bending to hug them both. "You know I love you two," she said. "It's like Claudette said. Just an empty building."

Now, sitting in the crowded lobby with Gina, Louisa, and Lurlene, Claudette uttered the words again. "An empty building."

Gina turned. "What?"

"Nothing."

A moment later, Lurlene said, "Geoffrey looks lost."

Claudette saw his trembling fingers as he reached into his shirt pocket and brought out his cigarettes, then appeared to realize where he was, and put them back. He kept shifting his weight nervously from side to side.

"He looks like he needs a urinal," Lurlene said. "Is he on something again?"

He moved from the stone pot toward the doorway. A woman came pushing in, and hurrying by him, she dropped her umbrella. He simply observed as she bent over to pick it up. She was very slight, and had a large purse that appeared too heavy for her, and she dropped that, too. Her dismay was obvious; others turned when she uttered a distressed cry. Geoffrey bent and picked up the umbrella and the purse, and held them out to her, smiling, a man aware of his own gallantry. She nodded thanks at him and made her way to the check-in counter. Geoffrey looked at Claudette, then walked over and stopped about four feet away. He tipped an imaginary cap, and smiled almost clownishly. "Goodbye, my trouble and strife," he said, then turned and went slowly out.

"How can he be so oblivious," Lurlene said.

"Always was," Claudette said. "From the beginning. I don't know why I didn't see it."

Thaddeus

He saw them sitting together, and made his way there, carrying two paper cups of coffee. He offered it to them.

Lurlene took one and Gina just shook her head, not even quite aware of it, looking beyond him at the entrance, from which the glow up the street was visible.

"Not me," Claudette said. "I won't sleep. And I've *got* to sleep."

"Why?" he asked her. "What will we have to do tomorrow?" His voice broke.

"I'll have another one," said Louisa, extending her hand.

He gave it to her.

"Thanks, Young Fighter."

He pulled one of the plush velvet-cushioned chairs over and sat facing Gina, who still stared distractedly at the entrance, through all the others in the lobby. The crowd began thinning out. New thick storm clouds had tumbled in, blotting out the sun. There was a nightmarish chiaroscuro effect in the street, all the shadows again made by flame instead of sunlight.

Gina said, "Maybe more rain'll help."

Mona Greer came through from the check-in counter, holding a handkerchief to her mouth. She crossed in front of them and went out the door, and back down the street past the windows. They watched her.

"What'll she do, now?" Lurlene asked.

"What'll any of us do," said Thaddeus.

The rain started again, coming down hard. The Grausbecks and Frye came past. The lobby was emptying out, slowly. Mickey Castleton, Ernest Abernathy, Peggy Torres, and Don Seligman crossed and, after hesitating at the door, hurried across the street to the diner.

"Nothing to do but go," Thaddeus said.

"We'll come with you?" his wife said.

The tentativeness in her tone went through him. He stood. She looked at her mother, who moved to take her hand.

Claudette said, "I wish there was something any of us could do."

The Ruark brothers came over. "Arthur Grausbeck's called a meeting," Gregory said. "We're all supposed to gather somewhere Wednesday around eleven. The whole company."

"We have to find a place," said Malcolm.

"Maybe the Bland mansion?"

"What'll a gathering accomplish?" asked Lurlene, her features still showing distress, but her tone resonating with a kind of frantic hope.

"We've gotta figure the money," Gregory said. "Find a way to keep paying everybody."

"Ah, God. It's really all up in smoke, isn't it." Malcolm sat in one of the chairs. His brother put a hand on his shoulder. The others stared, silent. A last fire truck came roaring past the windows, siren blaring. It occurred to Thaddeus that he hadn't even heard the siren until he saw the truck with its flashing lights.

Gina had sat back down, and Louisa followed suit. "I don't feel good. I think it's my liver."

"Not now, Mother. Please. Let's just go home. Please?"

Thaddeus turned and moved alone to the doorway, and out into the rain. Beyond the cloud- and smoke-darkened sky to the east, the sun had broken through again, but the rain had become a deluge, slanting with wind off the river. Thaddeus went out into the pelting of it. The smell of burning stung his air passages. At the corner, he saw Geoffrey Chessman crossing Madison with a jerky, nervous, halting gate, and then turning around and going back. He did it again. It was like a choreographed marching back and forth; he repeated it, moving with the same tilting stride. Thaddeus crossed Main Street to meet him on his fourth trip back. Geoffrey stopped in front of him. "Can't decide where to go." His eyes were dead, glazed, seemed not to be taking anything in; there wasn't even any reflection in them—the light from the fire and the frenetic gleam of the police lights appeared to die at his jaw, which was clenched, and knotted. "Can't figure it—leave or stay." He began trying to unbutton his shirt; it was the custodian's uniform he had been issued. He started pulling at the shirt. "Off. You lendings."

Thaddeus put his hands on the other's forearms, stopping him. "Geoffrey, hey, buddy. This isn't the heath. You're not in the play."

The other straightened and drew a deep breath, then gave a wide, lunatic smile. "This is where I say, 'I'm cut to the brains.' And you say, 'You are a royal one.'"

"Come on, man." Thaddeus started buttoning the shirt. "Let's get you somewhere you can come down from this, whatever this is."

"You're goddamned right I'm not in the play, man. Nobody is. This is the end of everything, Thaddeus. My last job." Now the chaotic lights were gleaming in the other's irises. "Goddamn," he went on. "You'd think it was a bomb."

Thaddeus looked up the street again at the tremendous flash-filled agitation of the smoke. "Come on," he said. "Let's get off the street."

Geoffrey stared as if to appraise him. "I always liked you."

Thaddeus felt the urge to ask him if he understood any of what had just happened. "Can you get where you need to go now?"

The other shook his head slowly. "Are you my boss now? I haven't had it explained to me."

"It's all gone now, Geoffrey."

"Can't decide which way to go, Mr. Deerforth. Go to the left it's disaster. Go to the right, disaster. Go up there"—he pointed at the blaze still roaring skyward—"disaster. You know?"

"Terrible," Thaddeus said, for lack of anything else. There wasn't anything else.

"Anyway, I always liked you fine. It was Miles Warden I couldn't stand."

"Hey, Geoff," he said. "You're stoned, huh."

"All the rest of them—well, fuck. The Grausbecks were nice."

He said nothing.

"Claudette and me—I thought we might get back together, you know."

Again, Thaddeus was silent.

"I'm not stoned, man. I'm confused. Like you. Only you've got someplace to go."

"I've gotta go, now, too," he heard himself say.

Geoffrey went off up the street, trying to tuck in the shirt as he walked.

"Get some sleep," Thaddeus called after him.

"End of our world, Mr. Deerforth. Nothing we can do."

"We'll make it," said Thaddeus.

The other waved the hand that had been pulling at the shirtfront. "'Come, good Athenian.'" He turned and went on, lurching a little, being jostled by people coming the other way. Then with a final tottering step, he looked back, waved, and smiled. The smile seemed strangely arbitrary, so irrelevant that Thaddeus marked it as crazy, like the earlier one, and wondered what drug the man must have taken.

He walked down to his car, got in, and sat there behind the wheel. The Ruark brothers and Claudette were going down the street ahead, toward AutoZone Park, holding a raincoat over their heads. He started the car and let it idle to where they were. "Ride?" he called out the window.

"I'm right here," Claudette said, indicating her car. A few feet farther on, the brothers got in another car. Thaddeus watched them pull away.

It was over. Everything was over, as Geoffrey had said. At the efficiency, he stood dripping wet just inside the door. It was seven-thirty in the morning. Gina and Louisa would have returned to the house. He showered, put on fresh clothes, and still it seemed that his very skin smelled of smoke. He sat on the newly slept-in bed, and began to cry again, then lay back. It was as if all his inner surfaces had been seared, whitened by the burning, and he was numb, hands folded on his chest. The world itself was only facts, one fact. A new, pitiless reality, itself, ungraspable, terrible. He fell asleep, both feet on the floor. When he woke, minutes later, he didn't know how long he'd been under—didn't know, indeed, that he *had* been under. There was more light in the room, though it was still raining. And there was a knock at the door. He stood unsteadily, his legs having fallen asleep, and opened it.

Gina, alone.

VI

Glorious

Friday, July 31–Saturday, August 15

Thaddeus

"I'm so scared," she said.

As he reflexively reached for her, she walked into his arms. They stood that way for a long time in the sound of the rain. He felt her sighing and shuddering. "Here," he said, and reached behind her to shut the door. They moved to the reclining chair, and sat in it together, huddled close, not speaking, listening to the storm outside. He breathed the smell of the rain on her. "I'm so scared," she said again.

He sighed. "Me, too." He held tight, fearful of upsetting the balance of this minute, wanting not to say the wrong thing or do the wrong thing. He would refrain from trying to kiss her. He would be still.

"I wish it was last summer," she sobbed, low.

He waited.

"I hate my own mind."

"I like your own mind," he told her. "I'm dog-tired of *my* own mind." He had the sudden discouraging realization that, once again, he'd made it all about himself. He almost cringed, expecting the reaction. Then said, "Sorry."

"I took Louisa home," she murmured.

After a pause, he said, "Is Whitcomb there?"

She nodded slightly. "Probably under the bed."

He managed to keep back the laugh that started. "Is that where he was when you left him?"

"No."

Again, he waited.

"He kept yelling at us that he was in a fire, once, as a kid. Barely got out of the place. Had to jump. That's what he said. Yelled. He kept repeating it. Over and over. How he barely got out of the place and had to jump. Ten years old. Broke his leg, he said. He just kept on while we were getting dressed to go over there. Like if it was said loud enough, we'd decide not to go."

Thaddeus let a few moments pass while she pressed closer, as if trying to get inside his shirt.

"Kelly Gordon was sick," she said. "At a urinal in the downstairs men's at the Madison. We saw her through the open door. They opened all the doors. We saw her like that and then Louisa said she felt sick and I was short with her. God." She sobbed. "I took her home."

Another silence, a long interval. There were still sirens off in the distance.

"Think those are still about the fire?" she asked.

"Doubt it."

She shrugged. The little movement at his shoulder made him happy. The whole world could burn. He breathed, and closed his arm slightly on the warm, soft solidness of her there.

"I want you to come back, Wolfie."

He started to say, breathe, *Oh, yes*. He felt the letting go, a deep sighing as if, after an interlude of cramping in his diaphragm, he had recovered the strength to exhale again. The entire lingual apparatus of his ability to speak trembled with the will for utterance. But something stopped him. He couldn't believe it. He turned in himself and was appalled at his own failure to articulate what was there. She sat up a little, and gazed into his eyes.

"I'm scared and sad and I want you to come back," she said.

"It's the fire," he heard himself say.

"What?"

"It's the fire. The theater burning down."

She waited, staring.

"Think about it, Gina. You just said you want me to come back."

"I do."

"You didn't say you want me to come *home*. You just told me you're scared and sad. And you want me to come back."

"I know what I said. I want you to come home. There."

"I can't. Think about it. It wouldn't—I just can't. Not out of this awfulness."

"What're you telling me." She stood, now.

"I want to come home, Gina. Oh, God, like nothing I ever wanted before. So much. But not like this. I *can't* like this. In this—this awfulness."

She stood there, silent, staring.

"Don't you see? If you really look at it, you have to see. Can we just get through and be clear of *all this* just a little?"

She reached for her scarf. Crying again. "I can't help any of it," she said. "I didn't cause the fire and I can't fix it."

"Who said anything about fixing it?" he said. "I love you. You've got to understand."

"Everything's gone up in smoke." She sobbed. "Us and everybody."

He remained silent. She was standing there waiting for him to react, and again he didn't have the ability to utter a single sound. There was no pride in this dumbfounded silence; in fact, there was something of shame—even fear. He thought of what she didn't know, could never know.

She wiped across her face with her forearm. "I'll see you around."

"Don't," he got out. "Don't talk like that. We'll be okay. You'll see."

"Well, don't break your neck trying."

"Gina—"

She turned, strode to the door, and went out, hurrying to her car without looking back.

Malcolm

Before Claudette had driven away, he pressed her hands gently, a signal between them. He took Gregory home, then drove to the cottage at the edge of the Old Forest. He entered and closed the windows and the curtains, and got into the bed. Before he was asleep, Gregory phoned. "You okay?"

"Gonna try to sleep."

"I wonder what'll happen now."

"I don't even want to think about it."

"Well, we'll talk later today."

He sank into a deep, dreamless sleep, and woke with the phone still in his hand. He got up, hurrying, though he didn't know why there was any need for that now. He showered, stood in the water a long time, then shaved and dressed and put coffee on. It had become a bright afternoon, the window full of sun. He sat drinking the coffee, trying not to think. When he stepped out the door, he saw Eleanor Cruikshank on the porch of the big house. She lifted one hand in what seemed a hesitant waving gesture. He walked over to where she waited with one hand on the porch rail. She looked like a Victorian lady in her ankle-length dark skirt and starched blouse the color of a funeral lily with high, tight-laced collar. "The television people say it's a complete loss," she said. "What'll you do?"

He sat down on the edge of the porch, the damp boards there; even having slept for a period, he felt very weary.

She said, "Come inside."

"If I could just rest here a little."

She pulled the rocking chair closer, and sat down. They remained that way for a few moments. She rocked slowly, the chair faintly creaking. "You're out of work now?"

"I don't know."

"When will you know?"

He turned slightly and looked at her. "I won't fail to pay the rent."

"I wasn't worried about the rent, Mr. Ruark."

"Call me Malcolm."

"Malcolm."

"I'll find a way to keep it up. The rent."

She was quiet. There was only the sound of the chair.

"For all I know, we'll still be paid."

"I just said I'm not worried about it. So—" She paused, then: "*You* don't worry about it either."

"You're very kind."

Again, they were quiet. The little creaking-wood sound came from the chair. Her brother stepped out, wearing shorts and a white knit shirt. He sighed. "Arson."

Malcolm turned. Eleanor Cruikshank stopped rocking and raised her eyes to her brother. "Martin?" she said.

"The fire chief, just now. I saw it." He drew in a sobbing breath. "On my TV. Arson."

Eleanor Cruikshank rose from her chair. All three of them went inside to the small room off the kitchen where Martin's television was broadcasting the fire chief's news conference.

"No, we don't have that information as yet," the fire chief was saying in answer to a question they hadn't heard.

Martin turned the volume up with his remote.

"Yes," the fire chief said. "We do have a suspect. We're looking into it. I can't say more now. We think the same method was used that the so-called pillowcase pyro used in San Francisco a few years back."

"An inside job?" Eleanor wondered.

Claudette

She found Willamina asleep on the sofa, and Ellis in his chair with a book on his lap, also asleep. She entered as soundlessly as she could, out of the gray light and the rain, exhausted, wanting sleep. She went into her bedroom and without undressing pulled the blanket back and got in. She thought she'd never felt anything so perfectly relieving as that cool soft pillow when she nestled against it. But sleep wouldn't come. She kept seeing the glare of the street and the flames, the figures scurrying back and forth in the shuddering light, the confusion, and the trucks, the high arching columns of water disappearing into that massive wall of upward-tumbling motion. It was as if it were all burned into her eyes, a brand there, like the imprint from having stared at the sun.

Cars went by on the street outside. She watched the shifting light on her wall through the red lampshade by her window. It looked like smoldering. She closed her eyes tight, attempting not to see it, but it was on the underside of her lids. She saw Malcolm, with his stricken features, and the shimmer of reflected flame-glow in his wide eyes. Her wakefulness transferred itself into falling off, so that she dreamed she was unsuccessfully trying to sleep.

Her phone buzzed, startling her, and when she reached for it she realized that it was almost midday, and both Ellis and Willamina were awake. They had put on an old movie.

"Hello?" she said into the phone, still gathering herself out of the sleep she hadn't been aware of.

Arthur Grausbeck's unsteady voice: "Claudette," he said. "Are you all right?"

"Groggy," she said. "You?"

"Ah—" He cleared his throat. "I don't know how to say this, so I'll just say it out. Geoffrey burned us down."

She held the phone tight. "He—what?"

"He set the fire, Claudette."

"He was smoking in there," she said. "I saw him."

"Bub-bub—this isn't dropping a lit cigarette or forgetting to put it out. He intentionally and with malice burned us to the ground."

"I don't—" The words seemed idiotic to her. "Arthur," she said.

"He texted me, Claudette. And he—he actually called the cops. The police say he took a lot of alcohol and—and, I'm sorry. A lethal amount of some drug. A sleep drug."

"Lethal?"

"I'm so sorry."

"Oh, God." She started to cry. She heard herself crying.

"Did you talk to him at all, after the—during the—"

"Very briefly," she managed.

"Did you get the sense—" He stopped. "This isn't the time."

"Oh, God," she said.

"He put together some kind of device—I can't understand it."

She was silent for a moment. Covering her eyes with one hand. "You—you said, sleep drug?"

"Right. I wrote it down." There was a slight pause and a shuffle. Then: "Fentanyl."

"Accidentally?" She was sobbing, not even quite aware of what she was saying. "Is it possible it was accidental?"

Arthur Grausbeck was slow to answer. He sighed. "Not accidental, no."

Malcolm

Quincey Blair flew in Monday morning. He took a cab to the house at the edge of the Old Forest. Malcolm Ruark met him there. He was a tall, carefully groomed blond man with a close haircut and eyes the shade of a hot summer sky. Malcolm saw the cab pull in and went out to meet him. They shook, and Malcolm, marking the moistness of the small palid hand limp in his own, surreptitiously ran his palm across his hip as they moved to the porch. There, Eleanor Cruikshank took the handshake and then brought a hankie out of her jeans and wiped both hands, completely without stealth.

"Sorry," Quincey Blair said. "It's really humid here. I forgot how bad it can be."

"Would you care for some iced tea?" the novelist asked.

"That might be just the thing."

She indicated the rocker and the chair next to it, then stepped inside. Malcolm took the rocker, and as Blair sat in the chair they heard the little porcelain bell. Blair said, "Servants. Wow."

"Her older brother. How long did you know Geoffrey?"

"Couple years." He shook his head.

"Would you predict that he might do what he did?"

"Naw, hell, who'd predict a thing like that? I trusted him, man."

They waited. Eleanor Cruikshank brought out their glasses of tea, and stood there leaning against the porch railing.

"Look," Quincey Blair said. "He was a fuckup—" He paused and nodded at her. "Pardon. But I thought he was trying to make some kind of comeback, you know?"

"I think *he* might've thought he was doing just that," Malcolm told him.

"Fact is," Blair said. "The guy was a liar. He'd tell you one of your own stories as if it happened to him. Everything was lies. I mean, I thought it was his way of—I don't know—trying to be entertaining. But he always wanted center stage, always gave himself the snappy lines in every story."

"You're describing a type," Eleanor Cruikshank said. "There must've been more than that to him."

Blair shrugged. "Well, he said he got beat up a lot by his dad when he was growing up. But, I mean, that's what he *said*. Hard times. That seemed true. I don't know much else. He wanted real bad to be famous. And he got beat up as a kid. Those two things, basically."

"Do you know Chekhov?"

"I'm an actor, ma'am. Of course I know Chekhov."

"Chekhov's father was a brutal man. The boy's first thought every morning was 'When will I get beat up, today.' But his funeral was crowded with people who didn't even know he was a writer. To them, he was just this kindly physician who treated them without charging them."

"Yeah, I get it," Blair said. "It's not an equation—I got a few beatings, too, growing up. But I never hit anybody or ever thought of harming anybody or anything."

"Do you think it's possible he was coming back here to do what he did?"

"I can't say that, ma'am. Far as I know—I mean, what he told me—was that it was all just a matter of taking up his old life. He'd come home and his ex would take him back and everything would be fine."

"I know he still considered her as belonging to him," Malcolm said.

Blair nodded. "Convinced she'd fall into his arms, man."

There was a pause. Martin came out with the pitcher of iced tea, and offered more of it. The two men declined. Eleanor said, "I'll have a little, Martin." He nodded and went back inside, then came back with a glass for her.

"This is a beautiful place," Blair said. "I used to like driving by it when I lived here."

"We like it," Eleanor said.

"So, where's Geoffrey's wife?"

"Ex-wife," Malcolm said. "She's not involved in this."

Suicide is considered a crime, so Blair's apartment in Midtown was a crime scene. They drove there for an appointment with a Detective Weber. Malcolm told Detective Weber that he had urged Claudette not to be there, understanding that she wasn't up to involving herself beyond whatever questions the police might want to ask. "She's pretty upset."

"I already spoke to her," Weber said. He was a sallow, gloomy-looking, stoop-shouldered man with bags under his eyes. "She's just as much in the dark as the rest of us."

The apartment had been cordoned off. In the small living room, there was a chalk line on the floor, and Geoffrey Chessman's custodian uniform was strewn around as if he'd hurled it piece by piece from himself; the shirt had landed on a lamp, the pants on the television cabinet. Nothing of this had been touched.

"As near as we can make it," Weber said, pointing to the syringe and the half-empty bottle of vodka on the side table, "he came back here sometime the night of the fire, swallowed a good deal of the vodka, and then injected a lethal hit of the fentanyl. We don't know where he might've got the drug." The detective went on to say the dead man evidently hadn't even intended to be stealthy about the arson. "It must've been some sort of final act for him. He was on his shift, the building was empty, nobody'd be injured or killed. He put his little homemade device at the base of that giant velour front curtain."

"Device," Malcolm said.

The detective nodded. "Pretty simple, really. Something you can set up and walk away from. You light a cigarette and attach it by rubber bands to a box of matches with one match sticking out where the cigarette will eventually burn to, you know, the coal, and when that reaches the one match, the one match flares up, which ignites the matches in the box, and all this rolled in a handkerchief. The whole thing bursts and—" Weber made a motion of an upward rush with both hands. "You get the idea."

Geoffrey's text had said, *Thanks for the kindness, Mr. G, if that's what it was. It wasn't enough. I set the fire. It's the least I could do for Miles Warden and the rest of them. I'm over now. Last performance.* Sometime later, he called the police. He got through to the dispatcher and said, simply, "I'm Geoffrey Chessman. It's my fire. I set it. I'm at 139 Cooper. No need to rush."

Blair sat on the bed and put his hands to his face. "Christ," he said. "I didn't expect this—" He looked up at the detective. "This is hard, man. I didn't even know the guy that well. I'm an actor."

"I'm a homicide detective," Weber said. "You think I don't know this is hard?" He went on to say that the deceased had no family. Apparently, the only people directly connected to him were Quincey Blair and Claudette Bradley. "As I said, I spoke to Ms. Bradley, and upset as she was, she managed to let me know both his parents're dead—his mother nobody knows where, and his father, of an apparent suicide, when the boy was fifteen or sixteen. He wasn't in touch with any kin she knew of. Does this seem correct?"

"He never said anything to me about any family or anything about his father offing himself, either. He was just a guy to me. He talked about his father being drunk and hitting him with a stick. But mostly he talked about *her,* and how he was gonna win her back."

"Well, that's about it, then." The officer handed Blair a card from a little clutch of them in his wallet. "These people specialize in cleaning up after things like this."

"Thanks, man."

"From the guy's cell we traced some associations with several types known for trafficking drugs here in the city, but none of them had any history of retailing fentanyl, and none admitted to ever meeting him, or even speaking to him. We had a woman come forward to say she spent part of a night with him at the Peabody Hotel. On her dime. And that was that."

Malcolm drove away, leaving Blair and the detective and the mess. He drove to Madison Avenue and parked in front of the hotel. The arsonist was dead, and the new Globe was a smoldering shell of broken-down brick walls. It looked like one of those ruined buildings in pictures of war.

Later, he drove to Claudette's apartment. Willamina answered the door. "She took her father to a place they used to go on the river. Just the two of them."

"I'm sorry."

"You want to come in? They should be back in a bit."

"No, thanks. Can you tell her I stopped by?"

"Sure will."

He went back to the Overton Park house. He saw Eleanor Cruikshank in her garden, but decided not to disturb her.

In the cottage, he undressed and showered again (it seemed impossible to get rid of the smell of the burning), leaving his cell phone within reach, on the sink. Claudette didn't call.

As the sun was going down, he called her. Willamina answered. "Sorry. I've got her phone. Ellis is needing her attention just now."

"Can she call me?"

"The detective spoke to her."

"Yes. It's over. Pretty cut and dried."

"Not to her."

"I know," he said. "I'm sorry."

They ended the call. But Claudette called right back. "I'm sorry." She was crying.

"Nothing to apologize for."

"God, it's—ah. It's such a big part of my life, you know? The theater and—and everything. There were—we—I don't know where to put it, Malcolm. You know, he never really seemed sad. It was always rage. He would talk about it. I thought it was passion, you know? I saw him with kids, and he was always so much *with* them. Like one of them. I remember thinking he'd make a great dad." She took a slow, sobbing breath, then coughed. Malcolm waited. "Oh, God," she moaned. "Everything feels so final."

"I know," he told her.

Thaddeus

Since Thaddeus and his wife were not together, and the Cosmetics Tycoons were in Sonoma, California, there was confusion about where the Wednesday meeting would take place. Wednesday, Thaddeus thought—the day after what would've been the opening. Finally Arthur Grausbeck called everyone with the news that the meeting would take place in the big house on the edge of the Old Forest. Eleanor Cruikshank's house. She had offered, Arthur said, and Malcolm had accepted the offer on behalf of the whole company. Jocelyn had the flu. She would try to attend on Skype.

That morning, Thaddeus drank coffee alone in the efficiency, then showered and dressed, and drove to the Madison. In the Sunshine diner, he ordered eggs and bacon, and more coffee, paying attention to these humble things, which were finally, perhaps not so strangely, more important than they'd ever seemed; they were the necessary steps getting through: you fed yourself, and you tried not to think of the dark too much. The mood in the place was solemn. People were lingering on the sidewalk outside, staring up the street at the smoking ruin. Several of them talked and laughed as if viewing the aftermath of some sort of carnival stunt. It was destruction, and they were fascinated. Thaddeus, when he had finished eating, stood among them, watching the embers rise. The whole street looked wrecked, debris and ash everywhere, and running mud.

He called Malcolm, but got no answer. The same was true when he tried Claudette. Louisa answered Gina's phone. Gina was in the shower. As he disconnected and started down the walk away from the ashes, Malcolm called him. "I was talking to Salina when you called. She's up early. She says she'll Skype from LA at eleven-thirty. Our time. Miranda flew to Chicago last night. She'll arrive this morning at nine."

"And the Grausbecks?"

"She still has flu."

"Should I come now?"

"Have you eaten?"

"Just did. I'm at the diner."

"Pretty bad up the street, I'll bet."

"Looks like a bomb hit it."

"Come on over," Malcolm said. "No reason not to."

At the Old Forest house, the novelist's older brother introduced himself, letting him in. "We're still in the kitchen," he said. "This way."

They went into a high-ceilinged room that had the look of kitchens of the thirties and forties. Thaddeus thought of old movies. Malcolm was seated at the table with his friend the novelist, who invited him to have a seat.

Martin also took a seat. The remains of breakfast lay before them. Thaddeus politely declined the offer of some coffee or toast.

"You've been to the site," Eleanor Cruikshank said.

"Yes."

"Still smoldering, I imagine."

"Smoldering, yes."

"Dreadful." She rose and touched her face with her serviette, then dropped it over her plate of half-eaten French toast. "If you'll excuse me." She left the room.

"This is such a beautiful house," Thaddeus managed.

"How well did you know Chessman?" Malcolm asked him.

"I thought I knew him pretty well, actually."

"Claudette's devastated."

Thaddeus shrugged helplessly, looking at the room. "I guess we all are in different ways."

"She's grieving him."

He could only bring himself to say, "Well, they were a married couple, you know. And even after the end of the marriage they were still in touch. I always thought of them as—stormy, you know."

"He kept calling her his lady to me."

Thaddeus shook his head. "Last time I saw him he was crossing Madison back and forth, talking to himself. He quoted Lear at me. It was like he wanted to play a scene. Like he *was* playing a scene. We used to get along, you know. We were friends, Gina and me and Claudette and Geoffrey. I always thought he was a little—I don't know—*tolerant* of me, because Claudette and I got so close when I directed her in the Scottish play."

Light poured through the high windows of the room, and the bird and insect song was frantic; a dog yelped somewhere. It all seemed to come from alarm.

Malcolm got up and went outside. Thaddeus followed. The air was hot, even at this hour of the morning. Eleanor Cruikshank was in her garden, working there with the stand-up weeder, wearing her wide-brimmed straw hat. They heard Martin cleaning the kitchen behind them. Thaddeus thought of going in and offering to help, but remained where he was. Malcolm called to the novelist, "Get you anything?"

She answered, "Perhaps I'll have a little tea."

The two men went back inside, and Martin, having heard her through the window, had already poured the tea. He took it out to her. Malcolm sat at the table again, and Thaddeus did, too. He felt useless and in the way. Malcolm had drunk down what was left of his coffee. The brother returned and poured more, and then offered some to Thaddeus. Thaddeus took it, sitting there at the table in the quiet.

"What do you suppose he had in mind?" Malcolm said suddenly.

"Who? Geoffrey?"

His smile was rueful and brief. He swallowed, shaking his head. "God."

There was of course no reply to this.

Later, with the novelist and her brother, the two men helped make platters of sliced cheese and fruits, with an assortment of crackers, Martin deftly arranging the look of it all. Then he and his sister, with Malcolm and Thaddeus's help, arranged things in the big room with the palladium windows, placing chairs next to the sofa and just behind it, moving the dining room table, where they would place Grausbeck's laptop for Skype, to the center of the room, just in front of the entrance.

People started arriving a little after ten. The board, members of the company, and the cast—Mickey Castleton, Ernest Abernathy, Peggy Torres, Michael Cross, Don Seligman, Mona Greer, and the other actors, except Mundy and Claudette. Mary Cho and Lurlene Glenn came in together. Other members of the staff were arriving. Everyone entered slowly, even shyly, looking at the pictures on the walls and the many books. Thaddeus was watching for Gina, who came in with Claudette. Gina looked over at him, and without expression looked away. He moved to stand near her, and acknowledged Claudette's nod. Gina glanced at him again, and he lifted his hand in a little waist-high wave. He saw the lost look in Claudette's eyes, where her makeup hadn't successfully concealed the shadows from the crying she'd done and the sleep she'd lost.

Everyone waited in silence after the low greetings and separate murmurings; it felt like a memorial service.

Miranda arrived at eleven-ten with Arthur Grausbeck. Her flight from Chicago had been delayed. She wore a silk blouse and blue jeans with the cuffs rolled to midcalf. She looked like someone coming from a bike ride. "I hate flying," she announced to the room. "Every bump scares me." She moved around offering her hand to people, introducing herself when necessary, and smiling with those small gray, pushed-in-looking teeth, murmuring her condolences for the disaster. When she got to Thaddeus, she said, "I had a sense of foreboding when we left for California. I told Salina." Her breath smelled faintly of peanuts. "I felt it in my bones and blood. Did you have any inkling?" Even in this gloomy, atavistic speculation, her eyes were bright and friendly.

Thaddeus said, "None. I thought things were working out."

She said, "Don't worry," as if he'd spoken about worrying.

Eleanor Cruikshank's brother was moving around the room, holding out a platter of pastries and fruit. Malcolm went over and poured coffee, and then offered various juices on a tray.

Salina would call at eleven-thirty. Grausbeck's laptop was open and the screensaver was on—fishes crossing a coral backdrop. As the time neared, everyone began to assemble, and they kept glancing at the door and the sunlit windows out on the street for Frye and Mundy and Kelly Gordon.

At twenty after, Jocelyn Grausbeck FaceTimed on her husband's iPhone. Thaddeus thought it might be Salina. Grausbeck held up the phone so she could see everyone. She looked terrible, as though she'd been crying sleeplessly all night. She coughed, and then struggled to breathe through a long spasm. At length, after this particularly bad spell, she blew her nose, and with a wheezing apology, and a wish for good luck, signed off. Then they were all waiting quietly, expectantly, for Reuben Frye and the other two. At eleven-thirty, there was no call from Salina. At fifteen minutes to noon, Thaddeus said what he felt sure everyone else was thinking. "I guess they're not coming."

"Let's not rush," Miranda said. "There's no rush."

"As soon as Salina calls, we should start," he said. He was aware of Gina watching him.

Gregory Ruark arrived, a little out of breath. He had hurried over from the Brooks Museum, whose accounts he also managed.

"Where's Frye and the others?" he asked. Then, seeing Miranda, he reached to shake her hand.

"They're late," said Gina.

Finally, the Skype call came through. Salina looked impatient and irritable. "Everyone there?" she said.

"Not all of us," Miranda said.

"Bub-bub-bub, we're still waiting for Mundy, Frye, and Gordon."

"I texted them about it last night, and this morning."

"I did, too, when I got to the airport," Miranda said.

No one said anything for a moment.

Then Grausbeck said, "Me, too."

"And me," Thaddeus put in.

"Ms. Cruikshank," Salina volunteered, "I liked *White Hawthorne* quite a lot."

"Thank you," said Eleanor. "That's very kind. And I'm very sorry for this trouble."

"We're grateful for the use of your place for this meeting. It's saved us a lot of time and trouble."

"I'm glad I could help."

Salina said, "Let's hear it, everybody."

Applause came brokenly forth, then gradually increased as people understood what she expected.

"Miranda, have you filled them in?"

"I was waiting for you."

Salina paused, and took a deep breath. "Everybody. First, we're well insured. And even if we weren't, we'd do this. We're gonna rebuild. We're gonna put the Globe right back together, exactly where it was and *as* it was."

This caused an immediate general stir of approval, and applause. Thaddeus looked over at Claudette, whose expression hadn't changed.

When it got quiet again, Mona Greer said, very shakily, "How much time will it take?"

"Relax," said Salina. "I know you're distraught. We all are. But it's not the end of the world. Thanks to Miranda, we've already got permits and a commitment from the city. Everybody's on board. We've gotta get assessments and other paperwork, and settle the claim with the insurance companies, and we've gotta have the site cleared, of course. I'd say the whole thing's gonna take the best part of a year, give or take a couple of months."

Everyone was silent.

Eleanor Cruikshank asked quietly if anyone needed replenishment and, in the following silence, asked if there was any other news.

"We do have some," Salina said. "Some little bit."

Miranda, sitting in a chair next to the sofa, said, "Come on, Salina."

Salina smiled cagily.

"We've got to decide some things," Mickey Castleton said, then looked around, seeming surprised at himself.

"We're out of work," Mona Greer moaned, low.

"No." Salina's voice was patient, and the smile was still there. "Here's my other news, people. Miranda and I have decided everybody's pay'll continue without any interruption. According to the various contracts."

Now the applause was full, loud, and long. Thaddeus, applauding, looked over at Gina, and saw her say something to Claudette. Claudette was looking around at everyone with something like wonderment.

"Also," Salina said. "Also, also—" She waited for quiet. "Also, we've spoken to the folks at the Monroe School of Dramatic Arts, and they're gonna let us use their stage, the old City Stage, for our *Lear. And.*" She paused significantly. "The other two productions."

She waited until the ruckus of approval died down again.

"It'll all have to be truncated, of course—we'll only have it for Thursdays, and Saturday and Sunday matinees. And early mornings or late nights for rehearsals. We'll have to move the preview night to the thirteenth—that's eight days—but you're already prepared and ready to go with all the lines and you'll have a week to accommodate to the new space. And there'll only be the one preview night, before we actually open on the fifteenth. Of course you'll be working with a pretty steep minimum where sets and effects come in. But they'll be doing their senior class's presentation of *Measure for Measure* and—well—it's Shakespeare. And from what I understand the sets for our productions were fairly simple, even the *Lear.* Is it possible to meld them some way in a week's time?"

Grausbeck turned to Gina. "What do you think?"

She seemed momentarily doubtful, looking around at everyone. Then with a nervous little reflexive sound almost like a laugh, she said, "I'd have to look at it. But we ought to be able to find some way to adjust to whatever's there. The important thing's the words, anyway."

"The play is the thing!" Ernest Abernathy burst forth. It was like a cheer. Everyone applauded again. The room was filled with good feeling, a generous sighing of goodwill all around. Again, Thaddeus looked over at Gina, who was looking back.

Salina said, "And you can bet we're gonna have an extremely sympathetic audience."

"Will there be a way I can talk now?" Mona Greer asked, and because it looked as if she wanted to say something in the moment, the others waited for her to continue.

She gave forth a little weary sigh. "I mean, maybe I don't have to be mute?"

Mickey Castleton said, "Won't we have to see what Frye's willing to do?"

"Oh, fuck Frye," she said with a sudden shocking emphasis. Then: "Where is he?"

No one said anything.

"And where's Mundy?" Salina asked from the computer screen. "And where's the other one. What the hell."

Again, everyone was still. Perhaps half a minute went by.

"Well. As far as I'm concerned—this meeting's adjourned," she said. "Let's get back to work, anyway. We've got plays to put on. I've gotta be in court. I'll be back in town by tomorrow or the next day." And then she waved, and vanished from the screen—exactly, Thaddeus thought, like a fairy godmother in a fantasy for children.

After a brief pause, he said, "Here's to Salina and Miranda."

Everyone applauded, and Miranda stood beaming, hands in the pockets of her jeans.

He saw Gina hug Claudette. Eleanor Cruikshank walked over from the fireplace and offered her hand. "Congratulations."

"Thank you," Thaddeus said, offering his best smile.

"There's even room *here* to do some rehearsing," she said. "If you need it." And then she was moving past him, to Malcolm, indicating the foyer. Martin had moved to the door and opened it. Frye and the other two had arrived.

Claudette

The visit from Detective Weber had been excruciating. Ellis kept breaking in, first introducing himself—which he did twice—then questioning the poor man about the whereabouts of Esther and Meryl. Willamina finally suggested that the detective and Claudette take a walk outside, so she and Ellis could finish their James Cagney movie.

"Always liked Jimmy Cagney," Detective Weber said. And Ellis wanted to talk about that.

Finally, they were outside, and walking down the street, away. "He's not always this bad," Claudette said. "The fire upset him."

"Like it did everybody." The detective took a breath. "Was there anything about your husband's—"

She broke in. "He wasn't my husband. We were officially divorced in October of 2011, four months after he went to Hollywood."

"Forgive me." He looked at the little notepad he had. "But weren't you in touch with him?"

The tears started again. She stopped. "Yes. We'd talk on the phone."

"And how often would that have been?"

"There wasn't a—there wasn't any pattern. Sometimes he'd call and we'd talk."

"Did you ever call him?"

She ran her wrist under her nose and sniffled. "No."

"But you didn't mind his calling you."

"Most of the time—" She had to speak through a sob. "No."

"I know this is hard. I wish there was a way around it."

She shook her head, trying to gain control.

He waited.

"I'm sorry," she got out.

"No, I do understand. Just a—just a couple more questions."

They walked on a few paces.

"What would—what would you talk about on these occasions?"

She thought a few seconds. How strange that she couldn't really find a way to say what the conversations were about. "We talked about him, mostly."

"Anything you'd term as *concerning*, given what's taken place?"

She stopped again, crying. "No," she managed. "How can anyone know or suspect a thing like that. He'd say extreme things, like—like anybody. The last time I talked to him he was—he was reciting from *Hamlet*." She wept for an interval while he simply stood there. And when she started walking again, he did, too. Then she stopped once more. "I—I can't really tell you anything else. His father stepped in front of an oncoming car. His mother disappeared, and then his father went with several others. One of whom might've sexually abused him. He never had a home life. He never finished high school."

Very gently, Detective Weber said, "You think this might explain—"

And again, she interrupted him. "Oh, Mr. Weber, so many people have it tough growing up. So many—so many people out there with lousy parents and deaths and hardships. But they don't do what Geoffrey did, do they? I don't know the answer. I'm trying to put away from myself the feeling that I should've known or sensed it from the beginning." She sobbed. "At least he didn't kill anyone but himself."

"Well, people can change for the worst, of course," the detective said, almost apologetically. "Or I'd be out of a job."

She had experienced recurring images of Geoffrey in the times when they were good together and the laughter was easy. His boylike immaturity, which was something they teased about: all the things he wouldn't do, or bring himself to try. No boats, no motorcycles, no elevators or Ferris wheels. No green peppers, though he would eat banana peppers by the handful. The way he would stop everything, frowning, and then think of something else fun to do. His enthusiasms, and his willingness to go beyond social boundaries—playing with the expectations of the citizens, he called it. Faking a tic, or assuming an indeterminate accent and pretending to be from a made-up foreign country. His jokes about his gone schizophrenic mother, who left him with his father, and how both of them were batshit. The laughs when he would tell of his grandmother's fear of Martians and ghosts, and how those two fears eventually fused into one fright about Martian ghosts. Claudette saw the endearing silliness and eccentricity, and the marvelous look of him back then. That, too.

And then she saw again the way he looked at her that last time, in the theater, when they recited the lines from *Hamlet*.

Where had the lightheartedness and the happy wildness gone?

How had everything disappeared so far into ire and the sense of being imprisoned? Over the hours of sleeplessness, she consciously entertained images of the dissatisfactions, the recklessness, the destructive fits, and the indulgences—and even the boredom—trying to see through it all, to some kind of explanation for any of it. She went over different scenarios, a form of interior cataloging of instances where she had considered his extremes, where she saw him walk away from one disaster or another between them, and thought of him as someone headed into other settings, life somewhere else, as it had been when he moved to LA. How terrible to think of him raging so deeply in himself that he could bring everything down, all possibility of any other chances. She couldn't fathom the least element of that negation. He had been beautiful; *they* had been beautiful. He had died alone, and her sorrow about it had taken all the flavor out of things. But she felt she must go through whatever this was going to be, this new reality, alone. She hadn't even spoken to Ellis or Willamina about it, Willamina understanding without speech, and Ellis—well, Ellis simply wasn't aware of a lot of it. And she couldn't bring herself to burden him with the knowledge.

Malcolm had called, and she found she couldn't really speak to him about it, either. "You'll have to forgive me," she had said. "I'm just not up to anybody right now."

"Well. I'm here, okay? If there's a way we can—"

She interrupted him in a burst of tears. "Oh, can't we not talk about that now? Please?"

"I apologize. Forgive me."

Sobbing, and then coughing, she said, "I don't know if I can do anything just now."

"Will you come to the meeting?"

"I'll try."

"No pressure."

"Thank you for that." She couldn't help the cold formality in her voice.

But she had come to the meeting. She had seen him and nodded, while he moved around the room making sure everyone was situated and comfortable. She kept to one side of the hearth as the meeting took place, leaning against the wall; and now while the visiting directors and the lead actor were situating themselves, she edged closer to the hearth, one hand on the mantel. The sun, streaming through the tall windows in wide slanting shafts, made a bath of light where Mundy and Frye stood. Kelly Gordon had moved to the left, standing next to Abernathy and Castleton. The novelist's brother approached Claudette and held out a tray of cheeses and crackers, and she shook her head, forcing a smile. He kept nodding and staring in a friendly way, as if he'd seen into her complicated feelings, and wanted her to know he comprehended.

"I know, I know," Frye was saying, having interrupted Grausbeck's attempt to summarize Salina's news. "But there's another problem."

Mundy asked for everyone's patience, and then took a few seconds to collect himself. He stood directly in the brightest shaft of sunlight so it looked as if he were burning before their eyes. Claudette put one hand to the bridge of her nose and pressed, feeling the headache coming. She kept seeing the crazy back-and-forth of Geoffrey as the fire consumed everything.

Mundy cleared his throat and shifted slightly, then began: "I'm afraid I—well—I'm sorry, but I have to tell you all." He looked at Frye, who nodded slightly as if to give him leave to continue. "Friends." He took another breath, and appeared to be fighting tears. "I fear I have to withdraw from any further work on this production. I had thought, since there was the fire, that there'd be no way to continue. But in any case, I won't be able to."

A long silence ensued. Mona Greer held her hands over her mouth.

"My contract," he went on. "My specific contract does not allow me to take part in any—in what would amount to a—well, an amateur presentation."

"How would it be an amateur presentation?" Grausbeck asked him.

"It's in my contract with the corporation. I had enough trouble getting them to make an exception for the new Globe. No small venues. No community theater."

Claudette heard herself say, "This is not a community theater, and it's unethical of you to say it is, after what's happened." She was amazed at her own urge and ability to speak. She saw Malcolm studying Frye's face.

Mundy was unmoved. "*Their* people are telling me it *is*. The fire, perforce, has quite ruined us, don't you see. It's force majeure. And I have to abide by my agreements with those people."

"And I have to go back to Holliwell," Frye broke in. "Emergency circumstances at home. And the fire, I'm afraid, abrogates my involvement anyway. I had no idea there would be any way to continue."

No one spoke.

"It's been a pleasure working with you all," Mundy said. "Regardless of other considerations. And believe me, I'm deeply sorry about the fire."

Thaddeus

When it was all over, and everyone had dispersed to their various glooms of despair, he sat in Eleanor Cruikshank's bright living room with Grausbeck, the Ruark brothers, Claudette, Miranda, Michael Frost,

Mona, and Gina. The others, Frye, Mundy, and the young director, had skulked away, heading back to their other jobs in the world. Kelly Gordon would be in the world's Wherever. Salina had been informed of the exodus through a text from Miranda and a call from Arthur, and now there was another Skype call, in which she railed about cowardice, and talked about legal action. "That's bullshit about them not letting him do any community theater," she said. "He just wants out."

"I didn't believe it for a second," Miranda said.

"Good—let him go," Salina said, at last growing calm. "We're stuck with it." There was a note of resignation in her voice. "Right?"

"Bub-bub. Then, we're—canceled?"

Miranda said, "No," as if wanting to deny a sad fact.

And from Grausbeck's computer screen, Salina said, "*Hell,* no, Arthur. Wait. Look, we'll do the one play. You all can put it on, can't you? Pool the talent? You're all rehearsed up, right? We'll even make some money if we can pull it off. Do it like a cause for the city. Who wants to direct it? We'll pay what Mundy was getting. And we're gonna fire him for cause before he can officially quit. I've got him for the shit with the women no matter what his muckety-muck-bigwig-television-moguls say, *if* they say it. He won't get a penny more from this venture, that's certain."

"Well?" Miranda said, looking around at everyone.

"My husband can direct it," Gina said. "He's directed before. He directed *Twelfth Night* at City Stage, and he directed the Scottish play when Miles Warden was in Oxford that winter."

Claudette added, "He was wonderful directing the Scottish play."

"Okay," Salina said. "Then, we have a replacement?"

Thaddeus looked at Malcolm Ruark. "Well?"

"I'm all for it," Malcolm said.

"No—I'm asking if you'll play Lear."

He took a moment, glancing at Claudette. Then he nodded slowly. "Whatever you want. And maybe, in your version, Thaddeus, we can keep the ASL at house right, and let Mona say her lines?"

"Please?" Mona said.

"I think we can do just that," Thaddeus said.

"Imagine," said Michael Frost, with a small, mocking laugh, "We had to have the theater burn down to escape Frye's version of *Lear.*"

Everyone was silent for a moment. Then Miranda laughed, and said, low, "True."

"I'm gonna get to say the lines," Mona said.

Thaddeus looked over at Claudette, whose face was unreadable, the sad eyes merely taking it all in. He wanted to get up and walk over and embrace her. *Oh, my dear friend. What this has been for you.*

"We've got a lot of work to do," Malcolm said.

"I'll be back in town day after tomorrow," said Salina.

For a few seconds after Grausbeck's screen went dark, they were all quite still, as if unable yet to take in the scale of what had unfolded. The months of work and concentration and all the tensions and surprises and troubled hours seemed somehow present in the bright room. Thaddeus looked at his wife and shrugged, and felt himself seeming to pout. He wiped his mouth and forced a smile.

"This is how it should be anyway," she said. "You always wanted this."

They all began almost immediately planning things; rehearsals would begin in the morning at the space on Monroe Street and would reconvene here at Eleanor Cruikshank's house in the afternoon. They would begin with read throughs, acclimating Ruark and Mona in their new roles. Thaddeus would spend the rest of the day and into the night, and maybe all night, redoing the playbook. They would all have to rework the blocking as they went, given the smaller stage and the fact that the Fool's role would now essentially be the original one. Gina would rethink the sets, with her husband's input as director. As they worked on, exchanging different ideas concerning the necessary changes and accommodations to the new situation and the new space, an excitement gripped them. Eleanor and Martin Cruikshank ordered wings and pulled-pork barbecue from Corky's. They all sat in the big room with the palladium windows as the sunlight faded and more thunder rumbled far off, and ate their dinner. And worked through ideas about addressing the difficulties.

Miranda, the source, the one with the funds, sat silent through it all. As the meeting was breaking up, she said, "This just might be all right."

Thaddeus and his wife walked out on the porch together, then stepped down into the darkening, sultry air. They drove separately to the house. Neither of them remarked it, quite. It might've been any pass of the year before. They came to the street, parked in front, got out of their cars, and walked silently up the walk to the porch. Through the dining room windows they saw Louisa and the Reverend Whitcomb sitting in the light of the chandelier over the big table. They were eating takeout. When the old lady saw Thaddeus, she stood and reached out her arms, and tears came to her eyes. "I'm so sorry about these horrors, Young Fighter, but here you are." She glanced at Gina, then seemed to push through whatever doubt arose. "You're home."

Gina looked the question at him.

"Glad to be back?" Whitcomb said. "In spite of everything?"

"We've got a whole lot to do, now," Thaddeus got out.

"Thaddeus is going to direct *Lear,*" Gina said. And now *she* teared up, explaining what had been decided, and what the afternoon and early evening had been. "I think we actually got excited about it." She turned to him. "Don't you think so?"

"Yes," he said, scarcely able to find his voice.

"Oh, Wolfie. You're gonna direct *Lear.*" She put her arms around him. And Louisa kissed the side of his face. Whitcomb stood and offered a handshake. Then Gina hugged him again, and leaned up to kiss him.

Malcolm

Late evening, alone in the cottage, he was pacing and thinking about calling Claudette, or Mona. He thought of drink. The shock of the last three days had begun to wear off, and there was a woozy hypersensitivity in him. Every thought, every image that came to his mind distressed him. Almost with a kind of spitefulness or pique, he sat in one of the heavy chairs with a cup of strong coffee and the playbook, and read through the part, aloud.

Lear.

"Fuck," he spoke the word into the silence, addressing himself. "You can't do this."

Finally he called Thaddeus. "I'm feeling a little shaky about things."

"Me, too," Thaddeus told him. "All of it."

"Can we meet about it, maybe?"

"Well, we're—yes. In the morning."

There was a pause.

"I meant now. Where are you?"

"I'm not in the—I'm at the house."

After a brief silence, Malcolm said, "That makes me very glad, Thaddeus. That's a ray of light." Immediately he felt silly. "Well, listen to *me*," he added. "Cue violins."

Thaddeus laughed softly. Then: "Did you speak to anybody else at the Old Forest house? Gina and I just wandered away."

"Everybody seems fairly numb. Though I don't feel quite numb."

"No."

"Jesus Christ," Malcolm said. "Numb. I'm terrified. I wish I *was* numb."

"We've got to get it all up and ready to go right quick."

"You didn't talk to Claudette?" he asked.

"No."

After they ended the call, Malcolm returned to the words of the play, saying them again, simply reading them. He stood and paced, and made another coffee. He remembered Salina saying, "I'm glad I don't drink like you did, so I *can* drink."

Yes.

His cell buzzed. Mona. "Thank you," she said. "I thought it was all over. And now it couldn't be better."

There seemed nothing to add. He thought of the terrible reason for this change—about which she was so glad. But then, she was young, and hadn't known Geoffrey Chessman. And he, Malcolm, was going to play King Lear.

Her voice brought him back. "I'm through with Dylan Walters."

"That's good news."

"I'm hanging out with somebody I never met before who's not interested in theater. I plan to teach him about it, though." She gave a little laugh.

He heard music in the background where she was. "You'll be great," he said.

"I hope so. Anyway, thanks." Then she was evidently speaking to someone else in the room with her. "Not that way, silly." And the connection was broken.

"That's correct," Malcolm said quietly to the empty room. "Not that way, silly."

He pressed Claudette's number. It rang a long time. He would leave a message, but she picked up. "I was in the kitchen, with Ellis and Willamina. She's getting ready to go home."

"You holding up?"

She sighed. "Barely. They've—they're holding me together."

"Can I do anything?"

"No."

He let this stand.

"I'm sorry," she said. "That didn't sound right."

"It's okay."

"I'm just not—" She paused. "I don't know if I can act in a play now. Or ever again."

Again, he was silent.

"I keep thinking I should've seen it coming, the whole time," she said, and once more he heard tears in her voice. "I'm sorry. I can't stop going over it. He'd call me and it was like we were a couple of snarky old friends, even when he was—when we'd been apart for a long time and he would say things to annoy me. 'Get a rise' out of me. That's what he called it."

Malcolm listened to her sniffle, and sigh.

"I'm sorry," she sobbed.

"Nothing to apologize for," he said.

"But everybody's—so busy *going on* with things, like it didn't happen. It's awful. I keep seeing him. These images. When none of it was so hard to do. The—the fun we had."

Again, Malcolm simply waited.

"There was a time when I did love him, you know. And my father can't keep it in his mind that it's—" She stopped, breathed, then went on: "That Geoffrey's—it's so hard now. I keep feeling like I have to tell him again."

"Of course."

"And I simply can't do it anymore. Not one more time. Dad talks about him like he's coming over any minute. Jesus. I'm sorry, I can't see myself falling into anyone's arms—"

This hurt. He waited, sighed, and then managed to say, "I just called to see how you are."

"Oh. Please don't take this the wrong way, Malcolm. Please."

He didn't see a way to take it other than the way it was expressed. He said, "Of course, no. Not at all."

"I need peace. I need sleep."

"Will you make it, tomorrow?"

"Yes."

"I know this seems like 'going on with things,' but I don't see how we can do otherwise. Isn't that, finally, what we're all supposed to do anyway?"

"I hate the silence," she said. "The—the awful final quiet. The endless not-hearing of that particular voice again. Even a voice you thought you didn't want to hear so much anymore."

"I've always hated that, too," Malcolm said.

She had said something else as he spoke.

"Pardon?"

"I was saying goodbye," she told him. "And I'm sorry."

He said, again, "No need to apologize," but she had ended the call.

Claudette

The great play, she believed now, was actually all about blood love. There was no other way to see it, and Thaddeus, in his gentle direction, had her playing Goneril as acting out of rage at not being loved enough. He asked her to play the scene with Oswald not as the scheming Goneril, but Goneril as at least partially an aggrieved and exasperated daughter whose father's excesses have brought her to wit's end. When the king rails at her, in the first scenes of their estrangement, Thaddeus requested that she react as though the man saying these things, this raging king calling all the power of nature down upon her—*into her womb convey sterility, and if she must teem, let it be a child of spleen, that it may live and be a thwart disnatured torment to her*—is also breaking her heart.

"Can we play it," Thaddeus said, "so that her evil isn't so much a *plan*, as a reaction? A developing tantrum? This is the king, with all his power still making its aura around him, or he couldn't command the loyalty of the hundred knights. And Lear's part"—he looked at Malcolm—"is also a fit. His own tantrum. Which of course sets the whole disaster in motion. Actually, from then on, the entire play's a procession of impulsive actions." Thaddeus paused, and looked at each actor, it seemed, in turn, and said, quietly, "Storms."

"Damn," Mickey Castleton said. "We should've had you from the start, Thaddeus."

Everyone applauded.

"From my banishment of Cordelia and Kent," Malcolm said, "to Gloucester's pursuit of Edgar from Edmund's lies, it's a parade of tantrums, isn't it."

Thaddeus smiled at him. "The only real *planners* in the play are Edmund and, to some extent, Edgar. Nearly everything *they* do *is* a plan. In Edgar's case, it *has* to be. Because of his scheming brother. 'Edgar, I nothing am.' And there's Kent, too, razing his likeness. There are those lines about some conflict possibly afoot between Albany and Cornwall, but the emphasis is all on the plotting of Edmund, and the tactics of Edgar."

The others in the cramped space of the smaller stage, with its fake trees and its canvas of forest greenery, were excited. Mona Greer with her broken heart (her expression) was saying her lines with a strangely compelling sorrowful evenness, and you could see that when Malcolm, raging at her, reached the phrase "My sometime daughter," there was a wrenching at his heart, the scene playing in these makeshift rehearsals far better than it had played with Cordelia signing all her lines.

"I'm getting the feeling he'll be better than Mundy was," Claudette said to Willamina, as they were eating their dinner out at Flight Restaurant. "And Thaddeus is so intelligently leading us all. And there's Gina sitting and watching the whole thing with her mother and the poor Reverend Whitcomb, who's trying so hard to understand it. Today he had—no kidding—one of those Cliffs Notes pamphlets with him, studying it as we all proceeded. I thought it was cute."

"Cute," Ellis said, then frowned. "Cute."

She looked at him. "Sweet?"

"I didn't recognize the damn word."

Ellis had grown faintly less tolerant of shifts in the hours of the day, and of the little deficits which were sometimes remarkably simple, now, and therefore exasperating. Franny had visited twice, and sat with him, and you could see her trying to be patient when he called her Esther. Willamina's grandchildren visiting made him jumpy, and snappish.

Willamina went past these little fits of temper by teasing him, calling him grouchy.

"The surest way to make me grouchy," he began, and then seemed to lose the train of thought.

"Is to say you're grouchy?" Willamina said.

He pointed at her. "There."

Now, at the restaurant, he said to Claudette, "How's the play coming?"

"You know, it's actually going really well."

"I'd like to see it with Claudette in it."

She glanced at Willamina.

"I understand she's good in it," Ellis went on. "That's what I hear."

"We're gonna be there at the preview night," Willamina said. "It's gonna be glorious."

"There's a word. I know that one. Willamina, your Irish chicken soup is glorious. By God, you are—" He stopped. "Hell. Where was I?"

"You were embarrassing me," Willamina said. "With your generous nature."

"Claudette," Ellis suddenly said, loud.

"Yes, Daddy?"

"Where the hell have you been all this time?"

"Let's order Irish coffee," Willamina said.

"I have to use the bathroom."

Willamina stood. But Claudette reached for her wrist. "Let me. You relax a little."

"You sure?"

"I'm sure."

Ellis said, gruffly. "Hurry up. One of you."

Claudette took his bony elbow and walked with him around to the hallway where the two doors were. The solidness of him made her wince inwardly; she felt his body as a separateness, he was a man, and for an instant, it was as though she didn't know him, quite. She saw the silvered hair on his forearms, the rucked look of the backs of his hands.

She had to go, too, so she guided him to his door and he pushed through, then she went into the ladies' room, hurrying. When she came out, he was at the far end of the hall, heading the other way from where their table was. She rushed to get to him. "Daddy? This way."

"Where's Esther?"

"Let's go sit down and eat."

He took both her forearms, squeezing. "Don't ever let anybody go if you can help it, Little One." His eyes were welling up. "Don't let them leave your happy life. Keep them all close. Keep everybody as close as you can."

"I won't let anybody go," she said.

"And try not to let unhappiness in."

"No."

"Never forget where love is."

"Daddy."

"Hey," he said, and smiled. "Claudette."

"Yes."

"Where's Geoffrey?"

"Away, Dad. He—he couldn't make it."

"Always liked Geoffrey. No sand, though. A little weak in the knees, I think."

"Let's go eat, Dad."

"Sure."

They made their way back to the table.

"Hello," he said to Willamina as he sat down. He pointed to the side of his mouth. "You know I was wounded in Korea. Right here."

"Is that so," Willamina said, with a glance at Claudette.

"We're gonna have a glorious evening," he said. "Aren't we? Don't you like that word? Say it."

"Glorious," she said.

"There. See? Glorious."

In rehearsals, she had thought Malcolm was tentative at first, especially in the play's opening scene, and she attributed it to the situation between them. Thaddeus was patient, and managed to be encouraging without soft-pedaling what the role needed. It needed what the company's oldest member, Terence Gleason—who had wanted so badly to play Lear, and was now in the cast playing Kent—expressed as the thing the disguised Kent says he sees in Lear: *authority*. Though Gleason played Kent's scene with Malcolm in a more shrill manner than was necessary, his will to be useful was clear, and Thaddeus carefully talked him down, with what

Claudette heard as a request to go easy on the rusty TV journalist. When Thaddeus saw that she had witnessed the exchange, he shrugged and gave a little sideways grin as if to say, *Anything that works*.

But in truth the new, reduced version of the play *was* working. They'd had to do away with the delusional mock trial in the hovel of the evil daughters, and a good deal more of Edgar's ravings as poor Tom, but the whole thing was gaining in momentum and power with each day. It would come in at just over two hours, and the whole company had begun to feel at home with it in the new space. The storm would be managed as it had been in so many past versions—by bending and rebending a large metal sheet, and rolling back and forth across the backstage floor an iron ball that Malcolm had borrowed from the Metal Museum.

She saw him at the rehearsals, of course, but she had gone straight home afterward. Ellis needed more time with her. Since the night he told the bear story so wonderfully, he seemed to be slipping. She had bought one of those devices parents with small children use to monitor their sleep and placed it on the desk across from his bed. At the time, he bridled about it—"I'm no baby, what the hell"—and she had explained that it was so she could hear if he needed her. One early morning before Willamina arrived, he said, "Are you spying on me? You're spying on me. Heh. Think of it. My own daughter."

"I'm not spying on you," she said, through tears.

He apologized, but sullenly.

She asked Malcolm to understand that she required space away from the play and the theater. She was having nightmares. The nightmares woke her, and kept her awake, but she couldn't remember them; there was only the fearful residue of them in the dark, as she lay awake.

After rehearsal on the seventh day, she took the mile walk over to the Madison. At the top of the street, the big tractors had begun removing the rubble of the Globe. She stood for a moment, gazing at it. Dust was rising where an earthmover was going back and forth. She entered the hotel, and through the lobby window saw Malcolm coming along. She went to the elevator and took it to the rooftop. He followed. She didn't know what to do about it, and then admitted to herself that she'd half consciously supposed he would do so. She saw that several others were already there—Seligman and Abernathy and Peggy Torres at one table, and Mickey Castleton and Terence Gleason at another with Lurlene

Glenn. Claudette took a table along the wall overlooking the street, and sat down, and he came straight to her. He asked, simply, "All right if I sit?"

She nodded. Everything was gathering in her soul.

He took the chair back slightly and then hesitated. "Is it—is it that you feel like you have to keep me in character in your mind?"

"It's fine," she said, trying not to smirk.

Once he was settled, the server approached them, already holding a tray with two glasses of water on it. The server was very dark, and had a tiny jewel in the side of his nose. He set the water down, took Claudette's order of a salad, and then asked for Malcolm's autograph. "Remind me when we settle up," Malcolm told him. "And I'll have the cheese plate."

"That was a bit brusque," she said. Then quickly added, "I'm sorry."

"I know it's been hard," he murmured. "You're doing wonderfully as Goneril. It's a privilege to be on the same stage with you. Actually, I'm a little unable to believe it. If I'd been told that night at Shelby Farms Park that five years later I'd be acting with you—and it would be *Lear*, no less—well—" He stopped.

"I think Thaddeus has the pulse of it."

"Can we talk?" he asked.

"About the play?"

He looked down and sighed. "Sure."

"No," she said. "Forgive me."

It occurred to her that restricting their talk only to the play and their respective roles would be a form of deceit. She had been sorrowful and low and wanting to avoid everyone, but there was also Ellis's incremental faltering. It was all she could do to haul herself into the old Monroe building to work. "Forgive me," she said again. "Since Ellis told the—the bear story so well that night, he's been slipping a little more."

"Sorry to hear that," Malcolm said.

For a space, there seemed nothing left to say.

"Well." He breathed. "Just—just wanted you to know I get it. I won't bother you again."

"It's not that, Malcolm. Can we just get through this, and—and then see where we are?"

"I'll be wherever you want me to be," he said. "On out. All my life."

She saw tears welling in his eyes, but he quickly ran his hand over them, feigning a tired yawn. "I haven't slept more than three hours a night since I took this on."

"It's an exhausting part. I think you're doing it better than Mundy did. And I thought Mundy was excellent, much as I disliked him."

"We'll see."

"It's going to be glorious," she said, and felt as if he might think the remark superficial. "Ellis and Willamina have been saying that. Sorry." But then she felt the rightness of it. "No," she went on. "That's what I meant to say."

He smiled. "That's your story and you're sticking to it."

She smiled back. The moment felt natural and relaxed.

Their food arrived, and they ate quietly, watching the others go back and forth to the coffee counter. They talked about Goneril and her father, the sad king.

Thaddeus

Miles Warden called from Australia at the end of that week. He'd got the news from Arthur Grausbeck, and was exercised about it.

"Why the hell didn't you or Gina call me?"

"We've been in a state of shock, to tell you the truth."

"Geoffrey Chessman. Christ. That narcissistic—but who'd've thought?"

"He was pretty much down to the nub," Thaddeus said. "Whole year's been a strain on everybody. We separated, you know, for a time. Gina and me."

"You're kidding. Because of Chessman?"

"No. Take too long to explain. Maybe we'll talk about it sometime."

"But it's over. I mean your trouble—the trouble between the two of you is over."

"I hope so, yes."

"You *hope* so."

Thaddeus gave a small sigh of vexation. "We've just been through this catastrophe of a summer that ended in suicide and the destruction of the new theater. We'll talk about all of it later, Miles, okay?"

Warden left a pause. Then: "So you're directing *Lear.*"

"Right."

Silence.

"Anything you want me to know about what to expect?" Thaddeus asked him.

"You did great with *Mackers*. And no matter what happens, Shakespeare manages to get through. It's all in the *language*."

He wanted to chide the other for voicing yet another all-too-familiar expression. Instead, he gave a weary sigh. And said, "We miss you."

"I'm not making as much progress on the book as I'd like."

"Well, after this one show, we're dark for at least another year."

"How's Gina?"

"Gina's okay. Louisa's staying with us, along with her boyfriend. I mean, her beau."

"I bet that's her term for it."

"That's Louisa's term all right. And I like it. *Boy*friend is ridiculous for anybody older than sixteen."

"Well," Miles said. "I thought we'd keep in better touch."

Thaddeus was silent.

"My fault, I know. Can I say hello to Gina?"

"Louisa took her and the Reverend Wrong out to lunch at Otherlands."

"The reverend what?"

Thaddeus explained, and they went on awhile longer about the way things seemed to be unfolding. He was spending the first hour of each morning with Lurlene, organizing for the thirteenth, the first and only preview night, the reception of which would be held in the old gymnasium of the high school across the street from the Monroe School of Drama. Invited guests would gather there, and spend an hour moving among tables bedecked with fare from several Memphis restaurants, each of whom had been prevailed upon by Miranda to step forward and provide for the occasion. And after a relaxing social hour of food and wine and conversation, with a few brief toasts, tributes, and gratitudes to the restaurateurs, and a salute to Salina and Miranda, followed by a special one to Lurlene for her part in arranging the event, everyone would cross the street to the old theater for the performance. As he was describing this part of the planned evening, Gina came in with Louisa, carrying shopping bags. Louisa had helped her pick out what she would wear to the opening. After the food was put away and Louisa had started to prepare a fried egg sandwich for Whitcomb, Gina gave her husband a tilt of her head and murmured, "Walk?"

"Sure," he said.

They went out as Marcel—true to form, snapping at them—came in. They strolled down the street, keeping to the mottled shade of the oaks on the one side, crossing when the sidewalk played out, and going on. He looked at the side of her face, the strands of her hair trailing down, flaming with intermittent flecks of sunlight, as though part of the sun itself. They talked about the job Malcolm was doing, and Claudette, too.

That night of his return, they'd had their first alone time together in weeks; Louisa and Whitcomb agreed to risk taking the dog with them to spend the night at the neighbor's house. Louisa pulled Thaddeus aside, leaned close, and murmured, "Remember, Young Fighter. 'Life, liberty and the pursuit of romance.'" She kissed him on the cheek, and then put her bony hands on either side of Gina's face and kissed her forehead.

"I think she's happier than we are," Thaddeus said, after they'd watched the two cross to the other house.

Gina shook her head and murmured, "We've got everything but hope." She smiled sadly at him. "Hope is what she's always had. So much so that she can see something to love in a fascist."

"He's trying," Thaddeus had said.

"Think of it," she mused. "A gentle fascist."

He decided not to respond. They went upstairs and indeed things went quite like a honeymoon night, as if neither of them had much experience. Afterward, they lay side by side and talked a little. He told her how much he had missed her, and she spoke of her loneliness during all of it. "Everything was so draining."

He was quiet, thinking how far away they had been from each other, and how far they still had to go in order to get home.

Home.

With an inward rush that almost brought a gasp from him, he saw how the possibility of a return of this trouble of hers would always loom now. He took a breath, caressed her hip, striving to trust the present moment, seeking to put away all thoughts of what sorrows they'd been through, together and apart. Trust could become such a fragile thing, finally, and he had the notion that it should not be left to people, then smiled to himself at the absurdity of the thought. *Ridiculous.*

She sighed. "I do have hope, you know."

"I hope so," he said.

And they both laughed softly, almost politely.

Now, walking down the long street toward Poplar Avenue, they talked about using the Monroe Street stage, and the work she'd done making accommodations to the place and its already finished sets. "I think it's gonna be really good," she said to him. "What a job you've done."

"I feel like I've aged five years."

"I feel younger," she said, and smiled at him. "I really do."

"Remember this moment," he told her, "the next time the darks come."

"Of course, and you know I probably won't."

"Well," he said, "I'll stick around if *you* will."

She took his hand. "Officially, we're an old married couple."

"Well, no," he said. "We're the couple that put on *Lear* in a makeshift theater with a makeshift cast."

"We are that," she said. "Mr. Director, sir."

He took her elbow, the lightest pressure, brought her to him, and in the bath of sun on that part of the sidewalk, he kissed her. It was a kiss that originated in his blood; its tenderness rose up from there, instead of descending from his mind.

Malcolm

It amazed him how light Mona was. Like a child; indeed, like a preteen boy. She played Cordelia with a grace and fluidity that everyone remarked on, and Peggy Torres was delivering Regan, in that high-pitched voice, so that the shrill sound of it actually enhanced the part. Mona's delivery of her lines didn't surprise him at all. Indeed, the surprise was simply how easily everyone moved through the complications and the darknesses of the great work. Thaddeus's touch was quietly, insistently encouraging, and when he asked for a repeat of a scene, his manner was nearly apologetic; but he had great command of the text, and a reverence for it that was stirring. It was good to see Gina and Thaddeus working out how to make one panel for the other play work for this one by a simple shift of the angle of light.

Mona had broken with her newest boyfriend, and was corresponding with Dylan Walters's ex-fiancée. She reported this to Malcolm with a sly smile, and he kept from expressing any curiosity about it. She and Abernathy were spending a lot of time together in the evenings, at the Madison. He heard them talking about dinner in the rooftop bar after the day's rehearsal.

Claudette had managed to put herself entirely into the work, though it was clear enough that she was using the intensity of it to compensate for what she was going through. Her friends were attentive, but kept the slight distance she seemed to require.

During full dress rehearsal the day before the preview performance, after doing Goneril's line to Albany about the betraying letter to Edmund—*the laws are mine, not thine. Who can arraign me for't?*—she felt lightheaded, and had to be helped to the chair where they had earlier practiced Gloucester's blinding. Everyone gathered around her. She took a moment, collecting herself. Malcolm stood with the others but kept his distance. Later, he sat backstage with her while Thaddeus had Don Seligman and Michael Frost working once more on the scene at the fake height of Dover between Edgar and his blinded father.

"You all right?" he asked her.

She nodded and sighed, sitting forward a little. "Thanks."

"How're things with your dad?"

"Don't ask."

"Sorry."

"He's started wanting to wander out. And Willamina's got to keep track of him all day."

Malcolm was quiet.

Beyond them, Seligman's voice rose, saying Gloucester's line: "*'As flies to wanton boys are we to the Gods, they kill us for their sport.'*"

"He still thinks Geoffrey's always about to arrive."

Malcolm wanted to take her into his arms.

"And an awful lot of the time I'm Esther now. Oh, I don't know."

Seligman's voice again. "*'If I could bear it longer and not fall to quarrel with your great opposeless wills.'*"

And then Thaddeus's voice: "Let's make it closer to the book of Job, here, Don. You know Job's speech? Job says, 'I know my redeemer liveth,' but he isn't praying, really. 'Yet though he slay me, I will trust in him.' That's really equivalent to 'I don't give a damn if he kills me, I demand that he explain, and I believe he will. I trust that he will.' Can we get some of that tone in this part of it? What do you think?"

Malcolm leaned slightly to Claudette and said, "Our friend Thaddeus is in his element."

She smiled.

"Can we be all right together?" he asked her. He hadn't known he would say it.

But she hadn't heard him. Mary Cho had walked up. "Claudette, can you stay and do the scene again when they're through?"

"Sure."

"We'll need you," she said to Malcolm, "for the last scene in a few minutes. Day before preview night and we're three weeks behind."

"So we are," Malcolm said. "But you'll no doubt recall we lost our venue to flames and our star to cowardice."

"You're the star," Mary Cho said, simply. She glanced at Claudette, then went on to the other end of the space to give Abernathy some notes.

"What'd you say before?" Claudette asked him in a tired voice.

"Nothing," he said. "Sorry for that crack about the venue."

In the last scene, he carried Mona out, and howled, and felt it, and laid her down gently, experiencing the strength of the moment, knowing that he could do it, and could say the line "'Cordelia, Cordelia stay a little.'" And as he looked down at her closed eyes, her lovely face, he understood that she was a young woman who liked to be admired and that he had admired her, and now, in the moment, he was admiring her talent. In the great force of the play, he felt redeemed somehow, freed, as she was freed, to be herself, and not the object of his fantasies and fevered dreaming. He said his last line, "'Look there, look there,'" and lay down along her body, and when he heard the line *"'Vex not his ghost, O, let him pass. He hates him that would upon the rack of this tough world stretch him out longer,'"* he felt an elation unlike anything he had ever known. In the long silence that followed the end, as everyone looked around at everyone else, he looked into Mona's eyes and was proud, and told her so.

"I think I was good," Mona said. "Wasn't I good?"

Claudette

Willamina arrived early with her mind made up to accomplish a general ordering and cleaning in the apartment. She wanted to make the whole day a celebration. Claudette felt anemic, and only half awake. Willamina made coffee, and began cooking bacon, and making toast.

Ellis was still asleep. Claudette sat in her robe at the table with her coffee. Willamina had brought a change of clothes, and her makeup kit. She was planning to spend the night. "I'm making enough for all of us," she said.

"I'll wake him."

"Tell him it's preview night. Or I will."

Claudette rose and went into the little room, where she found him asleep sitting up in the bed, with the biography of Roosevelt open on his lap. His head was down as it had been in the window of Memphis Commons that day with the sun beating through. Yet something about this moment filled her with gratitude; she had awakened dreading the day, fearing the sorrow when he wouldn't be able to make it to the theater, but he was *here*, where she'd had the courage to bring him. (Though now she didn't think of it as courage, but more as a sort of lucky stubborn will. Almost possessiveness.)

"Daddy," she said, touching his shoulder lightly.

He lifted his head and put one hand behind his neck, rubbing it as though to massage away a cramp. Then he looked at her. "I'm pretty sure I know you."

"Yes, you do, sir."

He smiled. "Sure, I do." He nodded. "Am I driving?" And he actually winked, as if this were a private joke between them; there had been a slight lessening of sensitivity about how such teasing hurt her.

Willamina came to the entrance of the little hallway. "Breakfast is served."

He rose and Claudette helped him to the bathroom, where he shooed her away and closed the door. "Go on," he called. "I'll be out."

She went in and sat drinking more coffee with Willamina, the two of them being very quiet, listening for him, both beginning to accept the gathering unlikelihood that he would be able to make it for preview night.

He came in wearing his dark blue suit jacket, with no shirt and no tie. Claudette's heart sank. He said, "This thing still fits," and took it off. Then he sat at the table and took a bite of the scrambled eggs. "Delicious," he said. "I don't remember the last time I had a breakfast this good, Esther."

"You want butter or jam on your toast, Captain."

"No toast." He looked at Claudette, chewing. "Hello," he said.

"Good morning," Claudette got out.

Squinting, leaning toward her, he said, "Franny's often annoyed. You seen her lately? And where's Geoffrey at? I saw him just a few days ago. We had too much to drink."

"How 'bout some more coffee?" Willamina said.

"Sure." He kept eating. "Don't know when I've had a breakfast this good. It's positively—" He stopped. "What the hell's the word?"

"Dad."

"Don't tell me!" he said.

"I know," said Willamina.

"Glorious!" He brought his fist down on the table. There was a morsel of egg on his lower lip; Willamina reached with her napkin and wiped it off.

Claudette left the table and went into the bathroom to take a shower. There, she let the water cascade over her like thoughts, crying quietly in the sound of it.

She had to leave for the theater at two. The reception was to be at five-thirty, and the play would begin at seven. Ellis fell asleep in his chair, with TCM on, while Willamina sat doing a crossword puzzle in *The Appeal*. It was a usual tableau, lately. Willamina reached for her hand as she went by to leave, and then stood to walk out onto the stoop with her. Claudette saw tears welling in her deep brown eyes. "We'll be there," Willamina said. "I swear we will."

"Don't—don't tax him."

"No, honey. I'm just believing. He wants it so bad."

"He doesn't remember me," Claudette said.

"He's just had a rough morning. You'll see. Look for us."

"No—no extremes, though."

"Go on, girl."

She drove away with a measure of irritation at her friend for putting the hope in her heart; it might've been better to be shut of the worry about it. After all, receptions, previews, and shows were events she had done many times without his presence. Tonight was only one more, she told herself. She wept all the way to the theater, thinking about playing rage, playing spiteful, hurt connivance and evil intent, while grieving about the whole bad year.

The reception at the old gymnasium was a blur. Malcolm Ruark was surrounded as soon as he entered, rather indecorously more for the TV celebrity than his coming debut as Lear. He seemed to take it with less dismay than she knew he must feel. Others moved among the gathered patrons and sponsors; the old gymnasium was crowded. Mary Cho and Jocelyn Grausbeck stood behind a long table with linen sheets draped over it, on which delicacies from the various restaurants were arrayed, with the respective signs and crests displayed at each station.

Arthur Grausbeck gathered the players and the tech and staff people, along with two members of the Monroe School of Drama faculty, and got them all to stand to his right as he stepped to the podium that had been placed at one end of the big room. He announced that as chairman of the Memphis theater board, it was his privilege to present the two ladies who had done so much to bring about the coming renaissance of theater and literacy in the river city. Salina moved to the microphone. She tapped the end of it, which sounded like separate thuds of a hammer, then made a short speech about the fire, and the Phoenix that would be the Globe Shakespeare Theater of Memphis. Applause and cheers went up. She gave a salute to Miranda, and then presented Wolfgang Amadeus Thaddeus Deerforth (pronouncing the whole name) as the director of *King Lear.* He bowed slightly, then indicated the cast, all standing in a row to his left. Salina followed by introducing Malcolm Ruark as Lear, which brought forth another cheer.

Claudette ducked out shortly after this, before the other actors exited, and made her way across the street to get ready for the performance. In her dressing room, she met Marjorie Appel, the staff member in charge of makeup. Marjorie was small, wiry, compact; she had tattoos all up her left arm, and on her right forearm. All of dragons. Claudette had worked with her through many productions, and liked her without ever really learning much about her. (Marjorie preferred it that way.) But the woman knew her face, every single line and gradient of it. Claudette got into the chair and, while Marjorie began working, held quite still, breathing quietly, mentally going over her lines, entrances, and exits. It was the kind of peaceful instance that always settled her nerves before a show. As she relaxed into it, she heard footsteps in the hall. She held up a hand, and Marjorie Appel stood back. At the open door of the room, Malcolm appeared. "Wanted to tell you," he said. "Your father's here. Walked in with Willamina just after you left. The two of them. Claudette."

"Oh." It was all she could find the strength to say.

"Arthur and Jocelyn actually got a place for them in the wings."

She got out of the chair and walked to him. "That's such happy news, Malcolm." And the tears came again.

"Not yet, with that," said Marjorie Appel. "You'll run."

"Can you excuse us, Marjorie," Claudette said to her. "Just for a minute? Please?" She took Malcolm's hand and pulled him toward her, closing the door behind him. Then she put her arms around his neck. "My friend, my love. Here's to us, now." She drew him to her for a kiss.

The play, the performance of it, unscrolled as if taking place in her mind, a dream of violent passions and immense failures in a world bereft of clemency. A powerful king throwing away with both hands the love that might save him, brutally demanding fealty and raging with petulant fits of nonunderstanding, faltering and losing everything of himself. There was his face, Malcolm's lined, enraged face, right in front of hers, saying, *I prithee, daughter, do not make me mad. I will not trouble thee, my child. Farewell. We'll no more meet. No more see each other.* And she felt the tears come, that she could use to express hurtful and vengeful anger. It was a beautiful night, everything working to a kind of exhilaratingly astonished exquisiteness of effect. And in the last scene, as she sat on a padded bench in the wings with her father and Willamina, she watched Malcolm, her love, with all his troubles and failures registering in the sad eyes of the old king down on his knees, looking into Cordelia's unseeing eyes and saying, *Cordelia, Cordelia stay a little*. And a breath later: *Why should a dog, a horse, a rat have life, and thou no breath at all? Thou'lt come no more, never, never, never, never, never.* And then, in the softest, most tentative and unkinglike voice, saying to Albany, *Pray you, undo this button.* While Mona Greer as Cordelia lay draped in his arms. It moved Claudette, as it moved the crowded house, and so, for all the stumbles and distractions of the night, and the ashes of the burned-down theater only a mile away, there was the prodigious magic of the great play once more, registering among the gathered many. And her father was with her, backstage, holding her arm tight with both rough hands, tears in his eyes. There would be time, still; there might even be years for her to keep loving him. She leaned over and kissed the side of his face, and he turned to her. "Did you like it?" she asked.

"You were so good."

She had to go out and stand with the others, and bow to the applause, and the cheers. When she came backstage again, he was standing with Willamina, who applauded, and who had tears in her eyes, too. "Great work," she said.

"Thank you," Claudette said simply.

Her father sat down again. People were moving back and forth and embracing and chattering and cheering, laughing; it was all the excitement of the just-after, as Claudette had always thought of it—that place where everything glowed. She leaned down and kissed Ellis on the side of his face. "Thank you for being here."

He smiled. "You know," he said. "The whole evening, all of it, it's been—" Pausing, he made a fist and held it against his knee. "Don't tell me. It's on the tip of my tongue. It was—"

"It's all right, Daddy," she said through tears. "I know the word."

—Memphis, Palo Alto, Edale, London,
Paris, Nice, Orange 2012–2021

Acknowledgments

To my friend Tom Bradac, who generously gave me valuable advice drawn from his years as the founder and director of Shakespeare Orange County, and who has played King Lear and also directed the play more than once. And to John Benitz, for putting us together at Thai Towne Eatery in Old Town Orange. They are both my colleagues at Chapman University. Any mistakes, blunders, or fault lines that exist about these fictional people in this made-up theater are mine alone.

And to Henry Dunow and Jordan Pavlin, who know why.

Note: The Memphis you find here is almost wholly of my imagination; I moved some things around in service of the story. For instance, I planted the Globe Theater on Madison Avenue, up the street from the old Madison Hotel. Anyone seeking to get from one part of the actual, beautiful city of Memphis to any other part of it using this book for direction would very likely wind up hopelessly lost.

A NOTE ABOUT THE AUTHOR

Richard Bausch is the author of twelve other novels and nine volumes of short stories. He is a recipient of the Rea Award for the Short Story, the PEN/Malamud Award, a Guggenheim Fellowship, the Lila Wallace–Reader's Digest Award, the Literature Award from the American Academy of Arts and Letters, and the Dayton Literary Peace Prize for his novel *Peace*. Three feature-length motion pictures have been made from his work. He is past chancellor of the Fellowship of Southern Writers, and his short fiction has been widely anthologized, including in *The Pushcart Prize: Best of the Small Presses*, *The O. Henry Prize Stories*, *The Best American Short Stories*, and *New Stories from the South*. He is on the Writing Faculty of Chapman University in Orange, California.

A NOTE ON THE TYPE

Pierre Simon Fournier *le jeune*, who designed the type used in this book, was both an originator and a collector of types. His types are old style in character and sharply cut. In 1764 and 1766 he published his *Manuel typographique*, a treatise on the history of French types and printing, and on what many consider his most important contribution to typography—the measurement of type by the point system.

Composed by North Market Street Graphics,
Lancaster, Pennsylvania

Printed and bound by Berryville Graphics,
Berryville, Virginia

Designed by M. Kristen Bearse